IN ... OF BATTLE

*   *   *

HAYDEN STRAKER, *star captain*. Even if all Amerika calls him a thief and coward, he will brave an enemy empire to complete his mission.

ELLIS STRAKER, *trader*. His schemes to shape Amerika's destiny have made him infinitely wealthy —but cost him everyone he loves.

HIDEKI SHINGO, *samurai*. He wants to command worlds, but cannot control his own passions.

ARKALI HAWKEN, *Hayden's fiancée*. Frightened of space and terrified of men, how can she survive the inescapable horrors of war?

AZIZA POPE, *MeTraCo Controller*. Her craven greed will lose her a planet—and endanger the stars.

HU TSUNG, *Kan general*. To deal with this warlord, a man needs a strong will—and stronger stomach.

*   *   *

Please turn this page for raves
for the saga of YAMATO.

THE WAY OF THE WARRIOR

PART 1

KEN KATO

WARNER BOOKS

A Time Warner Company

WARNER BOOKS EDITION

Copyright © 1992 by Ken Kato
All rights reserved.

Questar® is a registered trademark of Warner Books, Inc.

Cover design by Don Puckey
Cover illustration by Royo

Warner Books, Inc.
1271 Avenue of the Americas
New York, NY 10020

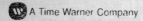 A Time Warner Company

Printed in the United States of America

First Printing: May, 1992

10 9 8 7 6 5 4 3 2 1

KNOWN SPACE

Known Space is the name given to the sphere of interstellar space centered on Old Earth, with a current radius of approximately three hundred light-years. Its boundary encloses all of humankind. The remainder of the universe is referred to as the Beyond. Since the exploration wavecrest of Known Space is expanding at almost the speed of light, its volume, and therefore the number of discovered worlds, is increasing as the cube of its radius. Exploration of Known Space continues, and will do so indefinitely, until the whole of the Milky Way galaxy is embraced.

Two key technological developments have allowed mankind to colonise Known Space: the first is the discovery of a means of faster-than-light travel, utilising "nexus points," small space-time wormholes that can be created within any star system; the second is the technology of "terraforming"—the fast transforming of suitably sized, suitably placed planets from chemically hostile environments into quasi-earthlike environments with atmospheres, oceans, entire imported ecologies, etc. Thousands of worlds have now been stocked with engineered flora and fauna, millions of diverse species all originating from the genetic pool of Old Earth. No true xenobiological life has so far been discovered in Known Space.

The creation of Known Space began in A.D. 2100, with the launch of six von Neumann pioneer drones, automatic ram-jet spacecraft capable of traveling at near-cee. At a constant acceleration of 100 gee, it takes these "pioneer drones" between three and four days to reach 0.9 cee, and about the same time to decelerate once they encounter their destination. Typically, a four- or five-year journey lies in between. During this time the ship's organix computers close down and hibernate.

Once a pioneer drone has arrived at a nearby star system it "detonates" the nexus, a quasi-stable space-time torus. The drone then replicates itself, and the daughter drones move on to the next-closest systems.

As soon as the new nexus becomes quiescent, it is possible for near-instantaneous communication from other systems containing a nexus point. By the time the first ships arrive, TF techniques have begun to transform the new system and start the work of terraforming. All systems based on a single (nonbinary) Main Sequence star, with a spectral type in the range A to K, are searched for planets. If suitable bodies exist in the "temperate orbits," they are mass-engineered using gravometric techniques to give a planet close to a one-gee gravity. Then chemical transformation, atmospherics, thalassogenics and surface architecture phases are completed before ecostructuring is begun. The process is now so refined, it can take less than thirty years to engineer a world to the point of human habitability.

Known Space presently occupies more than 120 million cubic light-years, and includes many thousands of star systems containing terraformed planets. A typical star density for our vicinity of the Spiral Arm is 25 stars for every 10,000 cubic light-years, so Known Space contains some quarter million stars, of which half are multiple systems, and three quarters of the rest are dim M-type primaries. Only half of those that remain contain easily terraformable planets. Nevertheless, that still leaves more than 16,000 worlds, all linked together by a "nexus" network.

Known Space is divided up into twelve equal Sectors, each like the segments of an orange. The poles and equator of Known Space are referred to galactic coordinates, so that each slice occupies 30 degrees of galactic longitude, and runs from pole to pole, with Old Earth at the center. The Old Earth system itself is not considered to be a legitimate part of Known Space. Since the Catastrophe, it has been surrounded by a three-light-year-diameter Exclusion Zone.

YAMATO –
the story so far ...

A Rage in Heaven, the first volume of the Yamato cycle, explored events taking place between the years 2421 and 2441. Duval Straker, a weapons scientist, and Ellis, his psi-astrogator brother, accompanied an illegal Amerikan trading expedition of five nexus ships to open up trade with colony worlds of the Neutral Zone, a region of interstellar space recently annexed by Yamato.

Many light-years from home, the fleet was trapped by adverse psi conditions and obliged to take shelter in the space port of Niigata, on Sado, a world deep in the Neutral Zone, where they had no choice but to put down and begin repairs. While they were at work, a huge Yamato aurium fleet arrived and bargained its way down onto the port apron. It then treacherously attacked the Amerikan ships and overwhelmed them. Only two escaped. Ellis was aboard one, but his brother was captured.

To deter further incursions into their newly declared

Greater Yamato Co-prosperity Sphere, the Yamato authorities decided to massacre all captives. To prevent this, Duval revealed his secret to the administrator of Sado—he had been helping to perfect something called a singularity gun, a weapon of devastating power.

In *A Rage in Heaven,* the story was told of how Yamato planned an invasion of the Amerikan Sector and how those fleets were eventually smashed.

Following the war Yamato was stripped of her military power, and Amerika negotiated the dismantling of her Co-prosperity Sphere in the Neutral Zone. In the wake of the political settlement, a trading base inside Yamato was agreed to on the world of Osumi.

Now ten years have passed since the war. . . .

The great Milky Way,
Spans in a single arch,
The billow-crested sea,
Falling on Sado . . .

Matsuo Basho (1644–1694)

PROLOG

And so it was written in ancient scripture that the three shintai *came down from Heaven in a time beyond memory, and that these were the same* shintai *that were cherished by the sun goddess Amaterasu to give her her brilliance. But she gave them to her grandson, Ninigi, saying, "Adore these jewels, the sword Kusanagi, and the mirror, as the soul of the gods." And from Ninigi they passed unto Old Earth, and to the Land of the Rising Sun, so that henceforth the* shintai *would belong to the Kingdom of the God-Emperors.*

And so Jimmu Tenno, the First Emperor, said that only those without stain might wear the sword Kusanagi, the virtuous and the pure in spirit, and that whatsoever impure man took it would surely die. The First Emperor gave the perfect sword to his son, and he to his, and he to his again, and every Emperor since then has revered it at the Great Shrine. Thus Kusanagi remained in Old Japan until the days of the fathers' fathers' time, when the seed of Amater-

asu and of Suzanu was united, and the power of Men moved beyond the world. . . .

And so it came to pass that when the sun had mounted spear-high and the armies of Echizen were routed, this peerless sword was given to the Kingdom of Men, to Goro-zaemon, the Monkey General, by the vanquished, and he took it to himself with an oath that it would be a sign of unity and power and of eternity, though all knew it was to show his might as Shogun. And all on Edo who heard the oath and who saw the sword drew in their breath and said that it was rare as unity, shining as power, and sharp as eternity, and they renamed it Shori—Victory.

And so the matchless sword that had passed undiminished down thirty centuries was given by the Shogun, Gorozaemon, to his son, Jinzaemon, the Bloodletter; then to Yaemon, Whose Rule Cannot be Surpassed; and to Urashi, the Taker of Worlds, and to Ichiyuken, the Builder; and at last to Denko, the Lightning Warrior, in whom the blood of the Fujiwara still flowed strongly, and whom therefore no curse could touch. And in this time all Yamato bowed down before the God-Emperor and yet paid tribute to the power of his Shogun, even the gaijin who came to Yamato in their ships, and it seemed that the radiant power of the Chrysanthemum Throne would shine for ten thousand years. But it was not to be.

After six strong generations the line of the Shoguns was spent, for it takes seven generations of man to pass from the plow to greatness and back to the plow once more. And the radiance of the Shogunate dimmed, and though the sword, Shori, fell quickly to eight who called themselves Shogun, all died miserably, for they were impure, and the time of the sword's passing was at hand.

And so on the night when Shih Shen, the Chinese Butcher, whose name be forever spat upon, brought the Armies of the Kan to stand above the world of Himeji it was decided that the spirit of the sword should be invoked afresh, and that the words of the Emperor Jimmu should be renewed strongly, so that the Kan Butcher might take the sword as prize and thereby die in torment. So it was that the sword was brought with reverence to a holy monk who had been blinded by the Butcher, but the monk stumbled as he invoked the words, and the invocation was altered to a curse so that any man, pure or impure, would die in torment if he possessed the sword, and that henceforth it should leave a wake of blood.

The next day, ruin came upon the world of Himeji, and the Butcher's kusentei ships raged above the city of Aioi, and all there fled or were blinded or were burned alive, and the Shogun's firstborn son was carried off to the worlds of the Kan. But Shori was hidden in a body servant's obi and smuggled into the Home Worlds in great secrecy to Edo, the world of the Shogun, which was its proper home. And a lesser sword, the Seishin-no-Tsurugi—Sword of Spirit—was taken by the Butcher in its stead, and Shih Shen did not know the deception all the days of his life.

At this time, the Shogun was Sakuma Hidenaga, May His Name be Forever Remembered, a great and cunning lord who even then had ruled for many long years. And Sakuma Hidenaga brandished Shori. And those among his subjects that were samurai saw the sword and drew in their breath for they knew of its power, and those pure in the Way knew that they must obey its possessor in all matters. Sakuma Hidenaga consulted his advisers and his council, and those that were wise said that he must drop the sword into the deepest gravity well in Yamato, to have its temper broken in a blaze of starfire. But those that were corrupt said that he must engrave his name into the steel of the sword, that both samurai and peasant would know him as Shogun.

But Sakuma Hidenaga, the cunning lord, the clever lord,

knew of the curse that anyone who possessed the sword, Shori, would die in torment, and thus he drew aside the body servant and bade him give the sword to his foremost wife, and when this was done the body servant's limbs were struck off one by one, for did not the curse apply to him also? And therefore was it not inevitable that his death be lingering? And when this was done, Sakuma Hidenaga was content, for he knew that all must now believe his wife's husband was Shogun, but that she, being no man at all, would not die in torment. . . .

The Book of Earth

BOOK 1

OSUMI

First, see [Ref. Module MCXXIV-024.240354]
YAMATO.

Begins: #Gamma CrA is a multiple system of three stars
that mutually jeopardise each others' gravitational sta-
bility, but the systems of Alpha, Beta, and Delta have
operating nexi and well-populated planets. They make up
the Kyushu Quadrant. The world of OSUMI, orbiting
Zeta CrA, is th#

. . . HACK INTERRUPTED . . .

#Osumi, a terraformed and inhabited world in the YA-MATO Sector, lying on NEXUS chains AC349 and AD350 (Pure Brightness Chain). Principal star Zeta Coronae Borealis (Sp: AO/F9, Luminosity=50 sol), lying 220 light-years from the Origin. System contains five sub-Saturnian gas giants, sixteen other bodies of planetary size (all sterile), two prograde nexi (Teth-Two-Eight and Teth-Two-Nine).

The system was entered by pioneer drone craft A.D. 2349, terraformed A.D. 2349–2380, first settled A.D. 2382. Under successive Emperors, Osumi grew to become chief of the nine provincial capital worlds of the KYUSHU Quadrant (see also: Bungo, Buzen, Chikugo, Chikuzen, Higo, Hizen, Hyuga, and Satsuma). By A.D. 2410 Osumi had eclipsed KAGOSHIMA, which had been the Kyushu capital world since A.D. 2215, and under Emperor MUTSUHITO (b. 2421, a. 2442) has enjoyed special patronage.

The ruling Hideki famil#

. . . HACK INTERRUPTED . . .

#onditions of defeat imposed under the Treat of Frisco, (A.D. 2442) was the Lease of Kanoya, a small, continental region of 10,000 square miles, ceded to the American Merchant Traders Corporation (MeTraCor) of LIBERTY, for 100 standard years. KANOYA CITY is the entreport for all Yamo-Amerikan import-export trade, which has grown annually to date, last year reaching one and a half trill#

. . . LINE ABORTED.

1

Year of Our Lord, 2451—
(being the 39th year of Kanei,
after the fashion of Yamato).

It was a day of ill omen, a day when evil hung in the
sluggish air under the bridge dome, and orbit-demons
clung to the *Chance*'s retracting antennae and squatted on
the outer skin, howling. Hya-ji, god of reentry, was shaking the ship, raging his fire in the stratosphere, tearing at
them as they passed through the Domain of Meteors, and
surely every man on watch could feel his power. . . .

Their ship picked up the Chinese battle squadron with a
clamor of alarm klaxons. The enemy fleet rose up ahead
of them round the limb of the planet, coming out of the
dawn-red light as they caught it up, and the Yamato crew-
men aboard the armed merchantman *Chance* showed their
hatred at the sight of it as it hit their scanners. It was the

worst imaginable circumstance for the Amerikan ship and her young captain, the Sencho.

Hayden Straker counted eight Kan, powerful dragon ships: big, eight-thousand-ton hulls, each carrying forty or fifty beam weapons apiece, and, dominating them all, a huge White Tiger Class warship transferring orbits under minimum energy conditions. They were orbiting prograde, on the same landing track as the *Chance,* hugging the top of the thermosphere and showing twenty-thousand-mph real velocity against the ground. There was no doubt they were bound for Kanoya City, and that was a bitch.

"Sweet Jeezus, we've run into deep shit," he whispered, feeling his blood drain from him. "It's war with Xanadu, and we've run straight into them."

The sight of the indicators showing a high Index ruffled him. It was unstable and ominous and full of threat. Two *gishi*—native Yamato personnel—watched the forward monitors. He looked from them through the dome to the fin, along the ship's dorsal strake where drones worked tirelessly, at the smooth automatic retraction of external gantries that were already glowing red from the abrasion of tenuous hi-atmosphere gases. He saw the way the stars burned through the soap-bubble-clear blister above his head, and he knew that the Sencho of a trading nexus ship was a man truly alone.

He listened to the creaking complaints of the compensators, and could feel the Index fall again in the Osumi system. He was a tall man. A Yanqui, conceived and born in the city of Lincoln on the Amerikan capital of Liberty, but raised up in shame as a bastard whelp of an aristocrat's abandoned wife. And later, aboard his father's vessels in Seoul or wherever they cruised throughout the Zone, where he had learned hard truths about the universe.

He saw himself reflected in the dome, distorted and

standing at a strange angle. There he was, sparely built, in his mid-twenties, capless now and wearing a high-cut maroon jacket, long-frocked at the back, with cream breastings and solid argentium clasps. His legs were encased in cream tailored flexiplex to below the knee, then ribbed, black boots. Damned fine. Goddamned fine.

It was a face the Seoul ladies liked, fine and regular features, a white complexion made by shiplight and a thousand stars on young skin; long, dark hair, combed fashionably back and secured in a clip. He carried no Navy knuckle, but a heavy Wesson beam pistol jammed incongruously in his belt. He was an elegant man, endowed with poise and sensitivity, versed in the languages of the Zone and given to reflection, never born to work the nexi, much less to carry arms along the trade chains. Commerce is a filthy way to live, he thought. One step above raw piracy. But all in my father's glorious tradition.

He raised a hand to shade his eyes from Osumi's rising primary star. The sight of the Kan squadron gutted him.

"All hands stand to," he said, looking away. "Call alert. No, kill that. Just stand to, for the moment."

The *suifu*, head of the *gishi*, repeated the order to his thirds and the crew reacted to the talkback command. But as Hayden Straker watched the spinning patterns of cloud on the planet below, the color deserted his cheeks and he found he could not move. Suddenly the creaking of the ship's compensators filled his head, reminding him of the fabulous worth of cargo that the *Chance* carried, and the weight of responsibility staggered him. He began to sweat.

The *Chance* had come—very secretly until now—from Kagoshima, the lone terraformed planet of the Alpha CrA system of Kagoshima. The last thing they needed was trouble. Normally the Straker holds would be filled with Neutral Zone superheavy ore, finest-quality real mulberry silk, cakes of Malay "strap" from Penang II or cryogenic products from Yamato's RNA-DaiKoKu, the renowned genetic blenders—goods with a high trade value, with broad margins of profit and the whiff of illegality.

The house of Straker lived by Zone trade, but it could only grow by challenging MeTraCor monopolies, breaking into their lucrative and jealously guarded markets. That's why this trip was different. The holds contained Dover mulch and Honshu *meicha*—stomach cancer–retarding green tea—and other goods of middling worth, a nondescript cargo, some of it contraband, carried along the "Pure Brightness" chain, along the Zero Degree boundary and the Gunto, the arc of stars: Gamma, Alpha, Beta, Delta, and Zeta of what Amerikan Admiralty charts still called Corona Australis, the Southern Crown. Locally, it was "the Turtle."

He sank into his command seat and wiped away the cold sweat forming on his face. Aboard was the single most valuable item ever to come out of the old Prefectural capital world of Kagoshima. A thing so rich and rare that it might still buy peace where war seemed certain: a secret present destined for the daimyo of Osumi, the Prefect of the Kyushu Quadrant, Hideki Ryuji.

A glitter of meteors stippled the shield on the ship's beam; they soared, glided, fell back, bemusing the passengers that were watching them become entrapped by the ship's complex fields. One fist-sized chondrite had swooped in freakishly through the ventral skin field; it hung fixed and rotating just outside the dome, and one of the thirds ordered a maintenance drone to pick it up.

The passengers stared at it in wonder.

He watched the drone reach out a prehensile triad and grab the pirouetting meteorite, stilling it. Today's Friday the thirteenth, Universal Time, he thought, still paralysed by fear; the day we were meant to set down on the Kanoya City apron. The day Arkali and I were to be married. Sweet Jeezus, I knew it would never be. In my heart I knew this war would somehow come between us. Where in the name of psi are Commodore Vaile's ships? Psi, or Elvis, or the Adventer God . . . somebody tell me what I ought to do!

He stiffened as the *Chance* shuddered. In the guts of the ship the compensators were taking a buffeting caused by the uneven thrust of the engines. He put his hand out and forced himself to stand up. Underfoot, the flooring felt rubbery and spongy. The cold fetid aircon knifed at his neck. Ahead, a dozen *gishi* in white cotton headbands stood at their stations or stared at the monitors, chattering, watching the analysis of the Chinese ships. The old grizzle-haired engineer sitting by the bulkhead put his eyes forward and assumed an opaque expression, in shame for the captain who had shown pure terror at the appearance of the White Tiger. His loss of face was vast.

He walked back along the bridge, abaft the command console, where the Yamato *gishi* were not allowed to go. Here was Jeff "Red" Bowen, the astrogator, young Danny Quinn at the helm just seventeen years old, and the two racial Japanese passengers, one man, one woman, man and wife. He glanced in their direction, knowing their persons would be worth more to the Chinese than the prize they carried. They were not just Japanese, they were samurai, the warrior caste of Yamato. A daimyo's son in his robes, and by his side, his equally formally dressed wife.

He was Hideki Shingo, son of Hideki Ryuji, rose silk–wrapped, thick-limbed, powerful, cruel, infinitely arrogant, but sick-faced now despite his early-morning meditations. He was wrapped in a borrowed thermofoil against the cool ambient temperature maintained aboard the

Chance, vain and stiff with pride, impassive at the sight of the Chinese, but his liver could not stand the gravity variations caused by the laboring compensators—he was ship-sick.

His father was the Daimyo of Osumi, Prefect and ruler of the entire Kyushu Quadrant, probably the most powerful man in Equatorial Yamato and the man from whom the Amerikans and the Chinese leased the hard dirt on which their vital trading worlds of Osumi and Satsuma were built. Much had changed in ten years . . . maybe too much. . . .

It was now a decade since Ellis Straker had fought the Yamato invasion, a decade of political reversals that had seen an end to the aggressive policies of the Yamato government. After the smashing of her armed forces throughout that fateful week of 2441, Yamato had retreated into seclusion and silence. Amerika had not followed up her victory. She traded with the Emperor's domain only through the single Lease of Osumi. Immediately, Xanadu had demanded a similar lease, and it had been granted, on the Satsuma system, also in the Kyushu Quadrant.

On Osumi, Ellis had dedicated his energies to the building up of the Merchant Traders Corporation, the mercantile empire he had helped found in the years of uneasy peace before the Yamato invasion. But in the years that followed, all had not been well. Yamato's vastly populous Chinese neighbor had come to see her as an ailing power—one that might be used, accused, and then abused.

He recalled his father's long explanations of the political complexities that had led to his mother's death, his brother Reyson's death, and the wiping out of his uncle's family in 2444. Xanadu, or China, or Chung Kuo, or the Central Realm, as it was variously known, shared a boundary plane with Yamato along galactic longitude 330, and it was across this plane that the Dowager of Xanadu had moved her legions in the year following Amerika's great victory. The demand had been that Yamato open her nexus chains to Kan ships wanting to access the riches of the disputed Neutral Zone, but it had been a demand the *bakufu,* Yamato's military government, had had no option but to turn down. The refusal had led to war, and the war had been very bloody.

He shuddered. His eyes moved to the silent noblewoman—the Lady Yasuko. He did not know anything more about her than that she was Hideki Shingo's wife, but she reminded him a little of his dead uncle's Japanese wife, Michie-san. She was tightly swathed from sole to neck in *midori* green silk and carried a cute red *miko* fan with which she fended off the stolen stares of the *gishi*. In the whole voyage he had known nothing of her but her soft voice and a pair of extraordinary almond-kernel eyes that stared from a dead-white face on which bud-red lips had been painted. She was a samurai lady from the Home Worlds, samurai of the First Rank, refined and aloof, to Hayden Straker's eyes exotic, mysterious, untouchable. Her liquid black eyes darted away from contact with his own; they were lidded with the epicanthic fold that made their whites appear almost nonexistent. Those eyes had plagued his sleep every night of the voyage. They were calm now, calm and unafraid, and he could feel them searching him for an answer.

This Yamato lady likes nexus travel, he thought. She likes its terrifying uncertainties as much as any Boston Brahmin whose religion forbids him to transit a nexus twice. But however much she likes it, she can't like it as much as I hate it.

He glanced down at the ribbed black *duro* floor. In the owner's stateroom below, his father lay in his strap hammock, asleep—if ever a devil truly slept.

Ellis Straker owned the *Chance* and three lesser nexus ships that threaded the trade routes converging on the Yamato lease. He had made his son Sencho of the *Chance* only weeks before. Pridefully, Ellis Straker had done that. Triumphantly. Angrily. He had insisted.

"You're goddamed Sencho now, boy. Hear me? Hell, yes. Like it or not!"

A wave of sour regret rose up from Hayden Straker's belly and he forced his thoughts back to the ships that were blocking their landing. He was Sencho—captain. His father had said it. So he alone must make the decision.

"What's your reckoning, Mister Bowen?"

"Kan ships," the astrogator growled. He was a strong-built Virginian of Ellis's generation, closed as a clam, heavily tattooed and pitted by the Lebanon virus. That and taking snap and too much five-star had damn near ruined him before Ellis Straker saved his skin. He answered to no given name other than Red.

"And the flagship?"

"She's a fucken White Tiger, the bitch."

"Is that all we know?"

"Chinese-built, and Chinese-crewed." He spat on his hands and rubbed them together. "What else is there to fucken know?"

"C'mon, Red. Make some guesses!"

The astrogator fought his taciturnity to speak. "She's a warship. Plenty weapons, maybees a hundred. God alone knows what she and her whelps're doing in this fucken system, but it's bad psi to run into them."

Hayden Straker's stomach clenched, his fear haunting him. "Helmsman, what's your orbit?"

"Still tracking blue four-four-eight, Captain."

"Bring her up into a green hyperbolic transfer. The easiest one for the nexus you can get."

Bowen's pocked face was suddenly loaded with suspicion. "You're sheering off? Taking her towards Teth-Two-Nine?"

"That's correct."

"With the Index down as the Dead Sea, and a psi-storm coming on an' all?"

"We'll put on all power and outrun the Chinese and the psi-storm both." He put his hands in the small of his back and turned to his helmsman. "Please carry out my orders, Mister Quinn."

"Yessir."

The *suifu* had brought up his men to the bridge, and Quinn punched in the new headings sullenly. The engines fired and the compensators snarled in complaint. The starboard watch, all Yamato *gishi* from Osumi, braced themselves against the leakthrough, angling their bodies forward to accommodate the drag forces, then they moved to stand by the forward scanners. Most were bundled up in foils against the aggravating cold, moody with lost sleep and mouthing superstitions at the building psi-storm.

Inside, Hayden Straker felt the foreboding surge again. He saw Hideki Shingo watching him closely, and silently cursed the man. It was the samurai's fault they had lingered an extra day at Kagoshima in the system of Alpha Coronae Australis. The daimyo's son understood too well that his presence was pivotal. He had shown bloody-minded arrogance, challenging all requests as a matter of course, insisting as a samurai he was obliged to follow certain forms of etiquette before leaving the domain of a fellow noble. He denied that it was because Kagoshima was the old capital of Kyushu Quadrant and he was engaged in some private snubbing match with the ruling family.

Hayden Straker suspected that it was also because the crazy Adventers had for some totally incomprehensible reason proclaimed Kagoshima as the place where Adam and Eve had gone when they were cast out of Eden for their sins, and that an Adventer church to eclipse all Adventer churches must be built there. It was clear as glass: Shingo-san had wanted to take the opportunity to underline that Kagoshima was a part of Yamato.

He knows he's worth even more than the bribe we're carrying to his father, he thought as he eyed the samurai. And he's right, because in fact the whole future of the Amerikans in Yamato depends on him. Our trade in Yamato is essential, because without it the Kan would overwhelm them, and in time the Neutral Zone would fall under their sway too. I have no option but to act.

Suddenly Hideki Shingo spoke. "Your orbit is altering," he said in accentless Japanese. "Tell me your intent, Captain-san."

Hayden Straker understood and made reply—in faultless Japanese also. "We shall lose the Kan ships when we go through the nexus, Shingo-san. If our astrogator knows his business."

The samurai smoothed his moustache, his eyes coalblack, deep-set, and shadowed. His hand found the hilt of the *katana* bound at his side, and his hand began to knead the silver pommel. "You have my permission to proceed. We know our fate is already decided."

Despite himself, Hayden Straker was prickled by the man's certainties. He had heard a thousand other samurai talk with that kind of conviction about what was a matter of psi, as if they were personally under the protection of their damned gods, but Hideki Shingo alone of them had dared to assume a captain's prerogatives aboard his ship. He smiled shortly. "As you say."

Cadet Quinn made the final burn. Behind them, the flare of energy curved like a glittering sword; it began to straighten. The primary star steadied overhead. Then a roar came from the elevator shaft, galvanizing everyone on the bridge.

"What's this? What's this?"

Hayden Straker turned at the commotion, crushing down his visualiser, hating what had to come.

"You! *Hinin* excrement! Get out of the way, there!"

The *suifu*'s shouts heralded Ellis Straker pushing up the walkway. He was fifty-some years old and powerful as a bull, brooding, corpulent, buckling his belt around his girth and the gold-embroidered silk jacket he always wore aboard his ships. A black ginseng tobako cheroot was clamped in his teeth, half-smoked but unlit. He was foremost of the Free Traders, a man who had fought to build his fortune in Yamato as an independent trader, the only man who had dared to openly challenge the dominating monopoly of all trade between Yamato and Amerika held by the Merchant Traders Corporation.

He knuckled sleep from his eyes and glanced up through the dome at the primary. It was a blue-white furnace staring unblinkingly into space, and Ellis's huge shadow was cast long across the bridge towards his son. Then he fixed his stare briefly at the straggle of Chinese ships on the monitors and cocked the ruined, pale-blue astrogator's cap that his ten-year-old iron medals were pinned to.

"What's the goddamned meaning of this?" he demanded in the gritty Liberty accent he had never lost. "Cadet! I'll have my ship's head pointing at the Kanoya City apron, as I told you."

"But, Mister Straker, it was the captain said—"

"Red, replace this man at the helm immediately!"

Steeling himself, Hayden Straker stepped in. "Father, Quinn's right. I gave him that order, as Sencho."

"Did you, now, Sencho?" The cheroot jutted. "Well,

Captain, what were you damned well thinking on? Are you weak in the head, or what? Do your duty, Red, before I lose my calm. Bring her about to blue four-four-eight, and by the shortest route.''

"Yoh.''

"Put them on full alert stations, Red.''

"Yoh.''

The starboard watch scrambled under the *suifu*'s orders. Bowen shouted over the talkback in stilt-Japanese. They jumped for their weapons, climbing into their blisters and harnesses like monkeys.

"Stand by to burn!''

Ellis Straker strode over to his son, taking the bridge rail in his hand and peering into the visualiser. "Well, boy? I'm waiting.''

"I was attempting to take us away from that fleet, sir. I thought that tactically it was best to—''

"Psi damn your thinking.'' He lifted the heavy zoom disc to his eye. "The more a man clogs his brains with logic, the less he understands, the less he can feel out. Didn't I always tell you that? What were you doing? And why did you fail to wake me?''

Hayden Straker felt the cut of his father's words. The *Chance* was a five-thousand-tonner, built as a MeTraCor ship, one of the finest and fleetest merchantmen in the Zone. He had grown to manhood on ships like her, on the Lease and in the Zone. He knew nexus ships and hated them; he longed to get away from them forever. But his father needed a successor, and he had made his son captain. After an explosion of threats and promises, he had capitulated.

It was never in me to command any ship, he thought bitterly. Not the *Ylem,* which spends her days smuggling any commodity with a high duty. Nor a decoy ship like the *Plasma,* which tries to catch and destroy pirates whenever she can find them. I don't want command of ships like the *Aether* or the *Chance* that are expected to deliberately run against MeTraCor's monopoly. I don't want command of anything. I'll never be like him no matter how hard he insists, no matter how much he wants it. But he made me captain of this ship, and I agreed to take the job, and all so I could have Arkali. So captain I'll be until a proper legal discharge can be made on a planet of destination!

His anger boiled up. Why does he constantly taunt me? Why does he always try to humiliate me in front of the others? Goddamn! Before the Han Judges of Hell, I hate him! I hate him!

He had been a love child, the cause of his mother's shame. He had been born to a mother who was the daughter of a high officer of state, a woman already married for reasons of state to a wealthy but repugnant man. "She gave you life because of love, son, not because of duty," his father had told him hauntingly at her death six years ago. "Worship her memory as I do. And see there's fresh-cut flowers put on her grave whenever you come here when I'm gone."

Reba had died with her second son in the war when Koje Do had been overwhelmed by the forces of the Butcher, Shih Shen. As fortune had planned it, father and first son had both left the stricken planet for Seoul three days before. . . .

There he was. All pork belly and brandy fire. Standing there sure as shit on his damned ship bridge.

You treat me like a fool, he thought. The resentment welled bitter as snake bile in his throat. You dote on the memory of my mother and brother, yet you give your only remaining blood as much hell as you can. All my life you've towered over me, loveless as granite. Since my mother's death you've hardly touched me; you diminish me; though you bought for me a top Seoul tutor, you've no respect for my cultural learning. To you I'm still no more than an ignorant twelve-year-old boy. But I'm not that, I'm a man. Grown and ready to make a life for myself, in my own way, if once you'll let me be!

"I asked you a question—Captain."

The last word stung razor-sharp. "Yes, sir. You did. But you also told me that any fleet of more than seven nexus ships we see in the Perfect Brightness Chain has got to be Chinese, and therefore hostile. I didn't want to lose time before we started to run for the nexus."

Ellis grunted, one eye squeezed shut as he struck up a light for his cheroot. "So you edged her about, hoping I wouldn't wake, didn't you? Panicked by the sight of the Kan? Damn your ass, boy!"

Hayden Straker bit back his reply, feeling instead how his fear had been replaced by cold anger. Though they carried contraband in the holds, the real cargo was immeasurably more valuable. It was the prospect of peace. It had been a massive political gamble, a speculation on which the whole future of the independent trading house of Straker now rode.

"Yes, that and more," his father had told him before they left. "Without peace we're all ruined. Not just us, but Jos Hawken and all the independents. Yes, and the Merchant Traders Corporation itself. You can't trade in the middle of a nexus war. A year of seizures and unholy destruction by the Kan—that and requisitionings and commandeerings by our own Navy—ah, the consequences're not to be imagined. If it costs fifty *tranches* of aurium, we have to purchase peace, or face the end of all things. Don't you see that?"

A *tranche* was the term for a million in credit, convertible into refined aurium, and there were twenty credits to the subsistence unit. A man could live twenty lifetimes like a senator's bastard in the best parts of Lincoln on ten *tranches* of aurium.

Oh, Liberty! he thought. What a planet! What a citadel of learning and of progress! And the city of Lincoln: a place enlightened by the literary genius of Helm and Lamosangu, amused by the theater of de Sa and Wallenburg, where the fine architecture of Oulton Knebworth rings with the sublime music of Lukka and Xenik; where new scientific discoveries are made daily; where a man can study at RISC, or visit the Halls of the Void, or converse with men of intelligence and distinction in the *go* houses, or just let the wealth and power of the place seep into his bones. . . .

If only my father would let me take Arkali to Lincoln. Isn't that what Amerika's rights are meant to guarantee? That a man has an absolute right to do any damned thing he wants? With my father's blessing I could have taken her there. Taken her to live in the biggest, finest, most cultured capital in Known Space. Given success, this voyage could have brought my father's assent. Given luck, yes, but my luck has failed, just as I feared it would.

He caught the samurai woman's glance. Her eyes were on his own. For the first time her gaze held momentarily and he saw something smiling there. She understood his position; he saw that.

He turned. "I don't see how taking the ship away from an enemy makes me a fool."

"Then I'd say your comprehension is lacking."

He surveyed the forward monitors once more and tried again to quell his rising fear. The Kan ships were changing formation rapidly, hanging on the equatorial stations. The fearsome-looking Fort Baker, looking like a magnitude-zero star, twinkled in the visualiser and was gone. Fort Baker was anchored over Kanoya City itself, a massive weapons platform to discourage warlike attempts on the Amerikan lease. Moored in its standing orbit, it had now gone into eclipse so far as the *Chance* was concerned, and would not egress from behind Osumi's bulk for the best part of an hour. Once more Hayden Straker regretted bitterly the events that had brought him away from the marriage he should have been making today. . . .

It had been his father's idea to buy the cooperation of the Prefect, or overlord, of the Kyushu Quadrant. Ellis had put it to Controller Pope's Council at Kanoya: "If the offering's good enough, we might persuade Ryuji-sama to issue a proclamation that forbids the Kan to bring their psi-damned wars to Osumi. Our merchant ships are not sufficiently armed, nor numerous enough, to deal with a Kan squadron. But Kyushu Systems' Defense Units ought to be strong enough to smash them—if they choose to mobilize."

"And will they?"

"If we make it worth their while. Nothing's simple in Yamato, boy. That's why the Shogun's government made the daimyo of Osumi into the Prefect of the whole damned Quadrant. Only on the Prefect's say-so can the neutrality of the system be recognised—and backed with a threat of force. But don't forget, technically Ryuji-sama can decide to regard the lease as Amerikan territory and allow the Kan to interfere with us. That's because a state of war exists officially now between Amerika and Xanadu."

"Can he do that?"

"Yeah. According to that psi-damned fool, Aziza Pope. It's part of the treaty. She's stupid, and stubborn, with the soul of a stinking account drone, and she thinks inter-Sectoral affairs can be conducted on hardcopy and fair terms. I had to enlighten her six or seven times over about the Kan's attitude to treaties and fairness in time of war.''

Ellis and the Controller had met alone aboard the *Chance,* in secret except that Hayden Straker had been told to get on a pickup where he could overhear and so learn.

''All right, Straker, how much credit's it gonna take to appease them?'' Pope had asked coldly, hating Ellis Straker and all he represented, but knowing that the big man spoke the truth.

''No degree of credit can do that.''

''Then what are ye saying?''

''Just that I know of one thing Hideki Ryuji wants more than anything.''

''What?''

''A little gewgaw to be had at Kagoshima. A crystal. It's an amygdala—a power jewel, one of the forebrain thought amplifiers the great savant, Ramakrishnan, first brought into Amerika from Varanasi. The finest.''

''An amygdala?'' Pope had whispered, astonished. ''And the price?''

''Fifty *tranches*.''

Interest had decayed to anger on Pope's face. ''Impossible! Fifty million in aurium-convertible credit? MeTraCor can't underwrite half the cost of such a bribe!''

''Okeh, let MeTraCor bear half, and I'll underwrite the rest, by psi!''

''What? You?'' The Controller had been hugely suspicious. ''Why?''

''Because the trading house of Straker needs peace as much as MeTraCor does.'' Ellis had paused then, readying himself as if for a killing blow. ''And I want trading rights for Straker and Hawken Inc. to take effect the day the war ends. You'll use your influence to get me permits for my ships to enter Amerikan nexi with their bays fully laden.''

"No, Straker. MeTraCor has a monopoly. You know that. Only an Act of Congress—"

"Sure, a monopoly on trade with the home Sector. What if I found a loophole? You'd use your family's influence with the Directors on my behalf?"

"What kind of loophole?"

"I want a permit to trade from Yamato to Europa through Amerika."

"You want to ship Yamato goods to Europa?"

"Yep."

"Direct?"

"Yep. Without excise duty. Sealed holds. And no warehousing on Liberty or any Amerikan world. I want a permit to do that in perpetuity. And you'll get it for me if MeTraCor wants to keep Osumi as an Amerikan lease."

There had been a furious argument, but when Ellis Straker had threatened to withdraw his offer, the Controller had had no alternative but to agree, and that was the tacit deal the Council had finally accepted. Messenger craft had sped to the samurai capital at Miyakonojo, and Ryuji-sama had sent his younger son, Shingo, back with them to see the amygdala assayed and brought down to a safe planetfall.

While at Kagoshima there had been delay and further news of the war between Amerika and Xanadu: a powerful Kan squadron was to be sent into Kyushu, while the only Amerikan fleet beyond the Zero Degree Plane was five weary, virus-plagued ships under Commodore Vaile, last reported in the Scutum region, far away on the Amerikan lobe of the Zone.

Ahead now, signals were flashing up on the interrogators. Hayden Straker glanced at the forward monitors, then to his father, who made no move to reply to the threats. The enemy fleet have seen us turn and turn again, he thought. They'll surely open up on us as soon as we come up beside them and they get a good look at us, he thought, despising his father's unreasoning behavior. He trusts no one these days. Least of all, the Chinese. Kan he calls them, after the Yamato fashion. Kan for the people and Xanadu for the China Sector. It was the old name that had returned to usage after a hundred years in abeyance.

"Yellow four-four-four!"

The side curls of Ellis Straker's gray sideburns quivered under the flaps of his old astrogator's cap, his close-shaven cheeks star-pale and hard as ivory. He wore his scars like a fine suit of clothes: a badge of rank and a reminder of his past. He cast an evil look at the planetary limb and smiled a grim smile. "No, sir! There'll be no running from the Kan while I'm aboard. Red, put out the Straker ID!"

He faced his father hopelessly. "But we're at war now. At war! They'll fire on us!"

"Is it a little word like 'war' that troubles you, boy?" Ellis Straker's mouth pursed small. "Wars don't signify out here. There's always been wars, and there always will be. There'll be wars until the end of time because humans are made that way, because we're combative and we gang up in groups, and because we want the same things the other groups want. The only difference is the Kan have no stomach in a fight. Which is why Amerikans'll always beat them face-to-face. Don't you know that when you turn tail on cowards they're like jackals? It's then they rip you up, boy."

"Surely, surely you can't mean to confront a Chinese battle sq—"

"I mean to do my duty and touch down on Osumi ahead of them!"

"But they'll fire on us if we try to reenter. We'll have to descend through their formation!"

"Ha! We'll duel with any Kan that wants it. In any place, at any time, war or no war."

Ellis's jacket was glowing around his shoulders and purple-white fans of Vavilov-Cherenkov radiation were shining up from the *Chance*'s surfaces, drenching the bridge with ghostly light. Epaulettes of St. Elmo's fire made Ellis huge and menacing.

Hayden Straker forced his fists to unclench and held to his cool, reasoning self. "It was my intention to keep off the planet and give ourselves some time," he said. "Look at the Chinese flagship, she—"

"Stop your prattling. You have too much respect for what the Kan's beams can do, and too little for the state of the Index."

"But that monster'll blast us to plex shards if we come inside a hundred miles of her! She must have a hundred beam weapons aboard!"

Ellis laughed again. "Ha! She mounts exactly seventy-two. Sixty-five-kV heater units, made in Shanghai. And she'll not fire on us."

Despite himself, he felt astonishment. How could his father know that? But he did, and that was something real to respect and to try to fathom.

"Seventy-two, then. Does it matter? Still, we've less than half that number. Surely, once we come within range of her she'll—"

"Yellow four-eight-oh!"

Bowen bawled out over the talkback, echoing the order to the helm.

As the *Chance* arced into the new orbit Ellis Straker peered at the deep-scan monitors, his voice hard. "As I thought. Troops."

"Troops?"

"Yeah! For the taking of Kanoya City—I'd've staked

fifty thousand in credit on that fact alone. And that big bastard's the Pai Hu—the Western Palace. She's Admiral Hu Tsung's flag, out of Centaurus, and the others belong to the the Kan equivalent of MeTraCor. Wouldn't be surprised if Hu Tsung has scoured them from every apron in Xanadu against their captains' wishes. That corsair's a tough guy. Real loyal to the Dowager—I know enough about him to judge the delight he'd have in distressing us.'' He paused, watching, licking his lips and relishing the danger. Then his overwhelming gaze fell on his son again. "Did you think I spent all that time drinking five-star with those jug-bitten Korean sonsabitches in Kagoshima for the sake of my liver? No, boy, I was broadening my education.''

"They told you about Hu Tsung?''

"There's some that wish me bad psi, but there's plenty that still owe me favors.'' He split his devil grin. "I said we'd blood you soon, boy. Are you ready for it now?''

"But you never told me . . .''

He could feel his father's eyes looking through him, stripping his soul, laying bare his lack of courage. The electric air was dense, ozone-choked as the compensators hummed like blood in a fainting man's ears. He could feel the Index falling, oppressing them until the atmosphere was unbearable.

"Well? C'mon? Are you?''

"You never told me. You said nothing!''

"Okeh, call it a test. You've a belly full of contraband— half my life's work and every credit of your inheritance tied up inside this hull. You've a nexus spitting shit and pissing thunder, and a pack of Kan gutter rats between you and the Osumi apron. So, Sencho-sama, tell me what's it to be?''

He listened with astonishment and shock. "You can't

countermand me as you just have and then expect me to take back command! It's you who wants to close with the Chinese, not me! For psi's sake, I've no idea what you're trying to do!''

Ellis Straker's eyes narrowed. "Trying your mettle. Seeing what stuff you're made of, boy. And showing you what made your father number one in the Zone. Or anywheres.''

"You know my answer! Sheer off before it's too late. Take a line on Teth-Two-Nine and pray the Index starts to climb!''

"Pray the Index climbs?" Ellis pulled the cheroot from his mouth and spat disgustedly. A *gishi* in a pale-blue coverall leapt forward immediately to wipe it up. "And who'd astrogate the nexus for you?''

"Mister Bowen, or—''

" 'Bout time you gave it a shot yourself, boy.''

"Me? That's crazee. I don't rate as a talent.''

"Look at the state of you! Ah, you tell me till I'm sick of your whining that you want a man's rights. But are you a man? You can't run away now, boy! You'll have to fight! Or take the astrogator's cockpit.''

"But it's madness! What can I do?''

"You can show me you're my son.''

Hayden Straker shook his head silently. Burningly, he saw the helmsman's eyes nailed to the forward monitors; he saw Bowen mutely turn away. The samurai pair watched closely, fascinated by the older man's brisk aggression and enthralled by the barbarous displays *gaijin* were prepared to make.

"Now, take the cockpit, you yeller hobbledehoy!''

His rage welled up unstoppably at the humiliation. His "face" was in ruins.

"Take the cockpit, I said!''

"I will not!"

"Then you're the piss-ant coward I always took you for!"

For the first time, Hayden Straker raised a hand to his father's face in anger, his finger a dagger, his voice barely under control. "You made me Sencho, by psi! Yet each time you step on this bridge you shove me aside like I'm nobody! I'll not captain this ship, nor any ship of yours! You hear me? I'll never—"

Without warning, fireworks exploded in Hayden Straker's eyes. He reeled back and saw himself sprawled on the floor ribbing, on his back. His thoughts seemed suddenly to be three feet outside his own head, then he tried to speak and could not and he understood that he had been punched in the jaw.

"Get up, boy! Get up!"

His father's huge left hand hauled on his sleeve, and he staggered to his knees groggily. Every time it had ended like this, his fight knocked clear from him by a belt from a Navy knuckle. But not this time. Not this time, by God!

Six feet away his father had turned his back on him, laughing. He put his fingers to his bloodied mouth, his head ringing with anger.

"I said we'd blood you . . ."

The words blinded him. His red-slicked fingers grabbed the heavy octagonal knob of his blaster grip, ripping it from his jacket. He saw Bowen turn, notice him too late. Then the astrogator's cap was flying across the bridge, the iron medals jangling on it, and he felt to his shoulder the jar of his father's skull as the blaster butt slammed into it.

The ginseng cheroot fell smoking on the floor, then Ellis Straker crashed to his knees and pitched grotesquely forward onto his face. The wound in his bald pate was deep and white where the edge of the grip had cut into it. As Hayden Straker watched, it began to well with dark blood, and the sight of it stayed his terrible fury so that he began to shake.

"He called me a coward! You heard him?"

On the bulkhead the Index indicator dipped into critical, tripping the alarms.

Bowen's eyes were wide. "Jesus, psi . . . man, you've killed him!"

"What?"

"You've killed him! You've murdered the capt'n!"

"I'm the captain!" Hayden Straker raged. He was breathing hard now. He was cold as a corpse as every eye on the bridge stared at him. He staggered as Bowen went to turn the body over. "Leave him be, Red!"

"But he's—"

"I said leave him be! Don't you understand me? Touch him and I'll blow the heart out of you!" He reset the blaster menacingly.

Bowen backed off. Suddenly the orders he must make were clear in his mind. "Stand by to adopt blue eight-four-seven."

He saw Hideki Shingo watching him with astonishment. The samurai woman was clinging to the bulkhead rail beside him, those extraordinary eyes fast on the blood.

Bowen was shaking his head. "I cain't fucken believe it!"

"Psi damn you, repeat my order to the *gishi*, astrogator!"

"Hachi-Shi-Shichi Aoi!"

The *gishi* fired the ship's engines, sending her careering up away from the planet at root two times their orbital velocity, Osumi's escape velocity. He saw Daniel Quinn and ordered him back to the helm.

"Get a fix on the nexus!"

"Yessir."

"Bowen, give me a read on the Index."

"Low down and still falling," Bowen growled, his voice barely audible.

He pushed the Wesson back in his belt. "All hands to ready for action." He was quaking uncontrollably, his veins on fire, but he knew he must carry his actions through and impose his will. A gravitational judder smashed through the ship, and as the *Chance*'s compensators damped it she bucked, then the engines fired again and she sliced through the void, tearing away from the planet and the Kan ships. Two vessels were already maneuvering to follow them, firing long burns that trailed opalescence behind them, gaining like hunting dogs on a cybojack.

Silently, the *gishi* began to strap into their harnesses and break out rods and power looms inside their beam-weapon blisters. Hayden Straker knelt over his father's back and turned him. If only he'd let me be, we'd have run free and clear by now, he thought bitterly. Jeezus! What were you thinking, you monster? What plan was in that terrifying mind of yours? Hayden Straker saw the blood pooling on the underfoot ribbing, but the massive chest was rising and falling. Thank psi, he prayed. Don't let him die. Dear sweet Lord of the Void, don't let me be a murderer.

The primary's stare was suddenly extinguished, blotted out by the eclipsing fin as the ship jinked. Another gravitational anomaly shivered the hull, making the crew grab for the rails and shifting the shuttle in its hangar in the *Chance*'s belly. *Orim*—huge trails of phosphorescent light from the accelerating surfaces—lit up the dome as he cradled the bloody head, then he parted the eyelids and saw a naked eyeball roll up white. He tore off his jacket and shirt and began to staunch and bind the wound with the fabric. What have you done? he asked silently, hating himself. He'll never forgive you. Never.

He tried to cover his thoughts. Hardening his face, he spoke to his father's steward who had appeared. "Get him to the medicos. Gently, Nyuyoku-san. You're responsible, and tell me as soon as he wakes, d'you hear?"

"Hai!" The steward dipped his head in assent and translated the order. Half a dozen *gishi* jumped to the order. Then Bowen stood over Hayden Straker and spoke his mind as straight as he dared. "I wish you hadn'ta done that, Hayden."

"He had no right to hit me, Red. He had no right to call me a coward."

"I don't know about rights, but I known your father near on thirty years, and he ain't never been bested in a ship fight."

"You know the *Chance* is built for speed and maneuver, not for fighting Kan battleships. When I took the decision to run for the nexus, it wasn't cowardice." He stood up, naked to the waist. He felt the infrared leakthrough from the dome playing hot across his neck and chest as he faced the astrogator, man to man. "What you don't know, Red Bowen, is that we're carrying an amygdala aboard us, and that's a cargo short on mass and long on value. The *Chance* would have outpaced any of those Kan vessels."

"Maybe—if'n you'd wanted her squirted all over the system. I don't believe a *rashie* is any place to try to hide in."

Hayden Straker felt the shock of the word. It was from *arashi,* the Japanese word for a violent hurricane. All who traveled the nexus chains knew and feared the special stark-mad psi-storms that disrupted the communications of Known Space a dozen times each year. Unpredictable as chaos, these extra-deep instabilities tore at the fabric of space-time and overwhelmed any ship whose astrogator was insane enough to attempt a transit.

"You think that's a *rashie*?"

"Yep."

"By psi—so why didn't you warn me?"

"Hmm." Bowen's lip curled.

"Don't you laugh at me, you sonofabitch! Why didn't you speak up about it?"

"Ain't regular to badger the Sencho on and on. A Sencho's supposed to know what's what."

Another judder blasted them in a sudden power-sapping lurch, and hope deserted him. "It's too late to run from the Chinese now. We're all but caught. What was my father planning to do? Goddamn his psi, Red, what was it in his mind to do?"

The compensators thrummed and thrutched, filled the dome above them with waves of deep bass sound; the *orim* glowing against the shields made mirrors of the decks. "I sure as hell ain't no savant, Capt'n."

Bowen's sour reticence prickled him. "Psi damn you, Red, it's not my fault my father made me captain of the *Chance* and not you. I'm asking you, do you think he really meant to fight?"

"Like you said, you're capt'n."

The compensators howled, a terrible sustained force behind them now, and Hayden Straker's mind struggled against the panic rising in him. We'll still be able to fire our beam weapons whatever happens to the Index, but Chinese naval vessels'll have tractors ten times our power, and their dragon ships are big enough to pull us in, if we can't run for the nexus. They'll paralyse us and concentrate fire. A singularity gun could save us, but only the Amerikan Navy is allowed them now that Yamato have renounced them, and they're restricted technology to any ship leaving the Sector to stop the secret getting out. . . .

What about the amygdala? The daimyo's son and his wife? My vessel? My father? I have to get away. Think what'll happen if we're captured. That would be calamity. Calamity! The son of the daimyo of Osumi falling into Chinese hands would mean dashing all hope of bringing Ryuji-sama to our aid. He'd tell them about the amygdala and we'd be torn apart by Hu Tsung's men until they found it. I could eject it through a disposal vent, but that would do no good. I have to get the two Japanese and the amygdala to the daimyo's residence at Miyakonojo. I have to, or Osumi will fall to the Chinese and never be retaken. But there's no escape now. Unless . . .

"Ready the shuttle."

Bowen did not move. His eyes strayed towards the samurai.

"I said ready the shuttle for launch!" His hand gripped the handle of his blaster until Bowen snapped the order to the crew over the talkback. The hatches hissed open as the *gishi* went down the port, their thermofoil wraps rippling in the breeze.

"It's low pressure," Bowen said, looking up suddenly. "The hangar's bleeding atmosphere. We must be holed."

"What?"

"Ain't no other explanation."

"Shut the main hatch."

"We shouldn'ta opened it in the first place."

"*Dozo! Ki-te! Sugu!* Captain-san—I think Mister Straker-san he's waking now!" Nyuyoku, the steward, was coming up the elevator plate, a fresh shirt in his hand. Hayden Straker pulled him aside and pushed past, descending into the cabin where his father lay.

Once in the owner's stateroom, the shadows closed around him, and he shut and interlocked the cabin iris. "You're a bastard, hear me, Mr. Big-man-war-hero? And you deserve a piece of this through your black heart!" He hissed it through his teeth, as he pulled his blaster and reset it. The floor pitched, threatening to unbalance him, but he leveled the barrel at the ion lock of his father's Chinese safe and squeezed the trigger. The charge roared out of the snout, filling the cabin with noise and lightning and acrid blue smoke.

As it cleared, he saw that the energy bolt had shattered the ion lock and blown most of the front panel to smithereens. The sweet aromatic smell of the camphor wood lining drove out the sharp tang of ozone and filled his head when he threw back the hot, deeply scored door. It was a Chinese safe, all right; armored in limbozine, it looked like plex and was faultlessly plexlike in every way, except in two particulars: first, that use of a meson cutter on it would have fatally irradiated anyone trying to break in with neutrons, and second, that a simple blaster, useless against plex, was enough to melt it out.

"Yes, you're a bastard devil, all right," he said through his teeth to the bulk floating in the strap hammock. "Now let's see what else you've got."

Inside the safe were two fire-blasted copybooks, another volume bound in red skin, and three fine women's silk *yukata*, now spotted with glowing burns. He pulled them out and trod on them. Under them was a large tattered datachord from a ship-to-ship interrogator, pale blue, wrapped in its own cable. He threw it aside. Beneath that were some small flexiplex bags, and a large cheroot box packed with little quarter-pound Zwiss aurium ingots. They, too, were pulled out. The bags were tied with thread and meticulously labeled. The bolt had ripped open three or four of them so that small glassy lumps gleamed amber and red where they were strewn. Large living crystals and chrysoids, he saw: government-embargoed cyberbrain parts. Nothing above ten *mensa* in power. Bound to be the ill-gotten proceeds of some rogue dealing with the Kagoshima Koreans, he thought as he ransacked the safe, scattering everything until it was empty.

For God's sake, where is it?

A flash of light came from the corner. Shards of light showered down, stirring the smoke, illuminating a half-sized Bowen, but the stateroom apparition was just a holo, and though Bowen cursed and shouted and slammed the bulkhead with his heel, he could do nothing. Hayden Straker stared around him in the smoke-misted air. Nyuyoku had carefully laid his father's magnificent pair of blasters on the visualiser podium and hung his jacket on its shaper on the locker door. The jacket! Yes, of course! He would have kept the amygdala on him.

Footsteps rattled outside. The iris was tried, blows rained on it and the heavy control box. Bowen's voice raged and swore. He grabbed the huge jacket, ripped out the shaper, and put it on. He felt the microplex lining cool on his skin. The material was thick and full of authority, the clasps heavier than his own, and the braid on the sleeves hard with crusted gold. It smelled of his father. It bore the honors of a decade ago. Then he felt inside the deep, broad-flapped pockets. Nothing. Where did you put it, you sonofabitch bastard? He held his breath, sweating in the airless cabin, his jaw aching, as he began to feel along the seams of the jacket: the cuffs, the collar, where the sleeves joined the body, everywhere, meticulously, inch by inch. But still nothing.

By psi, maybe he's hid it in his astrogator's cap, he thought. The one that's on the bridge? He frantically redoubled his efforts, ignoring the shouted demands to open the cabin iris. Then he lifted the jacket's hem and his fingers felt a hard, round object the size of a peach stone and the gritty feel of a fine lion-metal chain, and he knew he had found what he was looking for. He ripped the lining and pulled it out. The amygdala was in his hand. He studied it, gasping with relief, turned it over in his bloodied fingers. It was cut into hexagonal facets, clear and hard and a deep malevolent red. He felt an insane desire to press it to his forehead and listen to his father's subconscious thoughts, but the urge passed off and he held it tight in his fist instead, knowing he must find the most secure place to hide it. A place so secluded that no one could find it and take it away, a place so safe that it could not be lost. He must wed it to him inseparably and take it off the *Chance*. Then he realized the perfect hiding place for the amygdala.

A sudden shaft of raw light sliced into the gloom from the center of the iris, then the plates bulged again under a huge kick. The mechanism half tried to shut again but then gave up. Bowen and two men behind him forced open its rubbery-lipped plates and burst in. They held, stock-still, stark agony on their faces. Then Bowen spat, clawed at the choking air, and he saw him go straight to the strap hammock.

There was a groan.

"Thank Christ!" Bowen whispered when he saw Ellis Straker was stirring, that he still lived. "He ain't dead!"

It was the blaster firing, and only the blaster firing, that
had brought Bowen here. Sickened and relieved that that
was so, Hayden Straker took up the pair of blasters from
the visualiser podium and pushed them into his belt.

"Let me past, Bowen."

"I . . . I thought . . ."

"I know what you thought. That I'd murdered my own
father in cold blood." His voice dropped, suddenly
drenched with disgust. "Well, you were wrong, Bowen.
Now get out of my way!"

3

The clang of ranging fire sounded against the shields:
Chinese warning bolts sent across the void to test the
Chance. The astrogator backed away a step, but as Hayden
reached the wrecked iris Bowen told him, "I been to hell
and back a dozen times for your father, Hayden Straker!
You ain't half the man he is, and you never will be, y'hear
me!" But Hayden Straker was already up the elevator shaft
and on the bridge.

"You! Take the helm!" he told the *suifu,* moving to the
tractor console and removing the keys from it. Then he
stepped across to the shuttle hangar emergency-egress
hatch and pulled the lever that cracked it open. A gush of
air swept past him into the shaft.

"Aii! The north wind!" a *gishi* shouted in Japanese,
using the nexus rat's term for a loss of pressurisation

aboard a vessel. "Sencho-san, maybe something is very wrong!"

Hayden Straker felt his hand falter on the hatch. Even so, his relief at getting the hatch open was enormous. A few more minutes and the interlocks would have sealed the hangar deck, requiring a specific override from the astrogator's cockpit—something Bowen might not have acquiesced to without spilling blood. He raised his voice above the sound of rushing air. "And you, Quinn, get two men and follow me!" He turned to the samurai and said in the man's own language, "I apologise for asking, but I would be most obliged if you would please agree to follow me down to the shuttle."

Shingo's eyes slitted and his squat, muscular body resisted. Cold moving air slashed at his face. "*Iye, wakarimasen!* I don't understand! Are you asking me to go down into that? Now? When the ship is under attack?"

"I must recommend that you do so, Shingo-san." The *Chance*'s belly-rolling maneuver sent the vast cloud-swirled face of Osumi flying across the dome from rim to rim. "As you see, the planet is close by. We are no more than five hundred miles above the surface now."

"You are mad. We'll all be killed!"

"Is it not true that the future is already set?" Hayden Straker held the man's appalled stare, knowing he must go through with it, at blaster point if necessary. Hopefully, it won't come to that, he thought. These samurai believe the entire universe is predetermined—but they also respect rank above everything. Perhaps I can use that. He adopted a formal tone. "As captain of this vessel, I promise you that the shuttle is the safest place to be. I ask you to follow me."

As the samurai opened his mouth to speak again, another warning bolt from the closest Chinese pursuit ship poured fifty gigawatts of raw energy into the shield halfway down the starboard dorsal strake, throwing up a dazzling plume of white light and clanging the *Chance*'s structure as if she were an enormous bell; a second later the sound of the electromagnetic shock wave struggled back to them in echo through the bones of the ship.

He tried again. "Honorable Sir, they mean to destroy us. According to our mercantile custom, as captain I have the right to insist you obey me while you are aboard my ship. I will not willingly subject you, or your lady, to the dangers of a bombardment by the Chinese. Therefore, I order you to get into the shuttle with all speed."

Hideki Shingo met his eye challengingly, then magnesium-bright St. Elmo's fire reflecting from the fin surfaces forced him to shade his eyes. "Such words, Captain, are easily spoken by a man who does not have to follow."

"You mistake me, Honorable Sir, I intend to come with you."

"Hoh?" The samurai stood aghast, holding to the support rail as the *Chance* juddered. "You will get off your ship? Abandon her in this, her hour of need? Did you not just proclaim yourself her captain?"

He shouted above the whine of escaping air. "It's true that a captain is responsible for his ship, but he must also take care of his cargo and his passengers! Since the value of these far exceed the value of my vessel, it follows that it is my first duty to see you safe to planetfall!"

"You think in terms of 'value' at a time like this? But your ship? Your crew? What about them? And what of your father? Have you no notion of filial duty?"

"Please don't speak of my lack of piety. It is our way. As for the ship, she is sound, and the crew are capable men. They must take their chance, as must we all."

The talkback chattered. A damage report. Hayden

Straker looked once more to the lights set into the plate at his feet, to the ranting pressure alarms beside the emergency hatch. Five had begun warbling. The interlocks were trying to engage. If he slammed the hatch shut to smother the leak, he would never get it open again. There was no more time. In an agony of indecision he went over to the elevator and looked down to the owner's stateroom. The smoke had thinned, and he could see Bowen's back bending. He saw his father's hand lifting from the strap hammock. Yes, I have to make planetfall with the samurai, he thought. I've got no choice. I can't send them alone, and there's no one else I can trust to go with them. He took Hideki Shingo by the arm.

"I must insist! There is no other way!"

The samurai was outraged at being touched. He drew back, his hand chopping out his words. "Your first duty is to your ship! And to your father! The ship is the safer place!"

"That is not so! Please go aboard the shuttle!"

"I told you: we will stay here!"

"*Iye!* No!" Hayden Straker's patience snapped. He's playing for time, he thought. He's scared of the shuttle and he's gambling that I'll surrender the *Chance* without a fight. He said, "If you do not leave, I will fight until the end, until the Kan utterly destroy this ship! But the life of your lady is more important than the *Chance*! And it is imperative you reach Miyakonojo!"

"Imperative only to you! The Kan—"

"You have no conception what their beam weapons can do to a ship like this once the shields are overcome—and to you, if you remain aboard!"

Shingo shook, furious over his own uncertainty. Only the ambiguity in their social rank kept his sword in its scabbard.

"You must do as I say, Honorable Sir!"

"If you were not an Amerikan—"

"But I am an Amerikan!"

"Then behave like an Amerikan! Surrender to them!"

Hayden Straker's mouth set hard, the rush of air plucked at his clothes. "I will never surrender this ship to the Chinese, Shingo-san! And I will never surrender you to them either! Do you understand that?"

The samurai turned away, seemingly entranced by the hatchway. His eyes burned, and suddenly Hayden Straker saw what the man had been trying to hide from him. It was intense fear. The admission came hard from him. "I cannot go into the shaft! I cannot face great heights! I am afflicted by vertigo!"

"It looks a long way down, but it's a poiseway. You'll float. Trust me!"

Another Kan bolt screamed into them, blasting high-energy X rays into the now minutely transparent bridge dome. They ducked automatically, and felt instantly foolish at their fossil bodily reactions.

"Quickly! And trust me, sir! Do as I advise!"

Hideki Shingo was jolted from his paralysis. He looked privately to his wife. Hayden Straker saw her nod, and then the *gishi* were watching their captain climb down the emergency-egress hatch poiseway and into the shaft that led to the hangar deck: the Sencho went first as a courtesy, as a sign that he had accepted a samurai's word, then two *gishi* engineers, then came Hideki Shingo, then the lord's wife, and lastly Quinn-san.

They were gasping for breath at once. The air, blasting madly, was steaming from a gash in the ship's plex skin near the place where the £127 drone port had been. The blast was transforming itself instantaneously into super-cooled flakes of solid nitrogen and oxygen frost at two hundred and fifty Celsius below. The *Chance*'s intrashield temperature was low enough to make a regular Nebraska II blizzard. It could only be a meson mine that had done that.

The meteorite! he thought suddenly. And the drone I sent to bring it inside. Jeezus, what if it had blown after the drone brought it through the port?

Why are there no drones at work healing the hole?

Because I cleared down external maintenance operations when I decided to run for the nexus, and I failed to reinitialise them. Shit an ingot! I hope Bowen's across the situation.

As he watched, the force of air ripped another piece of debris through the hole, opening it, increasing the gale, sending a big crack like a crocodile's smile across the fragile denatured plex at the fringes of the wound.

Quinn waited anxiously above, steadying himself in the gale. He was up almost level with the hatch, at the top of the poiseway. The samurai were climbing down far below under the curve of the *Chance*'s stern quarters, over the shuttle's top strake. Shingo's sword guards ground and rasped against the shaft sides as wind whipped him and the propelling grav waves carried him down.

"Now! Push off with your feet!"

Shingo jammed his long sword to the side of his sashed waist, and judged the air current and the next surge of the poiseway by instinct. He somersaulted and landed upright on the shuttle deck, turned, and immediately readied himself to receive his lady. But the moment had passed, the propelling field was falling away now after losing its load, and in sudden fear her hand groped out for help that was not there. For an awesome moment she dangled, legs constricted by her kimono and unable to locate her feet in the climbing holds. When the ship jinked she swung out from the side of the shaft and started tumbling; she threw her head back and her complex pinned hairstyle was plucked out by the rushing air. She began spinning faster until the knotted sash holding her kimono disintegrated. Obi and sandals flew off. Hayden Straker gasped as a shower of long pins and decorative combs rained over him. He pulled one of the pins out from his cheek where it had embedded itself like an acupuncture needle. His stomach turned over as he saw what was happening up the shaft and understood the danger. He signaled urgently to the two *gishi* attending the midpoint.

"*Ima! Sugu!*" Now! Quickly!

But instead of making a grab for her spinning body as it tumbled by, the men shied away from her. These *hoshi-gishi* were low-caste Yamato peasants or casteless *sango-kujin,* and he saw the horror in their faces. Planetside on Osumi, a disrespectful comment made within earshot of a samurai lady's closed vehicle was sufficient cause for instant execution. They refused to reach out to her.

"Grab her, damn you!"

The taboo was deeply ingrained in them. Despite the order, both *gishi* remained rooted to the rungs of the ladder. Neither man would look directly at her, neither dared touch her. Her speed began to increase dangerously under the force of air, threatening to spit her from the poiseway shaft and onto the shuttle deck with bone-crushing force. Careless of the amygdala in his keeping, he lunged up into the shaft and felt the peristaltic waves heave at him. Then he caught the woman twenty feet above the end of the poiseway.

She made a grab for his braided cuff and he pulled with all his strength on the handhold he had taken. For a moment their faces were pressed cheek to cheek and his hand slid round across her naked breasts so that he felt her firmness and the unmistakable touch of her nipple, then the field was falling again and he released her into it. She was naked apart from a pair of white ankle socks and the silk robe hanging from her elbows. Long black hair whipped about her deadpan face; the white makeup ended in a semicircle just below her collarbones; below that her petite body was golden, girlish, perfumed, and warm. She was groggy and distressed.

Quickly, he wrapped her in the fluttering robe and drew a fold across her middle to preserve her decency, then he guided her down to the shaft bottom. He knew that she had been disgraced in the eyes of her husband: true, a *gaijin* had seen her naked body, and held her, but her embarrassment at losing her footing in the shaft and her obligation at being saved from falling would far outweigh her concern over that.

He felt a sudden sympathy for the samurai noblewoman. She had been revealed to him by pure chance, and he had been affected by her. He knew that the glimpse of her had confirmed all he had imagined. Hers was the presence that had disturbed his sleep and invaded his dreams for a month. She was beautiful.

He entered the shuttle and dropped into the copilot's seat, landing heavily, aware that Shingo was staring furiously at him. He grabbed the stick—no autopanel, just a damned big hole where the unit should be—so now the shuttle required two pilots.

He activated the comscreen and shouted to the *gishi* to hurry down.

"Get down here! Quickly!"

They began to obey reluctantly, then Quinn shouted down fifty feet when he saw Bowen's contorted face appear at the top of the poiseway. The astrogator held a blaster in his hand.

"Get back up here, you sonsofbitches!" Bowen yelled.

Obediently, the *gishi* launched up out of the shaft again, squeezing past Quinn, who held on to his rung. Hayden Straker shouted angrily at the comscreen. "What are you doing? I need those men!"

"You're going nowhere!" Bowen blazed back. "You ain't abandoning! That's your father's orders! Or bad psi on you, you bastard!"

He thrust a fist against the shuttle's console. "Let go the hatch, Quinn!"

"Come back up here, Quinn! That's an order!" The ugly-snouted Wesson blaster came up, following him.

"Shut the hatch, I said!"

He could see the interlock latches jabbing crazily out of the hatch cover like the arms of a starfish, still attempting to engage. Quinn paused, then agonisingly pulled the lever that allowed the hatch to slam. Immediately the interlocks cycled and an urgent red light exploded in the hangar deck warning that the bay doors were opening in ten seconds. Quinn flew down the poiseway and jumped into the shuttle to take the pilot's seat.

"Attaboy, Cadet!"

"You sure you're doing the right thing, Capt'n?"

"We've no choice."

"I hope you're right, suh. I got an awful feeling . . ."

A tiny distorted Bowen blazed from the shuttle fish-eye coms and danced over their consoles. "I'm warnin' you! I'll open up on you if you don't get off that fucken shuttle! Your father's orders." Bowen's rage overflowed. He picked up a dynapad and began keying in overrides, saw it was too late, threw it at the screen. "Shut them fucken bay doors! Shut them, y'hear me? I'm warning you, you thievin' yeller whore's cur bastard! Y'hear me?"

The narrow-band link attenuated the astrogator's futile

curses as the dynapad was kicked uselessly across the *Chance*'s cockpit, and the great ship spat them out and they drew away from its bulk. Bowen ordered a beam weapon fired, but though it filled half the sky with neon pink it was an empty gesture, and Hayden Straker knew it.

Quinn nudged them forward at the slowest walk. Then they felt the softly tearing fields of the giant starboard lateral field as their own puny fields interacted with them, coalescing real slow, then pulling apart like plucking Velcro. And they were out.

Above the shuttle the raging turmoil of the planet's upper atmosphere drowned Hayden Straker's thoughts. He only knew there was young Quinn and the samurai lord and his lady, and that Bowen's gunner had aimed to miss, and that was all that mattered now.

He and Quinn had to work on the setup in unison. They selected a glide-path that phased the shell opaque and endured the gut-wrenching gees of reentry deceleration that would bring their speed down from 30,000 miles per hour to zero. As the shuttle's shell phased clear once more, a glorious but terrifying sight met them. A hurricane sunrise.

Here the Osumi terrain was mountainous. The planet was two hundred twenty light-years plus from Earth Central and had been terraformed a hundred years ago, long enough for the thirty-year ecological kick-start processes to have petered out, leaving a mature-looking ecosphere. Osumi was a moderately diverse planet; below she was mountainous, but soon chocolate brown began to alternate with the sapphire blue of an ocean.

Churning white clouds topped the atmosphere. It was these that worried him. These vast rollers of water vapor had traveled up out of the immensity of Osumi's temperature southern jet stream. They boiled up to seven miles high in a great atmospheric swirl.

The shuttle dived into it. They were thrust deep into its eye where they lost sight of everything, then out again into a gray world where threatening bluffs of nimbus cloud towered twenty thousand feet above them. Then their tiny shuttle was tossed up by turbulence, so their scanners lost contact with the Chinese ships and the *Chance* and the hurricane-shattered coast below.

Hail the size of grapes abraded the plex shell violently. Each time the craft was hit by lightning, Hayden Straker prayed that the organix would not be disabled; he held on to his control grip until his arms ached and the bones of his knuckles started to show through. Each time they were lifted up, high winds slammed them and he snatched a breathless moment to interrogate the navigation module about where they could land.

It was like an evil nightmare. The *Chance* and her Chinese pursuers were high above, stars of a night that had started to go out. No beam weapon would pick them out and evaporate them now, no tractor would latch on to them, Chinese or Amerikan. They were on their own.

The buffeting threw them about, and he told his priceless passengers to strap in. Soon there was another sound roaring higher above the comms static.

"The mountains! Thank psi for that!"

But the thanks died on his lips. He saw where the furious power of the storm met the skeleton of the planet where its fury was dissipated in wild mountain gusters. The valley into which they fell was long and broad, shallow shelving blocks of bluestone slag, then grasslands and a forest of great mature fast-gro trees, in patches blown flat as celery, and beyond that, lagoons of mineral green. But then they were rising again into the mountains and the god of plan-etfalls had set a triple barrier of shark's teeth between them and safety. No runway landing would be possible here. Just crevassed ice and certain death.

A deepening whine came from the shuttle's starboard side. Then the port engine cut out too.

"*Kuso!*" Shit!

"What'll we do?" Quinn asked, horrified by the sudden lack of engine noise and the rain pounding on the forward windshield. They hammered at the control, but the panel showed both engines were totally without power and un-restartable.

"Glide."

"Glide, Capt'n?"

"That and pray."

"*Kuso!*"

This time the swearing came from behind them. Now the shuttle was completely in manual control, it bucked like a mule. Despite the samurai woman's efforts, she could not close her seat webbing and she was struggling angrily. He tore his eyes away from her to look at the broken teeth of the mountain range ahead. They were higher; some were capped with snow. The peaks shed manes of pure white from their tops, and it seemed they were horse heads coming in a death charge towards them. The incredible, deadly beauty of it almost paralysed him.

He fought the horrible weight of the shuttle's steering, the deadness in his arms. His breath came in gasps, his words almost lost in the roar.

"Keep flying, you bastard!"

"We can't make it without the engines!"

"We'll get through!"

He committed them to their fates, praying that his timing was good, believing that somehow he could keep the nose square to the enormous peaks. Then they shot the gap and he heaved on his control grip, breaking his back in a last effort to turn the shuttle. Then they plowed into a hell of ice spicules and were pushed up into the swirling air.

Once—twice—three times they were carried forward on the wind's surges. Each time, when the shuttle crashed down again, both sticks were miraculously still in their hands and the flashing, twisting walls of volcanic slag had missed them. The thundering of the wind was suddenly deafening, its grip irresistible. Thirty, forty feet lower and the skids would ground, but the shuttle was still gliding in, down below the tree line and zipping over a forest of big conifers.

Suddenly they were lifted up, but this time the eddies caught them and threw them sideways. The seats were flung up out of their runnels. He saw the fearsome branches of a big pine arch over them and fill the forward windshield as they turned broadside to it, then ten tons of splintering timber fell on them and the world turned upside down.

He choked on burning fumes, broke into clean air, fought for breath. When his sight cleared he saw Quinn's pilot's seat was gone. Just wrenched out, like a giant hand had grabbed it. The shuttle around him was now just a shattered mess of crush panels above a boiling maelstrom; there was a gentle steaming along one side as highly corrosive fluorolube dribbled from a smashed duct. A tremendous weight pressed in on his chest. The samurai and his lady were a motionless mass behind him, also trapped inside the crash cage. Then Danny Quinn's head rolled from the upturned seat ten feet away.

"Oh, psi help you, Danny!"

A gasping scream bubbled in his throat, and the terror of the decapitation made his throat taut. Quinn's head rolled in the expanding pool of lube and began to be consumed in a hissing, spitting mass and Hayden Straker knew that psi could not help him, nor could anything, and that the next minute would see the caustic fluid spread to his own body and sear the flesh from him.

In a rage of despair he screamed, defying psi. All his life he had lived with bad psi, never truly knowing how to shape it. It was like living in the crater of a live volcano. Sometimes he thought he knew what it was; he knew he hated it. He had foolishly gambled everything on his fate, and now in one savage strike it had robbed him of his future, his honor, and his life. Now all would soon be lost.

"Wake up!" he shouted at the Japanese. "Wake up, or die!"

He tried and failed to throw off the crushing weight from his chest, saw the braid on the sleeves of his father's jacket begin to hiss and smoke powerfully as the lube reached it. Then he made one final effort to force the wreckage off his legs before abandoning himself to unconsciousness.

5

"This humble slave begs audience. Please have the goodness, Most Honorable Captain Straker, to accept the compliments of my master, His Excellency Hu Tsung, Governor of Yang-Mun' and the Fourth Canton of Wu-Chu, Admiral of the Fleet of Her Most Celestial Magnificence, the Dowager of the Central Realm."

The psi-storm had passed and Ellis Straker's mind was calm. His head hurt like hell, and the untreated wound throbbed in the cool of the Kan air-con.

They always stink like fried-noodle parlors, he thought. Never found out what it is, but Kan ships got this smell about them. Like rancid soy sauce and aniseed, and the damned singy-songy noises you hear. They got no sense of decorum.

The Chang Tai orbited steadily, her bridge busy with activity as the Kan flagship prepared to depart for the nexus once more. He turned a smiling face to the ship's officer and made his reply in formal Mandarin.

"I prostrate myself before you, Eminent Sir, in thanks for your cordiality. My treatment and that of my worthless astrogator, here, has been inappropriate to a humble trader of such lowly rank. Indeed, I am most shocked at the extravagance of it."

The Kan officer held an ornamented box before him.

Bowen stood hard-faced and brooding at Ellis's side.

He was running a violent eye over the officer's extravagant blue-and-gold uniform *pau,* the man's patrician face and stiff demeanor and the braided queue that hung from his half-shaved head. But when the astrogator's eye lingered on the gilded Imperial dragon that entwined the butt of his beam weapon, Ellis suddenly understood what was in Bowen's mind.

The decision to surrender the *Chance* without a fight had gone against his obstinate Virginia grain, and since coming aboard he had sunk into a murderous silence.

We're standing on a busy bridge, Ellis thought, just twenty paces from an emergency-egress hatch. A drop pod would be a simple way out for you, Red Bowen. But you forget it was a long time ago when I first set eyes on you, back when you and I were working the Zone for Jos Hawken.

Ellis stepped forward, his smile fixed, and abruptly addressed the Chinese officer. The officer's little fingers had nails easily two inches long. They were protected by silver sheaths.

Just like a couple of eagles on a Navy epaulette, he thought. A mark of seniority—maybe twelve or fifteen years in the service. He's a seniorish panjandrum; therefore, he's not been sent as an insult. Ellis's smile became indulgent; he knew he ought to offer a standard double-talk formula for "Okeh, pal, what do you want?"

"Eminent Sir, it is my misfortune that I cannot offer your rank greater respect, but—"

"Ah, this Unworthy Slave brings you a message. It is truly nothing."

"That I cannot believe of so august a messenger. Perhaps I might be permitted to know what is the nature of this communication you carry?"

"An inconsequential matter from the lord of this ship.

Admiral Hu notes that you have suffered some small loss. He asks if you will accept the present of this, his own cataplasm—to seal your wound from the harshness of the Osumi atmosphere?''

The lid was lifted, and the cataplasm oozed digustingly inside its box. It was a genetically bred—some said illegally engineered—Old Earth sea slug that liked nothing better than to sit across damaged human skin and divide healing time by a factor of anywhere from two to ten, depending on breed and quality. Ah, yes, Ellis thought. The Chinese have a regular fetish for them. The Celestial Servants sometimes wear the enzyme-free species at Court like a hat, and they say that there are special breeds kept at the Dowager's Forbidden City for sexual purposes—though that's a rumor I never had opportunity to confirm. What's this?

From the corner of his eye Ellis could see the warship's maintenance drones working steadily at their tasks, their installing and testing significantly urgent. Beside them two thick skeins of secure signal cables were being looped through to the astrogator's cockpit. Outside, on the Chang Tai's flanks, egress teams were out reconfiguring the antennas. Ellis smiled delicately, conscious of the goal he had set himself and of Bowen's lethal hair-trigger presence at his side. He nodded once, his face florid in the spicy atmosphere of the bridge, then, without warning, he launched an iron-hard fist into Bowen's unsuspecting midriff, doubling him up.

The Chinese officer stepped back and stared disbelievingly as Ellis took Bowen's upper arm and began slapping his back genially.

"Apologies, Eminent Sir. This pathetic minion has what you call a 'little bellyache,' " Ellis said in his best Mandarin. "And this is merely the Amerikan folk remedy for hiccups. Now, you may convey back to his Esteemed Excellency this message: 'I return his compliments two-fold and I thank him for his remarkable civility. Tell him I understand that the cataplasms grown from Xanadu cultures are generally regarded as of the highest quality.' "

He took the box and delivered a forty-five-degree bow. "I shall report your kind words exactly."

The officer dipped his head in a Xanadu bow of acceptance, still startled by the sudden blow. As he withdrew, Ellis slapped Bowen's shoulder. Yep, he thought with satisfaction, my name's well enough known among all the nexus rats of Yamato. It won't have taken long for the news to spread through the Chang Tai's wardroom that they've made a prisoner of Ellis. That belly poke'll do my reputation no harm at all. I'll bet they're like a bunch of washerwomen over what Hu Tsung wants to do with us.

When the officer left the bridge, Ellis lowered his mouth to Bowen's ear. The astrogator was gasping heavily.

"Get your wind back, Red."

"Fucken Jeezus—Ellis—what was that for?"

"You know damned well. Can't you keep up a five-minute pretense for the sake of manners? And lift your head up, Red. When you were without work, I gave you a berth on my ship. Yeah, twenty years ago, lubeneck, when you were suffering and I had my pick of a hundred like you. And I did it again after the war, when you'd pissed yourself and all your profits away. Don't forget you still owe me. Now—you all right?"

Ellis stared at him until he nodded his head tightly, still clutching his stomach. "I'm—all right."

"Good." He cocked an eye towards the drones. "Now, do you see all this quasi-coding and reconfiguring that's going on? I want to know what you make of it."

Bowen straightened up enough to watch the egress teams at work on the far side of the blister.

"She's been in action, all right—I seen her starboard fins—all new plex—her lateral's been retracked—and the blisters—along her weapons deck have been recut—she's taken a heavy burn from beam weapons—no more'n a week ago."

"That was my thinking."

Commodore Vaile must be close, Ellis thought, coldly calculating the chances that the Amerikan squadron was hunting the Kan marauders. By psi, if I know Vaile he'll be hanging off the nexus in Delta CrA, waiting for these dung flies to settle on Osumi. Then he'll come over the event horizon like a crack of thunder and smash them while they're sitting on the apron and helpless. Yep, that's sure to be Vaile's plan. I heard he's a good strategist and a fearless man. I wish I was in Seoul now, in a big bed with Su Lin or Eriko or pretty little Naoe. Shame about those silk *yukata*. They'll think I've forgotten about 'em and give me hell, as sure as shit, and—

Bowen suddenly growled a revolting oath toward a passing Kan engineer. The foul stream of words made the man start and drop his dynapad.

"For psi's sake, man," Ellis barked. "Will you hold yourself in check? And lift your mouth!" He lowered his voice. "By psi, you'll smile, all right. I surrendered to these *shoben*-heads for a damned good reason, and you're not gonna spoil it."

It was yesterday, Ellis recalled, with his skull split and pain eating at his wound and no balance in his legs, that he had been answered back by his dirty-mouthed astrogator for the first time in ten years. And for the first time, he, Ellis Straker, had seen fit to make an explanation to him.

"You'll send out an UnCon 40," he had ordered, knowing it was time for desperate last measures, a maneuver aimed at limiting his losses. But the order had shocked Bowen and busted his temper.

"You're fixing to surrender?"

"Yep. And to offer the Kan Osumi pilotage data, too."

"Fucken help them? But why?"

"Do your duty, man."

"But we're all fixed up for a fucken fight, eh!"

Ellis had stared him down hard. "Ah, shit. A fight's suicide. And you know it."

"That's not what you told your son! You lied to him!"

Then something inside had made Ellis trade words with Bowen in a way he had never done before. "Listen, Red, you sonofabitch: Hayden's just a boy who can't figure beyond running into a *rashie* or trading beams with a White Tiger Class junk. But I had myself an ingot of a plan!"

"So why didn't you fucken tell him about it? You made him fucken Sencho. You know he can make good. He ain't a fucken boy no more."

"I told him I'd blood him, didn't I? I said I'd teach him, show him his old daddy's way with anybody that stands in our path. He can run a nexus ship, all right, but that's nothing. It's how he recognises his talent. And how he gets himself out of a bind. That's what counts!"

"Yeah, and now you fucken know. He knocks the fucken shit out of you and shoots off with your fucken amygdala and your fucken hostages in a shuttle that's got no auto panel and's only quarter-powered—"

"Ah, zip it up, Red!"

"No wonder they say you've become a fucken wicked bastard that don't trust fucken nobody, Ellis Straker."

"I told you to zip your filthy mouth, Bowen!"

But instead Bowen had faced him, all vestige of his customary respect shredded. "Your son asked me to guess what fucken devil-trick you had in mind, but I couldn't figure it out. By God, he was fucken right about you. You are the very devil!''

Ellis had turned on him, his finger stabbing, his teeth still chewing on a burned-out cheroot.

"Now you just listen to me, asshole! You know as well as I do that the Kan're bent on taking Osumi. Don't you understand that with a shit-for-brains like Aziza Pope acting like the Queen of Sheba at Kanoya the place'll be overrun without a fight, and then the Kan'll possess damn near everything I've got. So it's devil-tricks my ass!'' He had snatched out his cheroot then. "Psi damn you, man, you should've stopped Hayden like I told you and everything would've been okeh!''

"I tried, by psi!''

Ellis had spat then, angry beyond control. "Ah, you let my son go to his death!''

"I didn't have the power to stop him! And you don't know he's killed, but if he is then it was you and not me who sent him to it!''

"Why, you bad-assed scum—''

Ellis's words had halted and he had grabbed two fistfuls of Bowen's jacket, but the astrogator had been a dead weight, unmoving, unafraid, and he had said, ice cold an inch from Ellis's face, "I'll not pronounce on you, Ellis. Nor on your son. But I know every man has his snapping point. And you pushed him too far, so you did.''

Ellis had broken off his stare then. He had put Bowen down. There had been a smoldering pause and then the order had raged out of him. "Do your duty with the UnCon 40, like I told you!'' And he had stamped below to sort the ruined documents and illegal chrysoids from his busted safe before the boarding party arrived and learned too much.

The shame of it. He had lost a cross of words with

his own astrogator, and that soured him and angered him because he knew that to lose a man's respect was a terrible thing, and irrecoverable. He had picked up the red-bound disc of Kan signal codes and ripped out its spline before meticulously erasing its pages one by one. Then he had smashed up the pale-blue datachord.

He had bought the disc last year from Kim Gwon Chung, the Korean privateer, knowing he might need it. He had had the counterfeit interrogation datachord made up by a shady Seoul chandler the same day he had bought those pretty silk shifts, one each for his little Seoul girlies. All of it for the price of two dozen bulbs of real Louisville bourbon and a couple of dozen canisters of Taipei's highly prized "white-blossom" ginseng and the canceling out of a big mah-jongg debt. He had planned to beam out the false ID if they ran across a Kan patrol, as he believed they might.

We coulda bluffed our way past Hu Tsung and the Chang Tai piss easy, he had thought regretfully, watching the smoke rise from his ruined booby-trap safe. Yep, piss easy. That's how things should've been:

> *Signal to flagship: humbly declare that I am the Xanadu private trader "Tiensin." If the Honorable Organ of the Imperium will please excuse my insolent caution, I was blind enough to mistake you for Amerikan warships. May I request permission to inject into Osumi orbit so you may chastise my gigantic foolishness?*

And that would've been that! A little fast reflex maneuver and we'd've been down on the Kanoya City apron an hour ahead of them, psi-storm or no psi-storm. Yeah, and with the means to prevent the Kan from pressing their siege. Instead of that we've got ourselves an irreparable mess!

A prideless course had been forced on them. The UnCon 40 had been beamed out and acknowledged, armed boarders had swarmed across, and he had been meekly taken off the *Chance*. All the eager Kan crew had found in the holds were containers of nondescript stuff and the stink of a charred-out safe in the owner's suite.

Once aboard the *Chang Tai*, Ellis had feigned ignorance of the state of war existing between Xanadu and Amerika to the ship's officers and formally protested his vessel's being confiscated as loot, but it had been a feint while he waited for the notoriety of his name to spread through the ship and arouse the interest of the Kan admiral.

Meanwhile, a personal promise of good behavior, given by Ellis to the Chinese captain, had paroled Bowen, but at his release the astrogator had considered himself totally betrayed.

"We could've taken 'em! Y'know we could've. Why did you surrender *Chance* an' all, ey?"

He had told him firmly but quietly, "Because, Red, politicking's my stock-in-trade, and I've got to get close to their admiral to do that. Now I've lost both the Prefect's son and the amygdala, this is the only gambit I've got left to play."

Since then, Ellis had watched and he had waited and, throughout the day, he had seen more than enough to interest his mind. The Kan ships had maneuvered a number of big shuttles to be landed south of Kanoya City. They were landing troops. He had estimated two thousand Kan regulars revived aboard the flagship and a further thousand in freezees—auxiliaries brought along in suspension to be resuscitated when required—and with them what looked like beam-weapon ground installations and some meaty 80-kV cell units.

So, he thought, watching the lit-up drones wander and

work over the ship's sturgeonlike upper surfaces, now I know the Kan have landed beam weapons and personnel. Those forces will keep in contact with the fleet as best they can, then they'll surround Kanoya City and reduce it and nobody'll have the power to stop them except Commodore Vaile and his squadron. I need to know what's become of him, and I'll have the chance tonight, by psi.

He brushed at a tatter in his sleeve, memories of the last two days still churning his belly until a fond thought quelled them.

Ah, Kim, you're a wily old Korean nexus rat! But so much for the so-called amygdala you've been trying to unload for years. What an irreplaceable asset I almost made of that dumb old chrysoid. It's now the thing Hideki Ryuji wants more than anything in existence. And why? Because the daimyo got quietly convinced of its power to lay a hex and a hoodoo. Because somebody real clever made him believe with all his heart there was an amygdala that could erase the death curse on Yamato's most sacred big-deal samurai sword.

Oh, yes, Hideki Ryuji wants that amygdala, all right. He's an ambitious man. Made a general at thirty by the great Shogun, Baron Harumi himself. Made daimyo of Osumi at forty, by his successor and Prefect of all Kyushu Quadrant a year later by the current Shogun. Ah, a big mistake! Sakuma Hidenaga's Shogun of all Yamato, Overlord of the Empire, the most powerful man in Yamato— more powerful, in fact, than the one man who formally outranks him, the Son of Heaven himself, the Emperor.

Ellis smiled inwardly, enjoying his own astuteness. Yep, it was good psi the daimyo of Osumi came to learn of that special amygdala. Yep, very good psi indeed. A stroke of genius, I'd say. And for me to think of making it Kim Gwon Chung's unsigned chrysoid, that was real clever too. Because a chrysoid metacrystal of a hundred *mensa* is capable of being programmed with a whole bucket of cheap side-show effects that'll convince a man who wants to believe.

An unsigned hundred-*mensa* chrysoid's a rare thing indeed, and it was fortunate again that I happened to know of a man who wanted to unload one before all this started, and more fortunate still that the Kan were growing restless. I smelled ozone a long time ago. I knew there'd be a war and that I'd find a way to burn a credit or two out of MeTraCor's tight ass.

Ellis watched the planet slide by below with its big, swirling anticyclone of cloud. His flame of self-satisfaction guttered low. He almost sighed. Hayden's defection had thrown his affairs into worse chaos than a Korean's kitchen. It was a disaster.

By Elvis and all the Adventer saints, Hayden Straker, you've left your old daddy at a powerful disadvantage. If you had to run off I wish you'd have gone in your own jacket. You're a psi-damned coward and a thief, and I'll even pray to the god of reentry that by some chance you made planetfall so that one day I can find you and take the cost of my ruination from out of your hide.

However he looked at it, the losses were huge. On account, a jewel worth fifty *tranches* of aurium had had to be bought. Half of that—twenty-five *tranches*—was the sum Ellis had pledged to raise himself, a sum greater than his personal wealth and close to the limit of his credit. To keep the pretense he had had to show the aurium backing the *tranche* to Controller Pope, and to do that he had had to raise a loan part secured against everything he owned.

But knowing much more than he had told Pope, he had quietly put fifteen *tranches* into Jos Hawken's hands for safekeeping and stored the rest, ten *tranches*, innocently in the *Chance*'s cargo bay. As Ellis had expected, once the deal was moving Pope had started to hedge, then to go back on her word. Of the twenty-five *tranches* raised by MeTraCor, the Controller had insisted only ten *tranches* could go with Ellis to Kagoshima. The other fifteen was to be redeemed on a MeTraCor credit flag to be presented by Kim Gwon Chung in person, and would only be honored after the amygdala arrived and Osumi was effectively ransomed.

Though Ellis had expected it, he had not liked it. But despite the fact that it complicated matters he had reluctantly agreed, knowing that there would be plenty of Koreans willing to play-act the part of Kim Gwon Chung for him when the day to collect arrived.

That was a mistake, Ellis reflected sourly. Of the twenty *tranches* I paid Kim for that chrysoid, half was my own. In ten days I'd have stood to take five *tranches* free and clear off MeTraCor, without risk, and earned the eternal gratitude of the Directors for doing it. And I'd have got myself a writ allowing me to run trading ships direct to Europa that would have made me a fortune. Instead, without the chrysoid, I can't collect MeTraCor's fifteen, I've lost the ten *tranches* of my own that went to Kim, and ten of MeTraCor's, too. Then there's the interest on the loan . . . Jeezus, I'm worse than busted flat, I'm damn near inside out!

The hundred-*mensa* chrysoid was lost. The daimyo of Osumi's second son was killed—the man's wife into the bargain. There would be no forgiveness in Hideki Ryuji's heart now. And no means to secure his help. Kanoya City would fall and become Kan to the ruin of all Amerikan trade in Yamato.

The throbbing in Ellis Straker's head made him sick at the injustice. You've ruined me, Hayden, when all I wanted was to make a man of you. And after I fixed it for you to marry Arkali Hawken, who's without a sliver of doubt the most eligible female outside Amerika, by psi, and tasty enough to suit any young buck. Ah, it's all next to hopeless now. Better to have let you blitz us all to glory in the *rashie*, better you'd burned me as I lay, instead of running off with our whole future.

Now there'll be no marriage with Jos Hawken's daughter, and no merging of our enterprises, and MeTraCor's goddamned monopoly will go on—even if only out of Seoul and the rest of the Zone and only until the Kan choke trade off completely.

Ah, because MeTraCor's chock full of spineless flakers they'll surrender to Hu Tsung and lose the Lease, and that'll be the beginning of the end because if they lose Osumi they'll lose all Yamato trade, and then Seoul too, in time. And if that happens Amerika'll lose her revenue and the Kan'll gain it and the Dowager'll use all that credit to build for war, where we can't no more. By psi, within ten years we'll be fighting for our lives again, in Kalifornia and up along the Boundary and along the Thirty Degree worlds and in all the Amerikan dependencies, and before we know it they'll be strangling Old Glory herself and everyone in the Sector will have to speak the Kan's shit-gobbling language for evermore. Psi damn the Kan to the deepest ice hell! And psi damn you, too, Hayden, you thieving young cur, I wonder if you are dead, because, as I stand here and spit, I'd burn you through for what you did!

Within the hour the smell of Dover chow began to issue from the galley by the officer's wardroom and the flagship's talkback sounded off the menu in an echoing singsong. Bowen's mouth began to water. "Shall I fetch you back a bowl of something, Ellis?" he asked, respectful once more.

Ellis straightened and inhaled the air with satisfaction. The savor of *char siu*, marinaded pork, and onions fried in sesame seed oil made him smile. "Nope. I believe I've an appetite to preserve."

Bowen's jaw dropped. He saw Ellis's oddly easy mood, and knew it foreboded trouble. "Did I hear you right, Chief? You don't want none?"

"Ah, man! Did you not understand that gobble about the cataplasm? I'll lay you fifty *tranches* to a pail of piss I'll be dining on real organic chow with the Kan admiral tonight. Then we'll see where we're really at."

6

A huge Amerikan eagle insignia was phased into the plex of the dome, slowly bleaching to pink and pale blue under the burning glass of the sky, while beneath it Kanoya City prepared to meet the Chinese battle squadron now coming down onto the apron.

At first sight, the citadel of Kanoya was an impressive domed plex fortress eight years old and a mile across. It fronted the planet's main apron and was backed to the north by a huge sprawl of traditional Yamato-style peasant dwellings. At the center of Kanoya's western sweep the ornate portals had been slid shut, as had the hatches of all beam-weapon sites guarding the approaches, but their design was obsolete and their situation ill-considered. At the city's four corners diamond-plan weapons platforms thrust out, giving sharp casts of shadow to the plex walls, but those walls were patched and badly seamed and their phasing suspect, and no one was prepared to bet they would withstand a sustained beam-weapon assault.

Now the great white buildings within the city stood blinded by panes phased down against the noonday brightness. These were MeTraCor blocks, official buildings, residences and apartments, but one of them, the one over which the shadow of the eagle's eye was now passing, was peculiar. It was the third largest, adorned by an eagle also, or so it seemed—twice Controller Pope had tried to have that ''eagle'' removed, but it remained. A close look showed it to be a hawk. It indicated the house of Hawken Inc.

High up in the twentieth-floor penthouse, Arkali Hawken smoothed the front of her sheath of green silk and examined her face in an ultrafine-resolution macroscreen. Gray-green eyes stared back at her, offset by the viewing angle. The mac was useful for self-examination, better than a simple mirror because the detachable microcamera allowed different viewpoints and focal lengths to be selected.

She saw that her eyes were wide and clear; red tresses hung at her temples and fell across shoulders that were chalk white. She saw with approval that her carefully preserved pallor remained intact. It was the only compensation for the long voyage and the three months she had spent living within the Kanoya City lease. She pursed her lips in satisfaction, but as she looked closer at her delicate features, she saw that the events of the last three nights had left their mark around her eyes.

As she turned from the screen she saw her father surveying the Lease from the big seat in his executive suite. She felt her stomach turn over at the sight of him. He had hardly moved all morning, and the depth of his despair terrified her.

Jos Hawken was growing old, slight of build, private of manner and of speech, reputedly ice-hearted in all matters of business, yet now his palm sweated on a porcelain bottle, sweated just as it had three hours ago, except that now the bottle and the drinking thimble beside it were both emptied of rice wine. And though his gray-blue eyes were open, their gaze was fixed and he seemed to be in a trance. Her first thought was that he had poisoned himself.

As that fear began to cobweb her mind, she started forward, making her approach deliberately brisk.

"Father, are you going to sit here all day?"

A moment passed, then he was stirred by her rustling skirt.

"I'm sorry, Arkali. I was thinking."

Despite her fears she tried to sound kindly. "It's lunchtime. Perhaps you'll have a little something with me?"

"I'm not hungry." He paused, as if distracted by his inner vision again. After a moment he added, still without looking up, "But, please, have Mrs. Watanabe cook you something real to eat."

"Mrs. Watanabe is no longer here."

"What did you say?"

"I gave her leave to go to her brother's home in the township."

"Arkali, you shouldn't have done that."

She went back inside the airy office. Despite her father's recent redecorations, it was still tastefully period, she thought, with heavy classic Amerikan furniture from perhaps the first Rooseveldt's time—reproduction, of course, but well made, probably servant-crafted. It had the look of old-fashioned power: animal leather couches, a giant writing desk, patterned carpets, walls half-paneled in carved oakwood, an elegant typewriter ornament set on a silver tray, and in the corner a large mahogany coat stand for show, with a Homburg and a Washington tricorne and a "baseball hat" on it. Just like it might have been in, say, A.D. 1900. Overhead, a green tokage lizard clung sinuously to the high ceiling, still as a jeweled brooch, tropical and alien and a reminder that although the fake chimney breast showed off a genuine *New Yorker* cartoon and the wallpaper was Twentieth Century Manhattan à la mode, this was not the drawing room of some Old Earth salon, nor a quirky Lincoln mansion, this was an office in a bubble city on a stinking Lease across the other side of Known Space.

The lizard watched, motionless, as half a dozen ugly flies described endless square orbits under the brass chandelier, and suddenly Arkali felt very alone. Since the day three months ago when she had disembarked at the Kanoya City apron, she had been accorded the highest degree of respect by her father's staff, given every attention by his two hundred household servants. Even her Korean personal maid, Suzi, had been treated in an elevated way.

There's been, she thought, almost more fussing than a young heiress might expect or require.

But, though she understood her father's reputation, and listened to his pleas that she come to him instantly with the slightest problem, he had remained indefinably distant from her.

It's not, she decided, any lack of paternal love for me. There just seems to be some chill in his soul these days, a chill that will not thaw for my sake, nor for anyone's.

Jos Hawken hid his heart skillfully, revealing himself only in lapses, and therefore very rarely. She had seen the truest aspect of him yesterday, during the emergency. Then his charming politeness had faltered, and she had glimpsed a different man. It had been frightening when he had shouted orders at her like some coarse nexus captain, and sent her away. Frightening because she knew she had seen the reality of him, and that scared her.

Of course, she had shown nothing outwardly. She knew she must be prepared to make allowances for her father's past; his life had not been a usual one, nor an easy one, and she was proud of his success and his status. Her mother had told her how he had first gone out to the Neutral Zone as a spec trader after levering himself out of the Navy with a third lieutenant's rank. It had been a route followed only by the strong, the greedy, or the unwanted. Jos Hawken had been at least two of the three.

Jos Hawken turned it all over in his mind now like a plowed field. He felt as if he had been hit by a stunner. Drained. Knocked groggy. With all his life energy in a damned great puddle at his feet.

What does it all signify? he thought. Succeed or fail. Rich or poor. What does it all matter? What's the damned meaning of it all? And why are we here? Is this my trading empire? Is this my daughter and the heir to it all? God damn it, how fast life passes.

He and his brother had teamed up and prospered. As far as his brother and parents had been concerned, Jos's chief hope had lain in the notion of riches to be won by anyone willing to hazard their life in the Zone, forbidden though it was.

It was a fact that the Hawken family had certainly been in need of enrichment. They were a straggling branch of the lesser plutocracy that had been brought low financially a generation before, and by the time their third son came of employable age they owned little more than a tumbledown house on Liberty, a hundred thousand unproductive acres on one of the Dakota continents, and a rising tide of mortgage bonds. But the boy had shown hints of psi talent in his general-matriculation exam, and that had been enough.

Jos's father had indentured him to the Navy to learn about ships and astrogation, and he had gone willingly, though the Navy at that time had not been much of a service. He had learned and worked and performed like an average cadet officer, a certain native psi talent had been honed up, but it had not enough to get him into astrogation school, and he had despaired.

About then there had been a political putsch by the Expansionist tendency and Alia Kane had taken up residence in the White House, ousting the Henry dynasty. It had meant a revolution in attitude, and new opportunities, so he had used his Navy release credit to go in with his trader brother and purchase a kettle of a ship—a local lugger never built for long or difficult chains, but with a genuine Newport News hull. So it happened that he had lit out, determined to face the perils of the first outward voyage any Amerikan entrepreneur had dared to take into the Zone in fifty years.

What he had found there had shocked him. Almost the entire Zone had been Yamato-controlled and even Yamato-settled, but nobody seemed to be expecting an Amerikan and he had worked the first voyage for a good profit.

That first homecoming had been ecstatic. Despite suffering bad climates and tough conditions and the virus diseases that the new Zone settlements fostered, he had brought most of his crew back, and those that survived became instantly rich. They had endured everything, and all for a vanishing chance at wealth—but perhaps also the chance to feel a brand of excitement that had almost vanished from Amerika in the Henry years: the thrill of hard work and due reward in dangerous circumstances. It was a drug to hook any ambitious man. High commitment, high reward—just as he liked it.

Complaints from the Yamato ambassador had put Alia Kane in a difficult position. Her dilemma was this: should she go ahead and back Hawken as her heart said, or reprimand him as her head told her was the wiser course? Typically, she did what might have been expected of Alia Kane. She did both. Publicly, she forbade Hawken, or any private trader, to exceed the Thirty Degree line; privately, she summoned him and Billy to have dinner. And, of course, the Brothers Hawken had gone along—with their own chopsticks, just in case.

The President's dinner table was an infamous place of slaughter and glory. At that table confident magnates had been reduced to *jellosept,* Army field officers and Admiralty panjandrums demoted to instant civilians—Alia's autocracy was notoriously unpredictable, her moods famously variable, and her wit always acerbic. There had been some dangerous politicking before the coffee cake had come around, but he and Billy had walked out of the White House like a pair of kings. They had done the deal that made Jos Hawken, nominally, a Navy commodore. It had been what they wanted: covert backing.

The price had been heavy. A third voyage. It was only at flag-rank seniority that a man could be deemed to represent the President in matters of state. As a private merchant he could no longer trade in the Zone, but as a Navy commodore he had become an instrument of an independent Amerikan policy. Inside the Navy the chances of his reaching that status had been, at best, one in fifty thousand. He had become the first man in Amerikan naval history to go from being a third lieutenant to a commodore in one nexus jump.

Jos Hawken had seen the possibilities of the third voyage the very next day. He had applied himself diligently to his preparations, but even more diligently to working up further angles in the White House, and within six months he had devised a method of outfoxing the spies the Yamato authorities were running inside the Navy Commission. He had been clever enough to see there was a ship in it—if he played his discs right. He had talked to the head of grav-phys at the RISC Foundation, and had gotten his way in the form of a big old seven-thousand-ton battle wagon, the *Thomas Jefferson*. Another ship, the *Richard M*, had been added later. The catch was that he had had to take an entirely new weapon out with him to test in the Zone.

There had been many adventures on that ill-starred third voyage, and he had barely escaped with his life, but that weapon had shown him the way. It had been the singularity gun, an awesome device that fired knots of space-time— singularities like small quasi–black holes that would propagate through normal Euclidean space and penetrate anything made of matter—even plex. Those guns made Amerika the greatest threat to Yamato. They caused a war.

Suddenly, there had lain the key to the future, for all nexus ships no matter how modern needed to be reequipped now, and Amerika's Navy needed to be rebuilt. It had occurred to Jos Hawken to ask what Amerika should do to prepare for the coming war. If her Navy Commission was so corrupt that it was selling secrets to enemies and funneling funds into greedy men's private Zwiss credit accounts, something had to be done. But what? And then he had found the obvious answer. The executive power of Alia Kane.

Prompted by his brother and judicious "advice" made through high-level connections, he had gained a position as Joint Chief. From 2432 on he had ruled the Navy Commission almost single-handedly, to the chagrin of the parasites who had been sucking it dry. There had been several assassination attempts and a bomb at his mansion, but in the nine years that elapsed until the Yamato invasion he had worked tirelessly in the service of his Sector.

When it finally came, the invasion fleet was crushed. Amerika emerged almost without a scratch, but mighty Yamato was suddenly left without any defenses whatsoever. The Shogun's forces had had to retreat behind the closed boundary of their own Sector, abandoning their settlements throughout the Zone and retrenching beyond the Zero Degree line.

Jos Hawken had resigned his stewardship and gone back to what he loved best: commerce. Three years of Amerika running all trade in the Neutral Zone had followed, and even brooding Yamato had agreed to open up one city of one continent of one planet of one of her systems to lease to Amerika as a trade center. That had been Osumi, and Jos Hawken had gone right in there to stake his claim. An Amerikan vogue for Yamato culture had begun to explode across the home Sector, and Jos had understood at once how much could be gained just by giving people what they wanted. The stylistic fashions had meshed with concerns back home over substance, and the "real" fad had begun. Suddenly people wanted realfood and realwood and realcloth and realbooks and realeverything.

By the mid 'forties, Jos had owned a flourishing business. He had amassed enough capital to leave the enterprise to grow by itself. He employed thousands of Osumi silk workers and planters. His cargoes broke records, and the finished Yamato silk that made up half of the shipments was more than enough in itself to raise a tidy profit on each container when it arrived in Amerika.

But then the government had stabbed Jos Hawken in the back.

Following the war the vast Merchant Traders Corporation who had hitherto traded with the Europan Sector had gained the political ascendancy in Lincoln. Their pet aristos had got close to the President, and their trade-offs had swayed certain representatives in both Senate and Congress. The result was a merging of governmental interests and the designs of the Corporation. A declared monopoly was announced: henceforth, MeTraCor, and only MeTraCor, would be permitted to carry commercial goods between Yamato and Amerika. In one July day in 2444, the Trade Monopolies law had been enacted, and Hawken Inc. had been busted flat. Or almost . . .

Arkali sighed at the sight of her father combing out his memories. The story of her father's rise had been her delight as a child. The talk she had picked up from her uncle Billy had often concerned her father's status as a Hero of the Sector or his record as a successful businessman; rarely was there talk of Jos Hawken's later illicit dealings.

After the war, Uncle Billy had handled the operation at the Liberty end, but it had fallen to the Zone trader, Ellis Straker, to forge the last vital connection between Kanoya City and Honshu. Of course, the smuggling they had purportedly involved themselves in had been highly illegal, but no MeTraCor Controller had been willing or able to prove any charge, and though Jos had been attacked by MeTraCor for remaining unaccountably rich, others inside the Corporation were also getting their cut from his efforts, and so long as he drew no guns on MeTraCor and the bribes continued to flow, Jos Hawken knew that his continuing fortune was safe.

Arkali turned the macro on her father and examined him. He was careworn. Exhausted. But it was hard to believe he had fathered her in an act of obscene passion two decades ago, but then sex—copulation—was the greatest mystery of them all. What the Adventers called the "beast rite."

Kate shuddered involuntarily. There had never been any hope of persuading Jos to leave Liberty. Whatever psi instincts he possessed told him that the next year would be crucial, so she had upped and lit out for the New England Quadrant without him, taking her surviving children to live the genteel life of a Rutland absent landowner's wife.

Jos had not tried to prevent her leaving Liberty, not because he did not love her or value her, but because he had seen that her mind was made up, and because her final argument had been unanswerable: she had told him that he didn't need hostages to fortune holding him back.

That had been undeniably true. Much as she liked Uncle Billy, Arkali knew that he had been just as fond of political infighting as her father had been, only far less successful. After Kate had gone, Jos had been given the peace of mind to tackle greater things. Billy supported him loyally during the days of his fight against MeTraCor. He had delivered his notorious letter to the Court of Directors, saying that the Merchant Traders Corporation was a three-way misnomer. First, because it was a monopoly and not a corporation; second, because it didn't fix merchandise—only prices; and last, because MeTraCor's executives were not so much traders as quality deadbeats who never engaged in any trading in their entire lives.

Jos Hawken's attacks had been damning. He had said in the Senate hearings that MeTraCor existed solely to satisfy the greed of its own senior servants, and though he had for many years swallowed MeTraCor's corrupt ways, the time had finally come to denounce them and set about opposing the monopoly of trade with Yamato. Kate had spoken with pride of the clamor that had been raised in

Lincoln six years ago, and how the government, and even the presidency, had been rocked by the revelations.

So Arkali had left Liberty years ago, and nothing much remained of it in her memory. Nothing except a strange déjà vu, certain vivid textures and odors that were to be reawakened when her ship stopped over at Harrisburg apron on the way to the Zone. She had gone nexus-jumping just as her mother had once gone to Liberty to look for a rich husband. The human trade cycle had repeated, this time with herself as cargo.

The present aim, she knew, was an arranged marriage to formally amalgamate the trading houses of Hawken and Straker into a combine capable of spearheading the struggle for Free Trade, but for her it was a great life adventure. A blind leap into destiny. After the deathly quietude of Rutland it had been positively pyrotechnical, and the Zone a real shocker.

Everything about nexus travel had been strange to Arkali, and most of it more than a little frightening. She had undertaken a voyage across two hundred parsecs on a pan-Amerikan MeTraCor ship, the *General Lee*, seventeen jumps on a zigzag voyage almost as long as pregnancy, and during it she had fretted along with the other half dozen unmarried girls aboard. Despite her initial disdain for them, nexus sickness—stark terror before, light-headed astonishment after—the discomforts of her accommodation, and the exotic and frequently pungent cuisine aboard ship, she had gradually been drawn into shared confidences with the two companions whose social rank most nearly approached her own.

Not that that approach was close. Emylu Melnikh was an Army captain's daughter. She said that she had been sent out to join friends in Seoul, she was a nineteen-year-old of good position but low credit rating, who expected to be met and welcomed into a married cousin's respectable home.

Emylu had not been entirely innocent; she had had a hazy notion of what to expect, explaining that Seoul convention dictated a party would be held within a week of arrival. At it, she had explained knowingly, all the eligible Amerikan bachelors who wanted a wife would attend for her to choose between. Of course, there were many men who could not afford the considerable expense of an Amerikan wife. Those men took Korean mistresses, but the suitors she would select from would only be of high credit rating and of suitable rank.

Emylu's frankest worry had been over the ship's UV light balance and the maintenance of her complexion on the long voyage—she had complained that her freckles were multiplying to the point where they joined up—but on Seoul she had received the rudest possible awakening. The cousin on whom she depended had been reported dead of pinkeye.

Then there had been poor, plain Alicia Dutch. By her own admission, her prospects were dismal. Orphancy and a squint had blighted her, and her aristocratic guardian had disposed of her by purchasing a one-way ticket into the Zone aboard the *General Lee*. For Alicia Dutch, with no kin to take her in at Seoul, the future was pretty much what a wall-eyed girl orphan shipped out for convenience might have expected.

Arkali recalled the barbarous rendezvous, little better than a cattle auction, that Alicia and Emylu and the others had been forced to endure. The day they made orbit around Pusan, a dinner had been announced by Captain Jessop, and the girls recommended to put on their finest fabrics. Then the shuttles had come spiraling out to them, shuttles filled with elderly men. Each had looked, to a man, three times Arkali's age, each had been leeringly eager to see the wares brought out for his inspection. Captain Jessop had welcomed them, blue astrogator's cap in hand, urging them to go below to the after assembly where the girls had waited, first for offers of dinner and, before the soiree was out, proposals of marriage.

Arkali recalled how an aging man had mistaken her for one of those poor chattels with nowhere else to go. He had actually had the temerity to proposition her. She could recall the smell of his breath now, vile with snap and rice alcohol, his cheeks a mass of broken blood vessels, and her own stinging rebuff as she repelled his advances.

It had been just after the transit between Pusan and Ulsan that Arkali had learned with horror of the arrangement made in advance by the suitors that any girl who once refused an offer would not receive a second, and of Captain Jessop's strict warning to them that they must be off the ship within one hour.

The shocking education had filled her with doubts about her own fate. How terrible to end up like poor Emylu! What if Hayden Straker was dead of the pinkeye too? Or worse, a rude, uncouth individual. What if he was deformed from snap or designer diseases? Or foulmouthed? Or violent? Or just gross? Or . . .

Her father came in and she looked at him a moment before tears began to well in her eyes and she turned away from him. Then she realised that she was guilty of the trait that she found most difficult to understand in her father: the pathological wish to hide away true feelings.

That's the way of it, she thought. What else should I have expected? A man who spends his years in Yamato must eventually absorb Yamato ideas. Their norms must seep into a man's flesh through his pores, like the alien stink of this foreign planet. And I've always heard it said that in Yamato women are not thought of as fully human. . . .

Before transiting the Thirty Degree line, the nightmares had taunted her: could any father knowingly sacrifice his daughter's happiness simply to further his own financial interests? She now knew the answer to that. After all, it was the custom in most of Known Space from Hindostan and Izlam through the Central Realm . . . and in Yamato, too. Then could Jos Hawken do the same?

On the ship it had been a question to plague her relentlessly. As the beautiful planet of Osumi had drifted across the forward scanners she had contemplated the question, her faith shaken by the strangeness of everything, her mind made restless by all kinds of speculation.

Arkali remembered hardly enough of her father to recognize him the day the *General Lee* finally put down on the Kanoya City apron, but she need not have worried, for there had been a procession of servant attendants to escort the Hawken heiress, and poor little Suzi too, into the city through that strange light beyond the dome.

And her greatest fears had melted away when she met her intended husband, because Hayden Straker had proved to be as fine a man as any woman could desire: tall and tender, softly spoken and handsome in the face. She had fallen in love with him completely during those first embarrassed meetings at which they had coyly taken green tea together. And she had no doubt he had thought quite the same of her.

She looked at the Homburg hat on the Rooseveldt coat stand and the thought occurred to her that in the middle of that long-dead century of box TVs and vibrating metal ground-cars the ethos had been so different: to be free with sex and to fear death, instead of the other way around. How strange the shifting taboos. How true that the past is another country where things were done in ways incomprehensible to us in the here and now. Yes indeedy, quite another country . . .

She sighed. We should have been married two days ago, Hayden and I, she thought, her eyes filling again as she lifted up the lacquer-framed macroscreen and awkwardly took it into her father's business suite. I should be a lawfully wedded woman by now, no longer a virgin.

But instead the war has come and I remain virgo intacta. The ordeal of consummation is yet to come, but I will face that ordeal for you, Hayden, my love. Oh, where are you? Don't you know I put on my wedding gown for you? I offered myself, but you didn't come. Will you ever come now that a thousand Chinese soldiers are outside the city? Has there ever been a more cruel travesty of a wedding day?

Holding back her tears bravely, she slid aside the macro's cover and put her fingers to the selector to tune the device to the limit of its resolution. It began looking out beyond the ceiling and the confines of the dome to the celestial equator, to where shuttles and big, heavily armed Xanadu warships were hanging, half deserted now that most of their human cargo had come down.

Towards the zenith the Chinese flagship rode like a brooding bear surrounded by her cubs. Shuttles ferried to and fro, landing more men and more weapons and equipment on the apron from where she saw the beam weapons transported by ground-cars to freshly dug earthworks and emplacements that surrounded the city. And moving in columns, quilt-suited soldiers in bullet helmets and backpacks, with evil spikes fixed to their six-foot-long blasters.

Below, the normally thronging streets of Kanoya City were vacant. Everyone not in MeTraCor's employment had vanished to their sprawling slum township beyond the walls, to evacuate it and, with their families and belongings, to seek the safety of the wilds. All last night the inland surface routes had been packed with refugees, mainly Yamato peasants and casteless *hinin* fleeing the Lease. But there were also Korean artisans and Malais and *sangokujin*, all kinds of people from the Zone trade. By morning it had been quiet. Only the Amerikans and their personal servants and the Macau-Kalifornian mercenaries who policed the city for MeTraCor in their red leatherine uniforms remained. Three hundred individuals at most.

She put down the macroscreen and suddenly the ever-present aroma of Osumi was poignant in her nostrils—tropical tangs, spicy and chemical, cloying as snap smoke, moist in the humidified air.

The apple trees of Woodnorton would be bursting with summer's bounty now and . . .

She stopped herself, knowing she could never recapture the idyll of her unnaturally extended childhood, understanding it was useless to try, so she focused her thoughts instead on the responsibilities of the present.

"Father, what's happened to Hayden?"

"I don't know, child."

"But the Chinese appeared in orbit the day he was due to return, and they say there's been a huge psi-storm in the nexus—a '*rashie*,' they called it—or perhaps even a tsunami."

This time he did not offer her the self-indulgent smile he always brought out for her attempts at nexus-talk. Instead, his face was gray and cold as marble. "The trouble flared well after they were due to transit."

"Is he safe, Father? I could rest easy if I knew he was safe." She closed her eyes. "Oh, please tell me where he is."

7

The keen edge in Arkali's voice seemed to touch Jos Hawken, and he gathered himself.

"Easy, now. Haven't I explained ten times already? Hayden's aboard Ellis Straker's best ship, and the *Chance* is the best vessel in the Sector." He met her eye but looked away too quickly. "Hey, now, he's probably safe in Seoul, having turned from Kanoya City when he saw the Chinese fleet. He's sure to be waiting on the Index to fall at this very moment, snapping his fingers at the *rashie* and thinking of his wife-to-be!"

"Oh, do you think that's true?" She smiled bravely, wanting to believe.

"Sure!"

There was a long pause, then she said, "Father, if there's to be a battle, will we all be killed?"

The question seemed to amuse him. "No. We'll not all be killed."

"But there will be a battle? Those machines . . ."

"I don't think so."

She thought about that. "So there'll be a surrender?"

"That's right." He looked at her penetratingly. "You're not scared, are you?"

"Scared?"

"Of dying?"

"I trust to psi," she said automatically. "I came here, didn't I?"

"Good girl. Psi is psi, but in this universe you have to strive. That's what we all believe, isn't it?"

After a moment she asked, "Will the Chinese soldiers enter Kanoya City and take possession of it?"

"Probably."

Arkali's eyes widened at the resignation Jos Hawken could no longer keep from his voice.

"You seem quite sure."

"As sure as anyone can be."

As he looked at her he saw once again the incredible depth of those eyes. She was beautiful, but so fragile. He reminded himself that Arkali was no longer a child, she was a grown woman with a mind of her own, and ten times as willful as ever her mother had been. How could it be that she was at the same time so incredibly, so incomprehensibly, so innocently naive? And how could he tell his little princess what he had seen in orbit this morning? Knowing he could not help it, he fed her false comfort.

"My dear, when Ellis Straker delivers what he's brought from Kagoshima to the daimyo, a proclamation will come from Hideki Ryuji ordering the Kan to retire."

"And the Chinese will do as the daimyo says?"

"Sure. They must."

"But what if they don't?"

"Then a huge army will come from the rest of Kyushu and send them away."

Arkali's relief warmed him, but he felt filthy for lying to her. You decided! he told himself sharply. What did you promise? That she must know. Though it breaks her heart and yours too, she must know! But how can I tell her?

From the moment she arrived, Arkali had instantly charmed him and captivated him. From a plex-hard man of business he had been transformed into a mooning boy where she was concerned, and he had allowed her slightest whim to disrupt the Hawken household totally.

Though her courtship had awed the servants and she had made a hundred maddening demands each day, he had acquiesced to them all. He had been foolish enough to allow her to rule as she liked. He had even discreetly banished his native mistresses from the big house outside the dome—so she would not learn of them, because he knew that if she did she would fail to understand.

The Hawken mansion had stood apart from the other, lesser merchants' residences, amid watered moss lawns and lush formal gardens, two miles beyond the dome of Kanoya City. It was a pillared palace of fifty rooms, stolen from Luke van den Burg's architectural copybooks, with everything an equivalent Amerikan house possessed, everything except hologlass, which could not be had at any price and which would in any case have been an affront to local sensibilities.

When she had put on her red wedding gown for the fitting, she had made him put his hand on his heart and promise against his judgement that Hayden would return in time for the ceremony. And he had done it.

He did not know why, but on the appointed day he had promised her everything she had dreamed, whether Hayden was there or not, but the morning had soured and before noon what should have been the most magnificent reception ever to grace Kanoya City had been blasted by high winds. A hundred tables had been overturned in the garden and the wreckage pelted with heavy rain. The multitude had retired inside, but such had been the darkness of the sky that the lights had had to be lit in the conservatories, and the sound of wind and thunder had undermined the gaiety of the music that had played throughout the rest of the day.

That afternoon, with the marriage still unsolemnised, but with a thousand bottles of fantastically rare Europan grand cru and expensive rice wine downed by the many guests, he had begun to signal the abandonment of the festivities. Arkali had rebuked him then, and forbade him to let the servants, or the minister, stand down in case Hayden should still arrive.

And Jos Hawken had complied out of his fine regard for "face." Face—that strange strong social liquor, the Oriental concept that allowed everyone to keep their pride intact. Face was to protocol what spring water was to alcohol: a perfect mixer. Oh, yes, because Arkali could melt down any heart, he had indulged her. Just as any father who had missed his eldest daughter's young years would do on her wedding day. The waiting had gone on all night, and even the next day. When he had known Hayden could not possibly come, even then he had kept his two hundred servants stretched on tenterhooks, and called on his remaining guests by every means not to desert his hospitality.

He had, for her sake, taken steps to crush the circulating rumor that Ellis Straker had transited to Seoul deliberately to slight the House of Hawken, and he had absolutely banned the drunken gossips from embroidering a jilting tragedy out of the tale. But he had known full and well that he was making a fool of himself, he had not wanted his daughter hurt—no matter what it cost him in face.

But later that day, when the disastrous news broke that Kan troops were descending on the city, each of the guests, drunk or hung over, had bolted for his own house. The uproar had brought her to tears, and him to his senses. All the merchants' properties were exposed; outside the dome not one was tenable in a siege, and no one knew how long there would be to carry their possessions inside. He had wasted time comforting her, protectively propping up the illusion still, though he had known there was no longer any basis for it, because he had known that a war would ruin him, and now war had come.

To strip his own house bare had been the worst embarrassment. More than the betrayal of a man's word to his daughter. More than the collapse of his plans to unite the houses of Hawken and Straker. He had felt his stature shrink with every picture he took down from his walls, with every antique chair or trunk of clothes he helped carry into the yard. It had felt like the naked dismantling of all he was and everything he had built.

As a million refugees fled the Lease, out went the prize finned Cadillac, out the rare early plastic furniture, out the Turkmen butter-glaze porcelain, and the priceless pair of Twenty-first Century gullions. . . .

In the middle of the turmoil, he had ordered Arkali to go into the city, but she had refused, lingering as he and his trustworthy retainer, Kei-san, lifted the floor and buried the aurium from the strongroom in deep pits under the house. She had remained in her wedding gown, watching the servants frantically gutting the mansion of everything, and she had insisted on standing there at the tailgate of his expensive Bristol air-car, mindless of the shame it caused him to be seen in such total retreat. To him, then, in his agony, it had suddenly seemed that she was glorying in his fall, as if it was just repayment for her own bitter disappointment. As if it had been his fault that the damned rainstorm had struck.

That had hurt, and when she had pleaded to be allowed to take down the wedding decorations herself, he had not permitted it. He had shouted at her to change her dress and had sent her packing in an air-bus like the ones visiting samurai used, following two vehicles stuffed with all the precious belongings he had collected, and she had gone, so shocked at his sudden anger that he had felt even more ashamed.

He had followed late that night, entering the city by the last open portal, to take shelter at the spire that served as office to Hawken Inc. He had sworn to tell her instantly how sorry he was that he had lied to keep alive her hopes, but by the time he arrived her exhaustion had overwhelmed her and she had been asleep. In the morning, with the Kan ships gathered in orbit he had known that he could not face her without telling her the dreadful truth he had seen there. But it was inevitable. She had to know.

Suddenly, a loud hum echoed flatly among the buildings: a big weapon had been fired, one of the Kan batteries, trying a ranging bolt on the shields. Arkali jumped with fear as a violet streamer burst from the eagle's eye on the dome above. The bird's claw seemed to tighten its grip on the jagged cluster of thunderbolts it carried there.

Her face was stark with a pale, willowy beauty as she looked at him.

"Hey, now. It's only a test. A stray charge effect. Don't worry. That's Yanqui plex. Tougher than shiphulls. They can't touch it."

He lowered his eyes, knowing he was doing it again. Protecting her from the truth. Lying to her. He had to break the habit, but she was so vulnerable. So terrified. How could he tell her what he knew?

"I suppose they must have occupied the mansion by now," she said, her voice barely controlled.

"Perhaps."

"Will they billet their officers there?"

"I guess—Yes, I guess they will."

"You really believe Controller Pope will surrender?"
This time he did not answer her.

"You must believe so," she said, nervous as a doe. "Otherwise, why did you bury your aurium under the floor of the house? You would have brought it here."

"You're very perceptive."

"I hope you've kept some bullion here for our protection." The keen note had returned to edge her voice. "No one knows how Chinese soldiers will behave. Towards us, I mean."

"Calm yourself."

She wrung her hands and faced him. "Father, I want to know. Are they really as barbarous as the rumors make out? It's not death I'm afraid of, but pain. I couldn't face torture. I know I couldn't."

"Arkali, we're only at war. The Kan are a civilized people, and Yu Hsien, the governor of the Kan lease on Satsuma, is personally known to me. And I . . ."

Stop it! Stop it now! His mind shouted. You can't continue to protect her from the truth. Tell her what you know. Tell her now!

"And?"

"And . . . I know we'll be treated well."

She was silent for a space, then she asked, "So those are Governor Yu's ships on the apron? And those quilt-suited troops are his?"

"No."

"Then whose?"

"They're soldiers from illicit Chinese bases in the Zone. The ships are Admiral Hu Tsung's."

"Is he an honorable man?"

"Honorable?" His gaze was drawn to the other spires of Kanoya City's business district. He had watched the shadows sweep out the morning like ancient clock hands, shortening as they moved down Whorl Parkway. Before they lengthened again, he knew he would have to break his daughter's heart. He steeled himself to answer her truthfully. "They say Hu Tsung was a pirate. They say that though he now serves under the Kan Dowager's warrant, he's interested only in plunder."

She paled. "Then his men will take what they want from us? Even though we're Amerikan?"

He seized her arm and spoke deliberately to her. "Arkali, I have to tell you the truth. The Kan have come at the worst possible moment. You must know that they've been trading hard out of Satsuma in the last few years. Business has been bad. I'm close to debt." He stared as if stricken. "If I'm completely honest, I have to say that I don't know what'll become of us, or how the Kan will treat us, but I love you and I'll always try to bend psi to protect you."

She stared back at him as if seeing him for the first time. She had seen through him. "But the aurium? There's still the aurium! I watched you and Kei-san bury a *tranche* of it under the house. A vast sum of credit!"

He took her hands in his. They were trembling; his own were damp. He shook his head. Why had he ever trusted Ellis in this madness? But how could he have done otherwise? "The aurium you saw buried was brought here by Ellis Straker. It's neither mine nor his. It's the loan he raised for the enterprise Kanoya depended on. The credit, every last bit, is borrowed, and at a ruinous rate of interest that compounds the debt every day that the aurium remains in our possession. Without Ellis Straker's amygdala there can be no peace. Without peace I can't use Straker's ships, or anyone's, to trade myself into profit. Even if I could . . ." He shook his head again, searching for words, then picked up the macro and tuned it, pointing. "Arkali, you see that speck? There, the most westerly. That's the *Chance*. Somehow the Kan have got hold of her. Don't you see what that means? Straker's mission has failed. We're all of us at their mercy.''

"Oh, psi preserve us . . .''

Her whispered prayer was faint, but it bit through his heart. When she looked up, her eyes were red. "And Hayden? The wedding?''

"I don't know whether there can be a confluence of our blood now.''

"Oh, no! No! You promised me!''

Jos Hawken cradled her against him, racked by her sobs and her trembling as she fought him. Ominously, as if timed to the stroke of noon, the distant hum of beam weapons rolled across the flatlands and echoed like thunder from the shields of the city, scattering eye-hurting colors before the phasing shut them out.

The Kan siege had begun.

8

They were going to cut out his soul with a samurai sword.

Hayden Straker struggled to free himself from the violent grip of the devils that held him, but there was no way to shake them free. He opened his eyes and stared, but still there were the mean little Yamato-style huts and still the same huge shattered tail fin that reared up somber and silent and terrible over the village. And still the fear of those demonic traders who had been bargaining for his soul.

''Get away from me!''

The shout had been raw and loud enough to wake the world.

Hayden Straker found himself on his feet, awake, sweat drenched, and gripping the doorpost. It was less than half an hour UT to sunup, and the mean traditional timber-board houses of Kurihara huddled in pools of night, set apart at a respectful distance from the pagodalike nexus ship hull. Overhead the heavens were painted in brilliant pastels, an unearthly glow studded by the arid planet Kinsei and the slim, waning crescent of Osumi's close moon, as bold and bright as the ID devices of Izlamic trader warships. He shivered.

The great rearing tail fin amazed him. It stood a hundred feet over the village. How long it had been here he could not say, but a mass of foliage had overrun it, and a copse of huge chestnut trees seemed to stake it down and shelter it from view. The local people made offerings to it, as if it was a cathedral that had come down whole to them from the sky.

He looked out on a gloriously beautiful dawning—one he had not expected to see. But the mood stirring inside him was black and contorted, like the storm clouds through which he had plunged onto this fated world two days ago. His head swam, faint after the panic of waking suddenly from the horrors of night, he felt exhausted and utterly drained, but there was worse, something vile at his core. It was as though his heart was dead, as though there was nothing there within him but a hard indigestible emptiness as if his psi had been snuffed out, and that frightened him.

He deliberately set his thoughts on Arkali. I should be worried for her now, ashamed for myself, longing for her, but instead I feel nothing. Nothing at all. And I don't know why.

Perhaps my love for her only ever existed in the ideal

of conflating the trading houses of Straker and Hawken. Perhaps she never truly was a part of my heart. Perhaps I convinced myself I loved her when I did not. So many questions I can't yet unravel, but I know that the thought of her doesn't make me ache inside, and by all that's real I should be aching. . . .

He closed his eyes, as if shutting out the next thought, but still it swam into his mind. Could Arkali ever excite and fascinate me like Hideki Shingo's wife excites and fascinates me? Oh, but that was a fantastically dangerous thought. An unthinkable thought.

He stood up, fighting the stiffness in his thighs and back and side. Perhaps it's always this way after a man faces death, he told himself. Isn't that what those who have been there say? Everything's contrary. A void of indifference inside, when a man might expect to find only joy in psi at having survived. Was it possible for a man to lose his psi faculties and still live on? Was it?

A Basho haiku he had learned in his youth came to him and filled his head:

> In the total silence of a shrine,
> the cicada's voice
> penetrates the rocks.

And he listened to the words and astonishingly his mind began to calm, and he felt the fear dissolving, and with it the weakness and lassitude. He felt sensation seeping into him once more, and his sleep-fractured memories began to knit together.

Yesterday, on waking, he had stared at the numb corpse of young Quinn. He had been laid in one of the houses, stiff as marble in repose, naked but for a white winding sheet. The villagers' headman, Rosei-san, had wanted to cut juniper wood and incinerate the body immediately, but he had insisted that no one touch Quinn's remains for three days, on account of his Adventer father. "After which time the body must be buried."

"Buried? In the ground?" Rosei had said it not with revulsion, just incomprehension.

The funeral pit was already dug, and Hayden Straker knew it would be his responsibility to utter the Great Prayer and erect a bamboo cross over the filled-in ground. Poor Quinn, dead now at the age of—what? Seventeen? Never got a hold on psi at all, never knew what it was to be a man. That's not right, he thought, repelled by the duty. It should be Quinn speaking fine requiem words over me, then I'd be released from this life to atone as I should.

"I killed you, Daniel Quinn," he said quietly, remembering how yesterday he had put his own signet ring onto Quinn's finger as a token of faith. "It was I who chose to take destiny into my hands, I who tried to shape the path of psi to my own will. You obeyed me, and without your help we'd all have died—in a different crash, one much more tragic—so it was me who killed you. Just as surely as if I'd burned you down."

He put his face in his hands. "I promise you now, if you can hear me, Quinn, I will follow my fated path whatever the consequences. I swear I will!"

He caught his breath and coughed raucously, feeling the cool of dawn chill his flesh. The pain in his breastbone still throbbed dully where his psi had been ripped from him. The pale shadow of a ring banded his finger. It reminded him of his promise—and also of that other promise, as ruined as the crashed ship hulk now, the one he had made to a fine and innocent girl: to make for her a marriage in Kanoya City.

How could psi have spared me? he wondered. Why did

Hideki Shingo and the woman survive? And if we three, why not you, Quinn, who surely was the least to blame? Psi is the architect of all human events, but why can we so rarely see the reason of it?

He ducked out through the low door of the house, dressed only in one of his diminutive host's *yukata*. The faded black garment was made to reach from the shoulders to just below the knee, but instead of the belt wrapping twice around his waist it was hung loosely, just sufficient to preserve a giant's decency. He knelt and looked at his reflection in the big water gourd. He was unshaved and his hair was hanging free where the village women had combed out its length. It was now wild after turbulent sleep.

You must comb out your hair and find a shaver, or something to serve as one, he told himself sternly, still trying to marshal his strength. But there are more knotted matters to think about than a damned hairstyle.

You must try to come to terms with Hideki Shingo before his retainers arrive. Yes, that's important. He has a retinue of renowned bodyguards. Think, damn you! Think and think again! What about the *Chance* and the Kan fleet? Think about where we are. What about Kanoya City? What about the amygdala? Yes, most of all, what about that?

Hideki Shingo is determined to take it. What can I do about that? I must do something, because if I'm forced to give it to him, how can a dispossessed *gaijin* claim any reason to live? I've got no right to be here. This is not the Lease. This is Yamato. Inviolable territory. They can have me killed as soon as spit. You must find a solution, Hayden. And soon. Today.

Yesterday Shingo had made the entire village search the crash site for the officer's coat; he had been convinced that the amygdala must be inside, and when the maroon coat had been found close to Quinn's body Shingo's avarice had shone out. But his delight had turned to rage when the coat's lining was discovered ripped open and the amygdala gone.

Hayden Straker lifted himself up suddenly, knowing the full danger that surrounded him. He feared the change that had come over Hideki Shingo now they were ashore. He's getting more arrogant and more dangerous by the hour. I know he searched my body when I was unconscious, and I know he searched my clothes. So cunningly is the amygdala hidden that he could never have found it, but how long can it be before he demands it? Then I'll have to give it to him. . . .

Oh, but he won't get at the amygdala. It's impossible for him to do that. I made certain of that. Oh, yes, I got a start on Hideki Shingo.

A flush of satisfaction spread through him as he thought of his cleverness in concealing the stone, but it faded when he remembered the daimyo's son's temperament and the rumors that had been around of the excesses of his samurai bodyguard. When the messenger arrives at the capital of Osumi, Hideki Shingo's men will come here right away. Then they'll force the truth out of me.

I must try to play on Shingo-san's uncertainties now, he thought, feeling cautiously for the best way. Think, man! Think as your father would think. If that's possible.

What will Hideki Shingo do?

He'll demand the amygdala soon, perhaps today.

Then? When you refuse to tell him where it is—as you must?

He'll wait until his retainers arrive.

When will that be?

Tomorrow, at the latest.

And what will you do then?

Refuse again.

And if you do, what will Hideki Shingo do?

He'll almost certainly order them to torture me.

His testicles tautened as he thought of the infinite cruelties reportedly perfected by the Yamato samurai, of the chilling accounts he had heard. And because of where the amygdala's hidden it'll not just be a formal demand, nor even a cursory beating before I hand it over to them.

Could I suffer their tortures? he asked himself, dreading the certain answer.

He snapped his eyes shut, knowing suddenly that it did not matter whether he could suffer bravely or not, whether he could reason the situation through or not. Whatever happens, he thought, whatever I say and whatever Hideki Shingo believes, it is not in my power to hand over the amygdala. My life won't be worth a half-credit slottee once I reveal the amygdala's location, because Hideki Shingo's chief of a gang of blood-curdlers who love to inflict pain and death, and he doesn't willingly suffer anyone or anything to disobey him.

His father's voice came to him again: Does Hideki Shingo have the will to order the systematic disemboweling of personnel protected by MeTraCor?

Perhaps.

Didn't you see him administer two savage beatings with his own hands already?

Yes.

The first had been on a crazy *bonze*—a totally harmless monk—the second on the village headman's brother.

Well, then . . . don't forget, boy. These are Shingo-san's lands, not MeTraCor's. And who's to say MeTraCor still rules at Kanoya City, anyway?

Bitter psi, he thought, terror beating through him now

as he thought how his own cleverness had snared him. Bitter psi, I'll have to tell them it's inside me, that I swallowed it, and they won't believe me or wait for it to pass through me, they'll cut out my damned entrails before my living eyes to get at the truth of it. . . .

Sweat beaded his face, ran in trickles down his back as he fought down the evil thoughts. You promised, Hayden Straker! You promised to survive! You promised to bring that amygdala into the daimyo's citadel at Miyakonojo yourself! It's the only chance there is to make amends! Hold hard to that chance and believe! Maybe it's just the shadow of the nightmare that makes you think these dog-black thoughts. Hideki Shingo hasn't asked for the amygdala yet. Perhaps he won't. He's a bastard, surely, but that doesn't mean he'll order your guts ripped for the sake of a day's wait.

He shivered violently, feeling another feverish wave coming over him. He felt a sudden spasm in his abdomen. The gravity—or something—had loosened his bowels.

Sweet psi, this place feels as cold as death to me! And I fear the kami who live here. I should run. Run while I can. But I'm still so weak and I've no idea where I am. Oh, psi help me!

By now the village was beginning to stir. Old men were rolling from their futons, young men scratching and yawning, women beginning to chatter and go towards the river with big earthen pots hanging from bamboo yokes. A sharp movement caught Hayden Straker's eye. The leaves of a big fast-gro chestnut tree that grew beyond the last hut shimmered. An old man, his body robed in tangerine, his head shaved, bowed, then let himself down from a shrine platform built on one of its spreading boughs. The marks of Zen were tattooed on the man's brow, but his face was puffy and bruised where Hideki Shingo had laid about him with a bamboo stick yesterday. At the foot of the tree he picked up a begging bowl and a twist drum.

Just the old monk with his horn of plenty and his magic wand, he thought, reminded again of the beating Hideki Shingo had served out yesterday. Jodo-Ji—Pure Land Sect—they're wayfarers, possessionless beggars, mendicants, close to Zen but not strictly of it. Irritating perhaps, but harmless. Just world-hopping monks whom the villagers believe are in touch with the *kami*, the spirits of nature.

There was no need for the daimyo's son to beat him like he did. No need at all. Sweet psi, Shingo-san's strutting is terrible when he's angered. At least now the monk's stopped banging his drum; they have a strange hold over the people as soon as they start to chant their *nembutsu* dirges. Maybe that's what Hideki Shingo didn't like. He can't afford to lose control here, or even have his authority challenged—that's what he fears most.

Hayden Straker saw the monk approach, seemingly oblivious of his presence, but then the man stopped suddenly, a couple of yards away. He turned slowly and knelt, calmly putting his hands and forehead on the ground.

"Get up!" he hissed. "Quickly, before the samurai sees you. There's no need for that! Get away from me!"

But the monk ignored his protests. "I beg you, *gaijin-san*. Surrender your psi now. Surrender, and accept all you are given. It is too late."

He finished his obeisance, and stood up with slow dignity. It was as if he was willing the son of the Hideki clan to notice him. He had certainly succeeded in making his point to the villagers. They were silent in the way of people watching an air-car plummet from the sky. But here no one screamed and the tension endured.

Hayden Straker breathed quickly. Though the pain in his chest had lessened to a dull ache now, the bruises were still livid on his ribs where Rosei-san, the village headman, had used ancient skills on him. He had flogged the poisoned air from his lungs and hammered his chest to make his heart beat again. Any exertion now, no matter how slight, was painful. He leaned forward over the big gourd and poured a dipper of cold water over his head, gasping, then he dropped the dipper, and it fell with a splash.

A cockerel crowed out, and Hayden Straker realised that the villagers had begun to melt away. Automatically, his attention focused on the samurai's hut, and he saw that Hideki Shingo himself stood there, his twin swords bound jauntily into his waist sash. He had seen everything and he strode out, unsmiling, breathing the morning air deeply, taking a grim pleasure in seeming relaxed and at peace with the world when every muscle in him was tensed with the anticipation of violence. He walked deliberately and without interruption towards the monk.

So much fear has been loosed here by his coming, Hayden Straker thought as he watched. Perhaps the amygdala inside me is truly psi-cursed!

Superstitious fear bubbled in him, too, at that thought, a dark morass just below the surface of his mind, a hell of fears waiting just beneath his consciousness, and separated from his waking thoughts it seemed by just a thin membrane.

Kurihara—the village of the chestnut-tree field.

A strong spirit of terror pervaded the place, and he felt keenly the shameful oppression that Yamato imposed on the vast underclasses of its population. The denial of technology and education and travel, and the withholding of information about the outside, the corralling of most of its people onto lo-tech, subsistence reservations, the demands for absolute obedience backed by the threat of death. It was a kind of oppression that made an Amerikan ask: what government ever has the right to do that to its own people? Without the familiar fundamental beliefs in psi, people were reduced to ignorance. Without a knowledge of the order and lawfulness and logic of the universe—what could there be but an unknowable chaos, an unpredictable and terrible creation in which nothing could ever make sense?

Here, only samurai and notable talents taken from the peasantry by the monks of the various psi sects were allowed access to psi truth and psi training. For the rest it was like living in the Dark Ages.

In Amerika everyone was told about psi. It was the power of the Amerikan spirit that had fused those two half-worlds of cast-iron Occidental science and the dream philosophy of the East. Two hundred years ago in the enlightened Sector of Amerika they had refuted the power of pure determinism. Only in Amerika had they chosen not to believe that the Universe was with form and yet still void. They had kicked down the barriers and cast off the yoke of intellectual fear, and one hundred years ago in Amerika they had routed that fear forever, freeing, enlightening, and bringing understanding about the true nature of existence to everyone. He shook his head involuntarily. He was here now, back in the pit. How could he, a man of Amerikan heritage, protect these hard-won victories of mind? How would he be able to handle the limitless voids of Yamato thought?

He regarded the village darkly, his back straightening. That the crash has placed so heavy a burden on these people is monstrously unjust, he thought, clinging to that certain truth. To have brought any samurai down on them without warning would have raised panic and confusion, but to have brought a lord of the Hideki clan, so of their own liege lord, the man who owns them and everything around them—except the rivers and the sky, which are the gods' prerogative—who taxes them to skin and bone and sometimes to death, Jeezus, that was bad, bad psi.

Only the monk seems to harbor no terror of Hideki Shingo, and that's only because he's a sect man. Look at him, now. His insolence . . .

Oh, Jeezus! No!

Without any warning Hayden Straker saw the first light of the sun-star flash off Hideki Shingo's sword. Strangely it seemed to hang there in the dawn sky, curving, recurving, crossing the sliver of the old moon so that, for an instant, Kinsei itself studded the pommel like a diamond. Then the *daito* rose and stood poised to slash down over the monk and he found he could not shout, or stand, or do anything, except watch as the shaven head dropped and rolled in the dirt, as the headless body staggered forward a pace and crumpled down, gouting blood obscenely over the tangerine robes.

Hayden Straker watched as Hideki Shingo lifted the *daito* again, examined its length, then put a critical finger to the undulled edge at the place where it had bitten clean through the bones of the monk's neck. He wiped off the blade, carefully sheathed it, and stepped out the twenty paces to where Hayden Straker stood.

"So," he said, his eyes half-lidded. "Now there is one less insolent animal to bother the world, eh, *gaijin-san*?"

Hayden Straker could say nothing. His eyes searched to make contact with the samurai's universal humanity, and all the while his mind hammered at him, willing him to believe it had been some kind of accident, or an act of self-defense, or that it was done for some other reason. Any reason. There had to be a reason to kill a man. It was too horrible to believe the monk had been decapitated for pure amusement, because then Hideki Shingo must be a monster with no human conscience, and that meant . . .

The eyes Hayden Straker searched were not the shark's

eyes of an insane killer. They were liquid and alive and human, and they were very amused and Hayden Straker saw in them the challenge he dreaded. His own whisper was a croak, intense and full of revulsion.

"Why?"

"Because he disobeyed me. I told him yesterday that he must keep away from us. From me, from my wife, and from you, *gaijin-san*. Especially from you."

Hayden Straker shook his head. "But there was no need to kill him! He was a harmless old man."

"He disobeyed me."

"But you murdered him! Just like that! You're a cold-blooded murderer!"

Hideki Shingo's smile dropped away. "Don't tell me what I am, *gaijin-san*. This is my *han*, not yours. Mine under the laws of Yamato. This system and this world belong to the sons of the Hideki clan. The southern half of this continent belongs to me personally. Everything in it is mine—everything and everyone—and those who live do so under my sufferance alone. That applies equally to those born into it and those entering it from outside. Remember that, *gaijin-san*."

"I am an Amerikan!"

"Oh . . . yes." He smiled. "As for the Amerikan Lease at Kanoya City, once the Kan have overrun it we shall come to new terms with them. What will you be then? So sorry, *gaijin-san*, then you will be an unwanted stateless person, trapped by the misfortunes of war. A refugee person, with no status."

Then he smiled and turned and began to walk away.

Hayden Straker tried to control himself, stop himself shaking, stop himself looking at the hideous staring face of the monk. He gazed helplessly out on the old, smashed nexus ship whose hull had been made into a temple by the local people, and felt the terror dominating him. A crushing fatigue pressed down on him and he stubbornly stood up to fight it off, knowing that he must not give in to the nausea, that he must not vomit—for the sake of face. The agony of it continued until he knew he could not stand it any longer. Then the anger tore out of his chest. It was the same blinding anger he had felt just before lashing out at his father. Magically the crushing terror lifted and he knew that for a precious, crystal-clear moment his fear had gone. For that instant he wanted only to dive at Hideki Shingo and tear at him.

"You filthy Yamato barbarian!"

He had shouted it at the samurai's back, yelled it at the top of his voice, but Hideki Shingo was already twenty paces away and the fear had made Hayden Straker's voice hoarse and he had shouted in English and the samurai had affected not to hear nor to understand, and did not even break step.

Then, in the silence, the fear began to crowd him again, and Hayden Straker began to walk also. He walked away, stiff-legged and loose-kneed, towards the edge of the village, towards the ruined hull-temple, to put distance between himself and Hideki Shingo's killing sword. And he did not stop until he was safe among the huge vault of denatured plex. He felt himself shaking with fear, white-faced with shock, and he despised himself, because he knew that for an instant he had held a tiny spark of courage inside him and the chance to fan it into full flame had been his but he had let that spark die.

9

"You're a psi-damned coward! Y'hear me?"

It was his father's voice loud in his head. He stopped, surrounded by the echoing planes of plex, the ribs of a gigantic beached whale, and he knew they were mocking him. The makeshift god-house was bigger than a cathedral and infinitely grander than the flimsy dwellings that clustered around. The tail fin towered through the centuries, a reminder of mighty power, and of how easily the light of civilization could be kept from human minds.

He tore at a tree trunk until his fingers bled and the violence had robbed him of his hottest anger. Yes, I'm a coward, he screamed inside. And a fool! Is this how I should repay Rosei-san for my rebirth? By desecrating his damned temple?

Now I really understand why these people are terrified of Hideki Shingo, why they grovel in the dust before him when they cannot run—why they hide their children, and dare not look directly at him. By psi, I knew the samurai regarded their peasants as worthless chattels, worse than the dirt they stand on, but I never believed they could kill so easily. That was terrible!

Breathless and insensible to pain now, he stood up, every nerve screaming to him to run deep into the chestnut forest. To run and keep on running because all other options ended in horror. What shall I do? What can I do? I am no longer captain of any vessel. This is a strange place, a part of Hideki Shingo's own southern continental fief. He carries the ultimate power here. Sweet psi, what am I going to do?

He stumbled on inside the wreck and knew now why in his dreams he had dreaded the huge ruined tailplane. It's what I saw in my nightmares, he thought. In my sleep I saw the same shape rearing up over me. I felt the *kami* pulling at me—fearsome devil spirits—I saw them gathering about me in that weird storm light, like wild dogs drawn to a carcass. They wanted me to come with them into death, and I wanted to offer myself. I was starting to leave this life when Rosei shook me back to it again. . . .

He halted, the tailplane massive above him. The plex was weathered and friable. At some time its immaculate structure had been denatured by a meson blast, turning the material fudgy or chalky or flaky like blister metal or untreated stahlex, depending on its exact type. There were half a dozen ribs shooting up overhead like the fan-vaulting of an ancient gothic cathedral, surrounded by collapsed tree trunks and bushes uprooted by the hurricane. The hull was shaped like a longhouse or a loaf of Ruski *kleb,* the bridge tiered like a sharp pyramid and surmounted by a curious mushroom dome. She must have been a gigantic ship. From the time of the invasion. A globe-ship of a million men. A shattered honeycomb interior filled with freezee cells each with its dead soldier like a mummified robot in its niche, an orange light blipping on each, once a UT second, accurate to one part in ten trillion as a beacon.

But no distress signals were leaving this place. Each freezee had become a shrine. Some were intricately carved, most overgrown, and all filled with a dark power to enthrall the gentle people who serviced them so devotedly.

A monstrous devil-god leered at him from its crevice. A warrior gargoyle, dead a dozen years ago or more.

"Always meet your enemies face-to-face," he heard his

father tell him sternly. "Rush at them, boy, and they'll scatter like chaff in the wind!"

He staggered on alone through a waterlogged cargo hold wreathed in mist that lay about his legs and seemed to issue from openings and vents, and he sensed the danger from deadly Osumi paddy snakes—kraits—slithering unseen in the wreckage.

What a Satanic abomination this temple is, he thought, staring about him.

Loathing began to wash through him, and he felt the hairs rise in his skin as he fell under the shadows of the demon-winged tailplane. Part of his mind began to recite the Adventer's martyr prayer, twenty-third Psalm of David. "The Lord is my shepherd; I shall not want . . ."

As the echoes of his words filled the hull, he lashed out at himself.

Superstitious fool! Adventers are little better than these villagers, dominated by their beliefs and incapable of rational thought. They're constantly performing meaningless rites, making offerings to protect themselves from Wrath, or denouncing Flash to propitiate their god. They suffer the tyranny of their foul priests without the slightest understanding of psi. What hope is there for them?

Hayden Straker shook his fist, defying everything around him. Why do these villagers offer themselves so willingly to feudal bondage? Why don't they fight back? They toil and drudge the year round without rest, always scratching a bare living crushed down by the excessive tax revenues the Hideki clan imposes. They live within an inch of disaster all the time because of climate and plague and war and famine, while the Lord of Miyakonojo eats and drinks himself insensible using aurium-plated chopsticks each night, and pays a hundred *miko* girls to strew the paths of his wives and concubines with rose petals. Sweet psi, what have these people to lose by rebellion? They must hate Hideki Shingo. Why don't they rush him, all together, and destroy him? Why didn't they slit our throats when we landed? They could have claimed we'd died in the crash. Nine out of ten would have done that to strangers crashing out on Sweetwater, Wyoming.

His eye traveled across the jagged silhouette surrounding him, and he wondered that this smashed ship had stood unrecovered in this sheltered stand of bio-eng chestnut trees in the middle of hundreds of square miles of rice paddies for a decade or more. But the more he thought about it, the more it seemed reasonable. The hyperfast growing trees had given the village its name. They grew to maturity in one season. This had probably become a sacred grove since the crash, effectively hiding the ship from cursory searches.

And who was there to search? Men, of whatever kind, had seldom been granted permission to range at will in the domains of the Emperor. His worlds were jealously controlled, and Osumi, despite the Lease, was no exception. Official permission was required to go beyond the bounds of the Kanoya City hinterland, and the planetary government itself with a total land fief of sixty-five million square miles and twice that of ocean was hardly interested in combing the planet for useless trash. This wreck site was probably unguessed at by the Yamato power at Miya-konojo.

The ship was a mess. A heavy flux of mesons had slammed into it at some time, denaturing the plex and making it effloresce in all kinds of ways. The sight of it made his skin creep.

"Yea, though I walk through the valley of the shadow of death, I will fear no evil . . ."

He continued, picking his way deliberately through a

mesh of collapsed conduits, deeper among the weathered plex freezees. Devil-faced monkeys moved along the galleries of pipework. They were indignant at him, squatting to groom one another, or to suckle young, in the god niches. His eye moved among the snakelike creepers, searching the moss-mottled surface, and he realized with amazement that the plex shrines around him were not carved plex at all. They had decayed into a leathery material with natural convolutions. Natural joints. Natural seams. The whole ship was a fantastic structure, an immense piece of melted sculpture like the evolving forms of a limestone cave.

Then he felt it: a presence that drew him, that hung dimly in the corner of his vision. He turned. Incredibly, a samurai warrior in full armor was there, standing rock-still and ancient in the guts of the ship.

Earthen pots had been placed before him, garlands of purple flowers, offerings of food laid there, and the polished plex where knees and foreheads had kissed the deck before it. Hayden Straker knew with certainty that he was the first Amerikan ever to intrude here, the first man ever to approach without deference or due ceremony, without invitation, and his sense of unease turned into something close to panic.

The warrior regarded him malevolently, and the shock of its stare almost stopped him from going on, but he felt the overpowering force emanating from the empty eyeholes of the face mask, the winged war helmet, daubed in dripping grease and suggesting a gigantic power. It was as if the veneration and worship of a decade had concentrated a supreme godhead here, a godhead in being that saw him and recognised him and drew him on.

As he closed on the plex warrior, he was filled with awe. His head swam and there began in his ears a roaring like the ocean in a conch, or the wind ruffling leaves. Suddenly, his sight dimmed and he faltered. It was as if the world had contracted to a distant point at the end of a long tunnel, but still he forced himself forward, brazenly erect.

"It's empty," he said aloud. "It's nothing but an empty suit of samurai armor that the villagers have been worshiping."

He reached out and saw his pale hand touch the petrified warrior.

"Sonofabitch," he said, and thought how absurd it sounded, then he screamed as the arm came up and seized his elbow.

10

Rosei the Headman bent closer over the foreigner's terrible hand weapons, feeling doubts rise in him as he touched the Wesson's selector mechanism. The headman's eyes were yellowed in his wrinkled leather face. He was clean-shaven, slightly built, and very dark, with the wiry strength of the Kurihara people in him. He wore a dark green-and-black-check *haori* that covered his upper body, and a white band bound up his hair. Still he couldn't get the horrible sight of Shunjo the monk's severed head out of his mind. It was stomach-turning, but not as revolting as the *gaijin*.

So that's what they look like, he thought. Real blue eyes and hair like dead grass. Then all the other stories about them must be true!

Was it my fault? he asked himself. Are the gods punishing the village because of me? Did the highly favored god, Hosho Nyorai, see me steal the *gaijin*'s treasures and cause the monk's death? Or was it just his karma to die that way? Who knows, in truth? It's so hard to make sense of the complexities of this illusion we call the world. How strange that the other *gaijin* wanted to bury his dead companion in the ground like an animal, where he would decay and slowly pollute the earth. Strange that he would not permit the purification by fire. And what a shameful waste of a blue-metal ring it would have been to have buried it with him.

He looked automatically skyward. There was nothing to see, but strange things were happening in the zodiac nevertheless. More ships than ever were coming, and now this second crash. Out of all the places in the world it could have come down, why did it have to be here?

He clapped three times to attract the attention of the gods. Guiltily Rosei remembered screwing the ring from the dead foreigner's finger. He began to whisper a silent prayer, then broke off. Oh, Lord Kannon cannot save us from the war that's surely coming, he thought, drawing back his hand from the hellish weapons. You were wise to send a man to the *gaijin* city, Rosei. Hard times are coming and your people need more than blind hope. You were right to take the ring, because only blue-metal and guns can help us now.

The day before yesterday, at the height of the storm, he had warned them all. His kinsmen had crowded round the white man's corpse, their eyes drinking in the strange sight. Despite the wind, the smell of death had hung over the body like evil. None of them except Rosei's brother had seen an Amerikan before, much less a dead one.

"Give me room," Rosei had told them sternly. "Now,

listen to me! Do you know who that is in the next room? He's not just samurai! He's the daimyo's son, and the woman is his wife. I don't know what we've done to offend the gods, but that's Hideki Shingo-sama! In our village! Do you know what that means?''

"He's truly terrible!'' his eldest son had said, his eyes popping from his head. "Lord Kannon has decided to punish us.''

"You are a good boy, Kenji-san! Not greedy like your father.'' His mother-in-law scowled at her daughter's husband as she set down her ewer of water.

"Be careful, all of you! Shingo-sama's father is the Lord of the World! He'll demand proper respect and he'll cut you if you don't give it.''

"Curse you, Rosei-san, for saving them. Call yourself head of the village? Don't you know he's bound to bring evil down on us?''

"Hush, woman! Don't you know that he who kills evil men has the evil fall on him?''

She stared back, terribly frightened. "But there was no need to work so hard to bring the *gaijin* back into this world.''

"The Buddha said life is sacred. What joy in his death could we have? And now we will profit from this man. Aren't they all rich, these Amerikans? Look at his clothes. And look at his two killing guns. Surely he is an Amerikan samurai. Surely his retainers will show their gratitude when they learn where he is. Don't you see? They will protect us from the war!''

Rosei's brother snorted. "War, war, war! All you ever talk about is war. Oh, yes. They will protect us! Does this one? Does the other, the one who is alive? No. And why? Because they are just as powerless against the samurai as we are.''

His sister-in-law rocked her head in agreement. "Interfering *gaijin* are to blame for everything. Why don't they all go back to their home worlds and leave us in peace? Why didn't you leave that other one to die as he should have died?"

"Masae-san, what sort of peace have we ever had under the Hideki?" Rosei asked darkly. "The clan goes pillaging wherever they please. Their officials roam the world violating and looting at will. The various branches of the clan are always fighting one another. There is no law against rapine if you are of our caste. Daimyo are too busy intriguing with one another to care about *hinno*. And to finance their posturing and finery at Miyakonojo, they tax us into starvation. We are living in hard times. I say another big war is coming. I can feel it. And in war it is always the peasant who suffers. It is my duty to protect the village and the best protection is this."

Rosei held up the ring and they stared at it in awe, the wind howling in the darkness. "I believe this is the Lord Kannon's gift. A blessing. Just like the last time."

"But you stole it from a dead body," someone said.

"Why not take the killing guns also?" another said caustically. "They must be worth a thousand *koku* of rice!"

"If the killing guns are worth a thousand *koku*, then think how much more the man is worth."

"What if he dies?" Bokudo the ox-herder said mournfully, tucking his *fundoshi* tighter about his thin loins. "You are breaking caste rules—"

"He won't die!"

"That would be the best thing of all. If you want to know what I think—"

"Go back to the well, Masae-san! He won't die. I know about war, and I shall decide what's to be done. I repeat:

the ring is Lord Kannon's blessing on us. Now get on with your work and don't forget that anyone who looks upon a daimyo's lady will turn to stone!''

A sullen muttering had passed among them then, and they had dispersed.

I wonder if they still believe the ring is Lord Kannon's blessing on us, now Shunjo is dead, Rosei wondered, feeling a shaft of fear lodge in his bowels. How unfortunate that Shingo-sama came here! I still can't believe it. The daimyo's son, here, in our poor village! What could I do but send Kenji-san as messenger to Miyakonojo when he ordered it? What else could I have done but obey my lord? But if I sent my eldest son to Miyakonojo, I sent my younger son to Kanoya City, and that was even more dangerous.

Rosei saw his wife cross the village, poultry fluttering before her as she avoided the dead body of the monk. She's right, he thought. You're breaking the chief laws of life: know your place and stick to it. Manage the rice harvest and pay your taxes. Never ask questions. And never, never meddle in stations that are above you.

It was not my station to drag three strangers from the flames, yet I did it. How could I have known who they were? How could I have guessed that I was laying hands on my liege lord's son? And if I had known, I would have been bound to do the same. Shingo-sama is fiefholder of this land. It was my duty to rescue him and offer him every service.

But the village is my affair also. If war flares, Korean mercenaries who think nothing of despoiling our shrines will come here. For some of them, desecration is a duty, and the samurai lords of other worlds are no better. If war flares, the daimyo's soldiers will come looking for men for his army, and his taxes will increase again, and that will destroy us. The village is dangerously poor now. So what can I do? Good Lord Kannon, please help me to see the way!

Rosei's mind alighted on the most painful memory of his youth. Aiee! I know all about wars. When the Kan under Chu' Yuan came here in their bird machines. They burned every house and tortured my father to make him reveal where our holy relics were buried; he died three days after they flew away, leaving all we owned in ruins. Now I bear his responsibilities and I owe it to his memory to look after the village and the holy relics as he would have done—whether the Lord of Osumi's son is here or not.

He looked once more at his wife's tiny figure as she hurried past. She's a good woman, but she doesn't understand. Chu' Yuan's murderers may never come back again. And who can say for sure that this war will descend upon us? But one thing is as certain as the moon and stars: disaster will visit us this year, or next year, or the year after, or the year after that. One day the rice harvest will fail or be diseased or stolen, and without anything in reserve we will all die. That is why I saved the *gaijin*. That is why I'll send his blue-metal ring where it may do us some good. He had discussed his plan with his brothers as the rainstorm raged.

"But how can you get *gaijin* credit for him, Rosei-san?"

"By sending word to their City," he had said.

"Who will go now that Kenji-san has been sent to Miya-konojo?"

"I will send my second son with the aurium ring."

"But how can Yukimura-san go there? And what will he do when he arrives?"

Another had said, "Masakage-san, my wife's cousin's brother-in-law, went as a laboringman to the *gaijin* fortress some years ago. If Yukimura-san can find him, he will know what to do."

"First, help me put the foreigner inside," Rosei had said. "We must make him comfortable and then decide how to appease this great scion of the Hikedi clan."

"Appease our lord? Sorry, but I don't think that's possible. He terrifies my wife. He terrifies me, too."

"Yes. He's a monster, and dangerous. If he discovers what I've done, he'll kill us all. No one must know. No one. But listen, though he doesn't pay much attention to us, I think his lady does, so we must be very careful."

"Lord Kannon preserve us!"

What should I do? he asked himself now, still staring at the Amerikan's hand weapons. For the first time, both of my sons have gone from the village. The world is turning upside down. And a war is starting that will destroy everything.

I knew it from the moment we carried the living Amerikan from the wreck. This time it will not be like the last time, when we received the gift of the temple. When the One Living God ordered us to bury the heavy metal—like the metal of the *gaijin*'s ring—deep under our fields. Oh, no! This wrecked bird machine is one of ill omen.

North is Kanoya and the Amerikan fort; above, the New Bright Stars, and the Kan. A great war fleet of celestial fighting ships sails through the heavens each night from east to west, and now the son of the Lord of the planet, the most important daimyo in the whole Quadrant, has appeared from the sky. Whatever should I do? Lord Kannon, please tell me.

Weariness relaxed his mind, and he felt the power of his gods enfold him. Whatever you do, it will change nothing, they told him. Stop striving. Accept what is in store for you with dignity. Struggle will not avail you. Whatever you try to do, no difference to the cosmic plan can be born of your efforts, for what is is, and what will be will be. . . .

No! he shouted back at them. I don't believe that anymore! The Amerikans are strong because they struggle and they strive. They are strong because they believe they can alter the world with their hands and their wills. What if they're right? Thank the gods Yukimura-san and Kenji-san will both be back with their father soon. If my own honored father was here he'd say that the sons of men are just rice stalks bending in the breeze, that only the soil and the cosmic wheel and the great cycle of rebirth and the gods and the harvest continue. He would never have acted as I have acted. By all the gods, I hope I've done the right thing.

Suddenly, Rosei heard his wife crying out. She came running to him. "Come quickly! Come quickly! It's the foreigner. He's gone into the temple!"

BOOK 2

Material excerpted from "A Manuscript Found in
Space," by A. Hacker:
Ozma Vault Transmission Package KVFG #3352,
Copyright Synthetic Educator Corp. Orenburg, VIR.,
By Permission of the Central Authority, Old Earth A.D.
2450
[Ref. Module MMCDXI-078.952953 /Engl.]
[Cross-reference to other SEC modules in CAPS.]

PSI
First, see [Ref. Module MDCDXVII-507.873523]
FUNDAMENTAL HYPOTHESIS OF PHYSICS.

Begins: #unlike phenomena decribed by STATISTICS,
or more fully by certain branches of CHAOS THEORY,
which describe satisfactorily the interaction of inert,
nonliving substances, and the particles and waves (matter and energy) of the universe. However, the appearance of complex psychological decision-making, such as
may be found in even single-celled life-forms, is sufficient
to disturb the int#

. . . HACK INTERRUPTED . . .

#inherent in all human beings. The MATERIALIST doc-
trine of ALLER Z.H., KERGUELEN P.D., and FAULLS
R. et al. holds that in this respect, psi perception is
analogous to other intellectual capacities. The large size
and complexity of the human brain compared to that of
other biological animals is thought by them to be respon-

sible for such attributes as intelligence, self-perception, abstract thinking, etc., all of which require a minimum threshold number of NEURONE interconnections in order to manifest themselves; however, it is thought that individuals with so-called "magic number" genotypes are more likely to develop#

. . . *HACK INTERRUPTED* . . .

#lthough various complex and, as yet, unquantified psychological factors are thought to influence the results of studies that have already been undertaken to an extent that no conclusiv#

. . . *HACK INTERRUPTED* . . .

#eory requires a particle of imaginary rest-mass (called a PSITRON) interacting in the t2 time domain, in which the objective probabilities of future outcomes are contained as compresent dispositional factors, which incline or predispose the future to occur in certain specific ways. The multiplicity of virtual potentialities from which one emerges is #

. . . *HACK INTERRUPTED* . . .

#of psi itself. Also known as the ACAUSAL PRINCIPLE, psi is defined in an imaginary time domain by the psi-chi function. This function describes a fundamental universal physical quantity complying with the DOBBS-CHELYABIN CONSERVATION LAWS, and when projected in three spatial dimensions, and restricted to real time, it may be reduced to the well-known SCHRODING#

. . . *HACK INTERRUPTED* . . .

#solutely vital to the dissemination of Mankind among the stars.

. . . *LINE ABORTED.*

11

Ellis Straker threw open the iris of the MeTraCor facility house and paused as the mob gathered at his back. Two Macau-Kalifornian sentries in headbands and sloven jackets fled across the compound, and their sheriff covered his retreat with a brutish-looking 10-kV charge gun, running inside the building.

"Follow me up to the Trade Commission and we'll take our case to Aziza Pope in person! And if she won't listen we'll make her own Council declare her unfit!"

The answering cry went up.

By psi, I'll be lucky to get away with this, he thought, thanking whatever gods still ruled this godforsaken planet for the crowd of three hundred at his back.

Those who followed him were mostly independent merchants and their associates, men and women resident on Osumi, with families living in houses built within a mile or two of the Kanoya apron. Some, like the Solomon brothers, had prospered in Yamato and made themselves rich. Others were less successful, but, like Ellis, all stood to lose everything they had, and none of them felt any great love for the Controller, or for MeTraCor.

Jeezus, Ellis, he thought grimly, they're all with you and there's only one sheriff-at-arms to keep them out. Pity the Kan have stopped firing on us. You're gonna need all your best persuasion to convince Pope's yes-man Council and prevent them surrendering Kanoya. But keep your hand closed, poker player. Like the Kan say: honesty is a jewel, and those who spend it die beggars.

The crowd streamed along the atrium behind him and through the lobby, trapping the sheriff at bay against the great iris entrance of the MeTraCor Council Chamber. The soldier raised his ugly weapon, but when he saw the mob coming on regardless he turned and burst through the half-open sphincter, looking for protection from those it had been his duty to guard.

Ellis stood on the threshold, eyeing the seven who sat each side of the long white table before him. They were the Council of the Lease of Osumi, those in whom MeTra-Cor had vested all power concerning its affairs in the Kyushu Quadrant. They were the people who could slam the shields of Kanoya City shut against the Kan or lose the Lease forever.

Right away Ellis knew what they were about. In his nostrils was a stink he had met with too many times before—it was the sick smell of fear.

At the table's head, occupying the tall-backed Controller's chair and writing with an elegant stylo, was Aziza Pope. She was dressed in a severe black number and an out-of-style Egyptian cascade wig. To the Controller's right were her supporters: Embree Dzernic, also in black— a polecat of a man, then JJ. Foster, whose cheeks had grayed and hollowed with a practical-joke virus that she had picked up on vacation on Jaffa. Beside Foster, the apple-cheeked secretary, Fawley Beuze, held a perfumed sop-stick in his hand.

Opposite these, Ellis's eye took in the three men he knew were less satisfied by Pope's Controllership: Zeekyel Meredith, sanguine and straight-backed, a procedural stickler but a man who despised Pope and wanted her out. Next to him, Tung Hai Johnson, who the Osumi locals humorously called "gensui"—Field Marshall—because of his "snap" dealing, and the Chinese knew as Chang-Ching, "First Coadjutor" because of his past position as Controller of Kanoya. He had never forgiven Pope for supplanting him.

Careful, Ellis thought, outwardly he's a buffoon, but he'd burn anyone in the spine as soon as spit. Finally, the most junior but best connected of them all, the young aristocrat, Derion Reiner—three months in Yamato and at the board table because ten billion units of his father's MeTraCor stock had put him there.

So, Foster's still kicking, it's still three and three, Ellis thought, with Pope herself holding the casting vote that ensures her own survival, and the MeTraCor Mainboard Directors back on Liberty too remote from the jealousies and too far away to know the truth of what happens and what does not happen on Osumi—and I'll bet not giving a good goddamn so long as the profits continue to siphon home.

They all turned at Ellis's intrusion, startled rigid by the iris flying open and by the Kalifornian guard and the hub-bub of voices flooding in from the lobby.

More people were packing in behind now, and the commotion grew. That's good, Ellis thought, the pack of them are as jumpy as Arkansas II jiggers with that Kan fleet sitting up there. They know it's a crisis and they're in no mood to listen to this mess of whining MeTraCor megalocrats.

The echoes of the iris slamming open died away. At the head of the table, Pope stabbed the stylo into its silver toner well, her mouth set in a grimace, and she looked up shortsightedly.

"Damn ye, where's yer manners? Can't ye see we're in session?" She pulled on a pair of lozenge-lensed infraspecs, the kind that detected when a person's face was coloring up hot with fury or embarrassment, or cooling blue with fear, then she saw it was Ellis and rose from her chair involuntarily. Her hard Michigan Muslim accent was like grit. "By the Prophet, peace be upon him . . ."

Ellis advanced straight into the attack. "Ah, don't waste your prayers on my account, Pope! Or are you thinking I've come to depose you? Well, you can call this a revolt, and you sure as shit deserve it!"

Instantly there was uproar from the table, followed by a stream of obscenities and recriminations.

"What the . . . ?"

"Guard! Guard!"

"No! It's Straker, by Jeezus!"

"Straker? But how did he get here?"

"He's a renegade and a pirate!"

"Burn him, by Jeezus!"

"No! Hear him out!" Tung Hai's florid face darkened under his A-star-ruined skin. "Let's just hear him out."

Ellis's muscular bulk was the last thing any of them had expected, casting its shadow over their deliberations. Standing there with the flaming-red cataplasm covering his head like the mane of a Rhode Island lion, he guessed he made quite a sight to see. He knew they must have IDed the *Chance* orbiting among the Kan fleet. They must have assumed her taken as a prize, and with her their last chance to outmaneuver the Kan had gone. The Kalifornian sheriff-at-arms fought to bar the crowd from following Ellis into the Council chamber. He overrode the iris control, half closing it, and preventing them surging through, but it had jammed on a swarf bin that had been thrown into it, and twenty hands were trying to force it open again.

"Damn you, Straker, where's the amygdala?" Embree Dzernic demanded.

He brushed Dzernic aside, addressing Pope directly. "I've not come to banter with your pet monkey, Pope, but to report what happened to MeTraCor's credit, and to show you what can be done to save Osumi Lease now that your credit pinching's brought the defenses to a state whereby the planet cannot be properly defended!"

More indignation boiled up at the insult.

"Answer us! Where's the amygdala?" Pope shouted above the noise.

"Dust! Yeah, Jeezus! Lost like a burning meteorite! I warned you, Pope. I told you what would come of neglecting the garrison. I told you the Kan would come after your loose hide one day, but you wouldn't listen! Now I come here under a Kan truce signal—".

Pope recovered herself and plunged in. "A truce signal? Devils score him, and that's a Chinese medicoplast he's wearing! As the Prophet's my witness, he's in a filthy twisted deal with them! It's obvious—he's sold us to the enemy with our own credit!"

"But Straker he got no time for the Kan!" Tung Hai shouted. "Everybody know that."

"He loves credit more than he hates them!"

"C'mon, Tung. We been crossed and double-crossed!"

"I no believe that!"

The turmoil from the table rose again and the mob outside stirred in an ugly mood. Ellis waved the Controller down contemptuously, moving for control himself. "Now, sit down, Pope. And I'll thank you to keep your slanders to yourself. You knew the amygdala was a desperation measure. Do you think I'd surrender my own livelihood to the Kan willingly?"

"Ye're a pirate, Straker! And one that has stolen ten tranches of MeTraCor credit. What have ye to say to that?"

"Just this: you sanctioned the transfer and I've your signature print—and your worm Dzernic's here—to prove it." He swept out a sheet of hardcopy and brandished it in his fist. "Yeah, and MeTraCor's pledge is embedded in my receipt, so it proves you knew the gamble you were taking!"

"Ye're a pirate! Ye've sold us out just as sure as yer filthy heart can't be trusted!"

Ellis's anger simmered red at the insult, and his awesome stare cut the Councillors to silence. His war medals glinted on his cap, full of pride. "Careful, Pope! Don't you understand? The plan we agreed is in shatters. It's no fault of mine that the Kan mean to get us out of Yamato. If you'd moved when I said, instead of horse-bargaining with me for a whole week, then you'd not be squabbling among yourselves like a slush full of synthwhores now. I wouldn't have got caught by an adverse nexus, and an Index lower than a worm's belly. Nor would I have had to put out a surrender signal to Admiral Hu Tsung."

There was more dissent until Ellis banged the table with the flat of his hand. "I came here to tell you what's to be done now, and you'll all listen hard! I know your Controller ain't got the talent to see the way by herself. She'd give all Osumi away for a holdful of promises and a safe passage out. Yep—you may swear to that, all right!"

Pope stabbed the air furiously. "Satan! Ye rob MeTra-

Cor, ye insult this Council, and then ye dare to offer us advice! Well, ye'll freezee down for piracy, Straker! That or a summary burning by the Squad. I'll have yer atoms dispersed tonight, by the Prophet I will! Sheriff, get yer skin in here and arrest this criminal!''

Ellis turned to the rest, his eyes slits, sharply aware that the future of the whole Lease depended on what he was about to say. He steeled himself and addressed Pope straight. ''You might disperse me, but first, if you've any sense, you'll listen what I have to say—whether you like it or not. What's it to be, Councillors? Will you hear me out? Or will you decide in ignorance and lose everything, f'sure?''

The Councillors looked from one to another as more angry shouts came from the lobby. They all knew his reputation, and his legendary psi status. An astrogator's cape flew in over the sheriff's head and a Navy knuckle followed it.

''Anybody who dares to come across that iris will burn as Straker will surely burn!'' Embree Dzernic warned them. ''Lease law applies here, not Amerikan law. You should remember that.''

''C'mon, f'Jeezakes can't we make an exception?'' Derion Reiner pleaded, rising to his feet. Fear was on his face; his wife was pregnant with their first child, and due to give birth any day. She was outside, being jostled in the mob, and he was terrified she would miscarry. ''Surely we ought to hear Straker explain himself?''

''That fair, by gods!'' Tung Hai Johnson's voice scratched. ''Hear him talk!''

''Nossir!'' Pope shouted back. ''This is not a hearing. Straker is not a member of the Osumi Council. He has no business here. Officially, he—''

''No business?'' Ellis seized on Pope's words, turning

to the crowd triumphantly. "No business, she says, when two-thirds of my goddamned livelihood's on this planet? What about you? Now, are you telling me you'd see your prospects squandered by a weak-minded piece of shit who's anxious only to cover her own ass against what the Court of Directors might say? It's Pope who'd give up Osumi, not me! She's the one who'd sell you to the Kan! Is she your nominee in a crisis? I say no! I say we get rid of her, and then make a fight of it!"

Angry shouts for Pope's resignation burst in through the straining iris. A chant of "Fight! Fight!" struck up. The sheriff's *eboshi* cap was knocked off, but still he held them on the strength of Embree Dzernic's threat.

"Order! Come to order, and the Council will hear it debated!" Zeekyel Meredith shouted, despising anarchy. He pulled out his blaster, set it to 6.5, and fired a crackling bolt into the ceiling, sending down blobs of molten stahlex compound. The shock was immediately sobering. No one had thought members of the Kanoya Council might carry charged blasters into their debates.

"Silence!"

Embree Dzernic's glance was as sour as Iowa Chardonnay, but Ellis knew that where words were wanted he was always first into action. "Ellis Straker has consistently impeded MeTraCor by whatever means he could devise for twenty years. Of course he's trying to sell us out. He—"

"I want Straker placed under arrest," Pope insisted. "His treason's clear to us all."

"I still say we hear him talk." Tung Hai's snap-crazed jowls glistened with sweat as he got to his feet. He had been a taker all his life. The rough Korean genodrug, taken as green tea, gave a measure of immunity to the huge blasts of ultraviolet present in A-type primary spectra. Mu Ophiuchi, the hot Neutral Zone primary that he had grown up under, would have fried him had he not been an addict since the womb. "Now tell me you give permission, Controller."

"No. A thousand times. I will not!"

Johnson pulled out his blaster and slammed it onto the table. "Then this weapon yours. If I no have permission to defend the Lease with it, you take!"

More cries of dissent came from the iris where the sheriff-at-arms heaved at the front rank of the mob ineffectually.

"Straker's out of order," Dzernic told them, clinging to Pope's authority. "He can't speak here without the Controller's permission. Isn't that right, Zeekyel?"

Meredith's reluctance was grave as he acknowledged Dzernic's point. "Yes, Straker, we're in session. We have to proceed according to the rules or we're nothing. You will have to leave, and the lobby will have to be cleared."

Ellis planted his feet wide. He looked down the length of the shining table defiantly and tucked his thumbs into his belt. He knew the time had come to play his hand. "Yeah? And what if I tell you I just stepped off the Chinese admiral's flagship? That I dipped dough balls with Hu Tsung last night? That we had an understanding, he and I, and that this cease-fire is all on my account?"

A hush fell on the mob in the next room, but it began to swell again as the sound of MeTraCor troops running to the Controller's summons rose through the vents.

Pope seized her chance as the sheriff pulled the swarf bin free from the iris. "You see! Straker's condemned out of his own mouth! Sheriff! Arrest this traitor!"

Ellis half turned and hammered his fists onto the tabletop, his eyes flaming at the Council. "She'll destroy you, and it's a helluva pity when you're a wafer away from winning."

"For Jeezus's sake," Reiner said as the sheriff obeyed.

"Let's hear him out. What he knows may be of use to us."

The sheriff clapped a hand on Ellis's sleeve, then Fawley Beuze, the apple-cheeked secretary, flinched as Ellis's thumb and forefinger closed expertly over the official's wrist in a Chinese grip, and turned it slowly back. First the Macau-Kalifornian's wristbones, then his elbow joint, and finally his shoulder socket, locked out. His weapon slipped, clattering onto the polished floor. There was a grunt of pain. "No, man, please! You're breaking my arm! You're breaking it! Agh!"

When the man began to scream, Foster intervened. "That's enough! I move we hear what Straker has to say!"

"If there's the slightest chance—"

The iris fell apart and the crowd poured into the chamber. They began to engulf the stricken sheriff. Ellis stood unmoved. "Vote on it! That's fair, ain't it?"

"Yes," Reiner pleaded, as his wife ran gratefully to his open arms. "Let him speak, Aziza! Didn't he say he was practically an emissary of the Chinese admiral? If so, that changes things. We're surely obliged to hear his ultimatum."

"Yes, by Jeezus!"

"I say that fair."

Controller Pope's anguish was plain. Her voice rose to quell the tide of disquiet. "Okay, since ye appear to feel the Xanadu emissary has something to offer us, I'll give him two minutes dead. Then, by the Prophet, I intend to call on the guard to set their weapons to kill and send the whole lot of ye packing off to hell fire!"

"No!" Ellis stared hard at the Controller, despising her. "You can be sure I'm no emissary of the Kan, but we have vital business to transact here." He turned to the crowd. "That's business that concerns you all, and too important to be limited by a goddamned Controller's time clock. I told you that I shared dim-sum with the Kan admiral in the stateroom of his flagship last night, and so I did. That's the truth, and so is this: Hu Tsung means to murder you all if you surrender.''

There was a vast silence as he paused, then the sound of more MeTraCor troops arriving in the lobby. They were mollified by the quiet, and craned their heads to listen in.

"Yep," Ellis told them all, knowing he had won. "I talked with Hu Tsung, all right. But only so's I could know his mind. And what I found was plain enough. He's mortally afraid that Commodore Vaile's Navy ships will come blasting out of the Teth-Two-Nine nexus while he's helpless in orbit around Osumi. He's exchanged beam-weapon fire once already; that means Vaile's no longer in the Grus chain as the Council thought, but hereabouts. And if I know the Commodore he'll be waiting his moment to come out of Teth-Two-Nine like a jackrabbit out of a hollow log. Don't you see? If Kanoya City can outlast the Kan for a week UT, they'll be driven off!''

There was a shuffling and murmuring at that, and Ellis's heart fell. He knew he had played his best hand, but found only deuces.

When Embree Dzernic spoke up it was with a three-star lawyer's sweetest venom.

"Straker," he said. "I take it you're unaware that Commodore Vaile is dead?"

12

Ellis felt the color drain from his face. "Dead?"

"Yes. Dead. Of a contamination fever. We've known it here since a day after your departure to Kagoshima."

Zeekyel Meredith took it up. "It's true, Straker. Commodore Vaile's squadron is commanded by Captain Hart now. We have it that they clashed with the Han but that Hart was bested and has retired to Seoul."

It can't be, Ellis thought, reeling stunned by the news. The Amerikan Navy made to run scared by the rabble now sitting in orbit? When they've got the Merrimack County and four Concord-class frigates? That's not possible. Shit, if Vaile's dead that's bad, but if Hart's really lit out for Seoul that's disaster because it means he's a fool, or a coward, or both.

Ellis's mind began hunting desperately for an answer. Something, anything, to regain the initiative.

"I guess that means you have nothing more to say, Mister Straker." Embree Dzernic's inquiry was crisp. An annoying, tight smile played around his mouth.

"But that's crazee! Hart'd never do that. He'd know he'd be dispersed for dereliction of duty as soon as he crossed the Thirty Degree line."

"This is his drone message," Dzernic said, holding up the hardcopy. "In Captain Hart's own words. I believe it expresses his intentions clear enough."

The Council stared at Ellis as he read it. At his back, a crowd that seconds ago might have been persuaded to turn the Council table over and oust Pope bodily stood shocked and aghast. It was disaster. Then Ellis's great laugh rang out confidently.

"Ah, you're a pack of fools! It's a feint! D'you expect Hart to send you a message and send it through the nexus in a drone? Chapter and verse on his plan of surprise? When the Kan are roaming about in the system with every kind of sensor there ever was? Don't you see through that? What if it had been intercepted?"

Pope snatched up the hardcopy and shook it in the air. "What do ye suppose MeTraCor security codes are for? It's here in black and white, Straker! Hart's squadron's gone to Seoul!"

"Ah, Hart don't trust your codes—or your courage— any more than we do. That communication was meant for the Kan. Any half-clever synth'd see its real message."

"Straker!"

It was Jos Hawken, his daughter beside him, pushing anxiously through the line of MeTraCor troopers. "What status?"

"Megabad, Jos. This dumbass wants to surrender."

"Where's Hayden?"

"He's probably up there, selling us to the Chinese on his father's behalf!" Pope shouted.

"Didn't the Chinese capture you after all?" Arkali Hawken asked. "How did you get here?"

Knowing he must draw out the doubts from them all with his fieriest words, Ellis raised his voice. "Listen! Last night I played the broken-spirited man for the Kan admiral. I planted some deceits in his mind, and this morning he toured me around his assault lines before letting me go."

"Don't listen to him!"

"The idea was that I'd come and infect Kanoya City with despair, and that way I'd win the Kan a fast victory. But I'll tell you this: the Kan don't have the weaponry to reduce Kanoya City's shields inside a week if we choose to hold out."

"You can't trust Straker! He's—"

Foster's words died away as the crowd shouted her down.

Ellis struck off the points for everyone to see. "We have to get Fort Baker out of mothballs, and ready our other defenses. We can show them they'll not crack Kanoya in a week, a month, or even a goddamned year! We've got two hundred beam weapons and the power to supply them. We've got three hundred Macau-Kalifornian militia, and a hundred of them are trained gunners. We've good shields around us, built to keep any orbiter at bay for a week! It's a quick submission that Hu Tsung wants more than anything. He believes the Navy's waiting to pounce on him, so he won't hang around long. But the big one is this: we got no choice. That maniac'll put us all up against a wall—man, woman and child—unless we keep him off planet. Now where's the coward who'll say we should sue for terms?"

Ellis fixed Pope with his eye, infuriating her.

"It was never our intention to surrender Fort Baker or Kanoya City to the Chinese—" she began, but Ellis cut her off.

"Good. Then that's settled. If we're to fight, we'll need to enlist civilians as temporary militiamen. That means everybody who can sit up and talk. You! What's your name?"

A bluff young man in his early twenties, one of MeTra-Cor's junior staffers, put his hand to his chest. "Me, sir?"

"Yeah, you, sir!"

"Barb Eastman. Accounts personn—"

"Get yourself to the south side defenses, Barb. You're to oversee the batteries there and to get them in go condition. I don't want to hear a word, boy. Just do it. You, and you, soldier. Go with him. You're under his command as of this moment. Move!"

"Yes, sir!"

He hauled the sheriff-at-arms out of the crowd. "Get yourself busy running those three companies of asshole Kalifornians you call troopers. They're to man the West End and North Side beam weapons from Skid 34 on down. You're under the command of Councillor Johnson. So do as he tells you, or I'll bust your other arm."

As the soldiers left, Ellis ordered each of the merchants and MeTraCor officials he knew by name into makeshift inspection crews with orders to ready themselves and make reports on the state of readiness of all Kanoya City's protection batteries. Others he sent to the Western Hemisphere Equatorial Fortress, an outpost battery at the westernmost extremity of the Lease. He sent the remainder down into the underground arsenals to break out personal weapons, and to fetch and carry, and make arrangements as secure as possible against the bombardment that must soon resume. And all the while, as the whirlwind gathered force, Controller Pope sat rigid in her seat, seeing that she had lost the initiative utterly.

As Ellis led his followers from the MeTraCor building and towards the apron-side portal, the burning white sun of Osumi blasted him through the mile-high dome. His cataplasm wilted to indigo. The dome was phased to attenuate the residual hard radiation of an A0 primary.

Outside, it was steamy and lush. Osumi was no paradise, but no hell either: close on one standard dwelling-planet radius of 4,000 miles, but a denser core—giving 1.2 gee dragging at each elbow. Most offworlders living on Osumi had developed thighs like footballers. Osumi's primary, Zeta CrA, or a prominent star in the Kan constellation of Pi, the Turtle, scored almost fifty on the old solar luminosity scale—energetic for a dwarf star, and even with Osumi circling at a little less than seven AU it could get hot at the equator. The star's 3.63 solar masses threw Osumi round in just under 10 UT years, and the two-degree axial tilt imparted by the terraformers, plus the generous 2:1 oceanic distribution, gave equatorial Kanoya City a seasonless uniformity—what a citizen of Liberty would think of as "tropical" heat, broken only by the violent heat-transport flashovers that often gave rise to hurricanes at nexus quadrature.

Ellis looked around the jungly strip fringing the apron, savoring the green and blue jewel of Osumi's eco-mix. Some things were just pure Osumi, like here: striped blue-water buffaloids, with ever-present parasitic flies clustering black around open red sores on their backs, chewed placidly in the mud wallows beside the storm drains. The eye-hurting green of new shoots of distant paddies, and the needle-sharp detail of the pure white light that flooded them. Shallow lagoons that stretched in a Mandelbrot coastline to the horizon on the far side of the dome . . .

He got hold of himself. This was no time for reveries, but it sure helped for a man to remind himself what he was about to fight for.

He took a 65-kV Esandubya off a man and flipped the switches, hefting the sights up and jamming the brute stock into his hip. He had seen what he wanted of the apron. Not a lot there . . .

Ffffzzzzzt!!! FFzhang! Ffzhang!

Okeh . . . now nothing. He grinned. Let's see Pope get her pink ass out of here now.

Back inside the Kanoya dome all hell was breaking loose. Men and women were running around everywhere,

MeTraCor staff marshaling the effort, everyone shouting, organizing, doing, preparing for the siege. It was good to see, like old times, and Ellis noted it all with great satisfaction. Here he would create an operations room, on the ground floor of MeTraCor's biggest complex block, but first the silk containers and impex hold-cartons and swarf bins would have to be cleared out. He put Anderson on it.

He strode on, exulting in his assumption of power. Without formal declaration, or the taking of any official rank, he had become leader again, which was just as it should be. He thought of the batteries of heavy Kan weapons he had been shown set up to the south and west of the city along the fringes of Dragonfly Ponds. The ten heavily shielded Chinese beam-weapon batteries along MeTraCor's white paracrete apron would soon be readied for firing. He knew that with the Pai Hu's heavy guns bearing down from the zenith the Kan were capable of reducing the obsolete shields and foundation works of Kanoya City in maybe two days of continuous firing, but if they wanted the facility intact their infantry would still have to rush the breaches and make the occupation. And after taking casualties there'd be a real fighting spirit in the Amerikan men and women, and they'd fight to the death to deny the Kan their victory because that's the way things went when it came to it.

The weakest point's those damned raggedy-ass Macau-Kalifornians, he thought. I want to know how many of them're hiding out in the Yamato-style township. The sprawl's perfect cover for a Kan sneak attack. If the shield rampart were to be taken away those pretty little wooden hovels built against the north foundations would collapse, but it'll have to be done. Yep, we'll evacuate and fire the whole lot before nightfall.

The old excitement was mounting in him, just as strong

as ever. Death to the Kan, he thought fondly. Ah, that was a maxim good for an Amerikan to live by, but something Jos Hawken had forgotten. "An unreasoning hatred," he called it. But it was not without reason.

Within the hour Zeekyel Meredith reported over the com-net that of the three companies of security only two hundred MeTraCor troopers were fit for duty. "You know how Controller Pope saved credit?"

"By employing piss-head Kalifornian sentinels, vagabond deserters from the Sector military on Frisco and Sandyego."

"That's right. The worst people in Amerika to rely on, Ellis. We got a further thirty-four in the medicos, and thirty civilians at least who're too young or old to fight."

"Get them equipped, every one who can stand or hold a blaster. Pull in the Lease-living Yamato feudals, the customs officials, anyone with two eyes and four limbs. And bring me those *ronin* samurai who maintain order in the townships. If they're still there."

"The feudals are only fit for planting rice. They can't read, or even count."

"Train 'em!"

"They're beyond training!"

"They're human, ain't they?"

"Yes, but—" In the com-net's holo light Meredith looked small and less important than he had in the flesh.

"Then start thinking like an Amerikan again. It's only a question of will. C'mon!"

Meredith lingered. "The samurai won't like it, Ellis."

"Shaft them! This is MeTraCor's Lease."

"We don't want to antagonise them."

"I don't give a good goddamn, Zee."

"So what if they refuse?"

"Shoot a few of them. They profit from our trade, they'd

better be prepared to drill with us. Listen, some of these assholes have been riding on our charity too damned long. They're richer than me, some of them. Even extend me credit, some of them." He smacked his lips. "Well, now it's party time! They get their asses in the front line alongside us, or they burn."

Ellis felt an arresting hand on his shoulder as he broke the connection. It was Jos Hawken, and he was gray-faced.

"You lied to them, Ellis! I could see it in your eyes. My God, but you must hate the Kan more than I thought possible. You know fine and well what those beam weapons will do to us. Hundreds of innocents will be killed."

"Ah, we're all soldiers now. We've no choice but to fight." He lowered his voice. "You brought the aurium inside the shield, didn't you?"

"You'd ruin the whole of Osumi just to save that bullion from becoming Chinese, wouldn't you?"

Ellis faced him. "What's the matter with you? That's damn near all the credit we got left."

"You've no conscience! You'd murder us all and sell out your own son! I remember you coming on board Chesapeake. Norfolk apron—oh, ten, fifteen years back. You wanted it out with me, face-to-face. You had some kind of honor then. But, my God, you've become a heartless bastard!"

"And ten years has made you a broken down old man, Jos. Now get out of my way."

Hawken's daughter stood in shock, trembling at her father's side, her eyes accusing him. "Where is he, Mister Straker? Where's my Hayden? How can I marry your son when he's stranded aboard a Chinese ship?"

"Marry—Ladee, what the hell you talking about? Don't you realise what's going on here?"

"We're still in love. I still want to marry."

Ellis felt a pang of guilt, but angrily burned it up as he shrugged her hand from his arm. "You can marry Hayden any way you like once you've found him, Ladee, and to the devil with the both of you!"

Her voice rose. "But he's your son—"

"I've no son, by Jeezus!"

Hawken grabbed his coat and spun him as he began to turn away. "What do you mean by that?"

"I mean he's gone to hell in a bucket!" Ellis shoved Hawken easily away and tore off the writhing medicoplast to show them the scalp wound. "He did that to me and that's a death warrant for any man! He left the ship in a shuttle without my permission. Left his vessel a cowardly thief, with our only salvation in his pocket. He took the amygdala and the Prefect's son with him out in the shuttle, then dropped it into a hurricane and blew himself and Hideki fucking Shingo to dogmeat!"

"No!" Arkali's scream pierced the air.

Jos Hawken's face was contorted. "They're dead?"

"I don't know and I don't care. If he's dead, then the Lord God'll spit him out to burn in hell for his treachery, and if he's alive he's disowned. And you can be sure I'll find him one day and pay him real good for his sins. Now get out of my way, there's work to be done, and I mean to do it if you won't."

Ellis marched away into a confusion of ill-disciplined troopers, and Arkali watched him go as if in a nightmare. She shivered in the cool, eyes red and blinded by the intense light of noon, stinging yet numb, feeling only hollowness inside her. It can't be, she thought, her mind swallowing her in blackness. No. You can't be dead, Hayden. You can't be.

13

All was quiet in Hayden Straker's mind now. It was the morning of the third day at Karihara. There was a narrow winding track before him, covered in branches strewn by the storm. The broad sweep of flooded paddy fields sparkled ahead under a misty sun that was now half up. He walked towards it, marveling that so fierce a rage could be stilled to this calm beauty.

The sense of his own inevitable destiny filled his mind like a drug.

A quarter mile down the clearing, near the fringe of the grove, he came on the shattered craft that had brought him here, and the black rock mound the villagers had already erected on the spot where they had found poor Quinn's body. Instead of feeling pain at the memory, as he had done yesterday, he felt only the heartbeat of the planet and the firm black volcanic dirt under his toes and the warm breeze and the powerful radiance of the sun-star on his body. He nodded, knowing why he had come here, and sat down on the intact plex shell of the shuttle.

Before the crash the vehicle's conformable, slightly yielding surface had been like fish skin, micro-ribbed and barbed so it could be stroked only one way. Now the support system was dead, all lubes had stopped exuding and the slipstreaming mucus had turned waxy, shedding in dusty scales like the stuff from moth's wings.

An infinite peace had settled over him. All was ordered in his mind: the breaking away, the rescue, the coming back from death, all had been resolved since he had woken up.

He had no idea why he had blacked out. Must have been shock, he told himself. The beheading. Coming on top of what happened to Danny Quinn . . . A head without a body. A horrible sight.

He had never seen that before, not in his whole life. Now he had seen two. One after another. They say events come in multiples. Threes. Like echoes of one another. And it's not coincidence, its fundamental structure, the operation of psi. . . .

Somehow, it felt as if he had been knocked out of his track. He thought again of Arkali. She could never understand what had happened to him. She could never understand about his rebellion, about Quinn, nor about the amygdala. Yet he knew that, whatever she failed to understand, she would nevertheless forgive. She would forgive him anything and everything, and she would do it because she loved him blindly and unconditionally. Which was why he could never truly love her.

He felt a powerful desire to see her face again, to explain, and to have her smile for him just once, but he knew she would never hear his apology, nor would he see her smile, until he had put the amygdala into the hand of Hideki Ryuji.

He felt the new strength gathering in him. It was more than confidence, more even than conviction, it was as if he had acquired a weird sixth sense that enabled him to feel the flow of destiny moving like a river current around him.

Even the thought of the dead monk could not shake his certainty. It would not be long before the horsemen came from Miyakonojo, and with them the terror. He knew the immense danger surrounding him, because Shingo-san was a pacing tiger, but as he sat in the brightness of the new clearing and closed his eyes he felt the flow and knew he had only to follow its urging.

After an hour or so he got up from the sun-warming plex and turned his back on the shuttle, following the raised causeway that surrounded the paddies. Then he turned towards the village, his mind made up.

Rosei-san's people were out in the fields as Hayden Straker walked back. They labored stooped double in ground that had been hand-conditioned and irrigated with sweet water raised from the Oki River by a great spidery treadwheel. The village itself was a cluster of thirty or so mean wooden dwellings, each raised three feet from the ground on posts, with thatched roofs and lattice windows and a kind of veranda going around all four sides. As he reached Rosei-san's house he was met by the women and half a dozen tiny children who still gawped at him with fascination. When the older ones saw him, they stood still, their heads bowed as if in prayer. Rosei-san came out and his face took on its customary look of deference.

"Ohayo gozaimasu. Mokarimakka?"

"Ohayo," he replied familiarly. Though it was no longer, he agreed: "Yes, it is early."

The headman's anxiety was obvious as he drew Hayden Straker aside.

"Gomen nahai . . ." And there followed a welter of words that meant nothing to him.

He shrugged, not understanding the rural *hogen*. As a youth his tutor had given him standard Japanese, some Mandarin, and a little of the superpolite forms of Imperial Kyoto; he had studied all three, but it had been the written forms that he had concentrated on. His day-to-day business conversations rarely went beyond a vocabulary of fifteen hundred words—the lingua franca of Kanoya City was a shipney pidgin anyway—but the dialect Rosei-san spoke was hard to figure. It sounded as if it had come from Osaka, an old world in the Kansai, the part of Yamato less than sixty light-years from Old Earth. Osaka circled the A-type star known on Navy charts as Delta Normae. It had been settled for nearly a quarter millennium. Perhaps the peasants of Osumi had originally come from there? And what about Rosei-san? Wasn't "Rosei" the Japanese name for Sirius? That's a minor star in the Izlam Sector that would have been visible as a magnitude 2 star from Osaka, but certainly wasn't noticeable from Osumi. But then, "rosei" also meant "labor administrator," or just plain "experienced," and both those were reasonable names for a man born to a hereditary position like headman of a village.

"*Kami yo! . . . Uchi no omu wa do shita ka Taiwan no shumokuzame wo ke-girai shite imasu!*"

What it sounded like made no sense at all. He knew only the few *hogen* words he had learned since his rescue. Strange that the samurai woman could fathom the speech when her husband could not, he thought. Shingo-san probably considers it to be a peasant form that's not worth his attention.

The headman was trying desperately to make himself understood. "*Kanoya Si-ti!*"

The accented Amerikan word surprised Hayden Straker, and he smiled and pointed at his own nose. "Yes, I come from Kanoya City."

Rosei's voice dropped low. He shook his hand and stamped his foot, but tightly, as if afraid he might be watched or overheard. "*Gekihen! Okii abunaii pon pon!*"

When Hayden Straker raised his shoulders, Rosei re-

peated himself, emphasising his gestures, but then his wife
came to him with a small wooden tray on which tiny pots
of pickled vegetable and leaf-wrapped rice were set. She
bowed, whispering urgently, and Rosei-san fell suddenly
silent. He looked pointedly towards the house that the
gozen-sama occupied, and when he spoke again it was in
his usual quiet tone. He pinched his thin fingers together
and raised his hand towards his mouth, pushing the tray
forward.

"*Nan'gozaimahen ga go-en' nak' o-mezugari kuda-
hai.*"

Hayden Straker heard the bones of a formal invitation.
The form had always puzzled him: We have nothing to
offer you, but be so good as to eat it anyway. He bowed.
"*Itadakimasu.*" I don't mind if I do.

He realised he was very hungry, and sat down on the
bottom step of the headman's porch. He slipped on an
undersized pair of rice-straw sandals that had been provided for him, and drew the *yukata* tight about him like a
thin bathrobe.

As he savored the meal, he watched the men rethatching
their storm-damaged homes, and the women going to fetch
water. These people are as tough as leather and incredibly
diligent at their tasks, he thought. They risked themselves
to pull us from a smash, and they've shown supreme hospitality. Rosei-san gave up his own home to the samurai,
and gave his brother's home to me. I was blind to have
mistaken their quiet acceptance for docility. I never realised before why the samurai oppress their subjects so cru-
elly, or why they scourge the land to destroy accumulations
of wealth. Now I see they fear these peasants because of
their inner strength.

I wonder if Shingo-san understands that. Does he take
these people for weaklings because they submit to him?

Does he see that when they fall down and fawn before him it's just their way of resisting? It's not their way to stand up and fight oppression directly; they absorb it, draw it like a cataplasm draws infection from a wound, which is why they're indomitable. Yes, their strength is real, and their patience is astonishing, and I could not see that before. Rosei-san could have cut the throats of all three of us and dug our bodies into the rice paddies when he discovered who we were. Instead he agreed to send his fleetest man to carry news to Miyakonojo—on foot! He called out the entire village to search the crash site. And, through it all, he and his people have endured the strutting of their lord and his unspeakable violence without disturbance to their secret inner composure.

Could I have done so? No. Never.

Never in this universe.

He stiffened as he became aware that the samurai lady was watching him from the front stoop of the headman's house.

"Good morning," he said pleasantly, in Japanese.

There was no reply, except a downward tilt of her head. Then her hand came up to adjust the fold of fabric that draped to her feet.

"Won't you join me?" he said. "I'm about to have breakfast. *Ikaga desu ka?*"

Still she made no reply. Her eyes were downcast. Then a hand jerked back the screen that hung across the door, and Shingo appeared from the darkness, his killing sword no longer bound into his sash, but loose in his hand, the lacquerwork of the scabbard glinting menacingly. His stare was ice.

"Ah, I was just asking if you and your lady would care to—"

Shingo barked a curt order and his wife bowed, got up,

and obediently moved inside. The curtain was twitched closed after her, then Shingo strode forward to tower over Hayden Straker.

"Get up and dress yourself!"

He absorbed the abrupt command motionlessly, aware that the villagers were rooted around him, watching despite themselves. He swallowed his anger at Shingo's impolite speech form and looked up lethargically, aware of the amused insubordination that must be frozen in his face. Then, incredibly, Shingo swung his foot and kicked out at him.

"I said, dress yourself!"

"By psi—!"

"Get dressed! Cover yourself! Now!"

The blood surged in his chest, but he knew he had to swallow his pride and submit. Whatever the cost, do as he says! He holds the initiative and there's nothing you can do. You depend on him completely now. Forget the insult and do as he wishes. For Rosei-san's sake.

Calmness. Self-possession. Dignity. Hold to these things and you must win in the end, his mind told him, but also he heard his father's voice roaring at him to tear the heart out of the arrogant Yambo sonofabitch.

Wordlessly Hayden Straker got to his feet, turned, and with immense control went back inside the dwelling.

There he found his clothes as they had been left: washed, dried, and neatly folded on the wooden floor beside his sleeping place. His father's blasters had at first been taken to the headman's house, but now he saw they had been returned to him. He dressed methodically, while the anger flowed from him. He put on his leggings, belted them, clasped them at the knee, and slipped on a pair of white split-toe socks. The plain cadet's shirt was the one Quinn had died in. Knowing he must, he drew it over his head and tucked it into his waist, then tied the neck of the shirt up with a throat band that wound around and fixed at the back. After that he combed his hair back and secured it in its customary pony. Finally he put on his father's ornate coat with the braid and fancy breastings. The crash seemed to have dulled it, but the tear in the lining had been neatly and ingeniously repaired, the woven flexiplex fabric being caught with minute silk stitches.

Next he pushed his father's superb Wesson fighting tools into his belt, then went out into the sunlight and marched up to the house with the curtained doorway and rapped on the rough wooden frame. The curtain was swept aside instantly. Shingo's *daito* was drawn, the razor steel jutted, its curve deadly.

Hayden Straker took one pace back and bowed from the waist, and in his crispest Japanese he said, "Honorable Sir, I apologise if I have affronted you or your lady. No insult was intended. I humbly beg that you will take breakfast with me now."

The samurai stared at him in disbelief. Inside he churned with the prospect of swordplay, and his mind seethed as he picked over the dangers and insults he had been forced to endure because of this hated foreigner.

He looked the *gaijin* up and down. His outrage at his wife's loss of face was still tremendous. The rescue had been worse than death. These casteless *hinin* had dragged her away while he, their lord and master, lay trapped and helpless in the shuttle. Because she had been restrained from going back into the shattered wreck, Yasuko had been prevented from doing her wifely duty. They had laid their filthy paws on her.

Despicable *hinno*. Only physical exhaustion and the fact that they had been ignorant of his rank had prevented him from cutting them to pieces there and then.

"Well, sir? Will you step out?"

Shingo was instantly on guard. He had expected the invitation to fight from the moment he had kicked out, and he relished the opportunity to cut the *gaijin*.

Shingo's eyes searched the Amerikan's face, unable to believe what he had heard. Was it some trick, this craven and insincere apology? He saw village women watching slyly from their hovels. In due course this village would be taught a lesson. He would double their taxes for ten years, or maybe raze the village and blast their ludicrous ship-hulk temple to grains with beam weapons before sending them all into Miyakonojo to live as town lice. And so also would the Amerikan be made to pay—once he had given over the amygdala.

He said, ''You should know that on this world men are put to death for daring to look upon a samurai lady's palanquin. And yet you imagine you can insult my wife by speaking familiarly to her when you are not even properly dressed.''

Hayden Straker hesitated, scratched his chin contritely, then began to explain, ''So sorry, my lord, of course that was a mistake. You see, on board ship—''

''On board the ship you were captain! Here, I am captain. This is my land, and all that is in it belongs to me. The earth, the trees, the people. Everything. I am tired of explaining that to you. I am the law here. Do you understand? You are lucky I do not cut out your tongue for what you have done and said already, Amerikan.''

''Again, Lord, if I have offended you, it was not intended. Again I humbly apologise.''

Shingo faced the foreigner stonily. It was the Europans, was it not, who had the great reputation as duelists? Surely these Amerikans, just another of the Untrustworthy Races, should react in the same way to provocation? More treacherously, perhaps, but just as proudly.

''Don't play games with me, Amerikan.''

"I beg your pardon, Lord, but I am not, in fact, strictly speaking an Amerikan."

Hideki Shingo stared at him, hating his lies, his anger doubling. "You are not Kan. You are not Europan. Do you not come from Amerikan territory? And before that from Amerika itself? Is your father not an Amerikan? Are you not therefore an Amerikan?"

"I lived most of my life in the Amerikan Lease on Osumi. My father is Amerikan, but I, myself, am not Amerikan. Some years ago, for trade reasons, my father applied to have me registered as a resident of the Osumi Lease. The application was approved by MeTraCor. Therefore, it follows that I am technically of Yamato Sectorhood and so . . ."

Midway through the Amerikan's absurd gabbling Shingo's anger faltered, and fear began to seep up from somewhere deep inside him. The exposure of this remote village prickled his spine as it was always prickled when his bodyguard were absent. By the Emperor, he thought, if my brother, Sadamasa-san, discovers I'm here he'll send his men to snatch me. Time is essential. Thank the gods he cannot use power technology here—but then, neither can I. Oh, what a prize I would be if he could take me, and with Yasuko also in his grip he could make my father bend to his will. Elder brother must know I'll try to use the amygdala to force the succession.

I need absolute secrecy. That's why I had to stamp my authority on this despicable village from the start. That's why I beat the headman's brother and killed the monk. Without fear in his heart there could be no guarantee the messenger would go directly to Miyakonojo and follow my orders explicitly. There's no protection against betrayal except fear, and fear will work on this foreigner, too, as I proved when I chopped the *bonze*'s filthy head off. Still, there's nothing else to do now but await the sound of horses' hooves.

The Amerikan's voice droned on at him. "The fact is, where I was born is immaterial. In the Amerikan colony of Bunguran, in the Sector we call the Neutral Zone, where there are Japanese-speaking refugees from . . ."

He's trying to bore me to death, Shingo thought, his anger simmering higher again. I've never heard such nonsense! Then he saw the blaster butts in Hayden Straker's belt as he straightened, and his grip increased on his sword. By the Emperor, he thought, I should have been more vigilant. He has stolen them from me as he stole them from his father. Were they not lost in the crash? Were they not searched for at my command? And found on my land by my villagers, again at my command? Therefore, does he not understand that they now belong to me?

He stared at the beautiful blasters, unable to believe the audacity of the Amerikan thief. He must have removed them last night while I was taking *cha*, and now he wears them as if they were still his own.

But wait! Look at the indicator. There's no power to fire them; therefore, are they not completely useless? There's no reason for me to fear them. A sword needs no power, just the strength of *chi* flowing in a man's arm to wield it! By the Emperor, I shall strip the blasters from his belt and humble him!

"So? You did come here to fight!"

"To fight? No. Not at all, Shingo-sama. But I would be most honored if you would breakfast with me."

Look how the *gaijin* backs down abjectly, he thought, infuriated. This politeness can only be because he wants to insult me again! And how he speaks with hooded eyes! He will not fight because he has no honor. These barbarous Amerikans grovel like dirty peasants as soon as their ships and forts and beam weapons are taken away. You disgust me! All of you! Once I become Prefect of the Kyushu Quadrant instead of just ruler of this useless continent, I'll drive all interfering foreigners back where they came from! Yes, keep the empty blasters, Amerikan—or whatever you say you are. They are a symbol of your impotence and of no other significance. They and the intelligent jewel you stole from your father will be mine soon enough.

The samurai turned and marched back inside the dwelling, Hayden Straker watching after him with a half-smile. Yes, you can't help it, can you? he thought, pleased with himself. That's the way to disarm you. You understand cringing and servility well enough. What about flattery? I bet you're a sucker for that too. And thank psi for this good Amerikan jacket. These samurai respect rank like soldiers respect a uniform, and that's something else they can't help.

Fifty horsemen thundered into the village as the sun touched the zenith. All the horses were lathered and very tired. There were a further four riderless horses with them, and another that carried the villager who had taken the message to Miyakonojo. He was lashed across the saddle; his body had been flayed and was caked with dried blood.

Rosei's people, men, women and children alike, had

stopped their work at the first sound of hooves and prostrated themselves on the ground. No one except Hayden Straker dared to move or look at the bloodied body.

"Headman! Come here!"

The lead rider was one-eyed, a livid scar slashing his empty eye socket and trailing deeply across his cheek. He was armored in *yoroi* style and fearsomely armed with a long *daito* sword. A lance was holstered in his saddle. He was a *hatamochi*, one of the daimyo's personal bodyguard, big-boned, muscular, and deadly. When no one moved to his command, he dismounted and strode towards the cringing headman. He took off his winged helmet, revealing an overoiled hairstyle, graying slightly as was his beard. He folded the helmet's face mask inside with its cords and looked sharply around.

"Eh, you? What is this place called? Who is in charge?" he demanded, nudging the trembling villager with his foot. He looked about, grinning. "Ignorant *hinno* peasants, there is not a human being among them. What use are they to anyone?" He raised his voice. "I said: where are we and who's the headman? Interpreter, come here. Find out where we are, and how far we are from Kurihara."

Another of the riders dismounted and scrambled forward, his lacquered war gear catching the light like fish scales as he knelt. He was darker than the other, and his eyes bloodshot from exhaustion. Just as he came up from his bow, he caught a movement in the doorway of one of the hovels and froze.

There, emerging from the shadows, was a *gaijin*, a tall, unsmiling white man dressed in a jacket, and wearing a pair of blasters. He came forward without obeisance and seemed about to intervene when a stocky figure appeared from another of the huts.

Both horsemen went down immediately on one knee

before him. The one-eyed leader followed suit with slow dignity. He said with great formality, "May the gods be praised I've found you."

Shingo's reply was equally shallow. "May the gods be praised it's you who has found me, Gozaemon-san."

But Shingo's relief was far from total. No, he thought, motioning the men to rise, I'd rather anyone had found me but you. You're my father's man, a mercenary, and by all the gods, you're the most terrifying son of a *yuna* in the whole Quadrant.

"What is this godforsaken place? How far are we from Miyakonojo?" he asked.

"The road from Ninokata was difficult, while that from Haraki was worse. That pathetic lump of dog filth you sent to guide us here could not ride. First he slowed us, then he put us on the wrong side of the river, so I had to teach him a lesson." A passing afterthought overtook the *hatamochi*'s features. "You didn't want him alive, did you?"

Flies blackened the disfigured body on the horse. As they watched, the one-eyed *hatamoto* pulled out a small fish knife and severed the lashings that held the body. It slumped sickeningly to the dust and Haigo Gozaemon poked it with his toe, turning it onto its back. Then he knelt to hack off the head, which he did with butcher's cuts and held it up by the long hair to admire. Viscous gore dripped from the ragged meat at the neck, so he cast it aside negligently.

Fleetingly, Shingo considered the real reason why Haigo Gozaemon had flayed the villager to death. Undoubtedly to enhance his reputation among his cadre, probably for his own gratification, but certainly to maintain secrecy. Shingo thought of the amygdala, and a dreadful uncertainty flashed through him. That's the key to the stone in the Shogun's holy *daito,* he thought. More power than a poor standard bearer could hope for in a hundred lifetimes.

"Yes, I rode without stopping, Lord. Neither sleep nor rice delayed me, because I knew I had to find you. And now I have."

"You made excellent time, but I ask again, where are we?"

"Harusada!"

Another horseman dismounted and produced a scroll from his saddle. Although the inscriptions were in Japanese, the map had been made by an Amerikan survey satellite and was wonderfully detailed. It outlined the main roads and settlements south of Kanoya as far as Ninokata and west as far as the coast, but the location the samurai pointed to was not marked as a village.

"It's no more than two hundred and fifty *ri* from here to Miyakonojo, Highness."

Hideki Shingo calculated from the scale. There were 2.78 *ri* to the Amerikan mile. That meant they must be close on 100 miles south of Kanoya City.

"You brought a *hogen* speaker with you?"

"Of course, Lord. Interpreter!"

Another trooper stepped forward.

Shingo said, "Tell these people to fetch water and fodder. I want my men ready to ride again inside the hour." He eyed the Amerikan suspiciously and moved out of earshot. In a low voice he asked, "It was not you I summoned from Miyakonojo. Did my father send you?"

"No, Lord. That was my idea and my idea alone. You see my men have orders to be particularly vigilant in times of political ferment. The piece of filth you sent as messenger was intercepted long before he reached the gates of Miyakonojo."

Shingo's heart sank low. "I take it you kept your destination secret from my father and from elder brother?"

"Of course."

"And no one questioned that a detachment of fifty men was leaving the capital without explanation?"

"Oh, I expect it was questioned eventually, Lord, but I was long gone from Miyakonojo before anyone thought to question me."

The *hatamochi* showed his even teeth, and a blade of ice shafted Hideki Shingo's heart. He knew immediately what was meant by the smile. The autonomy that men like Haigo Gozaemon enjoyed was great. They were sanctioned by the Shogun himself and appeared as "gifts" to daimyo, whom he did not wholly trust. Some were simply spies; others irritant grains in the oyster politic sent out to grow a pearl for the Shogun; others still were parasitic lechers or men of huge appetite who ate and entertained their hosts into ruin. As warriors and intriguers, the *hatamochi* mercenaries had no equal. Many had risen to key positions in the armies of the daimyo. They were reckless opportunists, totally ruthless.

"Of course, our departure was expected," the *hatamochi* continued. "For a week now we've been awaiting the call to ride as your ceremonial escort from Kanoya, so we were in readiness."

"I see."

"It was common knowledge we would be summoned to meet you there as you stepped onto the apron—the son of the Lord of Kyushu Quadrant needs an appropriate bodyguard, eh? Especially when he's bringing back such a magnificent amygdala."

Shingo's blood froze in his veins as the huge offworlder samurai watched him closely. May all the gods protect me, he thought. I'm truly in the tiger's mouth. Haigo

Gozaemon's a fantastically dangerous man, and it wouldn't take much to incite him. How much does he know? Did Sadamasa buy him? I can't afford to let him know anything about the amygdala, and I can't afford to deny anything to his face. What can I do?

"You do have the amygdala, do you not, Lord?"

Cold fear began to flood Hideki Shingo's belly, but he forced his face to remain impassive. He saw the Amerikan staring in disgust at the headless, fly-blown body twenty paces away. Yes, that's why the messenger was flayed, he realised. To reveal the truth about what precisely has happened to the amygdala. Haigo Gozaemon knows. Oh, by the spinning fires of Jigoku, he knows!

"What did you say?"

"I said, Lord, that I assume you still have the amygdala."

"Unfortunately, there was an *arashi*. It must have sparked off a typhoon. When we tried to land, the winds turned us over, wrecked us, and we were almost killed. We lost a good deal."

"So the messenger told me, Lord." The *hatamochi* looked back penetratingly, his voice honeyed now. "You must have been very worried. Stranded here without any protection and with such a prize in your keeping. But no need to worry now. No one else knows where the amygdala is. No one else knows you are here, Lord. No one else in the universe but I, Haigo Gozaemon."

The *hatamochi*'s laugh was that of an evil *kami*.

"You have been with my father a long time," Shingo said, desperately trying to retain the initiative.

"Many years, Lord. I came to Kyushu with the armies of Baron Harumi. I remember the sack of Hainan and how we broke the Dowager's armies by panicking their fleet. We clothed our ships with high-ranking Kan hostages. And after, we showed the scum how a real ruler tolerates none of their sugary pity.

"Whenever we caught Confucian priests we used to slit open their bellies and then make them eat with us so the rice fell back into their own bowls. It's amazing how much they could consume like that! Then we'd kill them anyway, for being cowards. Oh, yes, we ransacked Hainan very thoroughly. One rich man, I recall, killed all his women-folk rather than let them fall to our soldiers, but when he found that his house had been missed, he ran outside and died at his own hand. Ha!

"Oh, there was excellent bloodletting that day. Our soldiers had a feast. Ah, well, what a man does out of sight of his family is his own business, eh? *Uchi ni icha hina-gai, soto e decha taka-gai,* as the *kotowaza* says. A chick when at home, but a hawk when abroad!"

Haigo Gozaemon's grin stretched the skin, knitting the wound on his cheek. "Baron Harumi was a good lord to work for. Plenty of plunder and plenty of excitement, eh? In one planetary siege we killed forty million and Baron Harumi ordered the nine thousand four hundred and twelve who survived to be blinded when they surrendered. I was told to bring the eyes to his tent in silver dishes, and the Shogun sat up all night personally counting them out with the tip of his *tanto*. He told me that if he found one eye missing I would make it up with one of my own."

"Is that how you lost your eye?" Shingo inquired politely.

Haigo Gozaemon laughed again. "No, Lord! I had made certain there were many, many more than the number he had specified. Ah, but Baron Harumi was a man amongst men! A great leader. You always knew where you were with him. And he, unlike some of today's people, knew which hand to wipe his backside with!"

"Hai," Shingo said quickly, recognising the razor edge in the *hatamochi*'s voice growing keener. He felt sweat spangling his back under his *haori*, and his breath caught drily in his throat. He decided it was imperative that he promise a reward here and now. "You did very well to get here before anyone else. I hoped you would. And you know it's my policy to reward loyalty. When we arrive at Miyakonojo, you must remind me to make you a present. An expensive present."

The *hatamochi*'s eyes remained dead. He said nothing. His hand was pushing down on the tasseled pommel of his *daito* so that the great curved sword thrust out behind him like a monkey tail.

"In fact, here, this is for you. Just a small token for the moment," Shingo said, his voice rising. He steered his fingers inside his *haori* to feel for the aurium and black pearl bauble hanging at his breast. He forced open the link and passed it to Haigo Gozaemon, who examined it discreetly in his palm before bowing and tossing the pendant back.

Shingo failed to catch it and it fell into the dirt. No one moved.

"That's most pretty, Lord. May the *nijuhachi bushu*— the gods of the twenty-eight constellations—crown you with mercies all the days of your life, as they surely will. But I have a better idea, why don't you give me my full reward now?"

Shingo tried to summon the courage to look the mercenary in the eye, but as he was about to speak he caught at the very edge of his vision a dark figure moving out from among the procumbent villagers. He cracked a sickly smile.

"Yasuko-san!"

She approached slowly, almost fawningly, with little

mincing steps, and when she stopped the *hatamochi* acknowledged her with cold politeness.

"Of course, you recognise my wife, Yasuko-san?"

The unexpected interruption had momentarily thrown the big man. "I . . . *Shibaraku desu ne?*" he said sharply, bowing from the neck—It's been a long time since last we met, has it not? "You are well I hope. But your husband and I were discus—"

"I'm very well, thank you, Honorable Bodyguard Leader," she replied imperiously. "I trust you'll be ready to leave the moment my husband orders it."

The *hatamochi* stepped back a pace. "The lord knows he has only to speak and I will obey."

"I'm glad to hear that, Honorable Bodyguard Leader, because my husband tells me you will have extra responsibilities on this escort duty."

"Extra responsibilities? I don't understand, Lady."

"Do you see the man with the two blasters?" she said, pointing him out deliberately.

He glanced slowly to his right. "The *gaijin*?"

"Yes."

"What of him?"

"As I'm sure my husband has said, he's a very powerful man. The owner of a particularly large amygdala. Of course, it's his property until he reaches Miyakonojo, where he intends to present it to my father-in-law, Lord Hideki. I'm sure he will hold you responsible if it does not arrive."

The ambiguity of her phrasing made him pause. Who will hold me responsible? he wondered with irritation. Hideki Ryuji-san? I do not fear him! Or does her "he" mean the foreigner? Who is he? And what's so "powerful" about him?

He regarded the blasters with searching interest.

"The *gaijin* will have to be most careful with his jewel, Lady," the mercenary said, his guile recovering. "I have heard there are many *goto* bands robbing and plundering in these parts."

She stood her ground, her heart hammering. At the back of her mind was the memory of the day fifteen years ago when a hunting jaguar had escaped its handlers at Court. She had been only seven years old when the snarling cat had fled from the firebrands into the women's quarters of the residency and circled about her. Then, to run would have been fatal. Now, she knew, she must hold to her inner strength and above all show no fear.

"What very special *goto* they would have to be," she said softly, "to overwhelm fifty handpicked men of the daimyo's bodyguard. My father-in-law pays you well to maintain adequate protection for his family. He has faith that you are a competent soldier."

You'll have to be totally convincing, she thought, frantic under her apparent calm. Your life and Shingo-san's life and the life of the Amerikan and much more than that all depend on what you say next. If only I knew for certain what the messenger said and what Shingo-san might have let slip. What can I possibly say to placate Haigo Gozaemon's greed and undermine his strength in arms?

"I'll say this, Honorable Bodyguard Leader, I pity the stupid *goto* who tries to rob the *gaijin*. For he has sworn to blow the brains out of anyone who touches his property."

The *hatamochi* stirred. "One man could not resist an armed *goto* band for very long. What *gaijin* knows the first thing about real swordsmanship?"

"I assure you this man is completely fearless. His blasters are amazingly powerful. They can stun a man at two hundred paces and cut him down at thirty, before any swordsman can get near him. I, personally, have seen him use his blasters in anger. His tactic appears to be to burn the brains out of the leader first of all. He says that followers always run about like headless chickens once their leader is dead.''

The *hatamochi*'s eyes narrowed. ''He is not the only one with blasters, Lady. Many *goto* carry the *teppo*. What use are his hand weapons against a *teppo* bolt?''

''Surely outlaws cannot have obtained such weapons on Osumi,'' she said, knowing well the implication of his words and knowing he understood her equally. ''All this continent is technology controlled. Any subject at all, outlaw or not, who carried a *teppo* rifle would be breaking the Emperor's law.''

''Outlaws are outlaws, no? Rest assured the *goto* hereabouts are well armed.''

''I agree there's nothing can protect a man against a treacherous and disgraceful ambush, Honorable Bodyguard Leader, but without surprise you must know that he would always have the advantage. Please correct me if I'm wrong, but his blasters are Wessons. Doesn't that mean they strike first time without an isolator ring such as the *teppo* requires? Of course, I can only speak from a woman's point of view, but even I can see he must be able to fire both his blasters before a *teppo* can even be leveled.''

Yasuko's palms were damp and she rubbed them together unobtrusively, knowing the *hatamochi* was backed into a corner, and therefore at his most dangerous. He's weakening, she thought. Strange how even the most violent of men needs an ember of rage to trigger his killing instinct. Dampen his ember with doubt and perhaps his fire will not catch.

She looked back at him ingenuously. ''Am I correct, or perhaps I have made some mistake?''

Haigo Gozaemon's doubts painted his face. He said gruffly, "That depends on circumstances and the man, Lady."

"I'm sure it must do, but Mister Straker is the finest shootist the Amerikan MeTraCor possesses. You know who his father is?"

"Who?" the *hatamochi* asked, clearly not liking the Amerikan's presence now.

"The famous Satoraka-san!"

"I'm sorry, Lady, but I've never heard of him."

"You must have. Oh, he's the Amerikan who destroyed six of Kim Gwon Chung's pirate craft in the Ulsan system five years ago. Don't you remember hearing about that?"

"Perhaps I did hear something. . . ."

"You know, that's why his son is charged with bringing the Amerikan MeTraCor's gift to the daimyo. It is he who agreed to this secret rendezvous with my father-in-law. It was a precaution against an early move by the Kan that might prevent a landing at the Kanoya apron. And how right he was to take it, don't you think so?"

Haigo Gozaemon straightened suddenly, sniffing a lie. "I understood you were wrecked here, Lady. The messenger said you made a hard planetfall and were almost killed."

Yasuko took his arm and began to lead him towards the veranda outside their hut, talking as she did so. The monstrous tailplane that reared up in the chestnut grove was clearly visible, and she knew the horsemen must have seen it from the western causeway as they approached, despite the hills.

"Ah, yes, a slight exaggeration, Honorable Bodyguard Leader. You know what these peasants are. They don't understand anything. There was a slight wreck. In fact, we came down in a severe rainstorm, the ship's over there.'' She waved vaguely in the direction of the globe-ship. "Here we are. You must be very tired after so long a ride in all your heavy gear. Please take off your shoes and sit down. Half an hour won't make any difference. It's best to recover your strength, isn't it?"

"So. But you were stranded in a small shuttle.'' He looked up at the huge ruined tail, and when he turned the jangling of his panoply made her fear surge again. She knew that the scope of her lie would have to increase still further.

"That's quite correct. It was a difficult passage through such high winds.''

He was thoroughly perplexed now. "So what is that ship?"

"Just an old wreck. You can see it's been here for years. Its beacon is the one on which we were erroneously guided in. The shuttle crew was skeptical our craft could be brought down without smashing the landing array; indeed, one of the men was lost, which is why the shuttle remains here.''

Haigo Gozaemon straightened. "The shuttle is still here?"

"Of course. Kan ships are in orbit. The Amerikans have decided not to go to the Kanoya apron, or back to their own ship, until the political situation becomes clearer. They regret the infringement of Osumi's technology laws, and in deference to them have chosen to close down here under radio black. They have, of course, already relayed news of our planetfall to Kanoya City.''

"It must have been most frightening for you, Lady,'' the big man said slowly, visibly crestfallen now.

"Oh, no. We were apprehensive, of course, and I wondered at one point if we would be killed, but as you can see we were not. Perhaps later I could show you the shuttle? Your men could help Mister Straker bring his equipment up if he hasn't already done so. Now, please sit down, won't you, and have some tea?''

"Just as you wish, Lady," he said, bowing his head slowly. "As I said, I'm your husband's to command."

"I'm sure my husband would like you to quench your thirst before anything else."

"Yes, yes, of course," Shingo said. "*Cha*. Bring tea here."

Yasuko moved away. The *hatamochi* shed his weapons in order to sit down. He loosened the *mogami-do* from his torso and took off his shoulder protectors and throat guard. He accepted a dipper of water and wiped his mouth, then stretched himself stiffly. Yasuko tried to see in his movements if he had made up his mind, if the intended treachery was abandoned.

"That's good. Yes. It was a hard ride. Thirsty work, Lord."

Shingo sat down also. "So," he said. "Do you really think there's a possibility of an ambush on the road to Miyakonojo?"

"As I've said, *goto* may still choose to attack us, Lord. As for anyone else, only your brother Sadamasa-san has the motive and the resources to mount an attack anywhere along the western causeway, but he's hawking with the governor of Kokubu somewhere out beyond Hanaki. He's at least four hundred *ri* from here."

"Excellent . . ."

Yasuko watched them talk from a respectful distance, the relief flooding through her. By all the devils of *naraku*, that was close, she thought, but this relief is false because it's premature. Now that Haigo Gozaemon seems to be appeased, Shingo-san's confidence is burgeoning, but I don't think the monster has truly decided yet.

What happens if one of his subordinates finds the shuttle, or if he chooses to cross-check the story with a villager? We don't have much time. If Shingo-san makes just one stupid mistake . . . And there's still the *gaijin* to consider. I don't know how long the deception can be made to last. We'll have to do something else.

15

As the *hatamochi* reached for another dipper of water, Yasuko took her chance and retired, moving towards Hayden Straker. He had walked away from the body of the dead villager, filled with disgust and anger, and he sat alone now on the steps of his hut. He did not look up as Yasuko approached him, and he rudely refused her offer of water.

"You are saddened by what the Bodyguard Leader has done to the villager," she said in a low voice.

Hayden Straker could not find it in him to answer her.

"Let me ask you, Mister Straker, what do you think are the chances of taking revenge on the Bodyguard Leader—with his own sword—while he sits distracted by my husband's talk?"

"Whaat?"

"Oh, please try not to react. I repeat, do you think there's a realistic chance of killing the Bodyguard Leader?"

Hayden Straker's mind reeled.

"What?" he said again.

She persevered. "That man is *hatamochi*. Also, a murderer and a thief. He knows about the amygdala. He is the only one who knows we are here, and I truly believe that, unless he is killed before he finishes his *cha*, he will murder us all."

Her words pierced him. The smell of the cooking fire was suddenly poignant in his nostrils. "You want me to kill him?"

"Yes, please. If that is possible. Before he kills us."

"Lady, you're insane. There are half a hundred like him watering their horses. Do you think I'm snap crazee?"

"I don't believe the others will matter once the *hatamochi* is dead." She struggled to still him. "We would all be dead now, were it not for the lies I told him about you."

"About me?" Hayden Straker recoiled. "What lies?"

"Please keep your voice down. I only said that you were an expert shootist who would blow his last eye out if he does not behave himself."

"Sweet Jesus! You said that? To that . . . that Cyclops?"

"His name is Haigo Gozaemon, and I had to say that. I know you are a brave and capable man." Her eyes traveled momentarily down the length of his chest and returned. "And I think you are a man of honor."

His voice fell to a growl. "Lady, you're mistaken. I'm no expert with a handblaster. These Wessons are not even charged. A professional swordsman would cut me to pieces if I even—"

"The *hatamochi* believes you are an expert, too. He believes the blasters are charged. Surely that's all that matters."

"And when he discovers I'm not, and my blasters are not? What then?"

"Within perhaps two minutes of that discovery, either he shall be dead or we shall be dead. That's why we must strike first."

Hayden Straker stared about him despairingly, detesting the calmness of her voice. "What about your husband? Uh—can't he kill him? He's got a sword—and he knows how to use it."

"A sword, yes, and some skill. But unfortunately my husband has no real courage in him."

"Oh, no. No. I refuse to hear this." His face hardened with ugly thoughts. "You're just trying to provoke me. It's an excuse so that I can be murdered within the bounds of your lunatic laws. There'll be fifty witnesses to say I deserved to die, so that the amygdala can be taken by your husband. Why should I trust you?"

"Excuse me, but that cannot be correct. We have no idea where you have hidden the amygdala."

"Uh-uh. I don't care. I don't trust you. The first sign of trouble and I'm out of here!"

Her eyes flashed angrily. "I said, I thought you were an honorable man. I was wrong. You are not. You are what your father called you. A coward. A boy. If you will not trust me, then I must show you proof!"

She bowed curtly, turned on her heel, and walked away from him, and he watched her go. He saw her cross the open ground slowly, taking small, deliberate steps until she was close to the hut where her husband and Haigo Gozaemon still talked. She moved round casually until she was out of the *hatamochi*'s field of vision and began modestly to readjust the silk obi that secured her kimono.

Hayden Straker saw the *hatamochi* turn, but he looked quickly away again out of decency. She was unwinding the obi as if to retie it more securely, but as Haigo Gozaemon turned his back on her, Hayden Straker saw the sash come off and her hands working swiftly to twist its length into a cord.

Hayden Straker watched paralysed in the knowledge of what was about to happen. She can't be, he thought. She can't be! It's madness! But he had asked for proof of her words and she had promised it. Soundlessly he willed her to stop before it was too late, but her course was set. In one motion, she looped the twined sash over Haigo Gozaemon's head, braced her toes between his shoulder blades, crossed her hands, and dragged the fabric tight against his neck with all her strength.

Immediately, Hayden Straker was on his feet and running. He saw the *hatamochi*'s powerful arms go up, clawing the air impotently. Then the bodyguard overbalanced and crashed backwards onto his back. The force of his struggles threw Yasuko clear, but she held tight to the sash, which remained hooked under his chin.

His eyes bulged and his teeth champed in a furious grin. As he tore at the strangling cord his face purpled, the vein in his forehead standing proud as the blood pressure in his head threatened to burst it. Yasuko gasped. One huge fist lashed out at her, sending the horned helmet flying from the veranda, and a flailing foot demolished the flimsy wooden board wall beside him. Then the *hatamochi*'s hand made contact with the scabbard of his *daito,* and he fought to unsheathe it.

Hayden Straker saw the terrible danger the woman had put herself in. She was like a cat attacking a Kebek wolverine. He saw Shingo rooted, staring at the *hatamochi*'s frenzied kicks, then one connected and he stumbled back, almost colliding with Hayden Straker. In another second the *hatamochi* would have the razor-edged blade out and Yasuko's legs would be carved to the bone. Her gasps were filled with terror, but still she refused to let go of the sash.

"Get him! Get him!" he shouted, but still Shingo did not move.

Hayden Straker's only thought was the sword in Shingo's sash. He made a grab for the silver and fish-skin hilt, and it slid free, but only an inch before Shingo's instinctive fury made him react to the ultimate insult.

He felt the bone-jarring shock of Shingo's blow to his shoulder, and the move sent the bright steel of the sword slicing up into his hand, a half inch deep through the soft side of his palm.

There was no pain and no blood, just the shock feel of parted flesh, and he almost dropped the sword, but caught it again and stepped forward into a slamming punch that Shingo was unprepared for. It connected with the point of his nose, flooring him.

Immediately, he turned to see the curved tip of Haigo Gozaemon's blade stabbing like a scorpion's sting into the dirt beside Yasuko-san.

The *hatamochi*'s sword was ripped free and flashed back again, making Hayden Straker sidestep. He could do nothing to prevent a second jab. This time it plunged into the ground between her knees, pinning her kimono. He knew he had to make his next stroke count, but he was unbalanced and he brought the sword down on the *hatamochi*'s chest, ringing the blade uselessly off the heavily laced lacquer breastplate. The Bodyguard Leader twisted now and raised his sword arm, and Hayden Straker made a desperate second swing, wild and wide with all his strength, that sent the *hatamochi*'s *daito* spinning away.

Horribly, he saw that Haigo Gozaemon's fist still gripped the hilt. The empty wrist spewed blood in pulsing gouts as it waved, spattering everything.

"Kill him! Kill him!"

"What?"

"Finish him!" Yasuko's plea was desperate. "Kill him, or his men will not follow you!"

Aghast at the duty, Hayden Straker placed the tip of his sword against the *hatamochi*'s exposed neck and shut his eyes. The sword slipped again and again as the giant threshed and wallowed in his own blood. Five times he had to reposition it before he could press it down, but when he did he pushed it deep, until he could make it go no farther. Blood lashed him and the man's body went rigid as if in a fit, then slumped suddenly. He felt the horror and pain of killing and heard the approving comments of the bodyguards who had surrounded them but who had made no move to save their leader.

He stared at them, the sword hilt still clenched in his fist, its point still embedded in the throat of Haigo Gozae-mon, and they stared back as if they had witnessed the killing of a man-eating tiger. He saw in their faces respect, excitement, a sly delight—but mostly respect. Inside him-self there was revulsion for the fact of the killing, regret for the necessity of it, and also shame that he had accomplished it. There was an equal shame, too, that dwarfing all these feelings was a vast and exultant sense of triumph.

He shouted. "*Banzai!*" Turning and swinging both hands above his head. "Long live the Hideki clan! Death to their enemies!"

And the guard raised their hands too.

"*Banzai!*"

Then they knelt to him and he saw what he had become, and he knew as the strength and life soaked away from Haigo Gozaemon that something had died within him, but that also something terrible had come alive.

16

The air in the women's bunker was as hot as an oven, and Arkali was exhausted beyond the point of sleep. She felt a trickle of sweat run down between her breasts and tried again to be grateful for the mercies of the moment. Soon the dread would start, but not yet. Not just yet. At least now the Council Member's tragic young wife had screamed herself to sleep, and the bunker was almost quiet. Even the flashes of Chinese beam weapons that had shredded everyone's nerves had abated a little so that most of the dozen women and score of children tried to snatch a spell of sleep before night fell outside the dome and the batteries opened up the terror once more.

Suddenly a shaft of light slanted down on her, low and acute, a beam trapped for a moment between the ramparts of the city and the frame of the bunker periscope. It picked out in scintillating motes airborne dust that had been shaken out of the crete by the bombardment, and the dread was pushed back.

The dust was beautiful, hanging in the air like purest gold. Yes, gold, she mused, gold in the air and gold in the bare white walls. Hang on to that thought and don't think of the dread that's building. See the gold illuminating the small, self-absorbed face of the baby in your arms, and think of this child's greater misfortune.

She cradled the infant awkwardly in the crook of her

arm, feeling close to tears. At first she thought it must be wrong to accept a synth servant's chore. It was inappropriate to be asked to sleep here, right among the others. But after the soldiers had gone away she had detected the hostility of some of the women building up, and she knew that her social position counted for nothing now.

"You'll come in with us, won't you?" the bigger of the two Solomon women had said.

"I . . ."

"Good. We'll appreciate that," her sister had said, and the matter had been settled.

But even these tough women had flinched when some of the refracting beams had scythed across in the street above last night.

"They got meson mines, them Chineeses," the oldest Solomon boy had said. "And my pah says their beams got the kayvees to come right down through even a self-seal dome like ours and all, and kill us here right where we lie."

"Zip your mouth, Jossie!" Loris Solomon's shoe had slammed into the boy's ear, but after that sleep had been impossible for Arkali. All night, beam after beam had momentarily found a mine pinhole and scattered down into Kanoya City to put melt wounds on the crete and pop out the plex cladding of the trade towers, and destroy the morale of the defenders.

Without her maid, Suzi, she had lain there in the pit under the empty city, bunched against the frame of a strap hammock, utterly terrified, knowing that the next discharge could kill her, or worse, perhaps burn her badly.

As the night wore on, the firing had fallen into a steady aurora of light, lethal and terrible: first the violet batteries on the northwest emptying their tubes; then the pink Crooke's beams from beyond the lagoon with their exploding scintillas that tested the shield fields; then heavy ship rays from the zenith, smothering the dome with crimson and making the foundations of the walls vibrate. Round and round us, she thought, on and on and on, night and day, without pause, robbing me of sleep, robbing me of the power to think until I'm driven almost insane by the terror of it. And then at night being locked in here with those who cannot endure, those like Floren Quint who go screaming mad. It takes a certain kind of anger or faith or some trick of the mind to believe that the death falling from the heavens can't touch you, or that if it does it won't matter, but I found that faith in psi.

Oh, Hayden, my *cher*. Now I know you're alive. I know you are. And I know I'm meant to marry you one day, and so I know the beams can't harm me because if I died what sense or reason would there be to psi, or to anything?

Concussions shook the building above as Arkali steered another spoonful of sodden Dover rusk into the baby's tiny budlike mouth, carefully wiping the pap from its chin. He exuded a nauseating sour-milk smell. She saw the pale-blue eyes widen as he noticed the spoon, the red ridges of his gums, the tiny hands and fingers that tried to grip her giant finger. He was hot and his face reddened like a beetroot and he bubbled with mucus, and she wondered what to do.

He was poor Elta Mundi's son, not weaned yet orphaned already. A tragic child. She was torn between pity and squeamishness, and suddenly she hated the responsibility of feeding the child. Maidless, she did what she could— Suzi would have fritzed out at the idea of feeding a new-born baby Dover-made goo. How this little one and the other children had screamed and screamed last night. And when the noise and terror of the bombardment had reached its height, Betrix Reiner's agony had done likewise. She had given birth to a girl, deformed and stillborn and shocking to the Korean girl who had acted as midwife.

Superstition had ravaged the *hinin* and the Koreans who still sheltered in the city like a firestorm: Did you hear about the wife of the young Amerikan lord? The new Council Member? The man MeTraCor was going to make Controller one day? Don't you know that his wife just gave birth to a two-headed pig demon? They say it had to be killed with an iron hook, but not before it spoke a curse!

Arkali shivered. Her maid had got herself lost. She probably ran away. All but one or two of the most loyal private servants had got the hell out before the shield was turned on, deserting their masters and mistresses. This data bunker, and other places like it, were the only places they could sleep safe from the leakage from the bombardment. It was a morass of tumbled calofoils and belongings and human forms. Women and babes in arms only down here, that was the rule Ellis Straker had imposed. Separate quarters for men and women. And when not sleeping, everyone to serve by turns however they could, sometimes unprotected—raw psi and chance your neck.

She wiped back a thread of hair and resettled the infant, scraping the remaining Dover morsels from the gray plexine bowl. She was desperately tired and suffocating in the sour air. It's exhaustion, she told herself. With my eyes open I can hardly remember Hayden's face; with them closed I can see nothing but his face. Oh, my *cher*, where are you now? Was it true what that terrible Bowen person told me yesterday? Why aren't you here to protect me? Psi steer me away from this horrible place. I hate Osumi and everyone on it! Soon they'll lock us in and the phobia'll start all over again. How long can this go on? How long can Ellis Straker ask us to cower in this hell? Until the Navy comes? When that might be weeks? Or months?

"Ah, nothing can protect you now, 'cept sweet psi!" Straker had shouted that at the assembled merchants and MeTraCor employees as the bombardment had reached its crescendo. "Make your peace with psi and together we'll give the Kan a lesson in how to hold hard on to what's ours!"

The man was a gung-ho lunatic. An animal! Couldn't they have just talked it out with the Chinese? Like civilised human beings.

She didn't care about Kanoya City anymore. Was it really a day and a night ago that her father had taken off his vest and rolled up his sleeves like a common laborer? How the emergency had turned Ellis Straker into a gloating beast of a man, striding here and there with a great black rod in his hand and that pocky-faced brute, Bowen, at his tail, and the Solomon brothers, one at each shoulder, all of them stiff-necked as samurai and shouting orders at everyone. Sweet psi, she thought, did I really consent to marry into his family? I must have been mad. How could a heartless devil like Ellis Straker have sired a son like Hayden? How could he?

A still, dead heat lay on top of her and she felt herself drifting. Already the memory of Hayden was distorting like the mercury blue that shimmered the dome with deadly patterns. Was he dead? No. She knew that much. He couldn't be or she wouldn't feel this certainty. Her heart would know—wouldn't it?

And there had been Bowen . . .

She began to meditate. Yes, Hayden, I know you're alive. Yesterday Bowen came to me with a wound in his hand and I seared it for him, and I pumped him on what'd happened. At first he told me to go speak to Straker, but I persuaded him. When he saw my anxiety he told me what I think was the truth, Hayden.

My *cher*, he thinks you must've gotten safely down.

"I'll say it weren't impossible." Those were his words. And if it was possible, I know you soft-landed. If I survive this night I swear to psi I'll go to your father and demand he tells me where psi must have taken you. Oh, soon this nightmare will be over and we'll be together again. I know we will.

The baby vomited abruptly over her hand and filthied her garb, and she looked up helplessly to the woman who had given the Mundi infant temporarily into her care. A huge woman, wife of one of the Filipino merchants, who fed her own baby from massive breasts. The two-year-old sucked on the big dark nipple lustily, eyes half-lidded, as the elder child cuddled her mother's side. The woman smiled impassively, her bovine contentment unshaken even here.

Arkali looked away, despairing that marriage must inevitably one day make a cow of her also. Hayden's seed will do that to me. After the pain of sex my body will be transformed into a bestial thing with bloated belly and udders, and I'll be a cow surrounded by rude infants, squealing and mewling and demanding and filthying and . . .

Another shuddering concussion woke her and jangled her nerves, then she realised it was the ion bolts being cycled home on the vault iris. Father, you promised you'd come to visit me here before six UT, she thought. You haven't come to me all afternoon, and now the guard have us locked in tight, ready for the hour when the orbiting ships reach conjunction. Oh, dear psi in heaven, I pray the Chinese troops don't breach the integrity of the city tonight—

"Zip yor mouth, you whining little bastard! One more word and I'll hang one on your ear, and that's me telling you!"

The tousled brood of Solomon children clung to their

mothers and aunts in the farthest corner of the bunker as
the eldest boy, ten years old, still brass-faced his mother
defiantly, fists clenched. Because his father and uncle were
absent he had chanced himself constantly, needling and
needling to be let out to hold a blaster, until the raucous
outburst came.

Arkali bit her lip, wishing Faya or Loris would give the
unpleasant little scumball his way. They were hard-bitten
women. Sisters. Not at all classy, though they tried ludi-
crously to affect a kind of refinement in their dress and
their manners because their husbands had made a little
trade money.

No, they were obviously bathhouse *yuna*, prostitutes
who swilled around ports everywhere like human scum.
These two had had the good fortune, if that was what it
was, to marry Art and Wil Solomon. And the match was
appropriate. Two harpies hard as rock salt for two tough
brothers who had prowled the Zone in a heavily armed
grabber for a decade, before turning trader and prospering
beyond the dreams of avarice.

"Most glad t'meet you, Arkalee," Loris Solomon had
said on their first meeting some weeks ago. That had been
at the Hawken mansion when she had danced with Hayden
and she had been presented as the new-risen star of Kanoya
City society. How many weeks ago? A lifetime. An age.
Loris Solomon grinned at the baby vomit, her crooked
teeth and shag of blond hair making her leonine in the
golden beams relayed by the periscope holo that filled the
wall with the street scene above.

"Fortunes of war, heh?" she said to no one in particular,
then the light extinguished, pinched out by the Kan admiral, and the moment was gone in the dulling red of a fast-
cooling dome.

The dread crowded her. Howling laughter came from

a distance. Undefined, feral shouting, men roaring and braying and the sounds of destruction, like Babylon in the days of Isaiah. Brawling and looting and sin. The baby convulsed and ruckled another milky mess onto her dress.

"You've t'wind 'em when you've fed 'em. Don't you know that much, Arkalee?"

"Won't you have him now?" she said, dabbing at the front of her pale-blue garb.

"Now didn't I tell you t'wear nothing but your under-liner?"

The brood smirked and shrieked around her.

"Just an underliner?"

The thought appalled her.

"Smatter, you not too hot?"

She became aware of the furnace heat. Close and hot and tropical. The purple dome, lit once more by Chinese beams seen through the bunker's camera, was vast and crazed with lightning. Here, in their shelter, dim lights were glowing, casting monster shapes on the white crete walls and pillars. A stylised eagle hung on the wall above the Filipino woman, paradoxical as an Izlamic crucifix. All around was a ruin of raw silk bales and half a dozen massive lead-lined plex chests like giants' coffins, each of 90 pounds tare weight, each made to carry 360 pounds of grade-one *o-cha* real green tea, tightly packed, stamped down by the feet of Yamato peasants. Dried leaves! The stuff that was one source of the Amerikan presence in this terrible, alien world. One of the real commodities grown in the mountains of Yamato, the demand of consumers to indulge themselves on variety, that's what all the fighting was about. . . .

Oh, Jeezus, this is the worst. Because we're women we're locked up in an airless cellar in case Chinese troops should get into the city. The safest place in the siege, so they told us.

Self-consciously she loosened the vomit-stained strings of her garb, unlaced it, and began dabbing at the stain.

"You'll have t'take it off, Arkalee," Faya said, laughing. "Don't be shy, now, you've nothing we ain't seen before!"

The hysterical laughter of drunken men came from the street above. It made her feel half naked. Last night she had taken off the three-quarter jacket with the mail epaulettes, but then the street-scene camera had attracted a bunch of roaming Kalifornian *ranbos*. They had grimaced into the lens and kicked at it. It had seemed as if the men could see right into the quarters as they made disgusting signs out of the holo. It could not be curtained off.

The yelling came again, much closer now. Braying and yawping. Foul drunken men with burred voices. Rough men, Macau-Kalifornian squaddies. A bad lot of men, without the acquisitive wit of the merchants or the starchy discipline of MeTraCor servants. Her father had said they were deserters, MeTraCor contract guards: Elayese, with angular faces and long moustaches, lazy, and fractious because they had run from their own officers once before and knew all the tricks. They were inventive when it came to mischief, cruel to the native prostitutes, they drank and fought or pitted fighting dogs against each other in the native town, for wagers and the joy of seeing a death struggle, and now they had loaded blasters in their hands, supposedly patrolling the service ducts for Kan breaches.

One of them aimed up on a MeTraCor wall box and deliberately fried it.

She panted in the breathless heat. Those men were moving overhead now like a pack. Laughing crazily, raw as hyenas. Footfalls on the plex six feet above. Betrix Reiner's face was haggard in sleep. The Solomons drew their children towards them. Arkali watched breaking glass, a bottle hurled at the camera so the scene occupying the wall shivered. The sounds were of the furniture of the office above being kicked over, and then the Filipino woman got up and crept past the pillars. She was holding a Malay parang, raised like a machete. It was sharp and heavy and could cut to the bone.

Loris Solomon hissed at her children. "Keep still!"

"But the door's locked," Arkali said. "They can't get in without—"

"Quiet!"

The hush was broken by the sounds of more feet, and shouts in the echoing air vents, incoherent voices mouthing obscenities in dog-Kalifornian, men thieving, looking for more whiskey. A flurry of kicks and blows rained on the plex iris. The blows became hacking, as with a bayonet on the ion lock, and the Filipino woman stood rooted, not making a sound for silence's sake and also to listen, but mainly out of fear. The vault iris was the only way in or out.

An adolescent girl began to sob as the fear transmitted itself from the women. The Solomon youth's face was a white oval now, his boy's hubris gone totally.

The crying gave them away.

"Eh, gimee gimee! You in there laydeez? You in there? Hey, c'mon."

"Quiet! Hush up!" Faya hissed at everyone.

"No!" Arkali shouted, getting to her feet also. "We ought to call for help. Call for an officer! We—"

Faya caught her shoulders and slapped her, then hugged her close to speak close in her ear. "No one'll hear us! Don't you see? They know it's the end. The Chinese're

coming, and the scum's got themselves rotten on five-star
stingo. The sound of women crying'll only serve to blister
them up!''

"But we must get help!''

"I tell you, I know all about it! They've cut the comms.''

"Eh, senyoraz!! You wanna jig-a-jig, eh?''

The man's voice was behind her, raucous and loud and
clear. It filled the room with cackling laughter. A huge
face loomed from the wall, hideously lit by the bombardment and distorted by being thrust too close to the camera.
Behind him another soldier, a bottle in his hand, knelt on
the ground to unhitch his dark-stained pants. They had got
tired of patrolling the sewers.

Terror and revulsion gripped her.

A bottle thrown by the first soldier shattered against the
camera, showering the scene with glass and fluid. Arkali
turned away, shielding herself, wanting to scream, to fill
the silence with her own voice, but she could not. The
younger children began to cry after the sudden violence;
they would not be soothed now. One of the women began
to whimper, and Betrix Reiner cried out.

"For Jeezus's sake will you quieten them!'' Loris Solomon hissed again.

Arkali clutched a wailing four-year-old to her and held
her tight. When she looked again at the holo the soldiers
were gone. The incessant roar of beam weapons filled the
bunker, flashes throwing the external world into sudden
silhouette. The ornate railings of an atrium shell fifty yards
away caught a stray beam pinholing in from the west.
Suddenly, as she watched, the wall of the building opposite
collapsed into ruin on top of a rack of parked zed-cars,
pushing over a slender tree into the street. She heard men
shouting in the distance. The luminance of their own weapons firing back across the blackness of the lagoon were an

intense poison green. What if the Chinese assaulted the foundations under the walls while these despicable soldiers who disgraced MeTraCor's red leatherine were all drunk? The Solomon lad climbed up to the air duct. She saw him struggle his head and shoulders into the hole, his shoes skidding on the wall below. Then a terrific bang on the other side of the bunker iris turned her head and she saw the Filipino woman flinch away.

The heavy dewlap of flesh that swung under the woman's raised arm shivered. She was praying aloud now, and Arkali saw the fear on her face. The bang had been a meson grenade and the plates of the denatured iris were being kicked in, the heavy cylinders tearing out from the now-cheesed brackets. Arkali ran forward to help. A tool-holder had appeared miraculously in her hand, but Loris Solomon seized it from her and Faya picked her up and threw her bodily behind the nearest tea chest.

"Get down there!"

"But I—"

"By psi, you'll keep your head down! You'll only incite them once they catch sight of that face! Some men like to really make a rich bitch like you beg."

She sank down behind the tea chest, her heart racing. Another flurry of kicks and the door began to disintegrate. She saw the Filipino woman jump forward, heard the sound of her struggle, of the parang ringing onto the crete floor. From where she crouched Arkali could see nothing. Then a big red-jacketed soldier pushed the woman back into the bunker, his hand around her throat, jolting her with tremendous force. He shoved her back against the wall like a rag doll and advanced powerfully into the sleeping space, a mad light in his eyes.

Others followed behind, ratlike. Three at first, then another and another. They looked around, smeared in filth and sweat, crouching with suspicion, then they began to straighten confidently as they saw there was no guard. Children's cries rose up as the big man unslotted the six-inch-long slitter from his weapon and discarded the mechanism.

"You wanna jig-a-jig?" he said, fixing Loris Solomon with an evil grin.

"Get out of here, you Elay mongrel!" she shouted defiantly, raising the toolholder.

He poked the slitter halfheartedly at her, turning to laugh and to invite his comrades to laugh also. Loris Solomon slashed the toolholder at his eyes and he dodged his head back, laughing louder now, but the second swipe was too fast for him and she caught his cheek with the cup.

He grimaced with pain and grabbed her wrist and pulled her to the floor, slitting her shift so that her breasts and belly spilled into view. Faya jumped out at him, screaming now. Arkali got to her feet, then the other men came forward and wrestled her away.

One of the men threw Faya to the ground with immense strength, concussing her, then Loris flew at him, madly tearing at his eyes and flailing her arms. The big man folded his slitter and took the toolholder from her as if she were a child. He said something to still them. He was breathing hard now. Blood was smeared on his face from the cut. He wiped at it, ordered the two youngest men to guard the door, then Arkali saw him grab Loris by the hair and hook the slitter round her throat. He shook her back and forth until she spun away, her hand going up to the raw wound that had opened up on her neck. Then she collapsed, gasping for air.

Arkali felt herself dragged out, she saw herself pummeling him with her fists, but he was huge and hard as plex and he grabbed her and subdued her with ease. Struggle seemed futile. One drag of his hand tore away the front of her garb. Then he gripped her painfully and he drank in her nakedness through blazing eyes and he told her in Satan's voice, "Now, I'm gonna cut out your throat. But first you get down on your knees and beg me to fuck you."

17

"Psi damn the Kan, and all the zitzy sonsawhores who think they're going to take this base off of us, and Hu Tsung and Yu Hsien in particular!"

Ellis Straker emerged growling from the smoke as it cleared from the ramp. He wiped the crete dust from his jacket and fixed an eye on the monitor that showed the Chinese batteries. A wisp of smoke curled up and away in the hot, optically boiling air amid a dark palm grove half a mile from the walls. A stray ray from one of the bustovers had lanced down to demolish the steps behind him and scatter his entourage.

A face appeared grinning in the blackness.

"Hope that squatting beam didn't heat you, Captain Straker!"

It was the young MeTraCor staffer he had put in charge of the beam weapons of the South Side reaching down to offer a hand. He sweated now in a dusty-red leatherine jacket borrowed from the quartermaster's store. He was crete dust smudged, but grinning and unfritzed by the near miss.

Ellis glowered up at him, but allowed himself to be helped onto the weapons platform.

"Devils break my legs if I'm heated by a Kan beam. And it's Mister Straker, if you please. Captains are what I used to be, and them who work for me now." He relit his cheroot from the crown of an argentium tube.

The other said, pleasantly, "A mite cooler now the sun's down, eh, sir?"

"Yep."

The spillthrough from the dome had been blistering, the Chinese fleet standing at conjunction overhead, with beams converging, their weapons firing in a rhythm now. Yeah, he thought, they're pacing themselves. Worried about running out of tubes, I'll bet, now they know they're in for a long haul.

He looked about him as the others emerged, coughing and dusting themselves from the accessway, and he drew in a mouthful of tobako smoke, pleased with the young staffer's psi-sure way and the ingeniousness with which he had lashed up his weapons with optimising software to keep them aimed and firing in the best sequence to keep the Kan siege at a respectful distance. It was true that the only real export MeTraCor made to Yamato was raw courage, and that would serve as currency anywhere.

"You did good here, man."

"Thank you, sir."

Absently Ellis head-counted his retinue: one Kalifornian sergeant; two Iowa corporals; the Teksas drunkard, Eckman, peppery and aged, swearing his mouth off; two of his own *gishi* who had not been on the *Chance* because of sickness, now recovered, good men; Nyuyoku-san, his steward, there for the sake of propriety since Red Bowen split his hand open on the task of barricading. Next was Jos Hawken and Cornelius Morgan and the two Solomons, the biggest independent traders, operators of nexus ships and dealers in silk and tea and whatever real stuff they could corner—rough bullets, the Solomons, but the stanchions that supported his bid to keep control here. Yes, tough men when their livelihoods were under threat and handy with beam or blade.

The three Council Members came up now, sickly JJ. Foster in the capacity of Controller's representative, stout, judicial Zeekyel Meredith, and last the cold-faced Derion Reiner, silent since his wife's ordeal, shocked raw by his inability to comfort her. So, he thought, twelve. But one of them's a dead man. The last bustover might have been a shade more psiful and taken out Foster's decaying ass. Give us all a break. She's here to spy on me and sell me out to Aziza Pope—if she lives that long. I wonder what filthy hash Dzernic and Pope are cooking up? They're hiding in some hole, I'll bet—psi pay their cowardice.

Young Reiner's okeh. Not like his father. Kurt Reiner was a sonofabitch and doubtless still is. I'll never forgive him for having mistreated Reba all those years. I doubt he'll ever forgive me for stealing her from him. But all's fair in love and war. Isn't that what they say?

Another bustover, the ten thousandth since the bombardment began, slashed across the city behind them. It threw up a searing light and made a roll of thunder. Then another got through, and another, rays dropping onto block and skid for half a second before the dome sealed. The city was scarred, the blocks disfigured, even MeTraCor Center holed. The excruciating terror of bustover beams stabbing down for a full twenty-four hours had turned those who could not trust to their own psi into twitching wrecks.

Last night had been sleepless for everyone. The Kan had shaped their bombardment to crack morale, and who but the psi-strong could sleep when each breath might be his last? He had seen men squatting over manholes with their ion guns, glancing nervously skyward as they waited for the patrols to make contact. In their quarters, and in the medivacs, tumbled bodies lay beset by fears. The remaining natives of the wooden city, too late to evacuate, lay under rigged flexiplex awnings, not trusting the buildings.

Wonderful how the locals surrendered to their idea of karma, knowing that what must be must be, the rest to their various notions of psi, believing that psi had locked their destiny long ago and that the suffering was neither good nor bad but just their appointed lot. They had huddled, these people, in family groups, mother, father, grandmother, uncle, cousin, and many, many children, wrapped in Yamato coveralls and cals and thermofoils, possessions bundled under their heads, arms and legs all tumbled together. There had been tension in their hunched forms and muttering, and then after midnight they had disappeared like magic. Two thousand of them had melted away, getting out of the city following secret smugglers' runs into the empty native town. A catastrophic loss of confidence had suddenly hit them, and they had hit the sewers.

It was strange. And eerie without them. They'd bribed their way out through the ducts and culverts, not trusting to any negotiated safe passage, and now there were just three hundred souls remaining in Kanoya City, all the more difficult for the Kan to kill with their electric blitz.

The inspection party cast long black shadows across the parapet as another flare lit up the sky.

"What's your name, feller?"

"Eastman, sir. That is, Barb Eastman, sir. I believe I've met with your son. We've spoken once or twi—"

A sudden pain seized Ellis's mind. "Mister Eastman!"

"Sir?"

"I was good enough to give you the command of this rampart, wasn't I?"

"Yes, sir."

"You intend to engage in small talk with me all night? Or will you make your reply to the Kan?"

The staffer stared back, unintimidated. A spline of brittle plex was in his hand, and he held it up for inspection as the garish flare light died.

"You can judge the quality of my replies by the heat of my weapons, Mister Straker. But I got complaints, even if you haven't. Look at this."

As the gun crew stood by, shouldering their power packs, the party gathered around the biggest of the weapons. Ellis regarded the staffer closely in the semidarkness. The man was twenty-one or -two, a spud—an awkward mover, thickset with a fleshy face that had been dyed tawny by the primary and most probably an excess of cheap fivestar, and made even darker now by the dust. His nose was blunt, and his eyes were set shallow under heavy eyebrows. As he walked around the weapon Ellis saw that the natural fall of his mouth was upturned at the corners into a false grin.

I'll bet that twist to your mouth makes you seem moody and insolent to your superiors, and you seem to have a grievance on yer mind. Yep, all in all, you've a face built like a bread pudding, feller, Ellis thought with faint amusement, but that's how your genes made you and you've got to live with it.

"So? What complaints?"

Eastman took the plex and braced it against his knee until it snapped drily. "See that! Rotten! Last couple of times I fired her, the squatting mounting damn near fell to bits. Despite all attempts to shore her up, I daren't fire this unit again in case the whole squatting shebang blows back off the parapet. Just look at this squatting gimbal: it'll be pulled free on the next firing for sure."

Ellis examined the flaking plex. "Ah, probably some kind of meson funneling edge-effect due to the shield. Nothing's been spent on these fortifications since they were put here," he said darkly, silently damning Pope as a tightwad. "You'll have to make do and mend as best you can."

"You can see I already have, sir. But all the weapons're the same. And see that!" The staffer kicked his heel at the cheek of the emplacement, the aperture that tapered back through the blister to admit the muzzle. The side crumbled where his boot made contact. It was cheesy and denatured. Old plex, never made right in the first place. "None of these barrels have been fired or tended to for above a decade. Half the squatting elevators were seized solid before I reamed them out."

Another crescendo of ultraviolet fire lit up the darkness and seconds later the bustovers sprayed down into the city, the nearest ripping into MeTraCor's buildings two hundred yards away.

"Some of these beam guides are a hundred years old," Jos Hawken said. "A hundred years in mothballs in Navy stores on Carolina. What do you expect?"

Eastman looked at the weapon morosely, hardly aware of the inferno raging a hundred feet above his head. The phasing was coming down with its customary swiftness and there was nothing other than the violence above to give them light.

"Fact is, it's worse than that. No external maintenance drones have been installed at Kanoya since the buildings went up."

"It's a maintenance-free facility, Mister Eastman."

He looked at the hated face of JJ. Foster, the Chief Agent. She was responsible for the staffers and junior posts, and Eastman's ultimate superior. He knew that to criticise was dangerous, but he guessed also that Ellis Straker would agree with him. He screwed up his courage further and said, "I don't think so. These weapons are a bigger danger to our crews than to the Kan. I'd call it filthy cheapness on some Controller's part."

"Mister Eastman!" Foster loomed like a hag in the darkness. "I think that you ought not—"

"Tell us," Ellis asked in a big voice. "How are you with a blaster, feller?"

"I don't know, sir."

"You don't know?"

Eastman shrugged, delighted by Ellis Straker's show of incredulity. The gaunt Foster watched him with a dead eye. And with good reason, Eastman thought, because the heresy he was about to speak was absolute. He wasn't going to support the charade any longer. "That's right, Mister Straker. We were never allowed to practise sidearms, or any arms at all. I think I speak for all the juniors when I say you can't believe the shit we've had to put up with here, sir. Between one ship and the next there's nothing to engage a man's mind. I would gladly have drilled with the garrison twice a week. Or taken a tester round our armor. Most of us would. And made improvements to the equipment at little cost to the MeTraCor, but they wouldn't—"

"That'll do, Eastman," Foster said sharply.

"With respect, sir, when we heard rumors of war we even sent a petition to the Controller to let us train up for the sake of our security here, just to relieve the psi-damned boredom."

"And the Controller refused?"

Another of the staffers, Bosco Shadbolt, had come to stand beside Eastman, a dark figure with an argentium tube held casually in his hand. "There was no reply to our memo," he said. "You can't believe it. It was MeTraCor's view that we were brought to Osumi as staffers, you see, sir. And staffers are here to regulate the trade flow."

Eastman agreed. "That's our function. Just to keep tabs and file reports and nothing else. It's a squatting crime, sir!"

Ellis looked around him with a hard glance, looking severely at the Council Members as they stood, black silhouettes, along the city's western ramparts and the bright opal of the sky. Then he turned back to the two staffers. "You're right. But you can be damned sure the ones who committed the crime won't ever be booked like they should."

"Look at it, sir: this is important to our survival! No upgrading of defenses to keep pace with the improvements in Kan technology. No antimine outstations. No upgrading of Fort Baker. Not even a regulation to prevent buildings being put up close by the apron. And the Kalifornian militia—"

Foster stopped short, her hollow cheeks stretched taut. "I said, Mister Eastman, that is enough!"

Ellis chewed down on his cheroot, ignoring Foster. "Militia, you say? Ah, it's a rag-bag of downworlder scum from Elay, and fit only to hang about the city for a quarter the cost of decent troopers. Sure, and the whole crew of them grand and petty larcenists and murderers too, I'll bet."

"Sir?" Bosco Shadbolt looked around the darkened faces, infected by the defiance. I don't care what happens now, Eastman thought, it's banzai for the man who dared to shake the Council by their golden balls. And it's sweet to shove the truth down their throats at last.

"S-sir?" Shadbolt stammered. "There's another thing—"

"Zip it!" Foster tried to hush him up. "Psi damn you, but this outpost's suddenly become a riot of hindsight and loose opinion! I got my eye on you!"

"Heh!" Art Solomon said. "These fellers are right to say their say. Let 'em speak up!"

Shadbolt quailed as they all looked at him. "I . . . that is . . ."

"What he wants to say, sir," Eastman said, covering his friend's confusion. "Is that this entire squatting facility's dropping out of its own ass, and it's big-scale corruption that's brought us to it. This Controller is nothing but a thief!"

"This is outrageous!" Foster's face slackened. Her jaw worked soundlessly, then she said, "Eastman, you'll apologise for that!"

"I won't, Miz. And that's a fact!"

Yes, a fact, Eastman thought, hating Foster, thank sweet psi for Ellis Straker. Why should I give my respect to some scumball who's been set above me only by years of idle time-serving and automatic promotion? These high-rankers demand respect, and that's wrong because respect's got to be earned. Earned by achievement. What's been your achievement, Foster? Doctoring the profits! Good-looking figures based on lies! By all that's real, how I despise your kind and everything you stand for! I'll call you to account, one day, you may swear to that!

"You'll hear from me again, Eastman. Your insolence is already known to MeTraCor. Well known!"

But nothing Foster said could touch Eastman. The Councillor seemed a small power now, pitiful and diseased, her personality diminished by the darkness in which no badge of rank was visible. Eastman thought of the time a year ago when the profound boredom of MeTraCor life and the claustrophobia of the dome and the constant pressure of disease and death had got too much, and he had pointed a charged blaster indifferently at his own head. He had pulled the trigger. Twice. And both times it had failed to fire. Though on the third attempt, when he had pointed it in frustration out of the window, it had gone off right enough.

"It's a MeTraCor sickness that some people grow famous through doing nothing," he said. "While others get infamous because of their honest work!"

"Your betrayal is noted, Mister Eastman!"

Eastman took the argentium tube from Shadbolt and threw it down at Foster's feet. There was silence, then another crack of violet lightning from somewhere overhead.

Ellis Straker glanced around the flare-lit faces, his voice thickening as he turned. "Betrayal is it? Now, I wouldn't call it that, Miz Foster. I'd say MeTraCor was trying to make folks in its own image—yeah, stamping them out by the dozen like counterfeit credit: soldiers who can't face war, merchants who don't know how to trade, chiefs who don't know how to rule! Seems to me your only business in Council is kissing ass and working your passage and simpering at the guy a grade above and doing nothing at all that's real! You forget the reason you're here, and why MeTraCor was set up in the first place. So don't tell Eastman he's betraying you because he's got the guts to speak the truth. Fact is, every Amerikan in Osumi has been betrayed, Miz Foster!"

Foster leveled a finger defensively. "You know we're limited in what we can do by the Treaty with the daimyo's Court at Miyakonojo. Ryuji-sama guaranteed our protection. He has always done so!"

"Ha!" Ellis shot an open palm towards the dome. "Why don't you tell that to the Kan?"

"The Chinese, sir, are breaking Yamato law!"

Another sizzling concentration of fire roared into the shields like dragon's breath, buckling the protective field inward. By the time it had compensated, a thousand more of the vacant thatched slums of the native town had been incinerated to charcoal.

"Well, now, wouldn't you say putting your whole trust in Yamato law is a shade blind as a policy?"

"Not if Ryuji-sama had been bought off as intended!"

"And had your field generators been strengthened! And had your plex armor been inspected annually! And had your people been properly trained, and had a squadron stationed here against eventualities! Then you'd have had no need for skin-of-your-teeth bribes to local despots. Nor any need to send a man on a wild-goose chase to Alpha CrA on your behalf." He turned to Eastman. "What else?"

"Just this, sir," Eastman answered wryly, and the half-smile came and went, "I like this red jacket. I'd rather be in MeTraCor's pay as a trooper. But MeTraCor's got rules about who can do what, and who can transfer where."

"I like the way you think, Eastman." Ellis took the samurai sword and a blaster from his steward. The blaster was Navy issue, good and well-made. "I can't get you enrolled in MeTraCor's private army, boy. But will a war do for you?"

Eastman took the weapons gratefully. "If it means work, sir! Hard work does a body good. I like to work. And at a fixed aim, where you know what's at stake and it's important and you're a main part of it. Something everyone can pull towards. I like it when there's no time to shirk. No time to languish and to think yourself into the pit." He smiled at the blaster and pushed it into his belt. "Work keeps the black thoughts off a man's mind."

"I know what you mean, Eastman."

"Yes, I thank psi for the war. It's brought me alive."

Another kick and flakes of cheesed plex were dislodged from the mounting. They fell at Eastman's foot and he picked up the biggest, hefting it and weighing the possibility of going all the way with his defiance. "That's Controller Pope and her people for you," he said, crumbling the flake. "Filling their credit accounts. Deliberate neglect is a crime!"

"One more word—" Foster began, but another bustover whined overhead and slashed a ragged black hole in the roof of the Halide Building and set a tree ablaze, stifling his objection.

"Time to press on," Ellis said in his psi-weird way, and the party began to move closely after him, knowing that something nasty was about to happen to the place they had just moved from.

Eastman took Foster's arm, causing her to linger. " 'All things come to he who waits,' that's what you told us, Miz Hypocrite," he hissed, knowing Kanoya City would be taken within the week. "Well, that's a filthy, squatting lie to keep a man down. Three years I've worked here for you, and every day I've thought the same thing about the Council and the Controller and the misrule of the Lease. And never once did I dare to offer my true opinion out loud. Until now. Well, you're rotting into your grave, Foster. Any man can see that. And you stink of corruption. If I were you, I'd stand right there and wait for oblivion."

"Let go of me!"

Eastman turned away in contempt as the inspection party moved off along the ramparts towards the next set of weapons blisters. Foster went after them and Eastman went back to his men as a bustover burned a crater in the ramparts where they had been standing.

"Lookee-look!" He grinned at his Sarawaki op, slipping

into Osumi trade pidgin. "Good good Navee shooter! And strong sword very okeh. Big give-me him come boss!"

"Yeh. Too good you, man!"

They congratulated him and he exulted as he brandished his gifts, stuffing the blaster into his jacket and the un-sheathed sword carelessly into his belt. He helped his men shore up the mounts and patch round the weapons blisters, and restrict the barrel travel on their recoil carriages. Yes, he thought as he strained to cross-complex the control system. The Chinese'll have Kanoya City inside a week and we'll all be in the same shit, so up where the sun don't shine with the squatting consequences!

"That Ellis Straker," he said out loud, full of admira-tion. "Now there's a real man. He calls me 'boy,' and I don't take that easy from anyone, but from him it doesn't sound bad. Compared to him, I am just a boy, just a MeTraCor staffer, the most junior of juniors. By all that's real, if only I'd had a father like him instead of—"

He bit back the resentment that burned like acid within him. The Sarawakis couldn't understand what he was say-ing, but he couldn't take chances. Never could.

The thought of Arkali Hawken sent a bolt of primitive passion searing through his guts. Sweet psi, she's just so damned beautiful! What I wouldn't give for a night with her. Just one night, by all that's real! Imagine it! Brushing back that hair, peeling off that sleek garb and then her looking back into my eyes like she meant it, wanting for me to kiss her. Just think of that!

Every man in Kanoya City has been looking out for her since the day she came. Those looks, and the richest *gaijin* heiress in all Yamato, too! By all that's real, with Hayden Straker rumored dead, and the city in chaos and her pro-posed wedding off, maybe there's hope for me yet!

But you're daydreaming, Barb Eastman. And where

does dreaming get a man? Did it get you one micron closer to anything to dream for a year and a day about it? He licked his lips, tasting the aldehydes of denatured plex, crete dust, and the salt of his own sweat. But just think of it. Suppose it was Arkali Hawken, wanting you—instead of her looking right through you as if you were an open window. Because I know Hayden Straker some, I had the chance to meet her—that is, to stand in the same room as her, though I'll bet she doesn't remember it.

By all that's real, some men have all the luck, some men are born pretty and dainty and full of aristo manners, and they're the kind that women such as Arkali Hawken are willing to look at. Not plain-faced MeTraCor staffers. No, not lumpish men like me. Men like me get ignored and it hurts like hell in the belly and boils up into violence and that's one reason I learned to fight like a wounded tiger anytime anyone trips my temper.

The inspection party was coming back this way now. He stepped up to Ellis Straker boldly.

"Sir? We picked up some movement. If you'll sanction it, I'll try these blisters out on the patch of ground above the sewer track at reference Az012.5/Rnge355.7, and I'll access MeTraCor city control subsystems to find the precise location data I need."

"Sanction it, boy? Don't ask for my say-so. You're in charge here. Do what you think's right."

"Yes, sir! I sure will, sir!"

Before he turned away, Eastman drew an illuminator from a wall bracket. He looked at Ellis, bright-eyed.

Ellis knew what the glance meant. He's got me down as a hero, he thought. And the boy's no fool: he's freely agreeing with me, so I'll have to say his opinions are of the right kind!

"Ever been assessed, Barb Eastman?"

"Assessed, sir?"

"For talent. Psi. You know?"

Eastman's chin fell to his chest. He stared at his boots. "No, sir. Never."

"Well, you're right to thank psi this war's come, Mister Eastman," Ellis told him. "That's your saving. You've got spirit, and you've got your own mind. Keep a hold on them both."

"Thank you, sir!"

Ellis walked off briskly, trailing his retinue of inspection. He was pleased with the crews and his choice of commander, and surprised by the unexpectedly generous feelings he had developed towards Barb Eastman.

Ah, you're psi-touched, all right, he thought as he led his group off the ramparts. But whatever you say, you're a slave to MeTraCor, and you'd have had no way out in peacetime. Two or three years more and MeTraCor, would've squashed the will out of you like the juice from a Colorado bedbug, and you'd be nothing but a stare-eyed zombee. That, or dead. Yep, I've seen it plenty of times before, and I know how the pressure drives spirited souls into decline, and those with most spunk into drunkenness and madness. Look what nearly happened to Red.

What a futile waste of all that's good in a man. It's a pity there ain't a few more like Eastman. A pity my Reba couldn't have lived to bear me a son like that back in Amerika. This war's been the ruin of me and the death of all that's mine, but it sure as hell has come as the salvation of that young man.

18

Barb Eastman crossed Kanoya Plaza with the illuminator in his fist. His thoughts were of the worrying vulnerability of the north side where the native town could give cover to a Chinese mine assault, or a means of getting into the conduits. Then, almost too late, he saw the shape running from the shadows of an alley.

He thrust the light beams out ahead, trying to make the shape out plainer.

"Hey, you! Stand still! *Sutoppu!*"

But the shape did not stand. There was something about its darting fearfulness that reminded him of vermin. Except that it was not running away, it was coming on at him frantically, fists flailing the air. In the dark the figure looked like it could be one of the undernourished *hinin* men.

"*Sutoppu!* Halt, psi damn you!"

He laid his free hand on the hilt of the sword but did not draw it; he lunged instead and the fugitive ran full-pelt into his thigh.

"*Itai! Yame nasai!*" he shouted, grabbing the scruff of his neck. "Where do you think you're going?" Then, as he pulled the creature off, he saw it was one of the Solomon boys, the eldest. He was breathless and in shock.

"It's the zoljers!"

"Soldiers? Where?"

"They're all crazee, sir, stone-mad and murdering!"

Eastman shook the boy hard. "Chinese troops have got in? Is that what you're trying to say?"

"No, sir! Them MeTraCor guards—they're killing my ma! Killing her and the others!"

He stared at the child dumbfoundedly. "Where?"

"In the bunker! In the bunker!"

"Are you sure? Show me."

He ran after the boy, trying to make sense of the garbled message, then, as he turned the corner, he stumbled over two men slumped in the street. He tried to pull one to his feet, but the soldier was limp and insensible. The insignia on the man's jacket told him that these were the Kalifornians who had been sent to patrol the north sector sewers. He picked up an empty whiskey bottle, stared at it. Both men were old-time stinking drunk!

"Psi damn their squatting hides!"

Then the Solomon boy was tugging at him, urging him on. As he rounded the next building he saw a ruptured methane conduit roaring a twenty-foot flame into the velvet blackness. It threw licks of flame across the bunker entrance. Then he heard the screams.

He told the boy, "Go bring help!"

"But I want—"

"I said, go bring help!"

"But—"

"Go!"

The boy's face was a grimacing mask, but his tough upbringing gave him the strength to do as he was told.

Horror consumed Eastman as he realised what was happening. Drunken mutineers have broken in on the women, he thought, and Arkali Hawken's down there! By psi, if they've harmed one hair of her head they'll pay for their actions ten thousand times over! He gave the illuminator to the boy and pulled out blaster and sword too, thinking there might be some quiet work to be done. The terrified screams spurred him like knives. He left the boy with another order to fetch more help before he fought his way into the darkness over a mass of tangled furniture, and dived down the crete steps and into the bunker passage, knowing he would have to murder.

Once off the stair his eyes were grateful for the blinking orange light issuing from the bunker. It seemed to him that he had stumbled into one of the caverns of hell. Two laughing devils were viciously slashing at women and girls with hand-held slitters, telling them to strip, taunting them with freedom but then keeping them back from the shattered iris. Younger children obeyed pathetically, cowering in the corners as their elder sisters ran back and forth screaming. The bunker's periscope camera stared at the gas fire, filling the wall holo with fire, turning the bunker into an annex of Hell. But Eastman came on into it, driven by savage rage, and drew back his sword instinctively. The blade soughed through the air and parted the throat of the nearest man, and the draw-cut went deep, severing the strings of his neck. The mutineer went down welling blood as the second man stared up at him, astonished.

Yes, bleed, you bastard! he thought, filled with limitless strength. Bleed and die and pay for what you've done!

The other began to turn to the attack. Without thinking, his arm straightened and he plunged the sword through the mutineer's shirt and a foot deep into his navel, withdrawing the weapon sharply before the abdominal muscles could spasm closed on the blade and hold it. Again, the man staggered down and lay useless, absorbed in his own agony.

He had not used his blaster, and neither man had made a shout of warning. It seemed that the chaos of screams

might have preserved his surprise as the women fell venge-
fully on the dying men, tearing at their eyes and faces with
their fingernails now.

He stepped past them, horrified at what he saw. He
crossed the entrance and flattened himself against the wall,
his blaster in his left hand. He was alive to the danger and
the need to tread carefully. There were shouts. How many
troopers were inside? Probably a whole kennel full of
them, drawn like curs to blood. How were they armed?

As his head came round the corner he saw three more
mutineers sprawling on their female victims, ripping at
their clothes and bodies, punching and shouting to subdue
them. Then he saw Arkali Hawken, and the hot dry air
turned to ashes in his mouth.

Her struggles were futile. They had stripped her naked
and the biggest of them had forced her bare back against
a pillar. Her arms were being dragged tight around it by a
second mutineer, a small, verminous man, who gripped
her wrists. Her pale, slim body was bucking as the big
half-naked soldier tried to part her legs and thrust himself
between her thighs. Her head tossed from side to side, but
he caught her chin and clamped his mouth over hers so
that her yells were muted. When the big man pulled back
she gasped and started to scream, but he hit her with the
flat of his hand, threatening her with growling commands
and the point of his slitter. He grabbed roughly at her
breast and squeezed until she shuddered, then he reached
down to smear his fingers across the auburn hairs below
her belly, and with his other hand he began to ready himself
to enter her.

For a long second Eastman gaped at the scene, shocked
to a standstill at the bestiality of it. Men were sprawling
on their half-naked victims, on the floor, on futons, against
the walls. The Solomon sisters were covered in blood,

strewn like discarded dolls across the floor. Faya lay dead. Beside her, Loris was staring sightlessly, her throat slashed open.

He tore his attention back to the big man who was obviously the mutineers' leader. He was barrel-chested, and his filthy shirt hung off him. It was ripped wide from the neck to the hem, and there were bloodstains all over it. More scratches and smears of blood were on Arkali's ribs and thighs. The mutineer's face was booze-slack and bleeding from a wound on his cheek, his eyes were fiery and sly, and as he pushed his breeches down, the dark stalk of his penis rose up grotesquely. He handled himself, and she screamed and wriggled convulsively trying to free her arms, but they were twisted back in an unbreakable grip and the second mutineer mocked her weakness as he waited his turn, pushing his face close to her ear and mouthing filthy promises.

''No, please!'' she pleaded hysterically, her fingers spikes. ''No! I'm a virgin. Please. I'm a virgin!''

Eastman bellowed incoherently. He burst forward and chopped his sword into the head of the man holding Arkali's wrists. The skull clove like a turnip, and he fell down.

The big man reeled off Arkali wordlessly, his dull eyes fixed on the blue steel of the samurai sword, his huge erection suddenly a laughable encumbrance. ''*Shoko!*'' he shouted. Officer!

The other mutineers had already found their heads and had seen what was happening. Now the women struggled out from under them and fled for their children and the unguarded iris as their assailants jumped to their feet.

Arkali stared, felt the red-jacketed officer grip her arm. She flinched, unable to believe he was really there. This was a nightmare that was never going to end. She saw the four drunken soldiers begin frantically searching for weapons, and the officer put out a protective arm to ward her away.

He shouted an order in Kanoya pidgin, but they were crouching like animals under threat, their eyes all white on the barrel of his blaster. She came out of her paralysis and grabbed up a blanket, bunching it reflexively to her breast. As she backed away, her bare heel trod in a pool of liquid and she looked down. It was the man who had been holding her arms. His brain had been laid open; colorless fluid coursed out of his cloven head, yet his eyes were pleading and he was begging for help.

She tried to shut out the hellish sight, tried to shout, but the air was pierced by a woman's screams that went on and on and on without stopping until she realised they were her own screams. She opened her eyes again and saw the danger the officer faced.

As if triggered by her terror, the four remaining mutineers had scrambled together. One held a table leg as a club, another had taken up the parang, a third found the toolholder, and the monster who had tried to rape her held his slitter. They were backed against the wall, but spreading out dangerously, more confident now, and eager to take the young officer who pointed his blaster at each one in turn to cover their slow withdrawal. Then she heard more footsteps in the entrance.

The panic rose in her and she tried to warn him, but as she turned she saw a Macau-Kalifornian sergeant armed with a blaster, and the Solomon men, also armed, and the horror-struck boy with them—and her father, at last, her father! He swept her up and swathed her in a blanket and held her tight and she saw that now Ellis Straker filled the doorway, and that he held a big knife loosely in his hand.

As soon as they saw him the four mutineers fell back, wild-eyed like pigs on an abattoir ramp, as if they knew what would happen next.

"Give her your blaster," Ellis told Jos Hawken in a strange, low voice. "Let her have her justice on them."

"No! Not Arkali!"

"It'll help to heal her wounds, Jos!"

"No!"

Ellis stared back at him, his eyes diamonds, then he nodded. "If that's your decision. Then you'll leave the bunker and leave us to do the rest in our own way."

Jos Hawken drew back, deeply horrified by the carnage in the bunker and by what Ellis's words meant. The wailing was muffled as he helped Arkali to stand, and she was steered from the bunker, stepping stiff and cold and shaking over the blood-spattered dead. At the door he lifted her and carried her up the stairs, still numb, and he thanked psi she was alive.

Below, there was now just the young officer who had saved her, the two Solomon men, and Ellis Straker left in the bunker with the four mutineers. Four on four, as Ellis's barbaric code of honor demanded.

Before they reached the street the screams started all over again. The first of the castrations had begun.

The horse ride to Miyakonojo was like a dream.

Hayden Straker traveled with a bodyguard of fifty of the daimyo's horsemen, with the Lady Yasuko, and with Hideki Shingo-san, the second son of the Prefect of Kyushu and overlord of this beautiful world over which their samurai banners flew.

He and Hideki Shingo were mounted on the two biggest horses, bay mares of fifteen hands, splendidly groomed and impressively caparisoned in silk and gleaming silver ornaments. The Lady Yasuko went ten paces behind her husband in a palanquin, a marvel of precise carpentry, carried across the shoulders of six heavily tattooed and almost-naked bearers.

He had still been in shocked condition when the column had left the village, his wounded hand bound up in a length of silk, his clothes spattered with dried blood and the rage of the death struggle still ringing in his head. He could not think straight. Events were impossibly mixed up: there was the Lady Yasuko getting to her feet over the body. The *hatamochi*'s flesh rippling with twitches even though he had been dead more than a minute, and the startling groan he made as they turned his body over to drag him away. At the same time, it had seemed oddly appropriate, almost comic, that the mercenary had urinated in death.

Hayden Straker felt a strong burn of guilt at that. To laugh at the indignity of a man's death is undeniably shameful, he thought. How could I have done that? But it was undeniably funny at the time also. And I did laugh, psi damn me.

Then—but it must have been much later—the hazy memory of Shingo-san kneeling with the blood streaming from his nose, in the sweet stench of decay. The unwound head of Daniel Quinn, now looking like a fat boy, skin marbled in death, bloating up in the heat.

Shingo-san had himself braved defilement to lever open the jaw, suspecting the amygdala was hidden inside like a coin of Charon. And when he found nothing under the swollen tongue he had stamped away angrily, leaving

Quinn to be laid to rest with a few chosen words—though what words he had spoken he could not now say. He remembered especially the grave being tamped flat, the dark brown, volcanic dirt of Osumi, and his promise renewed to the psi tripod of rough wood he placed above it.

He shook his head. It's like intoxication and the sickness that follows and the dull head after that, he thought. Can it be I was made drunk by the killing? But now I'm recovering.

Slowly, the memories knitted together in his mind as he rode. The distinctive smell of cremation had hung over the village. The twin pyres of the headman's son and his *hatamochi* murderer had sent up black smoke, rising in two pillars into the still air, to layer and mingle above the thatch roofs.

None of the riders had so much as glanced at the funeral fire of their ex-leader as they passed. Only the grizzled scout, Mori-san, the eldest of the riders and a man toughened by long years of rigorous service, had made any sign—and that had been to spit snap juice into the dust.

As the column picked its way towards the river, Hayden Straker asked himself again about the astonishing behavior of the bodyguard of the daimyo. He had thought he was committing suicide when he had leapt on Haigo Gozaemon and killed him in full view. The guard had been armed and close at hand, but they had done nothing to help their leader. Instead, they had gathered to watch, like men spectating at a fistfight. As he rode, he played with the paradox, twisting it inside out in his mind. Suppose it had been otherwise. What would MeTraCor's garrison at, say, Seoul have done if they'd discovered a Yamato merchant murdering their colonel? It was hard to believe Amerikan soldiers

would have just stood back and allowed it to happen—
even if the attacker had been in cahoots with the wife of
the Seoul Lease Controller!

But this isn't Seoul, he warned himself. Our rules don't
apply. This is Yamato, Kyushu Quadrant, and you'd better
take account of Yamato ways and samurai ways if you're
going to keep your promise.

After the killing the Lady Yasuko had looked to him in
triumph, the blood lust still firing her eyes. Then she had
thanked him. And Shingo-san had praised him grudgingly.
His nose had been streaming blood, but he had acted as if
nothing had happened. And the guard had watched him
with their strange bowing silence, expectant as dogs at a
picnic..

But he had been in no condition to pay any attention to
them. The fact was that he had killed a man, and even
though it had been necessary he felt revolted at what he
had done. The evil had been far too simple, and far too
quick and easy.

Trancelike, with the ache pulsing in his wounded hand,
he had ridden away from the nightmares of the village of
the chestnut-tree plain, and had slowly awakened to himself to find the bountiful land unfolding around him like a
lotus blossom. The verdant green of rice fields along the
Oki River were broken by dark wallows in which water
buffaloids waited out the afternoon. It was a landscape
dominated by the wide, shallow river, waters glistering
under the sun, and the fecund plain punctuated by distant
women, bright in colored coats, laboring in the fields. He
passed mud levees, clusters of thatched huts and the huge
yellowing leaves of plantains whose fruits hung in vast
pendulous green fists, unripe as yet.

All day the heat increased under the merciless stare of
the primary and the sky grew vaporous and heavy, turning

to the milky white of a blindman's eye, then the sun-star sank into the hills, red and blear, and Hayden Straker knew that this shallow Osumi season was pregnant with the onset of the rains.

Someday soon the clouds would break, the oppressive air would clear, and land travel would become impossible. The ban on technology in almost all areas of Osumi outside the Lease had the absolute authority of Imperial edict. No one—no one—broke the Emperor's laws, no matter what the emergency. Not even outlaws. He could be trapped here for months in this alien reservation, a stranger who understood too little—especially about himself.

He looked behind him, disappointed at their progress, irritated by the cumbersome and lumbering *kago* palanquin. It seemed to him the woman was imprisoned inside it. It was a screened and curtained traveling litter made without wheels and hung instead from a freshly cut thick pole of green bamboo.

No wheeled vehicle could travel in the mountains and plains of Osumi. No roads had been built for them. Only narrow, winding tracks that ignored contours. Fit only for bare feet, horses, and goats. Peasants had no need of the wheel; it made them soft. Samurai did not want the wheel; they had the good earth, and should the need arise, they had the air, too.

The riders had brought the *kago* with them from Miyakonojo, broken down into components and lashed across their baggage horses especially for the lady. He had seen their like often in the sedans of Seoul and Kanoya City's native quarter. Often when visiting that quarter the richer Amerikan traders went about in them, mainly to keep "face" in front of the local merchants and credit-brokers to whom appearances were all. But his father had never used one, saying that the only time he would let six men carry him around was on the last voyage of all, or when he was locked in a freezee and couldn't do much about it.

You're in Osumi now, he told himself once again. According to custom, it was the only mode of travel, except the *kura*, the saddle of a war tiger, that a Yamato noblewoman could respectably use. If only they'd rotate the poor guys carrying the weight of it more than once an hour, he thought, seeing the obvious way to speed their journey. The bodyguard could take turns. Rota the work with fresh men to act as bearers. Perhaps I should suggest it. He glanced at Shingo-san.

Shingo rode his horse silently, his pugnacious air enhanced by his quiet mastery of the beast. The breed was incredibly tough. These horses were from the Home Worlds, where Imperial princelings ruled their own personal planets in the Kyoto system and took an interest in bloodstock engineering. These were horses with distinctive ears that pricked inwards to almost touch; they had a reputation for endurance but also irritable natures due to their Arab blood.

"A fine horse," he said to Shingo, ruffling his horse's mane. "I was told that this breed has come about by chance from stallions escaped after a wreck. Stallions which were then crossed with local mares."

But Shingo only looked at him with fury in his eyes and then away, and Hayden Straker realised he had said something with a second meaning, something that had been interpreted as an insult.

Well, psi damn you! Psi damn your thinking in riddles and talking in riddles, he thought, suddenly riled by Shingo's irascibility. Yes, and psi damn your suspicious jealousy over your wife, too. You watch her like a falcon and treat me like an interloper, and, by psi, maybe you should because she's worth ten of you in every department,

and I'd take her away from you just to save her the trouble
of your morbid company!

The burst of angry thinking made him feel better. After
that, he sat up, and his strength of mind began to return
and he persuaded himself that he would soon be in Miyakonojo and the matter of the amygdala settled.

Where are you, Arkali? he wondered faintly. What are
you doing at this moment? Are you thinking of me? I hope
so. And, if you can hear my thoughts, believe that I'll
soon be back among sane people and I'll cherish you
and we'll marry as we should have done. Perhaps then
everything will be as it should, and I'll be as I was again.

But the piety of his own thoughts sickened him, and to
avoid thinking about it, he shut them away.

Before the dark came down they rode through Haraki
where the entire population of *chonin*—townspeople—
came out from their meal and threw themselves down onto
the ground until the column had passed. A little beyond
the town they took refreshment at a roadside inn while the
night camp was being erected. The Lady Yasuko came out
of the *kago* palanquin. She approached the inn dressed in
a style he had not seen before, a kimono still all-conceal-
ing, but made from a lighter, more yielding silken material
that fell in shapely folds. In her hands was an exquisitely
inlaid calligraphy box, one of the womanly belongings that
had been brought along with the palanquin.

He watched her for a long time. She took out a leaf of
some kind of fibrous hardcopy, unfolded it, and prepared
the ink block. Then she began to write. The movements
of her wrist were deft and graceful as she brushed the
symbols of the *hiragana* script, in columns, top to bottom,
right to left.

He watched her for several minutes more, then she noticed him and she put her writing stand aside. She followed

his eye to where the bodyguard were making camp. The junior men were disciplining the hapless staff of the *ryokan* with raised voices. She registered his unease.

"Please, if they are disturbing you, you should not hesitate to chastise them, Mister Straker. You must not stand for indiscipline."

He thought about that, unsure what to make of it. "They don't bother me, Lady," he said.

"Ah. Then you need say nothing."

A further moment passed and then she said, "For the present, we are quite safe. They will not try to harm you."

The lilt in her voice was one of amusement now, and prickled by it, he said, "Surely it was you who tried to kill Haigo Gozaemon. They saw you attack him first."

"Oh, but I am a mere woman." She paused long enough for one of the guards to pass by, and perhaps also to ensure he had appreciated her irony, then she switched to English. "You do not understand. These men are a kind of *ronin*. Mercenaries. Low professionals, like—what can I say?— like seventh-rank prostitutes. They work on behalf of whichever daimyo pays them most and they obey the commands of whoever they most fear. Because they owe no real allegiance to anyone, their loyalty is as the loyalty of bathhouse whores."

"I still don't understand. . . ."

She laughed. "In their eyes, Mister Straker, you were clever enough to send a woman to distract Haigo Gozaemon. It was you who delivered the death blow, and with Shingo-sama's own sword. Do not think the meaning of that was lost on them. It was not. As far as they are concerned, you dispatched their last leader quite legitimately and in a most novel manner."

He scratched his head, dumbstruck by her explanation. "But he was their officer, their leader!"

She shrugged. "Of course. They were all afraid of him. But you deposed him. Accordingly, what was his is now yours. And until someone deposes you, it is you who they will follow."

He felt fear frosting him again: though the paradoxes of Yamato had saved his life, still the strangeness of their customs remained outside his understanding. It made him feel as he had as a young boy, the first time he had got out of his depth in the swim pool.

Sure I drew Shingo-sama's sword, but it wasn't intended as a symbol, he thought. How can they interpret what happened in that way? Are they all snap-crazees? I've lived among the low-caste natives of Osumi for years, but I've never really understood them. The folks in Kanoya City's native quarter look different to us and they behave different to us, but I always thought that underneath they must think like we do. But they don't. They don't at all. No wonder I found their language so hard to learn, so crammed full of ambivalence and metaphor; it's because their whole way of thinking is totally and absolutely foreign to us. Psi help me when I get to Miyakonojo. What will it be like? Sweet Jeezus, they'll eat me alive.

He cast a glance over his shoulder at the half-armored warriors behind him. They unstrapped their jangling *haramaki*-style suits, took off their *nodowa* throat protectors, and unslung the *sode* shoulder guards in preparation for the night, yet none of them approached him. He wondered if the Lady Yasuko was hinting that he should give them orders, and if he did would they obey? Then he remembered how she had spoken delicately of "deposing," and he wondered if any of them was yet ambitious for promotion.

"Don't forget, you are MeTraCor's finest shootist," she said, the amused lilt returning. "You can kill any man at thirty paces. By now, it is probably fifty. But now you must please excuse me. It is time for me to retire.''

That night he did not sleep in the three-mat cell they had given him. Instead he ignored the universal curfew and sat for a long time on the steps of the inn, the din of frogs filling the dark that surrounded him. He was sleepless, because he now had the amygdala in his jacket pocket again and he was not inclined to swallow it a second time. He got up twice, the first time to look up at the brilliant stars and later to investigate the heap that was Haigo Gozaemon's tackle—the belongings he had inherited.

''C'mon, you sonofabitch,'' he whispered, ''I don't believe a *hatamochi* like you would've left anything to chance, not with an amygdala at stake, Imperial Edict or not.''

At last, he found what he was looking for: the slim Wesson 216i blaster snout hidden there in the left-side *kohire* of the armor, right where Haigo Gozaemon could have fired it unobtrusively to make good the extravagant threat of his reputation.

He ejected the clip of six tiny argentium tubes, inserted them into his own blasters, and put them beside him before he retired to sleep dreamlessly.

20

The next morning Hayden Straker woke to the sound of horses. The day was as close and humid as the first; away from the cooling breezes that swept in from the sea, the sky baked the land remorselessly and the *ka* bites he had collected on his hands and neck itched in the heat.

Halfway through the morning they left the river near another huge bamboo waterwheel—thirteen-sided and surrounded by a network of stilt-raised gutters—and followed the Shinto pilgrims' road north and west to Kin-Su, the Golden Rock. As they came to a lengthy rise, Hayden Straker turned to the grizzled chief scout and motioned sharply to him to come. Mori-san responded readily, so he explained his idea that some of the riders, the dozen assigned to bring up the rear, might lend a hand with the *kago*.

The scout's star-weathered face creased further. He was probably nearing sixty, old for his profession, his black lacquer helmet had seen better days, and he wore a stiff handlebar moustache. He was reluctant to comment.

"In that case, I order you to explain the situation."

"Hai." Mori-san sat up abruptly and began to stare into space, at attention though he was in the saddle.

"Well?"

"Excuse me, but what you suggest is not a solution," he said in Osumi *hogen*.

"Why not?"

The scout inclined his head quizzically. "So sorry, but such an order will not be seen favorably."

"Why not?"

"I don't understand, sir?"

Despite a growing irritation, he persevered. "Are you saying that they would refuse to carry out an order to help with the palanquin?"

"No, sir!"

"Then what?"

"They are samurai."

A long pause.

"Yes, I know they are samurai. So?"

The scout seemed at last to understand. "They are hon-or-bound to do only what the samurai class may do."

"They have arms and legs like other men."

"Of course you are correct, sir. But they have rank also. They should not be palanquin bearers when palanquin bearers are here in plenty."

Hayden Straker nodded. "And if I ordered it? Would they refuse?"

"Refuse? That's unthinkable."

"Why?"

Mori-san forced himself to explain. "Afterwards the shame would be too great a burden. Each man would ask himself why you had chosen to punish him with this humiliation. Perhaps some would ask permission to kill themselves."

"That's the most insane thing I ever heard."

He snorted, doubting the scout, but all the same he let him resume his place in the column, suspecting that in Yamato nothing could be made to work, no matter how important, if it overlooked the Way of the Warrior.

By midday they had skirted Kin-Su. And they stopped for rest and noodles. This was the Golden Rock, the scout told him, the most important Shinto shrine on the planet, one of the seven most holy places in all Kyushu, with its temples and sacred pine trees. Hayden Straker felt the magnetism of the place at once; an eerie whirlpool of religious devotion seemed to surround its lake. A depth of devotion inexplicable to someone like himself.

When he said so to Yasuko-san at the next halt, she hid her face behind her fan. "They come to seek one of the seven gods of happiness. Kin-Su is named after a huge nugget of aurium that resides in the shrine. Perhaps not so inexplicable after all?"

Thousands of pilgrims all with the mark of the god

Daikoku, a white *hachimaki* headband marked with a sack of rice and a hammer, were flocking in to choke the town, and Shingo chose a detour to avoid their handcarts and their tiresome and inevitable obeisances. He selected an inn six *ri* beyond the town as the sun-star began to set, and had it cleared of guests. Shingo-san had been in the saddle all day, and he posted three men as guards, then, once he had inspected the inn, he stomped away deep into the bamboo grove in back to relieve himself.

Hayden Straker sat down by the stone lantern. This was famously dangerous country at night. One of those places that made a person doubt the wisdom of the eco-programs of the terraformers. Here, the scout had told him, in the wooded depths, in dusty dry watercourses, the leaf nests of hamadryads were to be found. These were snakes that grew to an astonishing sixteen feet in length. But were not snakes that crushed their victims. These "king cobras" were Old Earth–evolved, no different from the creatures that had once roamed the jungles of that tragic planet. They were hooded, venomous monsters that could rear up above twice the height of a man to strike. They could move faster than a galloping horse and had no fear of men. Unlike most other snakes, the scout had said, they would attack without being first threatened: "Because, *gaijin-sama*, it is their way to hunt, and make their meals of other snakes."

"Why did the terraformers have to play these tricks, eh, Mori-san? Don't you ever ask yourself that? Why do they have to design ecologies that include mosquitoes and man-eaters? Why must there always be a serpent in Eden?"

"I'm sorry, *gaijin-sama*, I don't understand you."

"Oh, it doesn't matter, Mori-san."

He took ten paces into the gloom and returned. Tonight, he thought, I'll stay in my allotted quarters, but first comes *cha*.

The *cha* house was set a little way apart from the inn. The low cedarwood doors slid smoothly on waxed runners. He took off his shoes and entered, bending in the meticulous way he had seen Shingo-san do.

Yasuko-san was inside, delicate and elegant so that he felt like a cumbersome oaf.

"I hope I'm not disturbing you?" he asked.

"No. Please come in."

Four tatami were arranged in a swastika pattern round a central fire pit. The embers under the iron kettle glowed comfortingly as he took his seat cross-legged on the matting. Once more he took the opportunity of Shingo-san's absence to exchange a few words with the Lady Yasuko. Since the events of Kurihara he had felt a bond of trust that made words easier, and he had thought carefully about his best interests. On the one hand, she could be his guide and his best ally in this strange land; on the other, he could not fathom her mind at all, and he dared not risk infuriating her husband further.

"This is the best part of the day, I always think," he said as pleasantly as he could.

She did not reply at first, then said a little artificially, "Oh, yes, Mister Straker. Tea is the very heart and essence of civilisation."

She returned to her task serenely, arranging all the items needed to prepare green tea properly—porcelain service and bamboo utensils, whisk and bowl—after the fashion she had been taught as a child. The form of the ceremony created its own aesthetic, taking her into spiritual calm. This was a beautiful Zen oasis of peace in a universe of clashing sorrows. . . .

"Yeah. It's been a long day, and I'm as thirsty as hell."

Abruptly, she stopped her contemplations. Like a sleep-walker wakened in the middle of an action, she blinked.

"I'm sorry, but what did you say?"

"I was just saying: a tiring day."

"Dawn and dusk are indeed the best times on Osumi, when the sun-star is not so fierce."

"And which do you prefer?" he asked her. "The rising? Or the setting?"

She abandoned the ritual, turned her head, looking at him with clear, piercing eyes. "I enjoy the dawn for the promise it makes to the day. But I prefer dusk, for then the evening lies ahead and in my world the evenings are filled with music and laughter and the stars of heaven."

He nodded agreeably, stretching the weariness from his bones. "Your world sounds enchanting, Lady."

"So it is, Mister Straker. It is a woman's world. The world of the daimyo's Court. And it contains everything a woman could need or want."

He listened to her words, which were softly spoken yet definite and deliberate as was everything she said, but he noticed that the lilt had gone from them.

"You pronounce Amerikan most excellently, Lady."

"And you speak our tongue, which is very rare for a *gaijin*."

He accepted the compliment as graciously as he could. "Thank you, but I must confess I hardly think of myself as a foreigner at all."

"The Amerikans are a restless people, are they not? A nation of sky nomads? Unlike the other peoples of humanity, to whom we should long ago have taught the principles of how to behave. Ah, but despite our best efforts the Chinese and the Koreans have never learned how to be properly civilized, so what hope is there for Amerikans?" She stirred. "Will the Amerikans leave Osumi, now that the Chinese have made war on them?"

"I don't know."

"Ah, yes. But I forgot. You don't know about Amerikans. Officially you are a subject of Yamato. And yet you don't know about Yamato either. So, tell me, what do you know, Mister Straker?"

He smiled at her unexpected impishness. "I've lived on Osumi and other places, here and there, for more than twenty years, my father maintains houses in Kanoya City and also on Seoul, and I've visited many worlds of the Zone aboard my father's nexus ships. That has been half my life. The fact is, I know a little something about a great many places, but perhaps not enough about any one of them, except Seoul."

"Ah, yes. Seoul." Her voice became distant. "You told my husband you were taught Japanese there. But you can't take Seoul to be Yamato, nor the Lease of Kanoya City to be Osumi."

"You think not?"

"I think not." There was no guile in her voice. "If you lived in such places for a thousand years you would never become anything other than a *gaijin*. Perhaps you will turn out to be the kind of foreigner who can never really learn about Yamato."

He was disappointed by the remark. It seemed to him that another man might think her haughty tone was slighting, but he knew she was only speaking the truth as she saw it, and that, at least, was something he could respect.

"Perhaps you're right," he said, but he was thinking, perhaps the assumption of superiority is something these samurai are born to. Something they carry about them as naturally as their swords. He supposed he had succeeded in keeping his thoughts off his face, but then she spoke again.

"So sorry, but I think my words have wounded you."

He cleared his throat, looking toward the bamboo grove.

"Oh, no, Lady. It's just that . . ." He paused, guardedly, but then went on. "It's just that sometimes I envy those who know their place in life. Those who belong. You're lucky in that respect. I was born on a world I hardly knew. And I grew to manhood in wild places, not in a country that makes its own laws and that knows just one way. The worlds of the Zone have their own customs, but they are isolated and are always looking to other places for their culture. I grew up on ships and on aprons on a thousand different trading-post worlds. I have no great family spread around me, nor one single place I can call home. I know the bones of twenty languages but the flesh of none. Though I never thought of it before, I suppose that in truth I am a sky nomad. And rootless."

"Roots are necessary if the tree is to flourish," she said, proudly. "The Japanese always had roots. We are descended from the people of the islands of Japan on Old Earth, where the land was a chain of rock emerging from an ocean. The biggest island on Old Earth. Our people were harvesters; the sea was our prairie. Do you know that our Emperor is a direct descendant of the sun god? Yes, Mister Straker, it is a line that has ruled Yamato for over three hundred years, but it is a line that goes back for thousands of years before that. We came out of the Land of Nihon to conquer, and make these worlds our own. You should know that we are not to be dictated to by anyone."

He nodded cautiously, taken by the dignity of her speech. Then she relaxed. Her slim fingers laced and clasped her knee. He saw that the nails of her fingers were unpainted but the perfume she gave to the air was delicate as jasmine. Her kimono shimmered as she sat straighter to pour a little hot water into a bowl.

"You are anxious to reach Miyakonojo," she said.

"Yes."

"Then, if I may be permitted to counsel you in two ways: first, try to place trust in your own destiny, and second, learn patience."

"I'll try to remember that."

"Patience is the chief virtue of our Way, and it is a virtue that can conquer all. Never forget that Yamato is a universe of itself and unto itself. Nothing changes here. Psi exists here undisturbed. Here time is not measured in days or years or generations, but in the turnings of the cosmic wheel." She paused as if deliberating what more she should reveal to him, then looked away. "There are countless examples of patience on this world of ours, Mister Straker. I myself have seen, at the Shrines of Ninokata, a chain stretched between two stone pillars set one *ri* apart. That chain was cut from a single stone. You can hardly imagine the skill of the lone craftsman who made it, nor, I think, could you place a proper value on his patience."

She knelt forward, the licks of fire chasing the shadows from her eyes. In a darker tone she said, "I will tell you that, also not far from here, there is a shrine of twenty-one steps from a sacred lake into which the *ame no gawa* flows every year."

He looked up at her quizzically. "But the Milky Way is not a real river. It's just a trick of perspective, the disc of our galaxy seen edgeways from inside. It's only called the River of Heaven whimsically. How can such a river flow anywhere?"

"Each year, on the night of Cold Dew, the ninth of October in your Universal Time, millions of pilgrims come here to bathe in the lake, and as they gather and immerse themselves in the holy water at midnight, they marvel at the lake's surface rising higher from step to step of the shrine. It is truly a miracle."

"No, lady," he said, grinning. "That's only Archi-

medes' Principle. Of course, the water level rises when
they crowd into it, it's the same when you load a rowboat
and it sinks deeper into the—''

"Please listen to me," she cut in, still serene as a Buddha. "Listen to me with your whole mind and not just with
your forebrain. You must believe that the quality of psi is
different here. Here there is real Shinto magic. For your
own good, Mister Straker, believe that."

"Your pardon, Lady, I was simply saying that according
to basic science—''

Her eyes flashed at him impatiently. "If you will not
believe, then consider what has brought you here. The
belief in the Shinto magic of a stone! If it were not for
that, Ryuji-sama would have no use for the large crystal
you call an amygdala, and you would not be here!"

"That is the truth, at least," he muttered, not wanting
her to converse with him so intensely for fear that Shingo-
san would come back and overhear them.

"Mister Straker, in Yamato we believe that a man
should seek to uphold his rights under the law, but also it
is his duty to accept his responsibilities." She straightened
once more, and he saw the passion animate her. She was
frustrated by his ignorance and his cool politeness, and
that made her angry inside. "Like you, we also believe
that a man should strive to know the outer universe, but
also it is necessary to study the universe within. Know that
you cannot pursue these aims in isolation. You must pursue
them both. If you choose one alone, you will not attain
either of them. Pursue both simultaneously and equally,
and you will gain both."

He smiled. "Your philosophy is both ancient and honorable, Lady."

Silently he thought of his father's self-satisfied summary
of the samurai code: "Listen, boy, it's government, gods,

guts and genetics that interest them, in that order. You can add guns to that if you like. They've too much of all of them for my liking, but, thank psi, a shortage of the latter. Theirs is a crazy kind of Confucianism, soured and corrupted by hundreds of years of Shinto mumbo-jumbo, and you should keep clear of it. . . ."

The Lady Yasuko's eyes dwelt on his own, urging him. "There are things in Yamato that you could never explain in your science. Know that. In Miyakonojo you must think like we think, for if you think like a *gaijin* you will never succeed here."

"Allow me to thank you for your advice, Lady."

Her tone suddenly changed. "I think we shall reach Miyakonojo tomorrow."

He looked at her, uncertain what precisely she had been telling him, then Shingo-san appeared and they fell into silence.

Tomorrow, he thought, clinging to the real world where there was no Shinto magic and no foolish self-deceptions, but only hard psi explanations. Tomorrow, I'll deliver the amygdala to Hideki Ryuji. And tomorrow I'll claim his help in driving the Chinese off the Kanoya City apron.

21

Directly they entered Miyakonojo, Hideki Shingo's thoughts left the amygdala and turned instead to his two half brothers. The teaching of Zen is faultless, and the words of the masters are wise beyond description, he thought. That a man should have more than three wives is folly, even if that man is as rich and powerful as my father. The more wives a daimyo takes, the worse it is for him in his declining days, for then the number of his offspring is great, and the turbulence of their disputes multiplies also.

He looked steadily through the light-blasted timber arch of the gate, along the thronging street beyond, feeling that he had been away from the dispute too long. He ached to be back among those against whom he had sparred and struggled since childhood, and with those like Isako-san, his mother, who had nurtured and guided him. She knew that the turbulence was in his blood, that he needed to express it. She always understood that. She's still the most powerful woman in the Court, he thought, virtual ruler of the Residence, and only with her help can I become daimyo.

His thoughts explored the coming battle meticulously. Of the dozens of male offspring sired by Hideki Ryuji, only a handful were dynastically significant. These were the sons of his wives, for the spawn of courtesans and consorts could have no legal claim to power. Of this handful only two were old enough to be a serious threat: the elder, Sadamasa, and the younger, Noboru. So far, he reflected, Noboru has shown little aptitude for politics, and even if he had he would be an ally against Sadamasa, since Sadamasa is the man our father has named as his deputy, and the son he wants as his successor, and against the favorite there must always be an alliance. But even that will never be.

He glanced to his right and saw the *gaijin* looking up from the streets at the walls of the fortress citadel of Miya-konojo. Its thick plex walls rose up, black and seamless, above the rocky slope at their foot. It was big enough to act as a refuge for most of the important townspeople if an invasion threatened, or when filthy *ronin* pirates appeared in force. It was strong enough to withstand a lengthy siege by any but the best-equipped offworld forces. The population of the sprawling town of Miyakonojo was perhaps one million in number, mostly *chonin* or peasants, most of them uninterested in the power struggles that went on continuously in the daimyo's Court. They knew that whatever happened there was none of their concern.

But soon it would be, he thought. There will be a revolution in the coming months that will affect everyone. If my father is astute, then no son will win and perhaps three sons will die. But if he makes a mistake, then one son will win and two will die. Then Miyakonojo will have a new daimyo. He smiled, delighting in the prospect now that Haigo Gozaemon was no longer an obstacle.

How much does it matter to the great mass of people here which son will inherit the sword of power? he asked himself. To see them you would think it did not matter at all. In truth, it will matter more than any other single event in the whole of Yamato.

He breathed deeply as he entered the gates of the capital. It had taken every living decade of Osumi's history to confect this place. Here was the Ginza, the bazaar of the Old Town, rich with all the familiar essences of Yamato; the smells of continuous habitation were grained like pungent wood oils into these streets where the ways were crooked and narrow and hemmed in by tumbled hovels, where electricity wires choked the scene like the web of a giant spider, and buffaloids and scratching fowls and children with shade bonnets wandered about. One million people and decades of close-packed living. Their smells saturated the decaying fabric of the town: dust and spice and dried fish and incense smoke and burning rubber and animals and here and there a whiff of black stagnation and the pitiless sun-star in the sky fermenting everything.

The *gaijin* was looking about himself, sweating and uncertain, genuinely shocked by the way the guard kicked down the scum that raised inquisitive eyes to his stirrups. Oh, no, this is not Kanoya City, the wide streets and shining offices of MeTraCor. No orderly life of commerce here, no clean-swept straightness such as is found in the Amerikan city. Here, we tolerate every technology up to Twentieth Century. This is Osumi, past, present, and forever! My world! And nothing, Mister Amerikan, nothing you can do will ever change it!

The crowds swarmed and swarmed like locusts, many different people, but whoever they were, everyone averted their gaze and parted for his horsemen. The shouts of his guard rang out, the men who ran ahead with their long-bladed *naginata* switched at those who were slow to make way, and constantly the road opened before them. The town people of higher rank bowed or melted away as he passed, none daring to look directly at him, but their fear was shallow and their respect a sham. They were different from the rural peasants; these *chonin* had seen dynasties come and go. Even the young had that air of hard-faced wisdom about them. As if they had witnessed generations of rulers and ruled making what they could of their lives. When it came to it, what was a daimyo's son to them? But soon they would know the name of Hideki Shingo.

He shut his eyes, feeling the familiar smells thrill over him. The Ginza was a hive: a swarm of country peasants—toiling their masters' produce to market; women laboring with baskets on their yokes, or bargaining, or resting or gossiping. The young and the old, the poor and the prosperous, the strong and the weak.

Above the jangling bells of the horses, he heard the

brief sound of the *koto* introducing a public-service call to subjects, a reminder about yoke-tax payments floating out over the city from speakers.

Above them now, first-floor windows. The plain wooden shutters were drawn back. Behind the *shoji* the ranking lady of the Floating World knelt in profile, revealing a single white breast to the aristocrat while willowy, solemn-faced *kamuro* apprentice girls looked on like Siamese cats, pristine in Day-Glo silk. A little farther and there were holy trees, niches carved in them, Shinto idols, and women with a thread of beads looped over their hands, or clapping solemnly for the sake of a barren daughter or a sick father gasping in the meager shade.

There were the inevitable noodle stalls, sellers with their hair bound up like bundles of laundry. Across the road a ruined garden; a disbanded Ikki temple with sparrows twittering in the eaves. A monkey on a balcony and a fallow deer. *Chonin* women squatted behind cloths laid on the ground, laying out whatever they could sell: bunches of wilted leaf vegetable or *daikon* radishes. Here were men wearing *fundoshi* wrapped round their loins, *komuso* monks in blue robes, their heads enclosed in baskets, leaning on staffs, carrying shoulder sacks and flutes: rice sellers and tinkers, merchants and musicians, barbers and copper beaters, craftsmen of all kinds, and town lice—young men hungry-eyed for the opportunities of the street.

Yes, this is the Osumi I know, and the Osumi the Amerikans want to make their own. But I will not let it change. When I am daimyo I shall raise a huge army and destroy those who want to undermine samurai rule. Then we shall return to the great days of Emperor Denko!

They rode on towards the walled citadel, past the bigger houses of the merchant castes. The scum here think themselves superior and sophisticated and show far too little respect, he thought. They grow inappropriately rich by selling to the Amerikans. But that will stop. My father is despicably lenient. I will have no *chonin* in the Palace when I become daimyo. *Chonin* advisers and *chonin* guards and *chonin* raised to be samurai. All will go. The common people must be kept at arm's length or they will grow subversive and want power themselves. After all, does not history warn of that danger?

By the gods, the duty ordained by my nature is to purify the administration of this Quadrant! I shall tax the land and prepare for war. As soon as may be, I shall revoke the Leases of Kanoya and Satsuma, and expel the barbarians. As soon as may be, I shall follow the way of the kamikaze and throw the Kan out of Yamato!

Sonno Joi!

His glance darted to Yasuko's palanquin, and strong feelings began warring inside him again. By the gods, she tears me apart! I love her like a lunatic. I harbor passion and desire for her, but there's something terrible also. What made me hesitate when she leapt upon Haigo Gozaemon? Was it just my sense of self-preservation telling me not to move? And if so, why? Why that instinct at that particular moment? Truly, the gods lead astray whom they will and guide whom they will.

But then the *gaijin* blundered in and spoiled everything. What was it about Yasuko-san that made him jump up in her defense? The bitch! The beautiful, beautiful bitch! Oh, Yasuko-san, what a barbed gift you were from my father. Sometimes a man must accept wives as a matter of statecraft; sometimes they are forced upon him as gifts, or to cement alliances, or to emasculate a threat to the succession. Why were you my father's choice for me?

He closed his eyes again but could not close his ears. There was the constant noise. Vendors calling. Music on the public speakers, babies and bells and the yelping of a skeleton dog. The rumble of cart wheels. The swish of the *naginata*. More hideous music blaring in the distance. A crowd down a side street cheering a quail fight, clapping the twirling movements, another crowd gawping at a heavily wagered game of *shogi*.

He knew where he was, exact to the pace. Here would be the fat-bellied man, and there the old monk with the wisp beard who sat with hundreds of piles of bronze *koban*—local exchange units—built around him and the counting frames clacking in his hands. The call of the public-service speaker grew louder and they were soon passing by the Ebisu shrine and the cluster of temples where there lounged more filthy *komuso* and many, many beggars.

Here the beggars gathered like ticks under the dusty awnings. Did not the Buddha himself renounce riches to go amongst the poor? And how the *hinin* beggars knew it! For them there was refuge only among their many-armed gods of horror. There, crammed into the dark channels between high walls of plasterboard and timber were real living monsters! Not just *hinin* girls who borrowed starved infants to beg with, not just the hundreds of destitute mendicants crowding the steps of the temples and the shrines, but terrible human monsters. These were the lazar house creatures, the human freaks who showed off their fantastic deformities to make a living. There was leprosy on Osumi. On all worlds irradiated by A-type primaries, the mutation rates were naturally high, and when the mass of the population were not entitled to medical adjustments, what else could be the result?

Here was the man with gigantic testicles, like a huge brown pumpkin, that he pushed in a wheelbarrow before him, one leg normal, the other an elephant's; here again the spider-boy in his home crevice with legs and arms twisted up his back as boneless as serpents making his peculiar, leering smile at the world as he had for twenty years. There were the skin-cankered with their worn-down features and hands, blotched with sores but otherwise like newborn pigs, jangling their bowls. And among them, going in rags, such women as those of the casteless *hinin*, who would strangle their daughters and fit their sons for a life of begging by inflicting novel wounds that never ever healed, but jagged sharply at the heart of every passerby. Soft young bones broken and set at pathetic angles were too usual. Blinding was good for pity, also the sores of loathsome designer diseases, that and the application of hot irons to distort the features of the face. There was not a ruse to which some mothers would not stoop to equip their offspring for the ferocious competition of beggarly life. Thank the gods that I was made bodily whole and that I have a mother who makes me the center of her universe, he thought, idolising her. Isako-san is the only one in all the cosmos whom I can trust absolutely. She alone is perfect.

His thoughts turned bleakly to Hideki Ryuji. My father knows how much I want to be daimyo after him, he thought bitterly, yet Sadamasa receives his beneficence because he is firstborn and has the same-shaped face as his father. He should know I will never be satisfied with the parts of continents that are occasionally tossed at me. One day soon he will learn that I am not a cat waiting below a window for fish skins!

On my father's birthday Sadamasa was made his heir and deputy. But me? What of me? He gave me the governorship of Kirishima! Ha! The second city of Osumi, he calls it. Kirishima! I'm Taisho of a fortress built on a bare rock in the remotest southern tip of the planet's major land mass, a miserable system surrounded by jealous, semiautonomous families, a place with a small and insecure income and a reputation for being hard to govern. Kirishima! The place is a joke! An insult! But I shall redress that insult soon. With the gods' help I will create the ideal Bushido state.

Politics is simple. Power always goes to the strongest, to the most ruthless, the cleverest. But how to be all three? Perhaps I should put everything into a lightning dash for power, he thought, excited by the gathering idea. Think of it! If I spent everything I have or could raise from the credit brokers, I'd be able to buy my father's guards. Then a decisive strike against him in the dead of night. And, before anyone discovers what's happening, I melt-down Sadamasa's apartments with a meson device and surround them so that none of his people gets out alive. That would be perfect! My father's throat slit, Sadamasa turned to ashes, and that hag, Chizuru, his mother, burned with him. Absolutely perfect! I'd be daimyo at a stroke. Of course, I'd have to put out Noboru's eyes, and send him to a monastery once Sadamasa is dead, but that would be a minor detail—one to be left until the morning. . . .

He sighed inwardly, reining in his daydream. The reality of such a plan was not so attractive. Undoubtedly word would escape that he had tried to bribe the guard. He would be arrested, or at least forced to flee Miyakonojo. Sadamasa would slander his name, claiming he planned to seize power in the Quadrant in order to tighten the financial grip on the *chonin*. And because of Sadamasa's reputation as a reasonable man, everyone would believe him.

Oh, yes! Then I would have to go to Kirishima. To be holed up there with everyone on the planet against me. Ohhh! I cannot let that happen. What was it the accursed Haigo Gozaemon said? That Sadamasa-san was hawking at Hanaki? Well, if he was I bet he rode like the wind to be in Miyankonojo for the amygdala's arrival. He cannot bear to miss anything, even though this time it will mean witnessing a triumph of mine. I know he was behind Haigo Gozaemon's attempt to steal it.

They had come to the *torii* gate of the Residency. At the sight of it he felt an eagerness in the horse and his own mood lifting. The surrounding wall was black plex, and the gatehouse was tall and elegant, incised with rectangular patterns, and surmounted by two weapons blisters. The main portal itself was open, as was customary on ordinary days, but inside the way led up a steep ramp made of nexus ship skin scored across in deep chevrons to dissuade casual entry by wandering animals. Horses' hooves found purchase impossible until the skin was relaxed. The ramp was deceptive and deadly, a shadowed slaughtering ground. Any human being trying to enter the Residency uninvited would be trapped here as the ramp became a gauntlet bathed in hard radiation. Samurai guards patrolled the interiors with long-barreled *teppo* in hand, each with two swords also, as was the law. Others manned the inner checkpoint. Then a terrifying thought struck him. By the gods, what if there has been a coup while I've been away? What if Sadamasa-san has already made his move? Haven't the past weeks been the most opportune time? By all that's holy, my mother might be dead—or worse, his prisoner. What could I do?

Suddenly the panic rose in him. He searched rapidly for a sign that something was amiss, any clue that there might have been an emergency in his absence, but in every way the Residency of Miyakonojo seemed to be normal and as he had left it. The complex of black plex walls and austere graveled courtyards and halls and pagoda-roofed pavilions were in quiet occupation. Men he recognised as loyal to his father were still to be seen.

At the top of the ramp, outside the entrance to the dai-myo's official suite, Sadamasa-san stepped out from the shadows to meet him. He dismounted, and they faced one another.

"It is late, Shingo-kun."

Behind Sadamasa the residency guard stared sightlessly into space, the blades of their *naginata* glinting in the sun-star light. Sadamasa's face was somber, his eyes liquid. The moustache he wore extended over his cheeks and his sideburns were long and thin, extending to the angle of his jaw. He wore a crimson wing-shouldered *kataginu* over a long-sleeved, turmeric-yellow *kami-shimo* printed with leaf devices. It was loose, fastening across the chest from left to right, and a black sash cut it, taking two corded sword-hilts on the left side. He bowed.

Shingo bowed stiffly. His eyes tripped over his brother's form. Sadamasa was dressed in the same clothes his father had worn the day he had been promoted general in the Shogun's army. He was the image of Hideki Ryuji's favor-ite portrait, and he had dressed this way deliberately today. With the realisation, Hideki Shingo felt the tension be-tween them increase almost beyond endurance. Sadamasa avoided noticing the foreigner.

"Greetings, Sadamasa. You are well?"

"Excellent. And you?"

"Very well, thank you. My father is expecting me?"

"Naturally. We knew you were coming since you left the inn just outside Kin-Su. You will take refreshment?"

Hideki Shingo dismissed the escort, and at a sign from him the palanquin was taken on around the path towards the back of the Residency. The guard's lances parted and they entered the cool shadow of the courtyard, the hooves of the horses clip-clopping. His own led; the Amerikan's, still carrying him, came behind. He ducked his head under the *torii* arch, then he dismounted.

"Make the search thorough," Sadamasa told the guards.

The search revealed the two stolen blasters.

Sadamasa's wariness burgeoned. "Tell him he can't bring them any further. He must relinquish them."

He made no translation, knowing it was unnecessary. The foreigner spoke up, hard-faced now. "These weapons are my property, and it is our custom to go armed."

The words were in reasonably intelligible Japanese, and Sadamasa was surprised at them. "You cannot bring them any further," he said bluntly.

"It is also our custom to accept hospitality in the manner in which it is offered. Therefore, if I am fit to be a guest in your father's Residency, I can be trusted."

"So sorry. I insist that you relinquish the weapons."

"In that case you are insisting that I trust you when you refuse to trust me."

"In my father's Residency, yes."

"It is a point of honor with me to wear my blasters, just as it is for samurai to carry the two swords."

"The guards have orders to disarm everyone—even samurai."

Shingo intervened, sensing a chance to belittle his brother. "Sadamasa-kun, his weapons are not charged. Therefore, they are not quite weapons."

"Even so—"

But the foreigner shook his head, took out one blaster, set it to maximum, and pointed it into the air. He fired it in a long draining burst, then did the same with the second. And the smile on his face as he did so was so insolent and so self-satisfied as to be almost beyond belief.

22

The horses in the courtyard had been startled. A cloud of doves had risen up from the rooftops as the echoes of the beam weapons died away. Then, at Sadamasa's orders, the guards seized the foreigner and wrestled him to the ground.

An interesting spectacle to watch, the man at the open gallery thought. The view from the second floor had been clear, and the *gaijin* prophesied by Goro's *tayori* was indeed as arrogant and difficult as could be imagined.

"Oh, Sadamasa-san, my firstborn son," he said. "You will have to learn to understand and deal cleverly with the Amerikan mind before I can allow you to have Kyushu."

He had spoken his thoughts aloud, yet softly as if to himself. The austere hall behind him contained a dozen of his *fudai*, the inner circle—his closest generals, all of them within earshot. All of them had heard his words, but not one of them would dare admit it, for he was Hideki Ryuji, onetime General of the Shogun, and now Prefect of the Quadrant of Kyushu, the virtually independent ruler of nine provincial capitals and three associated territories, over twenty major nexus systems—and his word was life and death on all those worlds.

He summoned Goro, his *hisho*, his personal secretary, who knelt and bowed.

"My son and his guest will wait. Tell them they have

ample time to bathe and dress and partake of food before I shall require them. But have my daughter-in-law brought here at once.''

The *hisho,* a tall solemn-faced man, rose and backed away three paces before straightening and turning.

As his will was done, Hideki Ryuji smoothed the tip of his graying beard. He was fifty, a dainty man, slim and elfin, with sharp features and deep, soulful eyes. His skin was black-tea dark, his surcoat jonquil yellow. Everything about him was neat and quick. Intelligence shone from him. He wore, as did all the men present, the neatly oiled and tied topknot doubled back over his shaven pate. On his back, the *haori,* a loose jacket gathered at the waist by a sash, similar to the one Sadamasa wore, except that it lacked the stiffened shoulders. None of the men present carried swords in their sashes. The weapons were racked and guarded elsewhere.

Ryuji watched the gangling *hisho* go down the hall, his baggy leggings rustling. Being born of *chonin* parents, he never wore swords. It's just as well, he thought. He lacks proper bearing.

The audience hall was long and airy and built to take all the Hideki samurai and their allies in time of tension. It was raised in massive polished carpentry, flanked along one entire side by a huge painting of a river scene executed on silk. Along the opposite wall five windows admitted light. Each was cut perfectly square and latticed by a simple cedar wood grille. They transmitted the harsh A0-type light outside with a milky translucence. Along the opposite side, the lofty vaulted ceiling was supported by wooden beams, standing on pillars. The roofs were tiled in mock fish-scale slates, with wide eaves opening out onto a small, inner courtyard designed to allow the free passage of cooling breezes across the hall. Goro-san disappeared as he descended a flight of steps that split the hall, and reappeared as he walked towards the main entrance at the far end. It was guarded by two men and led into the outer apartments.

Ryuji thanked the god Marishi-ten for the *hisho* who was more than just a *hisho*. Goro-san was more even than a general at times. He was a consummate assistant, one of those rare men who possessed a gift from the gods. He was a grand master of an ancient science, a master of *tayori*, and therefore utterly priceless.

Tayori was precious. Crucial. Essential. The whole Empire ran on *tayori*. Across all Yamato, it was mixed with mothers' milk, yet it could feed the maw of government. It had the power to nourish, to placate or terrify high officials and the common people alike. *Tayori* could entertain and inform and educate. *Tayori* was the most efficient way to communicate; it moved subtly, yet faster than the speed of light, and it was always passed on the very best authority. No Imperial *horei*, or decree, could match the respect it commanded. It could proclaim or prophesy or vilify magnificently, and destroy the reputation of years in a single day.

Tayori raced in the pulse of the people. It was a currency more powerful than Amerikan credit. It reached everyone and, like credit, passed through the hands of everyone. Like credit it could be base plex or shining aurium. It could be worn down or dirtied or bent or twisted or adulterated or traded—but never hoarded, for *tayori* was alive, and it lived only so long as it was transacted. Those like Goro-san who knew how to orchestrate and to broadcast and to interpret *tayori* were jewels, for *tayori* was indispensable to a ruler. *Tayori* was propaganda, rumor, gossip, hearsay, information, and the nugget at its heart could be the truth, or it could be the kind of lie that revealed the desire of the people.

Goro-san had reaped the awesome *tayori* about the

amygdala and the joyful *tayori* that Haigo Gozaemon was dead. At first hearing, Ryuji had been distraught that the secret was abroad, but then Goro-san had lifted a bony hand and there had been shrewdness embedded in that cadaverous face.

He said that the knowledge had been taken by a fortune-teller from a scout who had sold it on to a pilgrim who knew a noodle seller who owed a favor to a friend who had ridden hard from Haraki to see his brother who was a Residency guard who had divulged it to a lady's maid to whom Goro-san often listened.

Ryuji had sat patiently while the *hisho* unraveled what he had heard, and finally he had discovered that the nuggets were nuggets of truth: Haigo Gozaemon was indeed dead. The amygdala was indeed coming to Miyakonojo, and moreover, it was in the hands of a *gaijin*, the same man who had killed the *hatamochi*. There had been a planetfall wreck of some kind, but the details of that were unclear.

"Our ship of state plunges unprepared into the nexus," he had whispered to Goro-san, fearing the downfall of his plans. "Don't you agree? If the knowledge of the amygdala is out, we are in danger."

But Goro had dared to give him a different opinion. He alone had that knack, to speak his true heart and mind to the Prefect of the Quadrant without fear of reprisal. To the learned and disinterested Goro the deceits of Miyakonojo were merely an academic mind-game—a game of *go*—and his own purpose was the accurate fathoming of them for his uniquely wise master. He had squeezed his hands, the bulbous joints of his fingers cracking. "Forgive me, Lord, but you are wrong. There is another way. . . ."

Hideki Ryuji had listened and stood up and paced the hall and, finally convinced, he had sanctioned Goro-san to operate on the rumor delicately and pass it back down among the people. In half a morning the Ginza had been buzzing with it: an embroidered story of murder and nexus-wreck and war, and magic—especially magic. How quickly the geisha would seize such ideas! Yes, and itinerant Kabuki actors would surely step out the story in a hundred evening gatherings throughout Kyushu within a month or two. And those who saw would love to add their own personal embellishments to what was in fact a perfectly simple tale!

It would be as if an entire campaign of disinformation had been ordered:

"Oh, wait till you hear this . . ."

"My dove, you will never believe it, but . . ."

"Listen! Have I told you about . . .?"

"Promise you will not say a thing and . . ."

"I have it on the very best authority that . . ."

Ryuji smiled inside. Without doubt, what is known today in the Ginza at Miyakonojo will be known tomorrow in all the Ginzas on Edo. The question of the Shogun's succession will suddenly be on everyone's lips, and the name of Hideki Ryuji will be linked to it. The Shogun, Sakuma Hidenaga, is growing infirm and soon he must die, for how much longer can an old man such as he live? There will be a power vacuum in Yamato. There will have to be, because Sakuma Hidenaga has held on to power by force of arms and then by craft and then by magic.

For too many years Sakuma Hidenaga has depended on the *kensei no katana*, the Master's Sword, second only in reverence for samurai to the Emperor's own sword on Kyoto. With it he has kept the samurai of Edo in awe for years, but now also the cynical *chonin* of the population centers of our industrial worlds, the surly *doso* class of merchants, and the other lower classes see him as their rightful master, too, because of the amygdala bound into its hilt. The magnificent jewel of power is reputed to confer the ability to read men's thoughts to the owner. All he must do is touch it to his forehead. Who knows if it is true? But if it is, how perfect a tool for getting and then keeping political power.

A potent jewel indeed, and also an influence over the mass of the people who believe that all inanimate objects are imbued with a "spirit"—which at the lower levels comes down to a debased belief that billions of invisible *kami* infest the material cosmos.

But the *kami* hiding in the Shogun's amygdala was supposed to be a jealous and vengeful sprite—cursed so that any ordinary man attempting to use it will die. Therefore, how can Sakuma Hidenaga rule, they reason, unless it is the will of the gods, and unless all the gods agree?

More informed opinion supposes the amygdala to be a very large chrysoid. One that has reached such a point of complexity that it has itself become psi-active. That its fields are dangerous and liable to lead to insanity in anyone whose own psi talent is insufficient.

Whatever it is, it's perfect for Sakuma Hidenaga! The lower people believe in the legitimacy of this man whom the amygdala's malign power cannot touch. Because of this, the daimyo of Honshu Quadrant pay punctual tribute and will not clash with him. Potential usurpers have been intimidated by the amygdala's baleful stare for years. It's an incredible stroke of political consolidation, but perhaps not quite perfect, because even Sakuma Hidenaga cannot live forever.

No, not forever . . .

Hideki Ryuji stirred, knowing that, irrevocably, he had made his move. The question was already being asked in high circles: "Who has the power to hold the *kensei no katana* when Sakuma Hidenaga dies?" And because no one could yet answer, fear was starting to grow.

Hideki Ryuji looked down the hall and nodded with satisfaction. The sweepers had kept the lower floor shining and spotless, as was his pleasure. It was important for a ruler to behave as a ruler and to appear to occupy a station midway between earth and heaven. For this, cleanliness and minute attention to the details of housekeeping were essential.

The hall was a marvel of subtle intimidation. To approach the dais, the *gaijin* would have to walk the length of the room. He would appreciate the symbolism of the pair of exquisite dragon fountains, for is not water significant in all philosophies? And is not its life-giving virtue understood by all men who have known thirst and the dust of battle? Because he is a *gaijin* he will certainly notice the gold *koban* coins scattered casually in the fountain. They respect wealth, these traders, these *beikokujin,* these People of the Rice Bowl. They are *doso,* merchants, at heart. All of them.

After the fountains, the *gaijin* would have to mount the eightfold steps, to the upper court where the floor planks were sheening with fierce light. Here was a geometry of wood that caught the light and returned it to the eye in a breathtaking way. The effect was designed to stun those who ascended, and so stunned he would pass by the *tozama* vassals and be scrutinised by them as he passed them. He would see their seriousness, and if that did not unsettle him, then there was Shirokuma, the hugely obese sumo exponent, who guarded the inner apartments with a permanently drawn *daito* and the stare of an executioner.

So, exquisitely, the meeting would lay low the hauteur of any petitioner who came here. It would ring every note in the scale of his emotions from trepidation to awe, until finally he would approach the dais, the simply adorned dais that symbolised a Prefect's authority. It was an impressive throne, with its highest-grade tatami and the real slow-

growing elm wood brought from the palaces of Kagoshima
when they were razed.

Kagoshima had been the Kyushu capital world throughout the Twenty-second and Twenty-third centuries of the
Amerikan reckoning. Kyushu, a realm perhaps fifty times
greater than Old Earth, occupying almost a tenth the volume of Yamato. As with all quadrants, a shift of capital
world had been made necessary by the relentless expansion
of Known Space into the Beyond, and the world orbiting
the A2-type star known to the Amerikans as Alpha CrA
had, two generations ago, given up its preeminent status
to another world 176 light-years farther from the origin of
Old Earth. At that time this new world had newly emerged
from the thirty-year settlement moratorium imposed by the
terraformers and it had been a brash new place full of
soilmakers and sulphur smells and still suffering violent
quakes.

Oh, yes, he thought, Osumi has developed over the
128 years of its heritage. It has changed greatly in three
generations of habitation, and this palace is the envy of
the sector.

The Amerikan is young, and he will surely be overawed.
And that is before the entertainments of the night begin.
With music and food and sake and seeing the eroticism of
my geisha, he will perhaps forget the price I have already
agreed to pay for his amygdala. And if that does not persuade him, perhaps a bribe of aurium and safe passage to
Seoul or the Amerikan Boundary will do it.

He felt a twinge of conscience. Bargaining with a *gaijin*
like a common merchant was not the function of a samurai,
and it was unthinkable to go back on a promise. But the
latest news out of Kanoya City had changed everything.

I have more than enough to occupy me here, he thought.
Squabbling wives and contending sons are tiresome. I have
too little time to muster my armies. How can I concentrate

on affairs of state? How can I deal with the main problem of how to wrestle the shogunate out of Sakuma Hidenaga's failing grasp? That's impossible if I am dealing with troublesome foreigners. Kan and Amerikan scuffling like children. I don't need distractions.

Hideki Ryuji returned to his dais majestically, and his generals knelt before him. They were his most closely bound allies, these hereditary *fudai,* his inner council of advisers, commanded by the number-one vassal, the *shukun*. The *fudai* included his sons and the others of his blood, the *ichizoku-shu,* whom he certainly trusted less than those men from families bound to his own by samurai traditions alone.

The closer the blood tie, the more acute the jealousy, he thought. It's foolish to trust anyone without a very good reason; to trust one's own blood can be suicide. Beyond the inner came the outer vassals, the *tozama,* daimyo from the other major systems of Kyushu. The other eight capitals were Satsuma, Hyuga and Bungo, Higo, Buzen and Chikuzen, Hizen and Chikugō. The men that ruled them had been chosen by him, and raised to their positions. They were mostly born samurai, but there were also men whose mothers—generally successful ladies of the Floating World—had bought their sons into the samurai class as children. These he regarded highly because their loyalty to him was uniformly certain. Others of the *tozama* were only controlled by a combination of hostage-holding and power bribery. These men would go their own way or have his head on a viewing table the moment they thought they could.

He looked at the faces that were ranked before him and he felt a sudden tiredness, a revulsion. It was crystallised in his mind as a strong yearning to go to Edo to attend the white chrysanthemum viewing.

One day soon I shall visit Edo again, he thought, getting

hold of himself. And it will be for a purpose more important than flower viewing!

He dismissed them with a single gesture, rose, and went into an anteroom. He sent his page on an errand, and sat down to wait for Yasuko alone.

23

Yasuko had allowed her two *jochu*, ladies' maids, to take off her undergarments in readiness to bathe. The main *furo* of the Residency was long and shallowly stepped and pleasantly set with sprays of flowers. It was cloistered and opened to the sky two stories above and catered to the *ichizoku-shu* of both sexes. Now it was empty of other female bathers, which was unexpected.

Yasuko was popular with her "sisters" and they had welcomed her back, wanting so much to ask her about the places offworld she had seen, but no one had followed her to the bathhouse. It's Isako-san's doing, she thought. Bathing in Lake Biwa itself could not purify that woman. She never stops arranging and interfering, and now it seems she's intent on hearing everything firsthand before anyone else.

Curls of steam came off the surface. She put her feet into the scalding water, pleased to have the chance to be alone with her two adoring *jochu*, to settle her thoughts and readjust to the ordered world of the Residency. Her two hundred "sisters" would be full of all kinds of wild *tayori*, none of it approximating to the truth—which was even stranger. Only one thing could have stopped them from following her to the bathhouse—a command by the queen bee herself.

Isako-san, number-one wife of Ryuji-sama, mother of Shingo-san and therefore her mother-in-law. She was the principal domestic power within the Residency, the one to whom all the women owed deference, even if they could not afford her respect. Her nearest rival was the equally proud, equally unforgiving Chizuru-san, mother of Ryuji-sama's firstborn, but only his second wife. There had been bare days between the births of Sadamasa-san and Shingo-san; even so, it had never moved Ryuji-sama that Isako-san claimed constantly that though her own son was second-born, he was nevertheless first-sired.

Yasuko cautioned herself that the politics of the Residency could not be ignored and reminded herself that much of consequence might have passed in her absence.

''What was it like, Honorable Lady?'' Sukiko, the younger *jochu*, asked her breathlessly. She was fourteen and wide-eyed.

Yasuko waded into the bath until she stood thigh deep, her golden skin desiring the touch of hot water after the stale airlessness of the *kago*. Against the turquoise and lapis lazuli of the bath, her body was like burnished bronze. Her long hair was tied up and pinned and she had shed her robe. There was only a silver anklet worn after the Hizen fashion—silver as a mark of respect to the goddess Tsuki-Yomi, Goddess of Moons, who did not approve of any other precious metal worn below the waist.

''What was what like, Sukiko-chan?'' she asked, using the affectionate form of address.

Sukiko's excitement overflowed. ''Kagoshima, of course! And going through the nexus hole!''

"Like diving straight into this bath," she said, smiling back. "Like diving in, but diving out again straightaway."

"Oh, Lady! How can that be? Weren't you terribly afraid?"

"I was at first."

"They say you were wrecked in a typhoon when you tried to land," Niso, the elder *jochu*, asked her, her eyes full of concern. "Now tell me: is that true?"

"Oh, you shouldn't listen to loose *tayori*, Bu-chan. You'll only upset yourself."

Niso was ten years older than she and was her oldest friend and companion. She had come with her to this world after Yasuko had been sent to Edo to marry. That had been ten years ago, when Yasuko was twelve. Niso was plump—Yasuko had given her the affectionate nickname of Bu-chan—and plain and childless, and the only time her pleasantly radiant nature showed any sign of cooling was when she thought her Yasuko-chan was not taking proper care of herself.

"I was very worried for you."

"And I missed you, too." She smiled again, broadly.

"Now, now, Lady Yasuko, you know that is not what I said."

Yasuko bent her knees and immersed herself, delighting in the burn of hot water over her back and belly and breasts.

"So you didn't miss me, hey?" she said, mock severity on her face.

"Of course I missed you. But I was very worried all the same."

"You're so beautiful, Lady," Sukiko said as her mistress stood up. "So graceful. You rise from the waters like a goddess."

Yasuko tweaked her nose playfully. "You're so kind."

"Oh, but I wish I had breasts too."

"They will grow. In time."

"In time for what, Lady?"

"In time for you to marry."

"Oh, I hope so!" She twisted about and put out her hand to stroke Yasuko's belly below her navel. Water coursed into the dark luxuriance of sable.

"Lady?"

"Yes?"

"Lady, why don't you shave down there, like the others?"

Yasuko answered her patiently. "Because, Sukiko-chan, I don't like the itching when the hair starts to grow again."

"Ugh! Does it itch?" She frowned. "Doesn't Shingo-sama object?"

"Why should he? This is how the gods intended a woman to be, not smooth and bare!"

"But doesn't Shingo-sama get the hairs stuck in his—"

"Sukiko! You ask too many questions, you horrid girl! Now go away with your silly chatter, and bring my best kimono. I want to put on something clean and light tonight."

She shooed her and splashed water and the *jochu*'s screams went echoing up as she fled from the bath. Then Yasuko laughed and turned to Niso, half-serious now. "It's good to be back, Niso-san. How was she?"

Niso-san understood. She made a face, meaning that Isako-san had been no more unpleasant than usual. She could have made it vastly uncomfortable for Yasuko's two *jochu* in her absence—especially Sukiko-san.

"You're sure?"

Niso was brisk. "Oh, don't trouble yourself about us. We know how to stand up to that old dragon."

"Yes. Please scrub my back for me."

As she scrubbed, Niso spoke softly, her mouth close to Yasuko's ear. "You should know what's been happening while you've been away."

"A good deal, I imagine."

"Yes. Too much. But that can wait. What can't is that Sadamasa-sama expects reprisals."

"You mean in revenge for sending the *hatamochi* to find us?"

"That was Chizuru-san's doing. I don't like it, Yasuko. There's something happening. That monstrous witch would do anything to get at Shingo-sama; maybe they will try to get at him through you. Yesterday, Hatsuko was listening at the curtain, and she heard—" There was a familiar rustling of silk, and suddenly Niso's face changed. Yasuko turned and saw that the Lady Isako had appeared, and behind her, silent as ever, the enormous fleshy bulk of the sumo champion, Shirokuma.

Isako's rustling approach terrified most of the women, though she was slight of build and dainty. Her eyes were very dark, the brows being heavily emphasised with black, and her lips were painted bloodred, but the whole of the rest of her face was astonishingly white. When she smiled, which was seldom, the joints of her teeth were seen to be lined with black, and she almost always kept her waist-length graying hair braided and hidden inside a formal wig. Today she wore a fine gold silk kimono, held in place by a starch-white obi, while the lapels of her undergarment showed white around her neck, and white *tabi* socks and high-block *geta* to complete the effect. They clacked now on the tiling as she approached.

"Yasuko-chan. How are you? I believe you had an arduous journey?"

"Yes, honored mother-in-law. It was a little tiring."

"Well, you shall tell me all about it."

"Of course. I've almost finished bathing."

The older woman inclined her head, sensitive to any hint of insubordination. "Your bathing will have to wait. Come out."

"I beg your pardon, Lady?"

"I said you're to come out of there now."

"I'll dry myself," Yasuko's voice remained honey-smooth. She lifted her arms and allowed Niso to wind a huge Amerikan towel around her body like a sheath.

"You'd better hurry, child."

"Yes, Isako-san." She stayed knee-deep in the water as Niso dabbed at her skin.

Isako-san's chin lifted. "My dear, if it were up to me you could stay in the bathhouse all day and all night. It is the Prefect of Kyushu who has summoned you. You are to attend him immediately."

Yasuko stepped out of the water. She dried herself and dressed with care, hardly aware of three elderly men of the Hideki clan who were seated on stools at the far end chatting and soaping themselves. She was more aware of Shirokuma's presence and his enigmatic stare, but untroubled by it.

As she followed him she wondered what such a look could mean. What thoughts went through a sumo wrestler's mind when he saw the ladies undress and go naked in the bathhouse? She felt a sudden great compassion. Of course, he had nothing in his head except wrestling. Everything in his life had been devoted to that, so there was nothing to feel sorry about.

Was that why Shirokuma and so many of the other sumo men were so huge? Because their energies had never been spent on women? Or was it the hormones they used to gain such prodigious size? The majority of this elite corps were

great sexless creatures who only thought about marriage
at the end of their competitive careers, and none more so
than their current champion. His life was limited to eight
hours a day at the training dojo, and ceremonial duties
for Lord Hideki. Sumo men were so impressive! Massive
thighs, massive upper arms, pudgy hands and feet, their
heads and necks and chins were clothed with flesh. Shirokuma's breasts were huge, hanging down over his big belly
like the goatskin sacks of a *hinin* water carrier. Pounds of
flesh hung from him; even his nipples were flattened into
ovals.

"What does he want, Shirokuma-san?"

"I don't know that, Lady."

"Is he alone?"

"He is."

If he's alone, then he's thinking, she thought. "Has he
been alone long?"

"Yes. And he has ordered *sake* for two."

She smiled at Shirokuma, liking him. Those breasts
curved round under his arms and hung in folds. Because
of the drugs his moustache was just an eyebrow wisp, his
voice high and fluting. But what of his desire? Did he,
hidden deep inside, have the fire of a man? What a terrible
thought: to have the fire, but never to have the chance to
quench it. A terrible thought! Far better to believe that
Shirokuma was no more than a thirty-year-old boy!

But that look he had given her as she dressed in fine silk,
that had not been the look of a boy for whom everything is
to come. It had been the special look of a sumo wrestler
whose days at the dojo are numbered, the lingering,
locked-away look of a boy-man emerging into a drug-
delayed adolescence.

As she followed him she made a conscious effort to
cheer her thoughts. Now I know not to wager credit on

Shirokuma's remaining champion for another year. See what you discover when you keep your eyes open! She smiled inwardly at the absurdly exaggerated roll of Shirokuma's gait. She listened to the way his legs rubbed together as he swayed into his steps. Undeniably there was a grace about him that was like the grace of an elephant, and though his sword was constantly in his hand, he had always seemed to her a gentle person. A devil in her couldn't help imagining him squatting like a woman to relieve himself. What must it be like? How did he function inside all that fat? Was there difficulty reaching his *dankon*?

Shirokuma took the ion key from his belt and unlocked an unobtrusive panel veneered in cedarwood; it was clear that, underneath, the portal was armored in plex. It led into a narrow corridor sixty paces long that communicated with the Prefect's private rooms, a passage most often used when Hideki-sama wanted to keep a meeting from being generally known amongst the *tozama*. At the far end of the passage was another door. As Shirokuma slid it open, Yasuko waited, reluctantly disciplining her mind to dwell on the coming interview.

24

"Ah, Yasuko-san! Come. Come."

She emerged from the doorway from the women's quarters and approached the center of the room.

"Lord Hideki."

"Come. Sit here by me."

The plain tatami matting was smooth under her socks. She knelt comfortably and clasped her hands in front of her attentively.

"Please excuse my lateness, and my appearance, Lord, but I was bathing when your order came to me."

Hideki Ryuji looked at her appreciatively for a moment. He wrote one more column of *kanji* on a sheet and stamped it with an ivory chop before laying the order aside.

"You may be at ease, my daughter-in-law."

"Thank you, revered father-in-law."

She complied with the order silently. Although it was usual for her to show a relaxed face to female members of the Hideki clan, and occasionally to their chosen guests, she felt particularly naked under the daimyo's eye. Now, she knew, he wanted her to relax so he could gauge the truth of what she told him.

"The journey on which I sent you did not go as smoothly as I had wished," he said.

"No, revered father-in-law, it did not."

"My prayers were constant. Tell me what happened."

She told him about the voyage to Kagoshima in detail, leaving out nothing of importance, and finished unhesitatingly on a warning. "Twice your son came perilously close to death, revered father-in-law. First a storm nearly killed him on landing, and then there was almost an attempt on his life by Gozaemon-san. It is my husband's belief that his brother, your first son, Sadamasa-sama, ordered his slaying."

"Soooh . . ." Hideki Ryuji said neutrally, watching her closely. "The caprice of the gods. Is that not so?"

She met his eye fearlessly, but still respectfully. "I think that the storm was because of the gods, for what else can a storm be? I believe it was inevitable that Kan ships would come and that it was our karma to be forced down from the Amerikan ship. It was also our fate that we would make a troubled planetfall. However, revered father-in-law, I do not believe Gozaemon-san was motivated by the gods. Perhaps it was his karma that he died, but he was sent by someone mortal.''

Hideki Ryuji stroked his beard thoughtfully. ''You said it was the *gaijin*, Hayden Straker, who killed him?''

''He and I both.''

''And do you believe as you say Shingo-san believes? That Sadamasa-san paid the *hatamochi* to kill him?''

''No, revered father-in-law. I believe Chizuru-san may have alerted him to the existence of the amygdala, but I think the rest was Gozaemon-san's own greed. He wanted to take the amygdala for himself, for its credit value in the Neutral Zone.''

He grunted. ''Then he deserved to die. Both you and the *gaijin* are therefore absolved of his killing.''

''Thank you, revered father-in-law.''

It was a formality, but Ryuji-sama, she knew, liked to be scrupulously neat when it came to his duty as lawkeeper. That's what makes him so able an administrator, she thought. Attention to details. That's why, if it is his karma, he will make an able successor to the Shogun.

''Now,'' he said, deliberately testing her. ''Tell me about the amygdala and about the *gaijin*. And tell me what you think Shingo-san has in mind.''

As a subject, Yasuko owed loyalty to the Empire, which meant to the daimyo personally. As a wife she owed loyalty to her husband. For Yasuko there could never be any question of which loyalty would take precedence. She took a deep breath.

''Of those three questions, revered father-in-law, the

last is the most urgent. Ever since you appointed Sadam-asa-sama as your successor, my husband's aim has been to kill him. I believe he will soon make a serious assassination attempt, and if he does he will have to include Sadamasa-sama's mother and also . . ."

"And also?"

"And also yourself, revered father-in-law."

Hideki Ryuji continued to stroke his beard, his eyes liquid. He had chosen Yasuko-san as Shingo-san's wife, and he had chosen well. Shingo-san had been a volatile youth, petulant and unstable and dangerously obsessed with the pursuit of power. He needed to be circumvented by a series of strategies, and one of them was the little dark-eyed girl he had brought down from Edo.

"How soon is soon?"

"Perhaps seven days. I believe he desires revenge as soon as possible. If you allow him to remain in the Miyako-nojo Residency longer than a week, he will have set in place everything he requires."

"How will he strike?"

She stated her predictions as dispassionately as possible, but he saw she was full of disgust at the duty he had given her.

"First he will begin to look for excuses to send Isako-san to Hanaki. I expect he will make attempts to corrupt your treasury officials. That is the only way he will be able to raise sufficient credit to suborn a large enough portion of your guard. After that I cannot say."

"Then you suggest I send him away?"

"Temporarily, yes, revered father-in-law. On any pre-text whatsoever, so long as he is far away from Sadamasa and yourself."

Is she saying that because she's developed a taste for travel? he wondered. Or maybe she's under her own pressures in Miyakonojo. How much trouble is Isako-san giving her? Or perhaps she means I should send Shingo-san somewhere alone? She's been exposed to him constantly for a month without respite, without the salve of other women's company. That's not good for any wife, let alone one who has otherwise remained in the capital since her wedding.

"And the amygdala?" he asked suddenly.

She fidgeted uncomfortably. "Perhaps that is more difficult. I assume, from the way the common people reacted when our column passed through the town, that the secret is a secret no longer."

He made an affirmative gesture, delighted by her sharpness. She had a way of offering more than was asked of her, and making the unwary give more than they wanted to give, but this time he indulged her. "Yes. You're quite right. Goro-san has released the story. You can assume that everyone of any importance on Osumi knows about the new amygdala and its power to counteract the power of the Shogun's sword jewel."

"In that case, you have announced your candidature. There will be a stir in Edo, and unless you desire to incur the wrath of Sakuma Hidenaga-sama you should keep your head low. It is said that the Shogun has a short way with threats to his authority. If I were you, I should wait and let the immediate consequences blow over. The seed has been planted, and it may be watered to spring up at any time in the future. If I were you, I would not involve myself in a power struggle with Sakuma Hidenaga's probable successors yet. I would wait until after he's dead."

He stared at her hard, confounded as always by the presumption in her voice, but liking—as always—the candidness and the perception of her answers.

"You would?"

"Yes, revered father-in-law. I would. That is . . . if I were you. Please excuse me."

She blushed, and he let it pass.

"The *gaijin*," he said, knowing he must summon the man soon. "Tell me about him."

As she spoke, he listened to her and watched her closely and he saw that she was telling him many things that were mere facts and that her true heart was shrouded from him. Therefore he only half listened and soon, sighingly, began instead to contemplate his son. Shingo-san was a dangerous fool. His hero was Denko, the last unquestionably great Emperor to occupy the Imperial Palace on Kyoto. Like Denko, Shingo-san would turn away from the wise accommodations that the Great Yaemon had reached with the low classes. Like Denko, Shingo-san would reimpose a breathing tax on *hinin*, he would expel the Amerikans whose trade made so much revenue for Kyushu, and he would purge the whole of Yamato with *kempei* and other vile secret police. If Shingo-san ever became daimyo of Osumi, there would be a bloody war that would start with an orgy of anti-Amerikanism and culminate in the destruction of Kyushu as a de facto independent fief.

He brought his mind back to Yasuko-san as she tried her best to describe to a lord who was not listening to her the motives of the foreigner, Hayden Straker. Can it really be worth destroying this fine, intelligent, excellent young woman just to cage Shingo-san? he asked himself regretfully. What a pity she has turned out this way. If I had known that twelve years ago I would have left her on Edo, or married her myself.

As he listened without seeming to listen, his mind ranged over his problems. What to do about the despicable foreigners and their irritating brawl? Didn't they know that his army, once raised, could crush them all out of existence as easily as a tiger could crush a pair of quarreling rats?

And what to tell the foreigner about Kanoya City? Should he be allowed to know that it had fallen to the Chinese and that the Amerikans were no longer a presence in Yamato? Sooner or later, Hayden Straker would have to know the truth.

So why not sooner?

It would certainly make the astonishing new amygdala cheaper, and it might just solve everything.

25

It was early, and the long shadows of MeTraCor's looted offices were thrown across the devastated fort. What the Kan had done, first with their white-hot bombardment and then with their occupation, had been ruinous. Now they had physically holed the dome as a precaution. There would be no more resistance.

Ellis surveyed it: blocks had been torn down, windows gaped, fissures and holes brutalised the surface-ways and the great buildings. The random rain of destruction was revealed in slanting daylight that picked out the blasted crete and tangled debris on the parade ground. Here an ironically tilted eagle motif, there a decorative tree burned neatly in two, its torn-down half drooping and browning on the skidwalk, its remaining half still thrusting up from the blackened trunk, unbalanced like one arm of a wishbone. And in Ginza Plaza—a stench powerful beyond belief!—where the foul water conduits had been ruptured, and their outflow splattered across a civic lawn, already crusted and flyblown in the shimmering heat.

Next to Jos Hawken's tower the Adventer cathedral. The skid was covered in thousands of diamonds and rubies and emeralds and sapphires and amber, and yet, miraculously intact, the beatific face of St. Anthony dangled, surrounded by a halo and surrounded again by a ragged gray snake of plex former where the stained-glass window had been shattered out of its gothic frame by intense heat.

Amid the counterfeit gems silent squaddies switched at flies, and down the street a pack of native *hinin* urchins had come out from somewhere and were rummaging through the contents of a building that had been burst out by one of the bigger blasts; hardcopy like ticker tape and thousands of datareels, the records of trade, their copper gleaming surfaces chaosed by the blast and warping under the merciless heat. There, too, were clothes and furniture and a great stock of priceless Satsuma china and a little girl's dolly talking grotesquely to itself in baby-language as two of the *hinin* children watched it gravely.

Ellis Straker's jacket was new, his cataplasm gone at last from a scarless pate covered now by his astrogator's cap—the one trimmed with his Order. The clasps on his shoes shone like blue silver.

Ah, you look as fine as old Ayrton Rodrigo did when he set you on the road to fortune, he thought fondly, remembering the Libertyman astrogator who had first shown him how to get across his talent and showed him the way to psi.

By psi, my wealth may be temporarily in abeyance, but I've still got my talent, and the same brain in my head I've always had. Yeah! 'Bout time to get serious here.

He rubbed his hands together vigorously, the incredible news that had come to him last night still ringing inside him. Nothing could blight the day now. Nothing. But his instinct told him to lock the knowledge away for now, tight in the back of his mind, and give nothing away about what he had been told.

The golden dragon emblem of the Dowager rippled on the underside of the dome as he looked up. One big round hole the size of a zingball alley had already been cut in it, and monads with meson gear were working away on the shield field gens. He spat in the crete dust and deliberately took the spring out of his step in preparation for putting his mind on more serious matters. Then he looked up at NeXt-UT Spire—''Home of Narwhal Brand''—and saw the damage inflicted to a building that had been inspired by the junk-revival Dai Ichi Tower on New New York. He grunted to himself. I must be one of the few people on Osumi who knows how to read an ancient clock dial. One of the few people anywhere—'cept the fool architect who dreamed it up. Fact is, the pointers of MeTraCor's dumb-ass clock are six hours adrift.

They were forked skyward where a Kan beam had melted their mechanism at five minutes before one, the infamous moment of Controller Pope's surrender.

Shit! he thought, instantly rancorous again at the cowardly act of the Controller. Ah, by psi, Pope waits until I'm all tied up with a mutiny, then she gets right on the hummer to Hu Tsung and invites the sonofabitch in by the front door! Ellis closed one eye and pinched finger and thumb delicately on his cheroot, dragging the smoke into his mouth. The stub was all the tobako he had left. It was dry and tainted and not substantial enough to enjoy, so he flicked it ahead and trod on it. Ah! You're a pathetic turd, Pope. I told you the Kan'd disgrace you.

Maybe I should've said they'd whip your bare ass through the skidways with a plex disc on your neck like they do to their own common criminals. Maybe that would've changed your mind, you vain piece of shit. Hot damn! If only you'd had the spine to hold out a day or two more.

He recalled what Barb Eastman had told him. He had been in the Controller's office when Dzernic told Pope about the mutiny. According to Eastman, Pope had listened silently to Dzernic's report of the rapes and killings, but then in a fury over the justice meted out to the offenders.

"He did what, the heavy-handed bastard? By the One God, Straker has no right to discipline MeTraCor people. If he's killed them, that's murder! Don't you see? When the rest of the garrison hears—as they sure as hell will—they'll mutiny too. They'll turn on him, and then on us! He's out of his mind with all this talk of Commodore Vaile's squadron and resisting at all costs. You know what that means? Our lives!"

Apparently, Pope had decided to skunk-out there and then. "To save further bloodshed," so she had said, broadcasting to the whole of Kanoya.

"I spoke out, but I couldn't stop them," Eastman had said bitterly.

"You did what you could. And that's all."

Now a jag of loathing lodged in his guts and he belched acidly. That disgrace had been three nights ago, and the victorious Kan had marched in the following morning, engines roaring, tokens waving and their colors lighting up the dome. Two thousand grinning Shantung troops, quilts belted tight and proud as samurai, and MeTraCor and its chief representative shown the worst kind of face-loser in front of everyone. Pope and Dzernic were both made to kowtow, then stripped and flayed with willow switches all the way down Main Skid. The kind of treatment that doesn't leave a hell of a lot of dignity to an individual—but serve the assholes right for selling us out!

Ellis rode one of the few functioning skidbelts up to the city's ramparts broodingly, a macro in his hand. His own parole was still good, giving him the freedom of the city, and lunch with the Kan admiral was in prospect. The sentries left him alone as he made his way along the runways to the place where four days ago he had shown his front-line people how to customise a bog-standard Dahlgren beam weapon into something the Kan ships would fear to overfly. "Their vessels're plex-hulled, same as ours, see?" he had told them. "We'll give them a bolt out of the blue to keep them orbiting at a respectful distance."

He had opened the guns and shown how the safety overrides could be disabled and pulsed, and how argentium tubes could be twinned so they quadrupled the beam power and started to overload into resonance, creating spurious ultra-high-energy particles over 10-to-the-power-20 electron Volts. He had shown the clerks and MeTraCor's cadet traders how to adapt their blisters to give total elevation to the guns, how to shield their own sites with heavy metal and blast the sky with cascades of unguessed particle power that would shower muons traveling at 0.995 cee upwards. It was the reverse of the natural cosmic ray effects that dogged nexus ships every time they traveled through the atmosphere, denaturing the plex of their hulls and giving operators a pain in the credit balance.

"See, those Kan ships're orbiting real low to give us as much hell as possible from their guns," he had told them. "They're skimming the top of the thermosphere, coming over in a half dozen different orbits, each one rotating over us every once in a while. Then, because of the orbital dynamics, every few hours they reach a kind of conjunction up there and all their beams open up at the same time, and they're able to give our butts hell. But with this—" He had patted the modification he had made to the Dahl-gren. "—we put a flux of muons up there that'll send their detectors crazy and their overrides'll cut right in and— *pzzt!*—out they zip to a safer orbit. It'll get them off our backs for a while, until they figure out what's going on."

He had warned them, on the price of their lives, not to point their glowing barrels at one particular ship orbiting among the Kan fleet.

His stomach heaved as he tuned the macro to the zenith and thought of the immense debt he was in. But like we say, he thought, despondency is the only real hell, exuberance conquers all. Fuck Yu Hsien and Hu Tsung, and fuck the credit brokers in Seoul who rated me flat, too. I can start a new career any time I want! There's always Kim Gwon Chung. A pirate and a more dangerous man than ever these days—now I'm legitimate and he's not, but he owes me a favor. I warned his ass a long time ago not to mess with me. After I snuffed six of his pirate grabbers, I let him get away from me in a seventh. Hope he appreciates it.

There again, I could join forces with the Solomon Broz, and we could hit the Zone and maybe split fifty-fifty with Kim—No, you're too old to be hunting down Kan trans-ports in a grab, and it'd be too much like a real surrender.

He sighed, seeing his beautiful vessel in Kan hands, but nothing, not even that sight, could take the shine off the day now.

The news he had received last night had jolted him. A native Osumi peasant, from one of the many forced-labor rice farms, a man with kinfolk south along the meridian, had brought a garbled story to Barb Eastman. And Eastman had brought the man straight to him.

Eastman's face had been full of pity and regret. There

had been no way to disbelieve the native because of the ring. A thick ring, with the Aquila Eagle, and the Straker pennant device of stars and waves. He had sworn that the ring had been pulled off the finger of a *gaijin*—an Ameri-kan dead from a skyfall that went wrong.

The news had devastated Ellis and he had felt like vom-iting. Damned ring had too much psi anyhow. It had a knack of showing up at evil moments.

For the first time he had been forced to believe in his son's death. He had felt it was time he sent Eastman away, not wanting him to witness his loss of face, but he had gone instead to his desk to settle a sum of credit on the native man.

"Go ahead, get what you need from any store you can find functioning."

Then something had made him look again at the wide-eyed man who took the credit chit, and he had called in his steward to question him thoroughly in his own language.

"What village is it?"

"A holy place far away to the south—I don't know the place he says—it means the field, or the plain, of chestnut trees."

"Did he come from the village himself?"

"No, Ellis-san."

"Then how did he get the ring?"

"From a brother's wife's cousin's friend who had a relative who saw it."

"And was the dead Amerikan alone?"

"Oh, no sir!"

"Then who else?"

"There was the ghost of a dead daimyo who rose up out of the holy grove, and a dragon with fifty heads and teeth that dripped blood appeared, clothed all in fish scales of iron—"

The steward had raised his hand and slapped the side of

the man's head with undue venom. "Tell the truth, you lying peasant!"

The young man had put his forehead on the floor and cringed. "I swear, Lord!"

"What's that he says?"

"He says he swears, but he's lying, Ellis-san. I know these people. Some nonsense about hundred-headed monsters from the sacred forest."

"Nyuyoku-san, just let him say his say."

Eventually, they had pared the story down. "He says there was a pillar of fire in the sky, and then the ghost of a daimyo and his consort and two white men who were Imperial servants came out, but the one with hair of brass died and the other did not. And something about fifty samurai on horseback."

"The *gaijin* who died?" Ellis asked. "Did he have hair of iron? Or hair of copper? Or hair of brass?"

"Hair of brass, Lord."

"And the servant who did not die? What about his hair?"

"He says that was most strange of all, Sencho-san. That one had human hair."

Ellis had snapped his fingers. Though the story had been relayed and exaggerated in the peasant way, through many credulous and creative minds, the germ was of a black-haired man surviving a stormy planetfall. Black-haired because Daniel Quinn's hair had been blond as straw, and that detail would have been passed in the tale for certain!

"Not a word of this to anyone!" he had warned Eastman. "Not a squeak. Now promise me!"

"Sure I promise you, Mister Straker. I won't breathe a word to anyone. But what about Miz Hawken? I—"

"Your promise includes her—on your life."

"On my life."

"That's good," he said, pulling the macro out. "Hayden alive, stars burn his thieving eyes! And Shingo-san too. Just as I was thinking they were maybe dead after all. Ah, Hayden, you're the best possible news to my ears, but dynamite in another way: what's the hope for my amygdala now? And the hope it'll get to the daimyo? We'll have to be careful over that. And very, very quiet."

Now what about you? he thought, squinting at the image of the *Chance*. The air was cooling now that the hole was in the dome. The sun-star was newly up and showing white in an orange sky, through the smoky skin of the dome, a good time for thinking and working on a plan. He swung the macro round and flipped the screen on again.

His ship rode overhead, unhappily putting out her loathsome Kan call sign, a mush of plinkety-plonkety noises, and with a Kan prize crew aboard her, getting their hands on her priceless Europan gewgaws. . . . He twisted the tuner up to max res. Her image in the macro smeared and speckled because of the distance, but still invited his inspection. Somehow she was no longer his pride, the ship he had struggled all his life to possess. He suddenly feared she was gone from him, and all he had amassed with her had gone too.

Stamp on that stuff, trader! he warned himself. How can you think bad psi on a day like today? There's no place for pessimism in your philosophy. Never has been! And you don't allow thinking like that on your ship, so why here?

Ah, but Free Trade, he thought, still loving the lifelong dream with a fierceness that hurt. That's the thing to dwell on. That's the Big One, and always has been. With Known Space open to anyone to trade past any galactic latitude they damned well please, there'd be real commerce, real competition, real advancement. And with it, real wealth!

Credit's everything, he had told Hayden many times. Yep, everything. It's power and it's freedom and it's contentment, and it's anything you want it to be. There's nothing you can't do when your credit's rated high. Nothing. And there's too much you can't do when you're down short.

And the Adventer myth that credit's evil is spun by pious fools who've never felt any poverty.

And the rumor that credit makes a man unhappy is spread by the credit-rich who fear that other people want to take it off of them.

And the word that credit's an impossible dream is passed on by those who're resigned and chained to serfdom or peasantdom or whatever you want to call it. Man, there's no need to fear wealth, or hate wealth, or slander wealth, when wealth is absolutely increased by organized manufacture and inter-Sector trade!

We can all be in on it! By psi, the wealth of every Sector would see a glorious increase if I had my way! Shiploads of credit, yeah, loads and loads of it, like the globe-ships of aurium and argentium the samurai used to bus around. That's what we want, and a stinking dose of bad psi on anyone that says otherwise!

That's what Free Trade'll do. If we had that there'd be purest aurium raining down on Liberty and the Delawares and even scummy Kalifornia as well as down on the bald heads of Edo, and every person in Amerika and the Zone and all the rest of the Sectors would have ten times the rating they have now.

If we had Free Trade there'd be a hundred trading houses plying into Yamato. All independent. All competing for the home market. And think about Amerika freed from MeTraCor's arbitrary rules and her goods freed from MeTraCor's taxes. Within ten years every world this side of the Forty Degree Plane and most of the rest, too, would be sending ships to Canton and Shang Hai and Osumi! And I'd be the King of Silk in New New York, and then the entirety of Known Space would be tied together with trade: Amerikan hulls filled with Amerikan manufactures and Zone metals, with Xanadu hand-products and Europan gen-stock and Slavian *gryaet* and Brasilian phytoplank-ton—but most of all, the wealth of the Zone: bullion. Think of it! A hundred Amerikan trade houses vying with each other to refine and transport aurium, and Straker-Hawken Inc. ahead of the pack, by psi! What a future that would be—and will be, one day!

He strode a little farther, sighing, patting his vest pocket for his cheroot, then realising he had smoked the last one. Poor Arkali, he thought suddenly, remembering the night of the mutiny. Your father says you cry yourself to sleep, and have hollow eyes since your experience. Eastman says you're distraught. Well, didn't I say your daddy should've let you get it out of your soul with a blade. You had every right to revenge yourself, and to put steel into that scum's flesh. I'm sorry for you now, girl, and I'm sorry for the way I treated you. I never wanted it to come out like this, for me or for yourself. But that's psi and there's nix all justice to it, though some men, good men, try to make it so. And I'll bring you better psi sometime, you can depend on it.

He doused the warm feelings that were starting to kindle in him again. Hell! And where in the name of psi's the damned Navy? Can it be that Vaile really is iced, and that the new commander really is the slimeballing coward that his message to the Council makes him seem? What if the squadron really has fled away to the safety of downchain? He slammed his hand onto the plex abutment, wishing he had a hand-rolled Kuba stogie with him to suck on.

Ah, you know the truth of it. Don't deceive yourself! You're all alone inside your head, so don't think lies any more than you'd speak them aloud to yourself! There ain't no Navy coming to your rescue, and you've always known it!

So, what price freedom now?

He returned the drifting macro once more, and his seasoned eye took a careful circuit around the hull of the *Chance*, then by habit he used his imagination to take his customary morning examination of the bridge. The sun-star lit her flanks through her gantries and aerials like white gold. By psi, her lines are fine! Finest craft east of the Zero Degree Plane, and almost the biggest merchantman, and she's mine, by psi! Mine! Yes, even now!

There were faraway shouts of delight as a big spherical triangle of dome hung for a moment, then came crashing down into the eastern district. The violet points of light had become specks—drones preparing to troll down off the dome now. The smallest breeze stirred the crete dust at his feet and ruffled his cap trim. Instantly he spat on his hand and rubbed his palms together, then felt for the light air and a smile split his face. All along the southern horizon a gray line of haze misted the junction of land and sky. The air was beginning to stir up.

He folded the macro and slid the aperture shut, seething with the desire to get back aboard his ship. He had seen what he had come to see, and the knowledge fired him up like a Dahlgren beam. First take stock, trader, he told himself sternly. Take a grip and see where you're about— all the debt accounted one item at a time—and search out any credit you can, and then you can go eat breakfast with Admiral Hu as his invitation requires and balance everything up on the bottom line.

26

You're a squatting fool, and that's a fact, Barb Eastman, he told himself angrily, putting the flask out of Arkali's sight. You never think straight in the presence of women, and that's why they consider you uncouth and ungentle. And you are uncouth because you really don't know how to act properly.

That's not surprising, given where I come from, and what kind of early schooling I got. But I never allowed that to be an excuse before, and I sure am not about to start with it now!

He had visited her each morning so far, but she had hardly spoken a word to him. Today he had brought a silver flask with some five-star Europan brandy in it for her, thinking it might ease her mind, but the stink of the liquor had only awakened raw memories of that terrible night, and tears had started to swim in her eyes.

"No, please don't. I only brought it to give you a little comfort. Really."

He offered her his neckerchief awkwardly.

"Please go away, Mister Eastman."

"Now, there's no pleasure in sitting here alone, is there?" he said as gently as he could. He thought he understood her melancholy.

"I would prefer it if you left."

"Don't say that, Miz Hawken. Your father allowed me

to drop in on you in the belief that I might be able to cheer you up some. Don't let's disappoint him, eh?"

She let his neckerchief fall into her lap.

"Perhaps I can persuade you to drink a little green tea with me?"

"It looks revolting."

"Try a little."

"I heard green tea gives people stomach cancer. I hate it."

"You shouldn't speak like that, Miz Hawken. C'mon, maybe try a little?"

She shook her head. Her coppery ringlets rippled in the harsh light. She was very beautiful, but her face was pale and forlorn and her eyes were almost sightless as they stared into space.

Perhaps I embarrass her, he thought. After all, I did come across her naked, and otherwise helpless in the most disgusting of circumstances, but by all that's real the least she could do is show me a measure of thanks for preventing a wholly worse outcome.

A sudden thought daggered him, drove him towards panic. Maybe she knows what I am. No. Can't be. And what if she did? What if she discovered I was no more than a . . . SHUT OUT THAT THOUGHT! Why, if it wasn't for me . . .

"I want to die."

He stared at her, unable to believe she had spoken those softly numbing words.

"What did you say?" he asked stupidly.

"I said, I want to die. Now that Hayden's dead there's no longer any—"

"Oh, no, Miz Hawken! That's a terrible thing to say! Put that out of your head. Please."

Her body began to convulse and her face puckered and

she began to cry. He hesitated, horrified, then took her shoulders and clasped her to him, patting her back. She was like a ghost in his arms, fragile and insubstantial. Her vulnerability brought out a ferocious instinct in him to protect her, a desire to infuse her with some of his sanguine spirit, and he knew he would have to break his word to Ellis Straker if he was to succeed. He'd have to tell her about Hayden.

Damn them, he thought, his tormented past flashing back on him. They did a real good job on me. A real good job. I hope to psi they broke the mold when they finished. DON'T THINK ABOUT IT!

He forced his mind to the pretense of manhood he was living. Today's my squatting twenty-first birthday, the day a young man comes of age in Amerika! That's a laugh. Look at this woman: by all that's real, the only time I get to be alone with her, and all she wants to talk about is killing herself over Hayden Straker. I'll have to tell her he's alive. I'll have to. A real man would.

But if you tell her that, a devil inside him said, she'll never look at you again. And you can't break your promise to Ellis Straker. A real man wouldn't do that.

He swallowed. But when I look at her, and I feel those sobs racking her whole body and I know she's so broken up inside she's lost her will to live—I'll have to tell her.

"Arkali," he said, holding her at arms' length and insisting she look at him. "I came here to tell you something wonderful. So wonderful, I don't hardly know how to begin with it unless I have a jolt of five-star first."

He took a slug from the flask and told her that he had taken a native man to see Ellis Straker, that he had reported a *gaijin* down and alive in the daimyo's domains somewhere south of Kanoya City.

As he spoke, her eyes began to flick back and forth

between his own, gauging him, then she took the flask from his hand and began to drink from it until she choked on its fire.

Eastman watched her with astonishment. From her aching listlessness she went into a flurry of indecisive activity, almost panic. She moved around the room, combing fingers through her hair, asking unanswerable questions and making wild resolutions.

"Where is he?" she asked.

"I don't know. All we know is that he was reported somewhere to the south of Kanoya City."

"But we must find out where! We must try to find him."

"Arkali, by the terms of our parole we can't leave the city, let alone the Lease. And it's only a rumor."

"No, it's true. I know it's true!" She suddenly hugged him and kissed him on the mouth. "Oh, Mister Eastman— that is, Lieutenant Eastman, isn't it, now?—you don't know what you've done for me. Thank you. Thank you so much. I must find Hayden."

"No, you can't do that!" But before he could stop her she had whirled from the room, leaving him to look at the flask in his hand and to shake his head, knowing that he had betrayed Ellis Straker's secret for nothing.

She ran out across the Plaza in front of hundreds of Kan soldiers, in the raw light of the star, in the fierce radiated heat that had replaced the dome's stifling atmosphere. At first the soldiers turned to stare at her, not shambling Kalifornia leatherjackets as on the night of terrors, but quilt-coated Chinese in smart uniforms drawn up in inch-perfect lines. Their heads snapped to attention as the Kan officer spoke at them from a gaudy dragon litter carried shoulder high. The men were superbly disciplined and drilled, clean and expressionless and identical—almost mechanical—so she did not feel threatened by them. They were not like the filthy rabble who had got drunk at the first sign of action and broken into the bunker. . . .

She ran down Main Skid, her heart thumping and her breath tight in her garb. What if he doesn't want me now, she thought. What if Hayden thinks I'm dirty and no good for him anymore? The thought only drove her on towards the Hawken block.

No, we're going to be married! He'll take me away from this place. He promised. He promised! Where's my father? He must be in the city somewhere. He must be told right away. "Father!"

Yamato natives had begun to trickle back into the city. After the bombardment and the danger, they were returning, as if nothing had happened. As if ownership of the city didn't matter. And the Kan were allowing them in, perhaps to start the work of clearing up and making safe.

She went into the beam-blitzed, heat-pocked building, crossed the black and white marblite floor of the lobby, and ran towards the great elevator plate that swept up to the offices on the higher floors. It was still powered, and the cushioned lifters took her effortlessly up. The big corridor was eerie without people, and echoed to her movements. Debris blasted from the ceilings and walls lay scattered, shafted by white light from windows that had lost phase. Then she ran into Ellis Straker.

"What's this, girl?" he said, gripping her upper arms.

"Mister Straker! Is my father here?"

"You're in a hurry, when there's nowhere to go."

"I'm looking for my father. I want to tell him about Hayden. Barb Eastman told me—"

"Ah, he did, did he?"

His sudden sternness made her doubt herself. "Oh, tell me it's true, Mister Straker. Please."

"It's only a report."

"We must find him."

"Now, hold on, girl." Straker gripped her harder. He made her stand still. "Tell me exactly what's been said."

She told him, words tumbling from her.

"Listen to me. You can't go nowhere. This city's under Kan control and the sentries'll burn some nasty holes in your hide if they catch you outside the ramparts."

"But—"

"There's no buts."

A flash of sudden temper lit her and she pulled herself free from him. "Let me go. Where's my father? You disowned Hayden. Yes, you devil! You don't want to help him. Or help me to find him. Isn't that so? Where's my father?"

Her screamed words hurt his ears. He gripped her jaw, and she stopped.

"I'm sorry, girl, but you'll have to hold that or I can't think. Now . . . ."

"Where's my father?" she whispered angrily, her fingers clawed against his big hand, and he released her.

"Your father's not here. He's talking with whatever Council Members he can find, trying to get up some foolish petition to Hu Tsung to have all Amerikan personnel, MeTraCor and independent alike, shipped out to Seoul."

Her eyes widened. "Seoul? But what about Hayden? What's happened to him?"

Her voice rose again, and he strove to calm her. "Now—listen to me!—I'll tell you where Hayden most likely landed, and where he's trying to get to, but only if you'll promise not to tell another living soul about it, and that you'll do nothing to interfere."

"Tell me why I should?"

"Because if the Kan find out what he's doing, he's

as good as dead. And you wouldn't want that, would you?''

Her eyes hunted about. "But why should that be?"

He tried to present a patient face to her. "Well, because Hayden has the means to bring a Yamato army to the Lease that would cause the Kan to leave, which is something they do not want to do.''

"Don't patronise me, Mister Straker! Where is he?"

"A'right, a'right. Your word, now?"

"You have it. Now tell me.''

Ellis had already weighed and rejected the possibility of telling her the truth. He was angry at Eastman's betrayal, but he blamed himself mostly for having trusted a man so obviously in love. Isn't surprising, when you look at her, there's something about her despite the flakeeness, and Eastman knows she's beholden to him for her life.

Yep, he's heartsick, out of control on hormones, and in that pitiful state a man'll say anything, do anything and spend anything—which I should know from twenty-some years ago when I was in just the same stage of insanity. But maybe there's still a way to recover, because she's just as lovestruck over Hayden. . . .

He told her, "By the meteorological reports I estimate that the shuttle came down somewhere around two hundred and fifty land miles south of here. That's in Hideki Shingo's own *han*.''

"He's trying to make his way here? Is that what you're saying?"

"No. He'd have seen the bombardment from at least a hundred miles away. Could have known sooner than that, if he met with any of the refugees who fled away from here.'' He paused, knowing he could not trust her with the truth, then he went on in a glossy voice. "No, it's my guess he weathered out and lifted off again. Sitting out there is a MeTraCor orbital station. Fort Baker's heavily armored, a walnut of a place, small but built as strong as any orbiting fortress anywhere. She was put there to guard against slimy dealings by the Yamato government—an offplanet bolt-hole to go to in times of crisis, where the records could be stored and people evacuated. Not much armament. Mothballs. Strictly freezee and skeleton crew. One big red handle. One big motor to thrust out to Teth-Two-Nine and through in a dire emergency."

"They have astrogators there?"

"No. No astrogation facilities, just computer best-guess."

She was appalled. "They'd go through a nexus without human astrogation?"

"Uh-huh."

"But that would be suicide."

"Maybe twenty percent chance given a placid Index."

"Who would pull the big red handle given that?"

"I did say dire emergency."

"You think Hayden would try to go there?"

"Why not? The Kan—that is, the Chinese—won't have the inclination to besiege it until they've made Kanoya City properly secure. Yep, Fort Baker's where he's gone. You can depend on that."

"You must help me to get to him."

He stared at her and laughed dismissively. "No, girl. That's not possible. The best course is for you to await events patiently. Do as your father tells you."

Her face was set now. Suddenly she seemed very sober, and Straker could see her mother in her.

"I've done with waiting patiently and doing as I'm told. And if you don't help me," she said it very deliberately, "I'll never see Hayden again. But I will see him again, and you, Mister Straker, are going to help me."

He cocked an eyebrow. "That right?"

"You've no credit," she said. "I know that. And I know exactly how much you're in debt. My father told me. But I know where you can find a fortune in aurium. Fifteen *tranches* of it."

Straker felt the bottom drop out of his plans. It was fifteen *tranches* he had left with Hawken, the aurium Hawken had sworn was lost to Kan hands when they had scrambled into Kanoya City just before the bombardment.

"Your father told me what happened to that," he said guardedly.

"Yes, he did. But he lied."

"And I say you're lying now."

"No. He's stashed it. And I know where. I saw him." She tossed her head. "Now you'll help me. Won't you."

He folded his arms and sucked on his side teeth, wishing he had a tobako cheroot, wanting to brush her off, but needing to know where the aurium was, and inside he was boiling up a powerful anger against Hawken, who had deliberately crossed him.

"Well, Miz Hawken," he said at last. "If you're determined to do this I'll help you all I can. But not a word of this to anyone, y'hear? Especially to your father."

"You have a deal, Mister Straker." She looked him squarely in the eye and added, "I may say you can trust a promise of confidentiality from me—though you've shown yourself to be a poor judge of others in that regard."

27

An hour later, Ellis Straker stood at Manpuku-mon the Gate of Ten Thousand Happinesses, dressed in his best suit of clothes. Jos Hawken met him, looking solemn and imposing with his posing-stick and skullcap and his silver-striped vest coat buttoned all the way up to his collar against a wind that was getting blustery. The Kan sentries challenged them on sight, and saluted when they were shown Hu Tsung's chop on the pass, and the watch officer was called to examine the smart. He looked at them suspiciously but allowed them both to pass as if they were Osumi natives and not Amerikan traders under a dubious parole bound for the new governor's residence.

Once outside they took a two-man *kago* with ten heavily tattooed bearers and a lead man wearing nothing but a riot of mythical animals all over his torso and the painful-looking loincloth that bared the cheeks like sumo heroes'. The ride cost an impossible trade on Hawken's favorite posing stick. The leader bowed obsequiously as he wrapped the stick in a dingy square of cotton and tucked it into his *fundoshi*.

"Robbery!" Hawken said.

"Yep, but the population has yet to trickle back to town and competition's thinner than *mizo* soup. We can't walk unless we want to lose face completely. I'm going to hate being lifted up by damned bearers worse than you."

Hawken grimaced. "Psi-damned usurers! Don't they know the daimyo expressly forbids rate fixing?"

"Yep, they know, but they don't care any more about that than you do."

Hawken shot him a deadly glance, then flicked a hand against Ellis's jacket. "Why are you taking us out, Ellis? And why the need for putting on good garb? If it's for the benefit of Hu Tsung, you can be sure it's wasted. He's the biggest pirate to come out of Xanadu. The Dowager gave him this command in order to control him, and he was made governor of here, there and psi-damned everywhere, for the same reason."

"You're forgetting I've eaten with him once already, Jos."

"And found him to be a like-minded piece of shit."

Ellis kept his voice level. "Ah, get off that pedestal, Jos. I don't recall you refusing to handle the cargoes I brought you in the early days, or inquiring too close where they come from. You don't smell so clean yourself—to those of us that really know you."

The swaying, jolting ride out from the city took half an hour, down along the Lagoon of the Dragonflies and along the dusty Matsubashi Road. Hawken was sour and silent crushed in beside him, turning his eyes away from the dust-laden wind, hurt by events and his losses. But he was playing the wounded party deliberately.

Ellis stared at the views with equanimity. To westward was Haka-oka, a hill on which the daimyo had built a neat pagoda. Kan banners flew over it vigorously. It was on the highest point of the Lease, where in the ossuary, a dozen bone urns contained the remains of the Hideki ancestors right back to a dubious skeleton from the Showa era that was reputed to have been dug out of Manchurian dirt on Old Earth in the days before the Edict. Ironically, that Hideki had died in a war against the Kan.

The thought of Old Earth brought a dampness to Ellis's eye, and he touched his fingers to the node of his forehead. He did not know why, and had never known, but the thought of what had happenend to Old Earth disturbed him. It was so sad—yet also good and just—that a three-light-year Exclusion Zone had had to be imposed in the center of Known Space, and that the only ones allowed within that sphere were the cloistermen of Earth Central.

His attention was caught by the Kan banners as they rippled out, and he breathed in the damp, earthy tang on the air. That the wily Ryuji-sama had sited his ancestral tombs inside the Amerikan Lease was a measure of his statecraft. If a bunch of old bones could be turned into a respectable reason for bringing ten thousand armed troops into the Lease every year, or at his whim, why not?

They passed close by a large, favorite graveyard, a shady grove that was holy even to the local people. The plex grave tablets were incised with names that came from Connecticut and Florida and Utah and Wisconsin and most everywhere else in the Amerikan Sector; men, women and children who had come here and died here, or who had fallen into Teth-Two-Nine on their way in or out.

The locals who worked the fields in the leased territory as free-croppers had begun to return to assess the damage to their longan orchards and to reclaim buffaloids and pigs and dirty, brown *shedelevenoids* that the Kan had corralled to butcher should the siege go on overlong. They passed a horse led by a quilt-jacketed soldier; it bore two men in Kan officer uniform who grinned toothily at them, their padded war-bonnets making them look like ancient Soviets or men from a kick-boxing spar.

It was refreshing to see something new here. Soldiers or not, enemies or not, it was good. Yamato will molder like the bones of its ancestors unless it opens up, breathes in a few new ways. And what better way than tearing down the Boundary restrictions against the Zone plane? The Zone is naturally cosmopolitan. From the Black Jews and the White Jews of the Sculptor Cusp to the misplaced Danes of Canes Venatici, all kinds of peoples had set up there to make trade or homes, and that's good and proper and how it should be. But once over the Zero Degree Boundary and, 'cept for this Lease, it's dour samurai worlds and just as much a political and commercial monopoly as MeTra-Cor. It's surely time for the Emperor to loosen his grip and let the place thrive. That surely won't happen if Hideki Shingo-san ever succeeds in making himself daimyo and Prefect.

He'd have his father's skeleton in a pot on Boot Hill before the flesh had time to brown on the bone. . . .

Ellis checked his thoughts there. He felt anger at Hawken's deception and the desire to pop the balloon of his silence. The news would explode it well enough. But it wasn't yet time to tell him. Hawken sat on Ellis's right, his hands clasped on his knees, his face set.

"You're still worried about Arkali?" he asked lightly.

"She's still not well."

"Ah, you dote on that young woman to the point of slavery." And I'll bet your wife did the same back in Amerika, he thought, which is probably how she grew up to be such a delicate sheltered flower of a bitch. Why, I had female crew on my first command, *Dwight D*, were five years younger than her. They'd knock blocks out of her when it came to spirit, or even good manners. Yep. Badly nurtured. Snooty and tight-assed and painful.

He said: "She's improved since she got here, and she's opened out some, but maybe that ordeal of hers has set her right back."

"Set her back? Set her back? It's damn near made her

a case for the headset! She won't eat, or go out of her room. I doubt if she's had the spirit even to thank young Eastman for saving her. I'm at a loss, and I don't mind telling you.''

''So, Barb Eastman's been seeing her, eh?'' he asked innocently.

''It's the only way she can be made to get herself up every morning. But her conversation is reduced to a word here, a word there. I must get her to Seoul, and soon.''

Ellis absorbed that quietly. ''It seems to me she don't know much about the world in general and men in particular, poor girl, and after what she's been put through I wouldn't be surprised if she has difficulty with all her urges in the future.''

Hawken shook his head sadly and fell into silence again, so, as soon as he could, Ellis deliberately switched the conversation, wanting to condition Hawken's mood before they met Hu Tsung. He hid his anger about the aurium stash, but he could feel the issue tightening like a fist in his chest. Soothing chatter was what was wanted now.

''Cool day, though. Windy, eh?''

''Don't attempt to small-talk me, Ellis.''

He nodded amiably and breathed in deeply. After a satisfied pause he said, ''Ah, now, Jos, did I tell you I had a communication from Newaven on Connecticut?''

''Hmmm.''

''Yep. Good to hear it, too: it said the new college received its presidential charter some months ago. Straker College, School of Astrogation. How 'bout that?''

''I'm pleased for you.''

''Seems to me we got a tradition in philanthropy to keep up. Beats paying inflated prices for some squatty old painting to hang on a wall, eh? All those young talents getting a proper teach-in.''

"If you say so."

"I do say so."

"If you ask me, 'Straker College' sounds like a bid for posterity. At least my squatty old paintings are worth plenty in resale."

"If ever you get a buyer."

Ellis nodded pleasantly. Despite the wind and the uneven ride, he took out a heavy-bladed knife and began to slice minute arcs from his fingernails, putting his mind deliberately on the past to defuse his annoyance at Hawken.

"It's a fine tribute to have a school named for you," Ellis said, still watching Hawken throughout his reverie. "Ayrton Rodrigo would have been proud of that."

Hawken grunted. "If you think that, why didn't you ask them to call it Rodrigo College?"

"Below the belt, Jos."

"You still haven't told me what's in your mind for Hu Tsung."

"Ah, just a little breakfast."

Hawken shifted his weight. The *kago* lurched, swaying as the traders' mansions came into view. The wind raked the trees, rushing like waterfall sounds in their tops.

"Just that, a little breakfast?"

"Yes, and why not? A nice dish to point a man in the right direction for the rest of the day. Something to cool the blood, and you'll need it cooling before the day's out."

Hawken looked askance, and Ellis saw that his suspicions were mounting.

"Yessir," he went on heartily. "Then a glass of Europan wine or two to buoy us up for the discussion, eh? And perhaps some business, eh? Waddayasay?" Ellis nudged him purposefully. "Yeah! Invited to breakfast in your own house! But you have to hand it to Hu Tsung! He has style and a sense of humor!"

Hawken boiled. "You said business?"

"Of course, what did you think? Look there! There's your mansion house full of fornicating Kan officers. And right there is your study with Hu Tsung himself in occupation. A house fit for an admiral, eh?"

Hawken turned to him with an intake of breath. Then his temper broke. "What's going to be enough for you, Ellis? Your own son killed. My daughter raped. What's got to happen to make you understand we've lost! Lost, d'you hear me!"

"Naw, we haven't lost."

"Open your eyes! We've got no credit and no credit confidence! We're wiped out. Our joint venture is totally ruined, our houses ransacked by the Kan rank and file, then confiscated by order of Yu Hsien. Our stocks are all worthless. The offices are smashed and deserted with nobody to work there, with five hundred hold containers of hi-val-ad goods slated for Honshu but destined now never to get there. A hundred chests of finest pekoe tea and a thousand gallons of priceless Imperial soy thieved and put aboard Kan hulls. And business in Seoul idle as shit without our agents. Ellis, you'll have two more ships laid up on the Seoul apron three weeks from now, with Rad Givens and Eph Geneva not knowing what to carry where. All the figures are deepest, darkest, bloodiest red, and still you talk about doing business! Why don't you accept it? Take it like a man."

Ellis's face held its half-smile. He threw up his hand carelessly. "Like a gutless worm, you mean? Well, I'm not built that way, Jos. I'll find a way. I always have."

"Not this time, by psi. According to my figures, if you trade from now till the pioneer probes reach Iota One Scorpii you'll never get yourself on a level. And the debts you've got now are crushing!" Hawken's voice was edged with the slightest tint of triumph. "Twenty-five *tranches*! The whole capital figure you borrowed from Ei in Seoul. You were stupid."

They got out of the grounded *kago* and climbed the steps to the main entrance. Hu Tsung did not show them the courtesy of meeting them in person, nor did he send a senior officer. They were attended only by kowtowing servants. Hawken scowled at the functionaries, liveried men with pigtails and pillbox caps. Ellis saw how his ex-employer was stabbed by the humiliation of being received as a visitor in his own house, but he saw also that he was wound up tight about the aurium that lay in a safe under the adjoining room. It must be that, he thought. Or else I'm reading him wrong and Arkali was lying to me. Could she have been lying?

"You can't show your face in Seoul, Ellis. Not when you're twenty-five *tranches* in debt to that sonofabitch Ei."

"Yeah, if he finds out I've lost it all, I'm a dead man." Ellis fixed him with a dour eye. "You did tell me the fifteen *tranches* I left with you were definitely gone? In the hands of Hu Tsung and his officers?"

"Sure!" Hawken lied badly and without hesitation. "I gave you no assurances, Ellis. You know that. The Kan came down on us so suddenly here there was no time to move the weight of bullion into Kanoya City, and even if there had been time, the aurium would still have been taken when the Kan got inside the dome."

"I notice you had time to take your artworks and your Chinese crocks and your other gewgaws away," he said, looking around him. Loose window shutters banging filled the house with echoes, making the house seem even sadder and more abandoned.

Hawken blustered. "That was—that was my servants.

They loaded a car or two after we'd gone and saved a few things. By psi, Ellis, what are you saying? D'you think I'd have left a fortune in aurium for the Kan if I could've got it away? I won't have you blame me for that aurium.''

"Who said anything about blame?"

"Okeh." Hawken simmered, then he said, "I advise you not to say anything to Hu about the bullion he lifted."

"That right?"

"He might take it amiss. Accusing him—Listen, if you hadn't let the Kan catch you—well, enough said, I think."

Ellis's forehead rucked and his mouth assumed a flat smile. "A'right, then, that's the entire principal of the loan to repay, and with interest charged at fourteen and a half percent per annum UT, that's—" He figured the numbers rapidly in his head. "—that's damned near a hundred thousand in credit per day, each and every day, including public holidays. There's nothing else for it, we'll have to go to Seoul like you say."

"You want to go to Seoul?" Hawken was on guard again, but Ellis played him like a game fish.

"I've a feeling Admiral Hu will give us leave to light out."

"What?"

"Sure! Why not?" Ellis said expansively. "He does owe me a favor."

"You? What for?"

"For doing my best to persuade the Kanoya City Council to surrender. Or have you forgotten?"

"But you didn't!"

"Whoa now. He doesn't know that. And, see, I've got hopes of getting the *Chance* back into the bargain."

As they waited, Hawken made a nervous aside, "Look, Ellis, even if you sailed for Seoul tomorrow, you'd owe another million in credit by the time you got there. And before the *Plasma* and the *Aether* set down, you'd owe another two million. That's if they come in on time! There's not a round voyage into the Zone that's less than thirty days, and okeh, so you've two ships? What single cargo can yield between one-point-five and two million profit? Unless you heard of a source of refined aurium you been keeping quiet about.''

''Sorry to disappoint you there, Jos.''

''Well, then. You'll never keep your damned ships out of Ei's hands, and that's on consideration of the interest alone. Think again, light out for Ulsan or Palawan and get yourself another line of work.''

Ellis peeled off his skullcap silently. The agreement with Ei and his bankers was for a minimum loan of two months, that was thirty days UT, with extensions of a month of twenty-eight days at a time, available by prior arrangement. Interest was two months down, which was already paid, and at each month's end Seoul Time on the nail for every month extended. To an Amerikan, it was nothing but usury. Nothing in the United Worlds approached it, except perhaps in New New York, but it was the way the whole of the Zone worked from Car Nicobar to Fatu Hiva.

''Let's see—so what you're saying is this: I've been away from Seoul seven weeks UT now,'' he said, wanting to give Hawken every last opportunity to repent. ''If I left tomorrow, by the time I got back that'd be nine weeks, give or take a day or two. Ei-san'd be screaming for his interest, and I'd owe him three million, even if he was prepared to negotiate a further extension. Added to that, if he's learned about Kanoya City's recent history, or has got suspicious that the capital has been lost, then he'll foreclose. When he finds half his security—that's our Kanoya City holdings and the *Chance* herself—have already been confiscated by Hu Tsung, he'll be an angry man.

When he's certain I'm uncreditworthy, he'll have me killed, if he can. And he can.''

That was putting the worst of it right in front of Hawken's face. But instead of the penitent admission he had half expected, Hawken adopted an air of moral superiority designed to magnify the tragic state of mind his daughter's ordeal and their joint misfortunes had created.

"You may as well give it up, Ellis. You've ruined us both, and all our futures. Bale out while you can.''

Ellis's disappointment turned to anger. By psi, look at you covering your sanctimonious ass for all you're worth, you piece of shit—when you know full well that my fifteen *tranches* of aurium are under these very floorboards. Makes me wonder about the time John Oujuku and me tracked you down for dishonesty in the Navy Commission and you convinced me I was wrong. Maybe you fooled me then, too.

"At least your daughter's alive," he said harshly, then, suddenly conciliatory again, "Like you say, Hayden's most probably dead.'' Hawken did not look up, but just remained slumped inside himself, and Ellis's half-smile came back. "But whatever is and whatever may be, there's still business to be considered, eh?''

"Why, you thick-skinned devil! Haven't you got a single shred of compassion in you?''

He looked at Hawken, the anger undisguised now in his eyes, and Hawken shifted, unsettled by Ellis's attitude. "Ah, don't tell me you've got a monopoly on the moral right, Jos. You can show the universe your nice manners and piety when I show it only fists and a hard face, and most of the time the universe believes you're a good man and I'm an evil sonofabitch on the strength of that. But I know you: we're alike in too many ways, except that you hide yourself with hypocrisy and I don't.''

Another servant appeared and ushered them forward. They obliged and were admitted to Hu Tsung's dining room to partake of *zao dian*—breakfast.

28

The Kan admiral was as Ellis remembered him. Just as impressive, but now since his victory, even more majestic. He had impressive finger cones on the three lowest-rank fingers of each hand and had probably started growing on the index fingers six months ago, making him not only a powerful functionary, but also ambitious and maybe premature in his expectations.

He was of middle height, the same age as Ellis. His coat was sky-black like the contacts that covered his eyes, and cut from the best twin-coccoon silk. The front half of his head was shaved and the hair on the back half pulled severely back to a clasp and apparently plaited into a long queue that hung to his waist.

Ellis wondered what Kuang-chou pauper girl had had her scalp shaved to make the extension. The admiral's face was clean-shaven, dark-complexioned, with a pug nose and lines grooving his cheeks that sculpted it. The fleshy lips of Ling-nan and narrow eyes, the whites a gloss black and the pupils small points of white in the centers. When the admiral spoke it was with the characteristic lisping singsong of the Kan.

That sure is a prize Kan haircut you've got there, Ellis

thought genially. And I'd be doing you a favor to cut your pigtail off for you.

Hu Tsung performed a perfunctory nod of the head as he was introduced, and grunted as he was told that Hawken was the previous owner of the house. It was clear that the discussion was going to be via interpreters and heavy-going.

The meal was a battle of face. Beneath a great silver candelabrum, several dishes of pickled chili pods and mouth-puckering beans in poker-hot sauce. In the middle, a decanter of ice water stood, with three plain glasses, glinting in temptation.

They started with cold hors d'oeuvres, and Ellis saw at once this would be a tough fight. A black "hundred year old egg"—"slowly transformed by a special chemical reaction by long immersion, Honorable Guest, in a bath of lime"—*you zha gui*—"devils fried in oil, to begin." Then a tureen of the most intense eye-watering Sichuan noodles was served.

Hu's personal feeder-taster lifted food to his lips. On the dizziest high rungs of the Xanadu political ladder the ideal was to demonstrate status by having body servants for every purpose. In Xanadu, extremity abuse had been in vogue for the last two hundred years, everything from bound feet in women and forehead flattening in babies, to the fetishes of nail and hair practised among Celestial Courtiers.

The game here and now was face through food. It sometimes got dirty, Ellis knew. The scorning of the first few hot dishes was crucial. The aim was to keep face, and hold to the conversation despite a mouthful of white-hot spice, never to decline another spoonful when the stakes were raised around the table, and never ever to so much as look at the water.

"No, no, it was nothing that I did for you, Esteemed

Admiral," Ellis said modestly, his eyes giving nothing away, his lips and tongue raging with hell's own fire. "Though I'll admit this: it did take me the best part of a week to convince our hellcat of an ex-Controller she couldn't stand against your forces for long. Ah, she's a termagant and a half, a virago, our Aziza Pope. Be careful you keep her closely under arrest, esteemed sir, and instruct your servants not to listen to a word the lying schemer tells you, or she'll have you tied in knots. And now, I would like to discuss when it would be convenient for you to give me my ship back. Hao?"

Hu Tsung lost his humor at that, refusing the next morsel from his feeder. "*Bu xing!*" He banged the table with the heel of his hand, sending rings shivering across the surface of the water jug.

"The Esteemed Admiral asks if you want to discuss this some later time maybe" was the translator's version. Ellis knew that "Screw you, pal!" was more accurate.

Then Hu flipped up another trio of fire pods and consumed them, saying that the unfortunate ship was a prize of war, and her profits already divided amongst her captor's crew. She would be resold into the internal trade of the Central Realm at Shang Hai, to a new Kan owner: the Kan would henceforth have need of good hulls, because the intention of the Immaculate Commander, Yu Hsien, was to double trade and double it again in Yamato. Might Mister Straker consider accepting a small freighter, the *Tongzhi*?

Now that the points from the first few courses have been shared more or less equally, Ellis thought, it's going to get rough. A man needs real guts for this game.

"An unworthy delicacy in your honor," the interpreter announced, indicating the steaming dishes newly arrived. "Glazed ducks' feet—or very juicy *hai shen yu du*!"

"*Hai shen yu du?*"

"Sea slug, soaked in spring water, boiled once a day to stop them from rotting and served with fish stomachs. A strong tonic."

"Naturally."

"Your choice."

"Choice? Too tricky. Why not both together?"

"Excellent! Partake freely."

Hu Tsung broke wind with Chinese gusto, while the interpreter added, "But regarding the freighter *Tongzhi*. She is, unfortunately, too small and too old to be of much use in the Yamato trade, but she might serve to transport Mister Straker and Mister Hawken and the people of the Council, and indeed all the Amerikan people, as far as Seoul, where they might apprise their compatriots of the sequestration of Kanoya City."

Ellis smiled and gritted his teeth; his mouth burned, his forehead and the orbits of his eyes were wet with dew. "Are not the Kan a justly famous people when it comes to generosity?" he said.

The rest of the glutinous course fell to crunching and slurping. When Ellis pushed away his bowl it was pushed back and a porcelain spoon in it, so he could drain the sea-slug juices.

"Next?"

"Swine flesh."

"Wonderful."

"We have a saying in Xanadu: we eat every part of the pig with the exception of its—what you say?—its oink."

"Ha ha."

"Funny, yes? Please eat."

Ellis grinned at his bowl as it was refilled for him. It smelled like crab turds in methylated spirit.

"Ordinarily I would be most honored to accept the Esteemed Admiral's exceedingly kind offer, and remove to

Seoul the troublesome Amerikans who're languishing to no good end in Kanoya City—or should I perhaps call it New Tian Jin now?—and also to bring the news to Seoul, even though it might make the morale of Amerikans there suffer—yes, indeed, I would surely do this favor for the Esteemed Admiral, if it were not for certain other considerations.''

''Other considerations?''

A trickle of spice-induced sweat emerged at Hu Tsung's temple. He dashed it away nonchalantly with a flick of his longest finger cone before it could drip onto his collar. Now that credentials had been established, the real business could be commenced.

''Soup?''

''Shark's fin, I presume.''

Yu's expression was one of great disappointment, then he guffawed.

''The Elevated One says he has a special soup for you, his Honored Guests.''

''Oh, yeah?''

''*Yan wo tang*.''

''Swallow's nest, huh?''

Hawken's pallor greened a little more.

''You have heard of it?''

''It's my favorite.'' Ellis put his hands together. ''It has been my good fortune, Esteemed Admiral, to have met with His Excellency, the celestially favored Yu Hsien, on several occasions. You may rely on me when I say I know what he wants with Kanoya City.''

After the soup came the bear's paw, and after that the jellyfish. Then the final test, the truly disgusting but genuinely traditional scalded donkey.

''How one kills it matters greatly, Honored Guest. It is said that fear releases enzymes that tenderise the meat.''

Ellis finished every morsel, matching the Admiral mouthful for mouthful. I've got his respect, he thought. But it's only a draw, and I need a victory.

When the dish was cleared, Hu Tsung looked unconcerned. He gestured to the silent Hawken and muttered to his aide.

"Water, wine, or five-star, Mister Hawken?" the interpreter asked.

Hawken was shaken. "Thank you. A Europan wine is my choice. No doubt you found my cellars satisfactory, though I'll admit that my stock is not purposely inclined towards the Kan palate."

The barb went unremarked. "Mister Straker?"

"Ah, well, let me see . . . Yep, I think a slug of Jos's best five-star, if you don't mind, Esteemed Admiral." He flicked a hand at the servant-interpreter. "And I'll trouble your footstool here for a light on the stub of this *hong xing Habana*." He flipped open the carved box and ran the cheroot under his nose. "Ah! I'd offer you one of mine, but my supplies are temporarily held up."

The table servants moved to obey, and, as they did so, Hu Tsung spoke in English. "So! You presume to know what the Functionary of Satsuma wants? Perhaps you do. What is that to me? I am governor here. It is my ships and my weapons and my troops that have taken Kanoya City."

"Yep, but Yu Hsien is still in charge. He called you in, and he has the Dowager's mandate in Yamato. And most important of all, he outranks you."

"I am de facto ruler here."

Ellis's flat smile reappeared. "Yu Hsien wants to level Kanoya City, you know that, don't you?"

"What do you mean—level?"

"Just that. He wants to flatten it until there's nothing but a li'l biddee patch of lava."

"That is not so!"

"No?" Ellis plucked the particles from his grin with a toothpick. "Oh, I almost forgot. I've brought you a little gift. A famous delicacy of ours."

He pulled open the flap in his jacket and pulled out a bundle of flimsy film with something gobby and yellow and malign at the center.

The serving staff looked at it in horror as he unwrapped it. They could not prevent their noses from wrinkling and their stomachs heaving at the rotting stench as the airtight wrapping peeled away.

Hu was stricken.

"You eat that?" The interpreter said, the disgust raw in his words.

"Mmmmmh. Delicious," Ellis said, hooking a finger full out of the stinking evil mass and sucking it.

"A little Kebek Camembert, anybody?"

Ellis knew the Kan detestation for milk products well. So much did it revolt some of them that they said they could tell if Amerikans or Europans had been in a room because of the buttery smell their skin pores left behind. No way was any Kan going to let the most gloopee, stinkee cheese in Known Space pass his lips.

Instead, what passed the admiral's lips was two syllables. "*Bu yao.*"

He had capitulated. The cheese was discreetly removed from the board.

Point, quarter and game, Ellis thought. By a knock-over and a stay-down. He leaned forward with renewed authority now.

"See, from Yu Hsien's viewpoint Kanoya City is nothing but competition. What happens when the Amerikan Navy comes out of Teth-Two-Nine—as it has to do sooner or later. Or if Kanoya City gets put back into the hands of the Amerikans by the daimyo Ryuji Hideki."

"That is most unlikely."

"Wrong again. I'll explain why if you like. And then there's your own nexus ships." He indicated the purple and yellow iris flowers that swayed on their long stems in Hawken's garden. "Wind's getting up. The season of southerly gales is here."

"The weather is of no concern."

"Should be. Don't forget there're two nexi in this system and it so happens that the rainy season down here just happens to coincide with quadrature and syzygy when the nexi interact most with one another, and that means the quasi-predictable cyclic local movements in the Index can be expected. It'll fall to its annual low in the next few days. Then it'll be hell getting out of the system. You can only escape it by lighting out before the Index falls."

The underwriters in Seoul were wise to that. Ellis knew to his cost that no insurance policy would cover ships attempting to cross into the Zeta CrA system from Teth-Two-Nine or Teth-Two-Eight when the nexi were lined up in opposition or conjunction or at ninety degrees to one another with respect to the primary. Some covers even loaded premiums at the quincunx when the nexi were at 150 degrees to one another, without any reason at all. Happy to take your credit, he thought disgustedly, but you try to shove a claim through . . .

"Mister Straker, I am aware of the constraints imposed by what our statistical pilots call the flow of *chi*, what our Tao mathenauts describe as the balance between the second derivatives of yin and yang. Also, I have not been deceived by the part you claim to have played in the surrender of Kanoya City. You are here because I have respect for your reputation. Therefore, in return, I would be grateful if you did not treat me as if I was a fool."

Ellis leaned forward, his half-smile broadening. "Okeh, let's get down to it. It's clear to me that you and Yu Hsien are vying with each other over who's got ultimate authority here. Yu Hsien is Big Chief at Satsuma, and therefore, in theory, once your troops made planetfall they became his to command and Kanoya City his to dispose of.''

Hu Tsung stiffened. ''I repeat. I am the de facto power here. While my ships are in orbit around Osumi they make me Cheng Huang!''

''Okeh, you can get up on that God-of-the-Ramparts-and-Moats stuff if it jollies you,'' Ellis told him, shrugging ash off the cheroot. ''But don't do it for my benefit. We both know that all you really want is your fair share of the spoils. But Yu Hsien doesn't want you to have it, does he? He doesn't want you to ransom Kanoya City back to the Amerikans, he wants to blitz it down flat, or at the least to keep it Kan, because that's where his power lies, in keeping Satsuma free of competition, right?''

Hu Tsung's eyes flickered to Hawken, who had sat bolt upright at the mention of ransom.

A slatted shutter banged against the open window. It had the feel of an omen to Ellis—and to Yu Hsien the symbolism was clear.

Doesn't need a talent to interpret it, Ellis thought. The link between fluctuations in the Index and anomalies in planetary weather had been established two hundred years ago. High-mass stars tended to stabilize nexi, which explained why the major inhabited systems had primaries more massive than the original sun, but even a mass like Plaskett's Star would not overcome the chaos resonance peaks of multiple nexus arrays. Nexus storms tended to coincide with electrical storms on livable planets, and big fluid mechanical disturbances in the atmospheres of gas giants. The first nexus detonation in the Old Earth System had driven the Great Red Spot of Jupiter crazee.

''The southwest gusters,'' Ellis said. ''The nexi could

flip into instability at any time. Then where would you be? Your White Tiger would be spewing out the other side of Teth-Two-Nine in bite-size pieces? You know there're bad systems all the way from the Honshu Corridor to the Three-Thirty Degree Plane, and there's no passage between Tsi-Tsu and Ki-Koan for a ship with as great a mass as yours. That's why Commodore Vaile's squadron didn't come back for you. He knows the Index will trap you here like beetles in a killing bottle, without the expense of him hurrying over. C'mon, why not settle now and get yourself and all your ships away. That's what your instinct's telling you, if you're honest about it.''

Hu Tsung remained fox wily. He looked at Ellis unreadably. ''I may leave Osumi soon. I may leave with all of value that Kanoya City contains. Why should I negotiate with you over a ransom?'' He raised his eyes in demonstration of his point. ''Kanoya City and everything in it is mine already.''

''No.'' The trap snapped crisply shut as Ellis sat back. ''Because I can hand you an additional ten *tranches* of aurium—that's ten *tranches* of aurium that you'll never get without me—if you'll agree to be gone from here before the end of the month.''

Hawken's mouth opened, but closed again.

Ellis's eyes never moved from the admiral's, he was at his hardest now that he saw the greed lighting Hu Tsung's features. ''There's just two plex-solid conditions, Admiral.''

''Yes?''

''Both what you might call personal points of face that I believe you'll have the civility to respect.''

''What are they?''

''The first is that you hand me back my ship on the day you light out, and the second is that you have the kindness to get your shiny butt, the butts of your hangers-on, out of Mister Hawken's house—immediately.''

29

The sun-star Zeta Coronae Australis was waning over Miyakonojo's Prefectural Residency, a fierce disc lost in a featureless high overcast. The Lady Isako sat with her maids on the tatami mats amid silk cushions and Chinese brocade spreads; Hideki Shingo lounged beside her, distraught.

''That is how it is with women, my son,'' the Lady Isako said, infinitely sad for him. Privately she thought: it is a hard way for women, but it's harder for men. Restless, worldly, ambitious men, never growing up, always ungrateful, never stopping to enumerate the manifold blessing of the Buddha—never stopping until those blessing are gone like the chrysanthemums that bud and bloom and then wither in the gardens of the Emperor.

A Burmese cat yawned and stretched before padding delicately away into the undergrowth, its tail high. The gardens laid out below them were extensive and minutely tended, the formal areas divided by gravel paths and moss beds and dark water that drank in the opal light of the sky. In the pavilion it was cool and shaded. Hiding the walls of this private world, gnarled trees, their branches trained and twisted by generations of gardeners. Only Shingo and his mother and her two well-disciplined maids were there.

"My son, what troubles you? Come to me, and rest your head on my lap."

He looked up at her. "It's Yasuko-san, Mother. I need you to advise me."

She took his head and at once felt the incredible tension in his neck and shoulders, and she began to salve him in the way she had always salved him. "How many times have I told you that your marriage was a political marriage, Shingo-san? A marriage decreed by your father, and his idea alone. I never would have agreed to it. He knows you are more able than Sadamasa-san in every way. You're a better swordsman. A better *go* player. A better strategist. A better leader. And that's why Sadamasa-san has only jealousy for you in his heart. Your father named Sadamasa-san his successor not because he is firstborn, but because he fears you."

His face contorted, and she gentled him.

Yes, she thought, your marriage to Yasuko-san was more than a political marriage, but didn't I tell you what to do two years ago?

"Do you really think my father fears me?"

She answered him at once, her voice silken but hard. "Why do you suppose Ryuji-sama sent you for the amygdala, and not Sadamasa-san? He told you that you were the only one of the clan he could trust to undertake so delicate a piece of diplomacy. And you believed him, my son. You believed him!" She whinnied. "That was false pride. You are many things, but you are not a diplomat. No, Ryuji-sama sent you to get you out of Miyakonojo."

He looked at her dully, unwilling to hear, but she persisted.

"And why do you suppose Yasuko-san was sent with you on the space voyage?"

"Because she knows the Amerikan language."

"My son, how this woman has the power to deceive you."

He twisted on the cushions. The comforting softness of his mother's lap was an unction, but inside he seared red-hot with remorseless passions that allowed him no tranquility. Now it was as if his mother's words had unlocked the dungeon of his mind, and the horrors he had kept pent-up came flooding out uncontrollably. He did not care that each image of Yasuko-san he heaped on the fire inside him threw the flames higher: the glossy raven of her hair half concealed behind a crimson folding fan. Crimson, the color of festivals, of happy time. Oh, the faultless gold of her skin, her fine features, carved by the gods, her lips, her perfect eyes . . . and the foreigner looking at her, drinking her in.

The Lady Isako shifted her weight regally. "You have two most beautiful consorts, and I have taken the opportunity of purchasing the contract of—"

He cut her off. "There are many beautiful women, but such beauty as Yasuko-san has is hers alone. It shows every time she moves. What strength is that? Deliberate grace. Mocking poise. A quiet, insolent composure. How the sight of her maddens me! I want to possess her, but always she retreats from me. She doesn't want me. She never has."

One day I'll close her eyes forever. Those eyes. Always so cool and guarded towards me. She doesn't want me. And it tortures me because I need to be wanted by her.

His mother touched his temple, and he whimpered.

Hasn't Shingo-san always had everything he wanted? she thought. I always took care of him. From a child, he has always had the best. I always saw that he was given the best, and everything he wanted. But I could not prevent his wanting Yasuko-san, or that vile marriage.

"Tell me," she asked him softly, probing his hurt. "How did she trouble you?"

He stared into the seamless white of the sky and imagined the perfect skin that stretched from horizon to horizon slit by a thousand small wounds, each a bleeding cut. He imagined a rain of blood, each drop scarring his soul.

"On the Amerikan nexus ship," he began, unsure how to tell it. "Whenever the *gaijin* and I were together, she would not retire as she should. And when I ordered it she would watch us from a distance. Even when my eyes challenged her she turned her head away, like this—haughtily."

"Yes, I can see that disobedience is in her, my son. She is willful and wicked."

The fire in his blood consumed him. "I saw it. I saw her doing it. She was comparing us. As men. As lovers. I know she was wondering about him."

"As lovers?"

Shingo heard the breath in his mother's voice. Oh, without doubt Yasuko-san was comparing us, he thought. And why? Only I could know the answer to that. It's because I never satisfied her. He said, "Nothing I ever did could touch her, really touch her. But it was never my fault. From the very beginning, whenever we lay together she gave her body but withheld her spirit. She never once gave herself—all of herself—to me."

At first she suffered me through duty to my father, he thought bitterly, then she learned how much it angered me to thrust deeper and deeper, and harder and harder. It only amused her. No matter how I hammered on the gates of her soul, never once did she open herself to me. Never once. Though I've taken her so many times, so many different ways, each time it was as if by force. And each time, afterwards, when I had loosed the pearls of my passion, her manner was always too knowing, always that

maddening mixture of hurt modesty and brazen imperti-
nence. "Now every polite word she speaks is spoken with
blue breath. But she never looks at the *gaijin* that way.
Oh, no."

The sky's wounds dripped blood, and the drops were
blossoms. They shimmered red in the bushes around him,
mocking his impotence.

"You really believe she has lain with him?"

He did not answer her question. It seemed too immense
to be answered.

"Shingo-san? Tell me. Do you believe it?"

He continued to look out at infinity, but then his stare
decayed.

"No."

"A pity."

The Lady Isako's words were soft and he hardly heard
them, but they jolted him.

"What?"

"I said it is a pity."

His eyes were orbs as he looked at her. "Why? Why
say that?"

"Because, Shingo-chan, if you had said yes you would
have had a way to escape her."

"What are you saying?"

"Don't you see? You must denounce her. Destroy her
before she destroys you!"

"Destroy her? I cannot!"

"You must!"

He tried to rise, but she took his chin in her hands and
twisted it so that he was forced to look up at her. "My
son, she tortures you. If you could prove she has lain with
the *gaijin* you could destroy her. Legally. Without redress.
And no one could prevent it, not even our Lord! Promise
me you will do that! Promise me!"

He closed his eyes, the sweat beading him.

"But I know they are not lovers," he said. "Though I know she desires it, still . . . still they are not."

She released him and he sprang up, making the maids flinch.

"So sorry, but you did say that you knew her thoughts." Isako lowered her voice to him. "Her eyes spoke, did they not? Did they not?"

"Yes!"

"*So desu ka!* And she is eager to learn *gaijin* ways? Did she speak with him in his language? She might have said anything. They could have shared intimacies in your very hearing. Don't you see how she enjoys taunting you?"

He turned, staring at the blooms on the passion flower vine that twined counterclockwise up the wooden post, astonishing structures of purple and cream more alien than any mind could devise. Their perfect delicate beauty enraged him.

"No!"

"Oh, Shingo-chan—it gives women like her pleasure!"

"No!"

"So sorry, but perhaps you know it does! In your heart perhaps you know I am telling you what is."

He ran from the pavilion, vaulting down the steps wildly, his madness jerking him like a puppet as he ran and ran. Then his sword was in his hand and he was among a mass of flowers, kicking and whirling and slashing until the space around him was a ruin of stamped soil and fallen petals. Even the carp had fled from the fury of his outburst.

A little later, the Lady Isako came to him where he knelt.

"You see, Shingo-san? You see now why she must be destroyed?"

"Yes!" He shouted it at the sky.

She stroked him and led him back to the pavilion and laid him down on the tatami beside her and she knelt and picked up her koto and plucked a soothing tune as she had done after his childhood tantrums.

Twenty years ago . . . Could it be that long since my little Shingo-chan was punished by his father for burning his favorite horse to death in the Imperial stables on Edo?

Hoshi—Star—that was the horse's name, I remember. How strange to have remembered such a detail. But horses are obstinate beasts.

She looked at her son's forehead, the same bulbous curve as Baron Harumi. He had been her lover in the great days on Edo before she had married Ryuji-san, and after. Great days. How she longed to be back there, on Edo, in those times, beautiful again and young again and so full of life. How she had made them dance to the tune of her koto then.

With a flick of her wrist she plucked the last infinitely sad dying chord. She dismissed her attendants, who bowed and backed away until they had melted into the scented shrubs. Now it was time for her to rouse Shingo-san, to bring him out of his melancholy. After the violence there was always melancholy. She thought of the gift she had brought him, the contract. It was the bond contract of Myobu, the most seductive courtesan in Edo. She had cost a great deal, she, her hair keeper, and her other attendants, five in all—along with the strange old woman she called her *obasan*, grandmother or aunty.

Myobu—her name meant Lady of High Rank—lived up to her honorary title. She had only agreed because the Shogu, the one who had promoted her to the Fifth Rank, was now too old to appreciate her, and Sakuma Kiyohide would not bid for her. Elsewhere in the Edo hierarchy, Honda Yukio's obsessional delight in sodomy had affronted her, and she had by her refusal offended him despite the conventions.

Myobu's knowledge was deep and very specialised. She

would be the one to disengage Shingo-san's affections
from Yasuko-san, if anyone could.

If anyone could . . .

30

He had been here two days now, and the tension was
gnawing at him unbearably.

Hayden Straker closed his eyes and lay back, trying to
take stock of himself. No Amerikan had ever ventured
this far into the closed society of Osumi. The occasional
political emissary or temporary ambassador had passed
into Yamato, usually on their way to a specially quaran-
tined compound on Edo, but most of the trade transac-
tions—both commercial and diplomatic—that passed the
few land miles between Miyakonojo and Kanoya City were
handled by a vast and insulating bureaucracy.

He had been given a suite of rooms in the part of the
Residency they called the *shinden*, a sanctuary of tranquility removed from gossiping women, remote from noisy
babies and children, and safe from the spying and schem-
ing of servants and priests. In the *shinden* only male *fudai*
were allowed.

Though he was alone amid the exotic strangeness of his
surroundings, he had begun to find them oddly familiar.
To be in an environment where women were segregated
was nothing new to him. Aboard independent nexus ships
entering Yamato, women were strictly controlled. No

working permits. No female crews. MeTraCor had deliberately appointed Aziza Pope their Base Controller at Osumi in order to demonstrate a point about Amerikan attitudes, but the gesture had not achieved a lot. There had occasionally been women passengers, and women had come aboard on various Zone aprons with entry permits for Osumi, but for the most part Amerikan women were rare in Kanoya City, and he had spent his adolescence separated from them.

Even on Seoul, his father's Korean mistresses had inhabited a separate house on the other side of the city, a house that, according to an unspoken but still mutually understood law, had always been forbidden to him.

"I sometimes believe they got it right in Yamato," his father had once laughingly commented about the samurai courts of the Kyushu worlds. "Yeah, women and men with a place of their own, and a Neutral Zone between where both sexes can meet as the desire takes them. Then up and off into tranquility again when either one's sick of the sight of the other! Perfect!"

Hayden Straker opened his eyes and looked around him. His rooms were light and airy and overlooked a graveled courtyard. It was a suite befitting a guest of ambassadorial rank, with attendants to bathe and serve him, and all the amenities of samurai life. They had taken away his clothes and washed them and brought them back to him cleaned. Silk shirt and pants all shining white, his jacket reconditioned and his shoes too. In the meanwhile he had worn a *yukata* and relaxed on the floor of woven rice-straw, meditating on the task confronting him, but he had held the amber gem of the new amygdala in his hand, fearing to let it out of his grip.

That's irrational, he had told himself. If anyone was going to steal it, they'd have stolen it before now. Perhaps that fact shows that in Lord Ryuji's court the protection of Lord Ryuji stands paramount. That's important, because if Lord Ryuji is weak then I'm as dead as Cadet Quinn.

He had put the big chrysoid down for a minute or two, but then had picked it up again quickly, feeling much better with it in the palm of his hand. The touch of it comforted him; the thought of what it represented filled him with despair.

Hayden Straker made an effort to fix his responsibilities clearly in his mind. He squeezed the golden light in the chrysoid hard, knowing that the moment of decision was approaching. Before dusk I'm going to have to formally hand it to Hideki Ryuji, he told himself. In return, I'll request a prefectural decree addressed to Yu Hsien in person, ordering the Kan to dissolve their blockade of Kanoya City trade. That's what's been agreed, but—

He heard servants moving about in the adjoining room then, and listened tensely, expecting his forebodings to materialise, but the servants vanished again, and after they had gone he got up and discovered they had returned his blasters. There was no explanation. He examined them suspiciously. They had been thoroughly cleaned, but the argentium tubes were missing.

Perhaps I can rely on Hideki Ryuji's honor after all, he thought. I wonder what sort of man he is?

He considered that while he dressed and ate a light meal of ice-cold raw fish and rice selected from a tray of similar delicacies, and prepared for the meeting with the Prefect.

Two days ago, after his first meal in the Residency, a poker-faced *joshu*—assistant secretary—called Gama had come to him with excruciating deference to ask if he lacked anything.

"The Excellency did not find his unworthy meal too disgusting?"

"The food was very—palatable."

"The gravity on Osumi suits the Excellency?"

"It is quite satisfactory, thank you."

"Then the Excellency is not too uncomfortable?"

"I am most comfortable, thank you. I assume the hour has been fixed for me to speak with the daimyo?"

The assistant secretary had looked at him in disbelief and spoke as if he had not heard the question. He explained that he had come to remind the Excellency what were the correct forms of a Prefect's Court. So he had sat down cross-legged and listened for an hour and accepted Gama-san's euphemisms and roundabout talk as gracefully as possible, then he had asked again when he would meet the daimyo.

"Surely the Excellency understands that such a thing is unknowable."

His irritation had increased, but he had smiled. "It seems to me a very simple question."

"It may be the will of the gods that one day the Excellency may have the good fortune to find himself summoned to audience."

"One day?"

"If the gods will it."

He had stood up then, nettled by Gama's cringing. "I want you to carry a message to the lord. Tell the daimyo I thank him for his kindness, but that I want to transact our important business as soon as possible."

Gama had stared at him again, aghast, but he had folded his arms until the man disappeared. The man had returned later, and brought with him a magnificent casket of antique Etorofu lacquer, as big as a boxed pair of monomachy blasters, saying that any gift the Excellency might want to offer the daimyo might be presented with exquisite effect when set against the delicate green silk of the box's interior.

"A gift?" he had asked, now completely exasperated by the runaround.

"Of course, the Excellency knows it is customary to make a spontaneous gift to a great lord such as the Prefect."

"Oh, yeah? Spontaneous, right?"

"Yes, yes, Excellency. A spontaneous gift is absolutely mandatory."

"But I don't happen to have anything worthy of a great Lord. I didn't exactly plan to—Oh, never mind."

Gama had simpered. "Oh, yes. Of course. Nothing could be a worthy gift to such as the head of the Hideki clan, but however insignificant the gift, the Excellency knows he must try to think of something."

That had been two days ago, and he realised that what Yasuko-san had told him about the virtue of patience in Yamato was true: without measureless patience there could not even be a beginning.

Now he resettled the lacquer box under his arm, praying that the waiting was over.

He watched the procession assemble in the spacious outer court with unhurried leisure, then the *joshu* led him into the reception hall, bowing continuously to left and right. The nominal reason for the audience, he was told, was the presentation of a new *kashira*, hilt piece, for the daimyo's sword.

A sword, Gama explained, might be nothing to an Amerikan, but in Yamato the sword was not merely a weapon. It had originated in Japan on Old Earth, when for five hundred years it had been the most deadly weapon in existence. It was one of the Three Sacred Treasures.

Hayden Straker looked about as he listened. Around him were fifty armored troopers and perhaps a dozen distinguished-looking men in the winged shoulder coats of office. Each coat was cut from a silk woven with his own distinctive *mon* crest. Each man was wearing the sword pair on his left hip, and the samurai were kneeling in a color-coded line, enjoying the wafts of air that came into the hall.

These, he decided, were Hideki Ryuji's *fudai* and *to-zama* vassals—the noblemen who formed the government of the Quadrant. Then, one by one, the daimyo's three sons appeared with their attendants.

They approached and bowed to him in order of precedence. He followed the promptings of the *joshu*, and with all the formality of a *noh* drama, the subject of conversation settled immediately and unshakably on the weather, as if all other topics were odious to one party or the other.

"There was wind last night."

"But I think we had more wind today."

"From the southeast, too."

"Yes. And cooling."

I guess it's safe ground, he thought irritably. Comments about rain and ultraviolet flux can't easily be misconstrued. But remember what happened to Shingo when I commented on his horses. By psi, they think there's a poetic meaning or an insult or a hidden message in every damned thing a man says, and how they take it depends only on their mood. How can they organise anything constructive thinking like that?

On a reflex he looked for Yasuko, then remembered that this would be an exclusively male gathering. By psi, there's no justice in a society that represses its women. I don't care how many Sectors work like that, it's revolting and . . . well, just plain primitive. I wish they wouldn't keep bobbing their heads at one another, he thought, annoyed at the unnecessary bowing. They're always nodding, but I should be doing it too. It's just one of the million differences between them and us they like to exaggerate.

Above the entrance arch was a great plaque with an

322 • Ken Kato

embossed motto in golden *kanji*. He scanned the Chinese
ideograms, reading their gate and pine tree forms from top
to bottom.

"An ancestor's virtue is shown by the conduct of his
descendants."

It was a famous Yamato proverb, he knew. And appropriate. But strange that it was not the other famous quotation defining the duties of a retainer that he had expected
when he had first looked up at the *torii* inscription.

Perhaps it's a good omen, he thought as they talked.
Perhaps it means that Hideki Ryuji isn't an obsessive *bushi*
like his second son. He certainly seems to want everyone
to know he thinks of himself as a responsible man. I hope
that's the truth. By psi, Shingo-san's temper is so brittle!
Pray the daimyo's more like his eldest son, sly and grave.
Or, better still, docile and slow-witted like the youngest,
what was his name again? Ah, yes, Noboru. Noboru-san.
I'll have to watch what I say and do, especially since
Gama-san was so much at pains to drum into me the
necessity of proper Yamato etiquette. They set incredible
store by ritual and ceremony. Best to humor their ways.
And vital not to upset anyone.

They started to move forward. The gathering was formal
and attended by great pomp, with lords and lackeys and a
column of half-armored soldiers and the beating of a huge
war drum with a skin ten feet across.

A white stallion preceded the column, with a small boy
of maybe six summers riding it all serious-faced and cute
in his miniature war gear and two stubby wooden swords.
The file was headed by the rider and behind him the *tsukai-
ban,* messenger corps, who strode forward carrying their
sashimono, or daimyo's long standards, socketed into the
back plates of their black armor on a bamboo pole.

With Sadamasa and Shingo and the youngest brother,

Noboru, going before him, and the Shukuro, or Chief Retainer, and his retinue immediately behind, Hayden Straker was at last conducted into the Audience Hall across a glittering courtyard of powdered quartz. He saw the *hinin* sweepers grovel abjectly. They were flanking both sides of the procession, down on their knees, heads tucked in as if making themselves as small as possible.

Poor pathetic slaves, he thought, climbing the steps. *Hinin,* also known as *eta*—outcastes, the nonhuman. Imagine the arid, barbarous power that makes so small of a man's life and soul; from birth their one duty is to care for the courtyard, to switch away the foot marks and leaves brought in by the wind, no more and no less.

Ahead, the stallion began to turn. Its tail went up and it dropped several moist balls of dung before the steps. They bounced and rolled, and the procession ignored them, and as the last samurai passed there was no rush from the sweepers. The gathering up of horse dung was the task of an even lower subcaste, which, Hayden Straker supposed, was the rock on which the self-esteem of higher sweepers stood.

They crossed a hideously spartan space and passed by a pair of over-ornate fountains. Their insistent sound made him feel like urinating. As they entered, each of Hideki Ryuji's tributary *fudai* lords slipped a golden offering into the water, token gifts of submission to Hachiman, the fearsome God of War.

So this is the Prefectural Government, he thought, and these men kneeling in rank and file are the heads of the planetary governments of all Kyushu Quadrant. So that must be Hideki Ryuji himself. By psi, look at that sword! There's no doubt who's in charge here. I don't know what I expected, but he seems a mortal enough man and by no means the demigod they make out. I can't say as much for his fat attendant, though. What the devil is he staring at? And who are those people squatting in the next room? Surely they can't allow servants to listen at the screens? A sudden piercing cry filled the hall.

"Shit!"

He turned his head sharply, but it was only the jarring scream of an albino peacock strutting and displaying on the planking outside the window. He felt suddenly self-conscious. No one else had moved a muscle.

The procession fanned out and stood in a rank before the dais. Hayden Straker waited, as Gama-san had told him he must, and he felt the levity drain away from him. These ministers fear the daimyo, he realised, wishing now that his own father were here to guide and support him. His father had followed matters connected with Yamato closely. He had attempted to share his knowledge of the samurai with his son on many occasions, but sons were often poor students, especially when their own passions were concerned with other places far away.

He reprimanded himself now for not having listened more closely. Knowledge is power, he thought regretfully. And wisdom guides, no matter who speaks it.

The solemnity of the gathering was tangible now. Tension was visible even on the face of the *shukuro*. The atmosphere became silent and uneasy, until the daimyo ordered his three sons forward onto the first rank. They, in turn, indicated he should follow. He knelt as they had, doubling his shins under him, and tucking in his feet. Bows were made low and held all around him, and he, as an honored guest, did the same. Hell of hells, my shoes! he thought suddenly. Slowly, respectfully, he reached behind him and prised them off.

After he was formally welcomed he bowed again, low like the rest, but with difficulty because of his clothes, which, being tight and stiff, did not permit the bending of any joint of the body much past a right angle. Slowly, as the formalities continued, he became aware of the deadening of his calf muscles. He felt embarrassment, knowing that in a very few minutes his legs would go dead, but he knew also he could not move, no matter how much it hurt. He felt his dignity was bound to be undermined, but to straighten his legs now would be unthinkable.

He took his mind off the discomfort as best he could by watching the daimyo's page prepare the snap-pipe. Snap rituals had become absorbed into the fabric of many A-type worlds like Osumi. The manners of these samurai had evolved from those of the old Kyushu Quadrant capital world of Kagoshima that revolved under the fierce primary of Alpha CrA, a star that burned with an effective temperature of 9,500 degrees Celsius and put out three hundred times the energy of the original sun. It was hardly surprising they took the whole business of snap with deadly seriousness.

He took the long, flexible hose of the snap-pipe and drew in a mouthful of water-cooled smoke, letting the pungent chemical taste linger on his tongue. Like the others, he expelled the smoke slowly from his nostrils, but did not inhale, fearing there might be something else in the blend. Relax yourself, yes, he thought, but you can't afford anything but the sharpest thinking here and now, some of the things they use to cut snap scrambles the higher mind and destroys the capacity for analytical thought—worse, it makes a man feel falsely intelligent, making him imagine great consequences from very ordinary things, so that he can believe he holds the secret of the universe in the palm of his hand, when in reality there's nothing there but a mote of dust.

Gama-san had told him to listen, and to make no remarks

when being spoken to. That it was the daimyo's prerogative to be heard uninterrupted. Privately, he had thought it was the best idea to keep silent anyhow, and watch carefully how the lord behaved towards his three sons, and how they reacted to him.

For half an hour he took no part in the conversation, but stole glances at Hideki Ryuji, feeling his powerful presence and appreciating his obvious intelligence. He tried to remember the history of the man and thanked psi he had at least half listened when his father had walked him round and round the *Chance*'s bridge and told him about the lethal politics that had set Hideki Ryuji on the hot seat at Miyakonojo.

Hideki Ryuji was the general who had been sent by the Shogun to impose his will on the Quadrant of Kyushu, and so end the bloody strife that had followed the Amerikan victory of a decade ago. The previous daimyo, Osumi no Choso Yoshinobu, and his army had been destroyed on Hizen, thirty light-years away. He recalled dimly that Choso-sama's first son had been killed in battle, burned down by Free Korean ships that had gone on to overrun all the worlds that the Choso clan had annexed in the Neutral Zone, even to the limit of entering the Zeta CrA system and almost reaching Satsuma too, and impudently extracting a ransom before they would withdraw.

Something of his father's concern with those lawless days filtered back from the depths of Hayden Straker's memory, something about Korean threats to burn down Jos Hawken's ships and waylay MeTraCor messengers and of bribes and dirty credit, certainly the histories of the Zone were rarely what they seemed, and never simple. What was it Ellis had said?

"Make no mistake, son, the Shogun's capacity to double-cross is unparalleled in all Yamato. That's how the sonofabitch got to the top in the first place. It's my belief he deliberately allowed the Free Koreans to sweep into Kyushu because he hated the old daimyo, and when the man's only surviving son, Choso Yoshisaburo, tried to take over at Miyakonojo, the Shogun withheld his consent. Of course, without the legitimacy conferred by the Shogun's word, the Choso's claim was flattened and the whole succession was thrown open again. You know what dirty, bloody family feuds can grow up over credit, son. By psi, you can imagine what it got like in Miyakonojo, where there's an entire Quadrant and all its great wealth to squabble over.

''Choso Yoshisaburo's boy was only four years old at that time, so he posed no threat to his father, but he had two psi-cursed aunts, and them and their greedy husbands both pounced on the prize.''

The memory flooded back bright and clear. These husbands had been Nenoi Kai and Shibata Junkei; the former was daimyo of Chikugo and the latter daimyo of Kirishima. Within the year Nenoi had murdered Yoshisaburo and proclaimed himself Prefect, but the nobles at Miyakonojo had set Yoshisaburo's son, now just turned five years of age, on the dais and Nenoi had had to flee back to the safety of Chikugo, his ship pretending to be a *kempei* ship.

This had been the crucial point at which the Shogun had intervened. He had sent Hideki Ryuji to act as Prefect until Yoshisaburo's son reached manhood. But the boy had been murdered only days afterwards, and the blame pinned on Nenoi Kai. Nenoi was still on Chikugo, and Shibata Junkei had been taken off by the Koreans, never to be seen again. Thus both of Hideki Ryuji's rivals had been swept away at one stroke.

A bloody people with an equally bloody history, Yamato samurai, he thought. Watch them, and watch yourself. And no more slipups, psi willing.

The ritual of the audience proceeded at a leisurely pace,

Ryuji-sama delivering a kind of homily. At first the address seemed to Hayden Straker to be good-natured, though strangely pointed. He struggled with the complicated Court Japanese, and saw there was more to the discussion than the small philosophic disputes and light teasing about abstract matters that seemed to fill the lord's harangue. After a while he heard himself referred to in passing, and knew he would soon be called to state his business.

Ryuji-sama called on his sons to join him on the dais, sporting with them—sparring, more like. He began to dispute with them about the color of the Shogun's moustache.

"But what is, is," Sadamasa told his father definitely.

"No, my son."

"How so, revered father? How so, can black be white?"

"Because my word makes it so."

"By what reason?"

"Because I am daimyo and Prefect. And a Prefect may not be contradicted, except by one of greater rank, is that not so, Mister Straker?"

He hesitated, remembering again Yasuko's advice and trying not to be lulled by the obliquity of the talk.

"I cannot disagree with you, my lord," he replied.

Hideki Ryuji nodded once, emphatically. "You see, I may not be contradicted. A guest has said so." The daimyo clapped his hands. "Therefore, what I command is. If I so choose, I can command that peacock to become a fox, and henceforth all subjects who see it will say it is a fox, because that is the command of their lord."

"Only until one of even greater rank commands that it shall be a peacock once more," Sadamasa said sullenly.

Hideki Ryuji stroked his beard. "What even greater man is that? Who may command that title here?"

"Only the Shogun, father." The title meant Supreme Military Commander.

"Or a too-favored son," Shingo muttered quietly.

For the first time Hayden Straker felt the bite of the brothers' animosity overtly. It sobered him. It was as he had thought. For all their polite words, this still remained a test. The father was watching, feeling out the attitude in his sons, and they in him.

Sadamasa took the wise course, subtly parrying and deflecting the cut. "Or by the Emperor. Yes, let us not forget the Son of Heaven on Kyoto. Or by the god Hachiman."

The eyes of the waiting ministers and nobles flashed to Hideki Shingo and saw that he remained impassive to the use of his guardian deity and the insinuation attached to it.

Hayden Straker watched, understanding enough to see the spider's web of hatreds waiting to catch the unwary. Something's happening, he realized. Something tremendously dangerous is moving just beneath the surface. Be careful! Remember what Yasuko told you: beware the Prefect's family, for they are always in ferment. No daimyo can afford to trust his own sons. And, in turn, no daimyo's son trusts his brothers. There's always a balancing alliance across the generations, a common cause between a daimyo and his weakest son, always directed against the appointed heir.

He began to sweat as his mind went over his huge task again, trying to get clear what he must ask for. What if the Kan have attacked Kanoya City already? he wondered with alarm. Do I ask that the Prefectural Edict should order reparations? It's only right the Kan should make good any damage they might have caused. And if so, to what extent? Should that include the trade they've interrupted and that we've lost in the meanwhile? And what about the dead? If there was fighting, there must have been casualties?

He thought of Arkali. She might have been injured, or even killed. If the Kan had landed troops they would have ransacked everything beyond the dome, including Jos Hawken's mansion. He tried to think through the consequences of that, appalled at the difficulties before him.

Perhaps I should seek long-term political ends, like trying to persuade Hideki Ryuji to limit the number of Kan troops Yu Hsien can station at Satsuma, or to fix the volume of Kan trade, now and in the future. Do I ask the daimyo to revoke their permit to trade in Kyushu? Can I insist on any point? How far can I afford to go? Sweet psi, what would my father have done?

Anxiety rose inside him. You're not made of the same flesh as he is, Hayden-my-lad. You're terrified. And you've no idea where to begin.

Another appalling thought struck him. What about the enterprises of Straker and Hawken? Maybe I should try to extract some special advantage for us if I can. What if the daimyo included a demand for the release of the *Chance*? Surely Yu Hsien could not resist such a demand, even though the capture had been made in a Lease traffic-designated orbit and was technically beyond the daimyo's jurisdiction. Even that's debatable, he thought. Even that. I don't even know for certain if the *Chance* was captured. . . .

He sensed that the wordplay was coming to an end. Finally, Hideki Ryuji's gaze slid away from his son and his dark eyes began to examine Hayden Straker critically.

"So, Mister Amerikan. You are a samurai in your own country?"

"No, my lord."

"No? Then you must do as a samurai commands." He paused delicately, drawing in a great sigh, and Hayden Straker saw that here was a man capable of refined cruelty. Did he really smother Choso Yoshisaburo's five-year-old son, as my father claimed?

"Tell me about Amerika. Does it have many worlds?

Do you have many peasants on New New York? Are there snakes in the jungles of your capital?''

''I fear that our capital is comparatively poor in snakes, my lord. Our capital world is on a small, cold continent— like Nemuro in wintertime, though without the great mountains.''

''And your villagers? They are prosperous?''

He considered, knowing the game the daimyo was playing was seem-the-ignoramus. ''There is one great city. Greater than all other cities in Known Space. It is full of poets and artists and men of psience and—''

Grave nods of astonishment and glances at his *fudai*. ''Greater than all in Known Space? It is called Rin-kun, is it not? Where the daimyo is a woman, no?''

''You could say so.''

''Over Rin-kun there is now a defense dome such as they did not have ten years ago.''

''Quite so.''

Hideki Ryuji nodded and leaned forward. ''Interesting that such a dome should have been built in peaceful times. How big is it?''

''That I don't know, my lord.''

''How can this be?'' Sadamasa asked like a man slighted. ''You must give my father an answer.''

''I cannot, my lord.'' He permitted himself a smile. ''You see, I have never seen the Lincoln dome.''

There was a flurry of doubting comment, turning to frank disbelief.

''But are you not Amerikan?'' Hideki Ryuji asked.

''As I have already explained to your second son, my lord, I was born in Amerika. On Liberty. But I have been a naturalised resident of Kanoya City since childhood.''

Hideki Ryuji absorbed the fact thoughtfully. ''Then what is your title?''

He spoke softly. ''I have no title, my lord.''

"He is a merchant's son," Shingo explained, pleased to diminish the foreigner in his father's eyes. "His father is Ellis Straker, a famous ex-pirate who calls himself a trader."

Again a flurry among the *fudai,* this time of indignation.

"Does my son speak truly?"

"He speaks half truly, my lord. My father does call himself a trader, for that is what he is. But he has never been a pirate."

The daimyo placed his knuckles on his knees, and all who watched watched his face carefully, knowing what was coming. "So. Shingo-san is a liar?"

"No, my lord." Hayden Straker's eyelids closed and opened slowly; an icy calm lay on his smile now. "I would prefer to say that Shingo-san is mistaken if he believes my father indulges in piracy. My father is a merchant."

"But is this not, therefore, only the assertion of a merchant's son?"

"It is without doubt the assertion of a merchant's son."

"I think," Sadamasa said, leaning back. "That for a merchant's son this man is not without honor. See, he has brought you a gift."

The queue of Hideki Ryuji's samurai hairstyle bobbed, and he stroked his beard. Then his chin tucked and he bowed a permission at Hayden Straker, who approached to lay before him the box.

As he tried to move, the pins and needles in his legs rose to a furious crescendo and he wished he could rub at the dead flesh below his knees to restore the circulation, but he still kept his face straight.

"May I humbly present this unworthy gift, my lord?"

"You have brought a gift for me?"

"Yes, Lord."

He offered the lacquer box, and Hideki Ryuji took it.

He placed it carefully before him and opened it so the green silk lining illuminated his face from below. Then a profoundly surprised expression buckled up his features. His pronunciation was crisp as he hooked out one of the two blasters by the muzzle guard and let it dangle.

"What is this?"

"The fine gift of an Amerikan merchant," he said proudly. "I can assure you that they are of the finest quality; they were made on Liberty and are both powerful and accurate. You know, of course, that Amerikan hand weapons are the best in Known Space, and it's blasters like these that protect our settlers in the Neutral Zone from the most savage—"

Hideki Ryuji stared at him in silence. There was total stunned silence in the entire hall. He burned with embarrassment, realising that he had foolishly allowed his mouth to run away with him.

The daimyo took out the other blaster and looked at them both together, mystified. Then he laid them portentously on the polished wood of the dais.

Hayden Straker's belly dissolved. Bad psi, he thought suddenly, I've made the biggest mistake I could possibly have made.

Now I understand! Gama-san meant me to put the amygdala in the box! That's the "gift" Hideki Ryuji expects. Of course! Now it all makes sense. It's beneath any samurai, much less the Prefect of all Kyushu, to negotiate a deal. That's merchant's work. That's what the talk about traders was all about. You fool! They were hinting it was time to bring the amygdala out, that I should offer it as a gift to the daimyo. Psi damn their idiotic ways! Why can't they speak plainly and deal plainly? Now I've insulted him. And what in the name of psi am I supposed to do about that?

Hideki Ryuji shoved the blasters forward with his fingertips. "Please. I cannot take your gift. It does me too much honor."

"If I have offended you, my lord—"

Hideki Ryuji's eyes dwelled on him. "You have not offended me. You are a *gaijin* and your lack of proper manners is to be expected, as with very young children."

"Your pardon, Lord." His hand strayed to the pocket where he could feel the heat of the one hundred *mensa*-rated chrysoid. "I apologise."

The daimyo's voice became infinitely patient, striving to repair the fabric of the meeting. He said, "Come and sit here, son of a trader, and watch. You will see how Yamato merchants do business." He nodded at the attentive pages.

Seconds later, a man in plain cotton clothing came groveling into the room. He had to be helped into the Prefect's presence, and was shaking so much he could hardly unbundle his rag. He was halted by the daimyo's secretary, the man whom the *joshu* had said was called Goro-san.

As the formalities of presentation were undergone, Hideki Ryuji whispered. "This man is a merchant. He has been waiting at the gates of the Residency for thirteen weeks. He knows he has just one chance to sell me a special sword blade. Both he and I know it is a blade by the Master Sadakiyo, of the province of Osumi in Old Japan, made in the reign era Geno, more than a thousand years ago. It is worth precisely eight hundred twenty-five thousand *koku*—our *koku* is an accounting unit of credit equal to the annual rice subsistence of one peasant family. The merchant knows that I have coveted the sword since I first heard of its existence thirty years ago."

It seemed an inconceivably vast sum to pay for a sliver of steel.

The blade was unwrapped with huge care. The seller brought out a four-foot length of gold-embroidered silk on which to lay it. It was a *katana* two *shaku* in length, but with neither handguard nor hilt, and the raw dark metal of the tang extended several inches from the polished part. "Please, Lord, this poor thing I bring to your Court . . ."

He described it in an awed voice, holding the corners of the silk with trembling hands. The silk rippled and the blade glinted, but the words of his description made small—excruciatingly small—of the piece. They were hastily curtailed as Hideki Ryuji yawned into the back of his hand.

In an aside he said, "Do you see how he avoids touching the blade?" Hayden Straker nodded, guessing that the acid grease of fingerprints might in some way damage the steel, but the daimyo went on, "It is our law that only samurai must bear swords. He must not touch the metal for fear of polluting it. He knows he would be put to death instantly."

The Prefect's nonsamurai secretary, Goro-san, took up the dialog with the merchant. "On behalf of our lord I will give you five thousand *koku* for the sword. You will take it and be gone!"

"A thousand thanks, Honorable Court Secretary. I am truly honored that so mighty a commander of warriors as our lord deigns to make so staggeringly huge an offer to so poor a seller of worthless trinkets as I. Our lord's generosity is a legend throughout the Empire."

"True, true. Very true."

"But, sir, this inferior *katana* is not worth even five thousand *koku*. I know this because when the agents of the lord of a Far Quadrant sought to buy it for five thousand *koku* only yesterday, I was forced to advise that were his master to buy it for ten times that sum, then his own people would say he possesses an inferior sword, and if for ten times that again they would say he can by no means afford the best. But . . .''

"But?"

"But had his master instructed him to offer one million *koku*, then his subjects would say he is truly a Great Lord. Of course, I had to say: please don't insult your master by offering a lesser sum than befits a Great Lord.''

Goro leaned in on the seller aggressively. "And was the lord of this Far Quadrant greater than our master?"

"No, Honorable Sir! That cannot be! This Prefect was as dirt beneath our master's feet! Our master is five times the man this other lord could ever become.''

"You think I should offer you five million *koku* on his behalf?"

The seller's eyes glazed. "The generosity of Hideki Ryuji's noble servant is utterly beyond contemplation. But, in conscience, I cannot accept so vast a sum.''

"In that case, motherless weasel, I shall allow you to sell me the *katana* for one hundred fifty times its real value—which is just five thousand *koku*—and you shall have in addition one tenth the subtotal sum, as a mark of my master's charity.''

"Our master's charity is at least as great as his generosity, Lord.''

"Silence! Both are infinite, and so cannot be compared.''

"It is as you say.''

Hideki Ryuji nodded, and his man produced the scrolls of payment. The seller crawled away from the dais abjectly, a promissory note for seven hundred fifty thousand *koku* of generosity in his right hand and seventy-five thousand of charity in his left.

Hayden Straker watched, disturbed by the ritual humiliation. He remembered Kurihara village and the caste rigidity that permeated every level of society here. He thought of the birth status that locked everyone into a false and immovable destiny, and the quotation from Lord Naohige that the head of the Hideki clan had chosen to adorn his *torii*. The trader was much richer than his customer. But only in terms of credit.

As the sword seller retreated, something in the back of his mind made him decide on a tremendous gamble. He took the amygdala from his pocket and placed it on the tatami before Hideki Ryuji.

All eyes went immediately to the metacrystal. A gasp went up, more at the outrageous breach of protocol than at the stone itself. Hayden Straker's heart hammered. The moment was upon him at last whereby Kanoya City would stand or fall. His face unmoving, his eyes on the daimyo's.

He said, "I am a trader's son, my lord, but I am not here to trade. Nor did I come here to enter into negotiations. I came merely to deliver this new amygdala into your hands. It is yours now. Please take it. Then, I believe, since you are not the descendant of despicable ancestors, you will do what your conscience dictates."

31

The women stripped Hideki Shingo of his *fundoshi* so that he stood naked before them. They led him to the steps of the Pool of Infinite Tranquility, and as his garment fell away he looked over the glassy surface of the water. At its deepest it was navel deep, nine paces square and cut into solid rock that had been lipped with granite incised with the galaxy-whorl *mon* of the Hideki clan. Here steps led down into it, and a small star-shaped notch was cut in the far end over which icy mineral water brimmed to feed an ever-running channel.

Without pausing he walked to the top step, descended it, descended the next, and the next, and once again, until the icy water reached his upper thighs and then he turned and, smoothly, as if lowering himself onto a tatami, he sat down.

He closed his eyes, anticipating the agony as he lay back and let the water of the pool swirl up around him. His shoulders and arms tensed on the stone lip and his head hung forward like the image hanging from the god crosses of Neutral Zone interlopers. He felt like a man baring his neck for the executioner's sword.

How important it was for a samurai to daily demonstrate unflinching control before others.

Hideki Shingo was of the pure line, and he had learned that this water flow was the grant given by the god Hachiman for the true warrior to train and adjust his mind. Here, ice-cold spring water issued from a natural vent in the floor of the pool; from deep below the earth it welled up and bubbled. As he sat there it jetted into the cleft of his buttocks, played directly onto his testicles.

Aaaaagh . . .

He suppressed the gasp that echoed in his skull and remained still even though the icy current daggered him. He stared stoically at the hewn granite of the walls and the rock ceiling, containing within his chest a bellow of shock. Then he clamped his teeth together, feeling the flush of cold-pain to their roots and knotting in his temples and lower belly, and with a supreme effort of mind he forced himself to keep breathing without interruption.

How can there be shock when I expect it? How can there be pain when I have chosen not to acknowledge it?

It was a simple release, a self-inflicted torture, but also a meditation, and one that he had lately come to crave. It was as if the all-pervading physical discomfort drove his most difficult inner problems to a deeper chamber of his mind, a place where they could be solved.

He knew that soon he would get out of the pool and feel his flesh burn with incredible heat. How foremost is the sensation of extremes, he thought. And how true the ancient wisdom that if a man would achieve an objective—any objective—first he must attempt its opposite.

Oh, yes. Tear down the Adventer church before you would build the Shinto shrine on its site, fight in order to make peace, humble yourself to achieve great heights. And freeze the body with pain to experience the true pleasures of the heat of fire. But the fire will come later, after the cold has served to focus the mind, hard like a Jewel of Power.

Isn't that what the *gaijin* said before that incredible interview with my father? A world like Nemuro, in the wintertime, but without mountains.

Cold Nemuro in the Neutral Zone was once a world that belonged to the Empire. For ten years it has not belonged to us. After the demise of the great fleet at the hands of the Amerikans, many new *han* worlds have been left without lords. So saturated with shame were they on Nemuro that there was mass *seppuku* of the samurai. There was no question of leaving the underclasses to live on, alone and out of control. Without samurai the *sangokujin* and *hinin* would have degenerated into savage animals, so steps were taken to poison the atmosphere.

Oh, the glory of those *teakiyari* retainers! How exact to the spirit of *bushi* to commit *tsuifuku* together when it became obvious that they would have to vacate the planet.

Hideki Shingo felt his muscles begin to spasm. The shivering was coming upon him, and he forced himself into relaxation in the rigorous way he had been taught by the Zen ascetics.

I, too, have seen ice, he told himself, gripping the thought in his mind so that it distracted the pain. Remember it! See it! Fill your mind with it. . . .

Ah . . .

Yes, it was on Kyoto, when I was a young child. My father was accompanying the Shogun on a visit to the Court of the Emperor Mutsuhito. It was a visit that turned out to be five years long.

All modern materials were, and still are, banned on the Emperor's world. No technology postdating the sacred watershed moment of 2 P.M. on October 21, 1600, is ever admitted. The sole exceptions are the landers that are allowed to touch down on elevated timber platforms on Chi-Ku, an island remote from the Imperial Palace. In its entire history, Kyoto had never known a single refrigerator or thermodynamic stasis pack.

I thought those floating diamonds that the nobles made much of were things of great value. One day I secretly took one of them from the bowl that was set beside the Shogun's lunch tray. When Baron Harumi surprised me I tried to hide it in my hand. But the harder I gripped it, the more the ice stung. The ice was hard and transparent like diamond, but more precious than diamond. And yet in my hand it magically dissolved into water. It melted away as I watched, but I can feel the panic still, after all these years. Water dripped from my fist, and when it was gone I was terrified that the Shogun would notice I had stolen it and demand it back. How many years passed before I learned that the Shogun's mountain ice was wrapped and boxed and brought swiftly to the Imperial Palace from Mount Asahi.

Yes, they told me ice melted away so quickly that though a full horseload might start the journey, only a piece the size of a rock-melon would arrive in the Palace. Ice, more precious than diamonds on Kyoto, but still used by the Emperor in high summer to cool his drinks and to soothe his headaches . . .

Aaahhh . . .

The pain climaxed, and his teeth began to chatter.

By the gods, he thought, biting his jaws together hard three times then relaxing them, I cannot do as my mother wishes. I cannot. The very thought of the *gaijin* and Yasuko-san sends me into a boiling rage. How can I plot to destroy her when I know I cannot live without her? I want her. Totally. Body, mind, and soul.

This pool is unbearable today! It's far colder than yesterday. But that's good, because such cold contains a lesson. It's the key to the Amerikans' success. They are cold-blooded peoples. They must have come originally from a part of Old Earth tempered by cold. That's why they are as they are. That's why Yamato has been invaded successfully through Osumi. That's why their President chooses steamy Osumi as a pore through which to infect all of Yamato. They are fierce and they know nothing of proper human behavior, because their minds have been focused by winter cold, focused to a star point, a bright cold, blue-white star point like the amygdala in the Shogun's sword. . . .

Aahh . . .

A sudden tremor struck Hideki Shingo, but he maintained muscular control over his tensing stomach until the cramp subsided. He closed his eyes, feeling the cold right to the marrow of his bones now.

Yes, I must learn to think how the cold-blooded *gaijin* think. That is important now. Events have turned out incredibly well for me. With a little careful planning I'll be able to apply my newfound leverage, now that the amyg-dala is here in Miyakonojo. Will my father eventually decide to throw the Kan out of Kanoya City? I hope so, because even a shit-eating *hinin* may profit from the fight between a dog and a pig. In the world through which a samurai must move, the penalty for not staying one jump ahead is death, but I will be daimyo of Osumi, and it will be Sadamasa-san's head that rolls in the dung.

Ahh . . .

To beat back the pain he fixed his mind on the Emperor Denko, knowing that he had more than a little of the great man's blood in his veins. A great man. The greatest. Denko had not scrupled to behead two of his brothers, nor to imprison his father. He had known how to deal with *gaijin* pirates who plundered the ships transporting the first set-tlers across the Zero Degree Plane—he had forced the Amerikan and Kan governments to render compensation for every Yamato ship taken. Soon the Amerikans will have to deal with such a leader again, he thought, and even the *sangokujin* scum who populate so many of our worlds will recognise me as the living incarnation of Denko. Soon. Very soon now.

He was suddenly roused by movement in the water. He felt the lap of ripples wash his chest. He did not open his eyes. Always the *mamaoya* sent the slave girl to him. It was the same each afternoon, the same slave, an exceptionally passionate young girl, skilled and ritually cleansed for his enjoyment, and specially selected, too. Chosen for her pure blood, her hot, strong sexual appetite, and her man-ners, which were those of a vixen.

But this time he kept his eyes closed, looking at her instead with only the third eye of his mind, imagining her as he knew she would soon be opposite him in the pool, sliding breast-deep across the water, her young and slender body hidden, her hair long and thick and black, the part framing her face still dry. She would betray nothing on her face, despite the pain of the cold, despite the fine hairs erecting in her dark skin. Her expression would be pure, just as he demanded. She must be as brave as he was in the cold, or he would send her away forever. She knew that.

He would meet her eye, then, and he would watch her come to him. He would make her wait until she could not control her shivering, then he would take her and lift her up into the warm air and lay her on the granite lip of the pool, or carry her dripping to the futons, and there he would run his fingers over her body, which would grow warm, and he would feel her but the pads of his fingers would be white and wrinkled with immersion and numbed, and her touch would be otherworldly, and all the time he would know that she was praying that this time his seed would flow and be barbed so that it would catch in her belly and put her with child, because then she would be honored and her position in the hierarchy would be enormously enhanced. When he felt the power rise in him she would straddle him and massage him so expertly, with such longing. Then they would couple and he would slip inside her and she would be like a raging furnace after the ice water. And so they would continue until he was sure that he had her entirely in his power, that she was holding nothing back, and only then would he dominate her and glimpse Nirvana.

He opened his eyes. Startled that he could feel no movement in the water. The slave girl was not there, but another, standing above the pool, reflected quiveringly in it.

This was not a girl, but a woman, older, and swathed in astonishing veils of ghostly silk, pale turquoise and as insubstantial as moonlight on spring dew. She had rippled

the water with her hand and drips fell from the red daggers
of her fingers like diamonds. He stared at her as if she
were a vision, and the shivering began to take him.

"Lady . . ."

He saw that she had undergone the sixteen rituals of
adornment: a dead-white face painted with bloodred lips
and eyebrows lifted high above her eyes, he could smell
the scent of her, musk and melon and sandalwood, her
hair flowed blue-black from a knife-sharp parting below
which the robes cascaded. Her eyes were sabers. She wore
tabi socks and high-platformed wooden *geta* only just visible at her hem, giving her the elegance of height.

"Lady," he said, and began to rise from the water.
"Who are you?"

"My name is Myobu. I have come for your pleasure,
Lord."

Her voice was like a fountain. She came towards him,
stepping into the bright sunlight that dazzled the pleasure
dome at the end of the chamber; her two attendants followed gracefully. The air here was cooled by the water,
and the perfume of the gardens made it as sweet as rice
wine. He stood before her dripping cold water onto the
rough granite and then the tatami and down-filled futons,
his shivering uncontrolled now. He knew without shame
that his *inkei* was shriveled small as a walnut. Her young
attendants toweled him, dried his skin and hair, whispering
promises, rubbing piquant oils into his muscles, oils that
gave a deep fire to him.

The courtesan, for that was what she must be, was
clearly one of the finest money could buy, fully skilled in
the erotic arts. Who was she? Who had been to so much
trouble to bring her to Miyakonojo for him. His father?
She was a miko come down from the Shrines of Nara, but
women were often the most lethal weapon of the powerful.

It was the simplest thing in the world to poison a man with a loving cup, for a courtesan's attendant to open a vital vein or to reach down with a glass razor when he was striving for the Moment and sever him. He pictured himself raving in anguish down the corridors of the Residency, naked, his lifeblood gushing away, his manhood irretrievable in some specialist assassin's crack.

The horrible vision melted as she began to reveal herself. Her attendants removed her clothing exquisitely, and he touched her and together they sank into the silken nest. Then the attendants were naked also. They turned their hands on their mistress, touching her, drawing their nails along the insides of her outstretched arms, her equal breasts and flat, muscular belly, so that her nipples budded and her eyes rolled up into their lids. They kissed and caressed her and fanned her long hair out over the pillows to invite him smilingly, and the music of koto and *shakuhachi* drifted from a far pavilion beyond the canvas *maku* camp curtains, borne to them on the hot wind.

He began to grow unbearably large as he watched them draw her legs apart to reveal the shaved mound of her *o-manko,* the pucker of scented flesh that glistened now and held his desire. One of the girls marveled at him, took him, her mouth succulent. The wavering screens returned the harsh light and patterned the contours of their bodies as they mingled, then the courtesan began to coo and moan softly and he knew he could do nothing but couple with her, not even if she had held a razor of glass in each fist.

32

She had been briefed that this would be the most difficult assignment of her career. She would have to break every rule learned during the long training of a geisha. From the age of seven when she had been a *shikomi-ko*, through her teens when she had assisted by pouring *sake* for other geisha, at her debut and defloration ceremony, and with every client since, always there had been a lengthy foreplay in which the aim was to make a man feel as much a man as possible. The gratification of samurai men, she had been warned, was three parts spiritual, seven parts intellectual, and two parts physical. She had been trained to understand that sex was the last act of a liaison, often never attained, and that anticipation was the keenest pleasure. And so it had been always. But this time she had been told to disregard all the forms.

"He likes it like this," the Lady Isako had explained, exactly describing the ways her son sought his pleasures. Then she had asked, "Do you understand me exactly, Myobu-san?"

"Exactly, Lady. But please understand that the price must be special also."

The glint of steel had appeared in Isako's eyes. "I have heard that you gave birth to a bastard son six years ago. It would be about the time you said you went to Sendai for six months."

"Your informant is extraordinary, Lady."

Isako-san had taken that as tacit admission, knowing. "It was also said that this boy's father was not unimportant—the scion of a family of particularly pure blood—but that the father would not or could not make provision. Do you not agree that, since your son is of samurai seed, it would be tragic if he were to end up without a fief of his own?"

"If only such a thing were possible, Lady."

"Perhaps it is not impossible. I wonder if you can imagine a world in this Quadrant that would be appropriate to his bloodline? Nowhere too onerous, you understand, else the whole idea may prove to have been ill-conceived. Please give the notion some detailed consideration, and I shall await your answer."

So now, outwardly, Myobu was a pliant, lusting vessel of desire. Each supple limb articulated at the perfect angle of temptation to invite Shingo-san, each sighing, writhing movement hypnotic in its power to hold him. But inwardly, she was dancing.

The moves she made were learned skills, every skill a natural talent that had been refined and brought to sensual perfection by years of study and practice under one great teacher and a great many singular clients. She knew she could perform this act exquisitely, utterly confident that her face and body were under total command, and sure also that her own private thoughts were completely invisible to the man who rode in her.

. She felt him come to her, lay his hands on her, and her intuitive response was precisely the response he most needed. She felt his bull-like weight, measured his desire, opened her lips with her fingers, guided him. He was gripped by her passion; her head tossed and her breathing modulated. She gasped, this time without deliberation.

Horribly, the cold of the pool was still in his flesh, his hair was lank, he felt like a man in death, a drowned man, but warrior strength was still in his thighs and biceps and they forced her down. It'll pass, she thought. The girls will anoint his back and buttocks, and massage the life back into him. She gave the subtle sign, and they began to manipulate him as he arched like a bent bow to position himself. Then she drew herself farther apart to accept him and he entered her, grunting deeply, with each heave of his muscular back.

Her cries whimpered higher as she matched her rhythm to his. He groaned as he rode her, but then, incredibly, his *inkei*'s strength began to fade. She redoubled her movements, monitoring her inner feelings with concern, drawing every last skill from her repertoire, making herself moister by a conscious effort, as the *genro* geisha had taught her.

So that was it . . .

She had felt it. She had suspected it when the Lady Isako had talked with her. His very special needs. That's what the old bitch had said. What special needs, she had thought, knowing that whatever it was she could accommodate him. The ones with special needs were usually the easiest to satisfy, and by far the most grateful. He seems violent, but it's an odd kind of violence. A kind of frustration. What is it he's searching for? It's so hard to understand men, even after so long studying them. They're so completely different to women.

She knew instinctively that she must concentrate her body's being in her most highly trained muscles. In the depths of her *o-manko* he began to stiffen again, his flesh burning now, his hairless chest slick with sweat, sliding against the erect flesh of her nipples. She smiled inwardly, blessing her mother for putting her into this most favored of professions.

"But, Mother, I don't think I'll ever understand the minds of men," she had said on a visit home one year after her defloration ceremony.

"Do you understand the minds of horses?" her mother had asked shrewdly.

"No."

"Then what is the problem? Ride. And earn your living."

It was true. Looked at like that, there was no difficulty. Men were so easy to ride and control, much easier than horses, and much more rewarding. What other profession could have brought her into contact so intimately with so many rich and powerful men? What other profession could have taught her to develop her private mind, and allow it to circle in the high orbits of ambition, with every chance of fulfilling that ambition? If only she could play the game correctly.

It was a pity she had had to leave Edo. The Shogun's establishment there had turned against her. His wives, and the wives of the other nobles, had seen her through suspicious eyes, then there had been scandals, and they had wanted to banish her.

That is why she had come here—before they could move against her. And Osumi had seemed a suitable temporary alternative, and the Lady Isako had convinced her that events were stirring here. Momentous events . . .

He continued to labor for his pleasure, seeking her depths, but his breath was husky in her ear, his heart pounding. What was he searching for?

As if striving for the ungraspable, he became furious and she responded again. Her professional mind was helping him with all her ingenuity, but her private mind was wandering. Why was she here? What possibilities were there for her with Shingo-sama?

Why was the thought of Kirishima, Hideki Shingo-sama's personal *han,* so insistent in her mind? What use was Kirishima to her, or to him? An impregnable polar fortress on a world laid waste physically by the close proximity of three raging nexi. The system was a major transport junction and a vital link in at least six of Kyushu's chains, but no world of ease and luxury—perhaps it was worth something as a place of last resort, a place to retreat to in time of war, but it was not a capital to rule over in splendor.

Is it really what I want? she asked herself. Now Kirishima is in the far reaches of Kyushu. But it will be a great transport center in future·centuries when the interface of exploration pushes it to a commanding position in the Quadrant. Now Kirishima is a complete backwater of political power, a place granted to the second son of a Prefect as a sop to limit his ambition, but it might make a suitable reward for my skills should Shingo-sama find success and become daimyo elsewhere.

Yes, she thought. That will be my answer to the Lady Isako. Kirishima. In the fullness of time. For my bastard son whose real father no one will ever learn, not even him.

Shingo faltered.

Yes, his moon's definitely waning before the full. He's not going to make it! Alarm thrilled through her. What's the matter? Surely it can't be me? Then her darkest worry. Please don't let it be me. Not yet. I've got years left yet. I'm at my peak. Yes, it must be him. Only him . . .

The part of her mind that never ceased to think shut out her fears. It roamed over the opportunities she had discovered at Miyakonojo as she coaxed him onward and feigned ecstasy for him.

"Oh, oh, oh, oh . . ." she moaned, urging him to spend his seed, raking his back with her fingernails, tightening her inner muscles again to maximize his pleasure on each thrust.

He pushed into her again and slid on her oiled body. She bit her lips together as if waves of pleasure were sweeping through her, driving her mind into oblivion. He thrust into her one last time, breathless, sweat pouring from him, and withdrew suddenly. His *inkei* was flaccid now, though he had not unburdened himself.

Myobu lay there shuddering beside him, gasping for breath, lavishing praise on his manly strength, on the size of his male root, and on his unmatched capacity to satisfy a woman. The attendants stared at their mistress, awed. But beneath her seamless professionalism, Myobu wondered at him. It was worrying, the first time she had failed to bring a man, any man, to the Moment of Unbeing.

Perhaps that's why he's so ferocious in his ambitions, she thought peevishly, then, more practically, I must consult my apothecary; her magics contain a cure for every ill. She will prescribe the powder of the blue lotus mixed with honey, or perhaps vinegar that has had the testicle of a ram or goat boiled in it. Once he has drunk of that he will surely gain in potency. It will help draw that rage out of him, then he will be brought wholly under my spell.

He sat up like a busy man of affairs, without looking at her or speaking to her or giving any indication, but she saw that all the muscles of his limbs and back and neck were incredibly tense. He dressed, declining the aid of her attendants, quickly wound his obi, and all the while she eyed him languidly like a woman so thankfully exhausted by a man's prowess that she could not even raise a full smile or move to close her legs.

Perhaps that's good, she thought as he left. Better than if he had spurted like a bull. No one knows except himself and myself, and since my own reputation is at stake, as well as his manly self-respect, I'm certainly not going to jeopardise everything by letting him know that I know that he failed. Let that be the bridge between us, and the hold I shall use over him if I should need to.

The music came to an end, and she began to repair her makeup and put up her hair. She wanted to wash herself, but that would have to wait. The cold water in the pool was disgusting. No good for washing a delicate skin. Still, the payment here is compensation, and there may be opportunities, just as the Lady Isako promised.

So what of Hideki Shingo-sama—he of the Flaccid Root? she wondered. How important it is to know history and to learn the lessons of the past.

Already the part of her mind that made political calculations was beginning to go over the situation again, giving her hope.

Some years ago, when the Choso clan had ruled at Miyakonojo, Kirishima had been ruled by a different second son. When Choso Yasumoto had died and his son Choso Yoshinobu had taken over the Prefect-ship, his brother had disdained to render tribute, and Yoshinobu had sent his own son-in-law, Shibata Junkei, to enforce the proper collection of taxes. Junkei had deposed the son and become daimyo of Kirishima himself, but then a glitter of possibilities had been opened when the Amerikans and Koreans had begun to appear in the Neutral Zone. Free Korea's marauding vessels had killed Yoshinobu in the first incursions, and they had gone on to lay siege to the Kirishima system where Shibata Junkei was holding out.

The triple nexus was vital because it was one of the few that communicated directly with the nexi of the Zone, and, like a mountain pass in the hands of enemies it would permit foreign warships access to Yamato's internal chains should it fall.

After three months the Koreans had been forced to withdraw, but their hostage had been none other than Shibata Junkei himself, and they had taken him to their stronghold of Ulsan where, for all anyone knew, he remained still.

So what if Shingo-sama kills his father and half brothers immediately? she asked herself. He will still have to persuade the Shogun to support his claim to power, and that could be difficult. There are two possible obstacles. Of the old Choso clan descended from Yoshinobu, Yoshisaburo is dead at the hands of his brother-in-law, Nenoi Kai. Yoshisaburo's five-year-old son was conveniently smothered by Ryuji-sama years ago, or so the Lady Isako swears. But there is still Nenoi Kai himself, discredited by Ryuji-sama after the child's death—that was clever of Ryuji-sama to blame the smothering on Kai-san, but the fact that he's still alive just across the Honshu boundary is something Hideki Shingo must not overlook.

The foremost threat to Shingo-san is Choso Yoshinobu's second son-in-law, Shibata Junkei, she thought. My maids have discovered that he is still languishing on a Korean penitentiary world, a horrible low-gravity, gas-giant moon in the Ulsan system. Ryuji-sama has been outmaneuvered in that regard. The Lady Isako says that when the Koreans first took Junkei-san they tried to hold him to ransom. Then they realised they would get nothing for a pretender's worthless carcass—why should Ryuji-sama pay for the release of a man who also trumpeted his claim to sit upon the Prefect's dais at Miyakonojo? To kill him, perhaps, but for Shibata Junkei to be locked up on a dark moon of Ulsan was just as good as his being dead, wasn't it?

From what the Lady Isako says, it appears that Ryuji-sama has always been willing to play a waiting game. It has been his potent policy to do nothing so many times. And in this instance he must have chosen to do nothing, because by doing nothing he was imposing an exquisite torture. Every year that Shibata Junkei spent in captivity would take him further from a return to power, and on a frigid satellite of only one-tenth standard gravity, his muscles and circulation would adapt over the years to the point where he would no longer be able to leave. The first ship he climbed aboard with compensators set to one gee would kill him.

When it became clear that a ransom would not be forthcoming, the Korean general, Jae-won Roh, made his turnabout. He stopped saying, ''Give me this much credit or I will hold Shibata Junkei forever,'' and began to say instead, ''Give me this much credit or I will release Shibata Junkei tomorrow.''

Sooner or later, Shingo-sama, you would be wise to buy Shibata Junkei's release, Myobu told him silently. Yes, and then you should kill him, or my plans and yours and those of the Lady Isako will never come to fruition.

She rolled over and put her eye close to the *shoji* screen. Hideki Shingo stalked down the gravel path of the formal garden. He was making for his own household and she could see he was in a turmoil of unfocused rage. The gardeners and the crones who huddled by the steps with gossip-hungry eyes made obeisance as he passed, and then he was gone, rage and all, to find his only wife.

33

Hayden Straker sat in the saucer vehicle, sickened by the ceaseless rolling of the vehicle's contour correctors as it overflew the ground. With less than six feet of clearance under the machine, it was somewhere between the motion of a crippled lander and a ground-car driven across open country, but ten times as nauseating as either. The thought that the battle for Kanoya City might be fought tomorrow—and that if it was he would be in the middle of it—did nothing to settle his stomach.

This was Shingo-san's personal war chariot, his *sorasencha*. Yasuko's presence there had amazed him. She has courage, he thought. She's exercised her samurai right to ride to war beside her husband. How does she stay so calm? It's as if this was a pleasure cruise on Disney World. She looks really strange in that black armor. I'd swear she's enjoying this! Jeezus, if she knew the dread I'm feeling she wouldn't think much of me.

He looked away at the horizon. They were skimming the surface, doing a very stately mile a minute, their vehicle gondola open-topped and unshielded. The sound of the wind was like softly tearing silk, tugging at the long edge of their huge *sashimono* banner. It's black galaxy *mon* was repeated three times vertically on a tangerine background.

The banners of the other war vehicles and troop carriers heading the Hideki army fluttered like Day-Glo flames. There were seventeen "sky tanks" leading the vast column. Sadamasa traveled in second place, chevron-right, after his father's leading vehicle; then came Shingo's, chevron-left. Specially chosen *fudai* followed in strict rank order. Behind them, the mass of the army followed in skimmers whose horned shapes reminded him of giant stag beetles.

The entire capital defense force had been mobilised. Everything bar three militia divisions and half a dozen specialist units. The Prefect's signal had gone out planetwide, warning all fiefholders on Osumi to expect a general mobilisation. The order was one of the few that had the power to partially nullify the technology veto, allowing samurai to be jetted to the capital. The hardware itself had appeared from an underground arsenal built beneath the Residency.

He had watched the forces of the Hideki assembling in Miyakonojo over a period of seventy-two hours. On the first couple of days, thousands of samurai, crazed on war chants and flying the banners of Osumi's twenty-seven *han*, had appeared in response to the Prefect's order. All had been regimented and fully equipped. They had started out from the Residency yesterday, and at Hideki Shingo's invitation he had joined the number-three vehicle, climbing high up the matt-black side of the saucer.

Beams had ripped into the air as they departed. There had been jubilant martial displays. He had looked down from the gondola of the *sora-sensha* and wondered how anyone or anything could resist the ferocity of the wild horde that swept around them like a whirlwind.

The transparent plex canopy designed to shade them from the weather had been retracted from the twenty-foot-diameter gondola, and Shingo's own *sashimono* undulating beside the comms whips had proclaimed their status. Their mount's engines were capable of local Mach-1 in an emergency, but for delivering their one hundred airborne infantry with minimum scatter it was necessary to slow right down, and he knew that the samurai fighting code placed a premium on displays of reckless courage like the "buzzing" of weapons emplacements.

The flanks of *sora-sensha* three were decorated with three horizontal white bars that shone brightly in the diffuse light. The armored pilot had sat in a pod on the leading tumble-home of the saucer, controlling its movements with deft stabs of his feet and hands on the four control plates.

At first the streamlined dignity of the sky tank, its impressive bulk, and their height above the fields made him feel like a mounted warrior, but he had not been able to relax and enjoy the experience. He was drawn taut by Yasuko's presence beside him. Her influence was tremendous. He could discern the womanly shape of her body beneath the lobster-tail armor she was wearing and hear the soft jangle of the corded plates. By psi, she radiates femininity even now, he thought. But it's a strong femininity that's sensuous and so distracting. I'd like to know her, but that'll never be.

When they had been about to depart he had wanted to speak to her, and when her husband had climbed down he had asked, "Are you going to come with us all the way to Kanoya City?"

"If the gods will it."

"But it could be very dangerous. There could be a fight."

She had looked away from him very deliberately. "Perhaps there will not be a battle."

"Why don't you stay in Miyakonojo with the other ladies?"

"I am ordered here."

"Ordered? By whom?"

"Mister Straker, that is not your concern."

And that had been the end of the morning's conversation, even though he had apologised. That afternoon, Shingo had casually produced a scroll bearing the Prefect's seal. "My father has honored you with this."

He had opened it and tried to read its archaic formula. "My thanks to your father, but . . . what is it?"

Shingo had maintained his unsmiling composure. "You are hereby appointed a Commander of Fifty Men."

He had digested that, unsure what to say. "Then I guess I'm greatly honored."

"It is of no consequence. A matter of protocol only to

permit you to accompany us in the vanguard, and to allow you to wear your blasters. My father is meticulous in matters of law. Now, when we engage the Kan, you will be able to come with us into battle.''

"Then there is to be a battle?''

"That is the favor you requested.''

"And this machine will join the battle order?''

Shingo had looked him up and down. "Please say what troubles you, Mister Straker.''

He had drawn himself up, facing the Prefect's son, his teeth gritted. "Nothing troubles me, Shingo-san. But do you think it's wise to carry your wife into a firefight?''

Shingo had looked thunderously at him, then suddenly he had laughed his ugly laugh. "On Osumi, as you have already seen, there are some women who carry men into battle. Don't concern yourself with our ways, *gaijin*. Samurai women have had the right to go to war.''

He had glimpsed the dangerous ground on which he was walking then. She had said she was ordered here. If that was so, then by whom? By Hideki Ryuji, her lord? Or by her husband?

Now, despite himself, he had begun to ask tentative questions of Yasuko-san, disguising them as curiosity about the way in which so impressive a force of samurai had been brought together.

"Our tradition is an ancient one, Mister Straker. When the planet's security is threatened and the army moves, all our important men move with it. Naturally, that means the lord also.''

He stared wonderingly at the scene around him once again, thinking that she must be right, that the Kan would surely be intimidated, and they would have no stomach or strength to resist.

"Then everyone in the government is brought along with the daimyo?" he asked. "The Palace of Miyakonojo must've been completely emptied!"

"Almost. No daimyo willingly leaves his capital for even one day when it contains every hostage of value to him. Especially when he is taking his main force of modern weapons away from it. Even Hideki Ryuji-sama cannot be in two places at once. Therefore, there is no option but to take everyone with him."

He looked away, back down the wake of dust their ground-effect fields had kicked up. The column of troop carriers stretched for more than a mile: a vast organism of nobility, officers, troops, and supplies stretching into oblivion, obscured at the tail by the cloud of their passing.

"See!" Shingo told him with fierce pride, meticulously pointing out the order of precedence. "This is the way our ancestors took their forces to war. We are descended from heroes who lived and fought constantly on the move. It has always been samurai tradition that we follow the Way of the Warrior. That is how it should be for us. How it will be on our journey to Kanoya City." He drew his short sword and pointed forward. "A day ahead of the column the route masters and advance parties will give warning of our coming and prepare the way. Their transporters contain materials to make camp just inside the borders of the Lease. With them go the servants of my father's household. They will erect the bivouac we shall occupy tonight. My father must have every facility for attending to this affair of state in the evening. The Kan commander will be summoned to attend him."

"Seems a lot of effort just for a parley with the Kan. And why make the approach at a mile a minute when you could cruise in ten times faster?"

Shingo turned on him irritably. "A Prefect must conduct himself in the manner of a Prefect. With the dignity of a Prefect. Is that not yet apparent to you? Did you have no conception of the magnitude of the favor you were asking of my father?"

"Maybe your father's hoping to scare the Kan back to Satsuma."

At that point Yasuko intervened diplomatically. "Think of the Prefect as a gardener who one day finds a snake in his garden. Once he has discovered it, he cannot allow it to stay. But it may be more convenient to approach and persuade it to leave than to kill it with his hoe."

"So we set up a war camp on the edge of the Lease. Just inside Amerikan territory, to show the Kan there's no doubt about the Prefect's right to enter it?"

"Correct."

"You'll just wait there to see what develops to start with?"

"If our lord decides so, quarters will be provided."

"Yes. Our quarters are easy to find," Shingo said. "They will be erected within a red *maku* cordon—red to remind those who might wish to violate it of the color of blood."

"I'll be careful to remember that."

He remembered the severities of Yamato law, but even that was insufficient to drive the curiosity he now felt about Yasuko from his mind.

34

The war camp was finished before their arrival in the second hour of the afternoon. An astonishing maze of head-high fluttering canvas screens of various colors each bearing the *mon* of a different family had been erected. Inside each enclosure a miniature *han* had sprung up, complete with a prefabricated dwelling and most of the requisites of samurai comfort.

The constant banging of war drums announced the daimyo's approach. He turned away from the head of the column to a point where his standard bearers and weapon carriers hovered to proclaim him. Immediately behind their own sky-tank the rest of the first-rank vehicles swept in, their gondolas loaded with standing samurai, and behind them transports similarly weighed down. The Prefect's armored bodyguard disembarked and scrambled into position on the ground, their *naginata* glittering. After them came a group of four solemn ministers whose high-tongued black caps made them look similar to the sinister officers of the *kempei*.

"These must be the keepers of the Hoko? The treasury?" he said to Yasuko.

"You are correct, Mister Straker. Those first four gentlemen carry responsibility for Kyushu's aurium, all the wealth of the Quadrant. Though they are not samurai it is important that they remain incorruptible, for while the daimyo controls that bullion no one else can use it to proliferate arms, or produce artificial food, or use other aspects of modern technology, and thereby create a rebellion. The officials are here because our lord will bestow a certain amount of bullion upon his most deserving warriors after the victory. Then there are also the masters of the armory. . . .''

As she told him of the other officials that awaited the Prefect, part of his mind began considering the complex way that Yamato maintained its finances. It was clear that the vast bulk of the worlds of Yamato were organised according to the samurai ideal, and run on an agrarian subsistence basis. Rice formed the stock medium of the peasant economy, and the *koku* was its unit. Suddenly he realised what the underlying purpose of the peasant economy was. It was to force-drive an increase in the population. The people were kept materially poor, but child mortality was kept very low also, big families were encouraged, and under those conditions human populations exploded.

Elsewhere in Yamato there were vastly industrialised worlds that contributed to a dynamic aurium-based economy. He thought of the yellow metal, gold, that had once formed the basis of the early industrial economic systems of the Nineteenth and early Twentieth Centuries back on Old Earth, and saw the parallels, but the aurium-based economy of Yamato was different. Unlike Amerika, whose sophisticated credit system was based on nothing except the ethereal notion of ''consumer confidence,'' the Empire of Yamato had chosen the more solid foundation of aurium.

Aurium was more logical than gold because aurium had a real and not just a notional value. It was scarce and hoardable, but it also had astonishing nuclear and electron chemistries that made it the basis of just about every mod-

ern technology it was possible to name. Modern weapons
would not work without it, not a single variety of plex
could be manufactured, Dover comestible units would not
function, nor would many medical techniques, especially
limb regrowth. Even nexus-ship grav control would be
impossible without it. He could see that the possession of
aurium, and to a lesser extent its sister element argentium,
would mean power to anyone with the knowledge how to
use it.

He pointed. ''I can see what must be a hundred palan-
quins assembled over there, again with a strong bodyguard.
What are they for?''

''Those are for the *fudai* lords.''

''Yes. Of course.''

''And do you see your own bodyguard?''

The question perplexed him.

''They have not deserted you, though you have been less
than attentive to their needs. Perhaps you have forgotten
them?''

He understood. This was the cadre of horsemen who had
been led by Haigo Gozaemon, the men whose allegiance he
had won. Am I expected to lead them in battle? he thought
suddenly. Oh, in the name of psi, so that's what the scroll
was about. Hideki Ryuji has officially recognised my right
to command fifty samurai, and now the scroll has made it
legal! No wonder Shingo-san was gloating.

She saw his discomfort. ''Do not be alarmed. As my
husband has said, this has been done purely for purposes
of protocol. A good lord wisely attends to details and
always ties up the loose ends of his affairs.''

He heard the humor in her voice. He said, ''At tonight's
camp I must thank him for his gift.''

''The soldiers are now your right to command, but also
your responsibility.''

He hesitated. "How much will I be expected to—pay them?"

"Nothing."

Surprise took what he was about to say from his mind: that he had no means of paying them. "Nothing at all? Then how will they live? What reason will there be for them to fight?"

"Ordinary soldiers are not usually given payment in Yamato," she said, amused at his puzzlement. "It is their duty to fight."

"But—for nothing?"

"Not nothing, Mister Straker. Ours is an old culture; it is three thousand years and more even since the golden days of the wise and beneficent Emperor Jimmu. That is a long time for simple ways and straightforward laws to tie themselves into complicated knots."

"Try me."

She pursed her lips in annoyance, but did as he requested. "Officially, soldiers go to war because their lord commands it. In reality everyone knows that if they do not answer his call they will incur his displeasure, and so earn their own downfall."

"Okeh, I understand. Blackmail. But what about pay? Don't they get compensation? How do they live? Wars can last a long time. How do their families get by?"

"It is all part of the *han* system. If you study your legal title you will find you have been awarded a fief, a small grant of land, whose taxes will enable the Hoko to finance your troops. You need have no worries."

"It's a strange way of organising credit."

"Credit does not enter into it. It is understood by all soldiers that war is made for a share of the glory they will take."

His stomach heaved at that. "They mean to win 'glory' in Kanoya City? By killing?"

When she did not answer him, he said, "To us, killing is not glorious. To us it's obscene. Only to be done as an absolute last resort."

"You have killed."

"Only because you made that a necessity."

"It was not I who made it necessary, but you."

He turned away, then after a moment, asked, "Do you think there'll be a fight?"

"I do not know what our lord intends, Mister Straker. Perhaps the Kan will choose to leave Kanoya City. Perhaps they will be asked to pay for their own eviction in blood."

As they watched, the main mass of troops, ten thousand strong, fell in behind them with swords and fire-blasters raised. In their midst were ugly, snub-nosed, brutal-looking vehicles, mounting huge and unwieldy beam weapons. The biggest, which they called "Daimyo of Jigoku," had an ornate pair of barrels twenty feet long. In the rear, a mass of *ashigaru* followed, half-armored infantry armed with heavy assault weapons somewhat like 75-kV Esandubyas, the lowliest and least-regarded troops in the entire army, but the ones who would form the main part of any assault.

There were horses here, and caged animals, and a thousand other things that seemed unconnected with their purpose. It was as if, in some alien sense, the outing was an end in itself.

It's incredible, such pomp and ceremony and encumbrance when the only important task is to get to Kanoya City and humble the Kan into leaving. This whole maddening, magnificent circus has been assembled, when it would have been much cheaper and more effective to have sent a simple delegation with a list of demands. Why this lumbering monster and all these diversions when speed is obviously essential?

"How long will it take to reach Kanoya City from here?" he asked her.

"When. When. Always when." She sighed. "You will achieve nothing without patience. Slow is of the gods, as our proverb runs, and hurry is of devils."

"Yes, Ladee," he groaned. "And in Yamato only the ways of Yamato can succeed."

"One day you will understand. Meanwhile, do not waste your time trying to foresee what will happen when we arrive at Kanoya City, or trying to comprehend the mind of our lord. There may be a battle, or not, as the gods will it. You cannot influence that."

Messengers and couriers thundered past the encampment at intervals, communicating the daimyo's orders to his commanders, or bringing in news of detachments joining the column. As he watched throughout the oppressive heat of the afternoon, he saw the scribes taking down order after order from Hideki Ryuji's lips. Always close by were the Chief Retainers with their war fans, and the men who hurried in relays bearing the Prefect's orders to his army. Lesser daimyo attended him incessantly, waiting like the cheetahs in their cages, or the daimyo's hunting hawks. Several times already a party of *fudai* had unpacked bows, mounted horses, and ridden off in pursuit of distant herds of wild game.

"I myself have taken part in the annual *tsuiseki*," Yasuko told him, referring not to the classic form of hunt where noisy beaters surrounded an area and drove game towards marksmen, but to individual field-stalking with bow.

"For deer? Or antelope?" he had asked, surprised.

"Neither."

"Birds, then?"

She had laughed. "No. Man-eaters."

"Sweet psi! You mean tigers?"

"Yes. Tigers. They abound in the south."

"That must be an—exhilarating—sport."

"It is not a sport, Mister Straker," she said, her eyes reproving him. "It is merely a matter of good land management. This world is young and needs a firm hand. Also, hunts help the lord's administration. When a peasant brings a complaint, it is the duty of the local *han* daimyo to protect his people. That is how he earns respect. So it is when the complaint concerns a tiger."

"Shame to kill them."

"There is no shame. When a large, solitary male becomes old or lame, and can no longer chase down his fleet-footed prey, he will begin to take children from their play, or washerwomen from the riverbanks, and then, of course, he must be killed. A samurai reputation is very much improved when—Why do you laugh?"

"It's just . . . a woman stalking tigers in Yamato a thousand years after the invention of firearms? Hunting with bows and arrows?" he marveled. "It's crazee stuff."

She stiffened proudly at that. "Why crazee? I assure you, Mister Straker, I can bend a bow as well as any man."

"That's not what I meant. . . ."

"I have samurai blood in my heart," she said imperiously. "And with that go proud hereditary responsibilities. Among samurai it is expected that a woman fits herself for battle by practising the martial arts, the sword and the *naginata*. Samurai women hunt just as men do. Don't you know that in the Quadrant of Hokkaido they have many women warriors? In Shikoku, too, there is a whole regiment of troops who are women."

"Yasuko-san, I meant no offense," he said, thinking that he had touched too heavily on another raw sensibility.

"What I find hard to understand is the way your people train in archaic methods. Crawling after tiger with bows and arrows would be considered insane on any of our worlds.

"Not arrows, Mister Straker. Arrow. Singular."

"Sheee! On Wyoming they hunt them with damned big guns, but one arrow . . . no way, Ladee."

"Here you would be little thought of if you were to hunt tiger with a flame-blaster. Here our fish poachers would never even think of annihilating a lake with sonic grenades just to make sure they caught all the fish."

And the thing of it was, she was right!

These people continually defy predictions, he thought, surprised by the impact of her words. Form is as important to them as content. Tradition is revered for its own sake. It's not what you do, it's the way that you do it. It's not the arriving, it's the getting there that's the crux. Appearance is everything. And yet nothing is really what it seems. My old belief was that Yamato women were just downtrodden chattels; now I'm not so sure. It's so confusing. I used to think they kept women chained up; now I don't know if it's the men who're keeping the women in their place, or the other way around.

He glanced at her and looked away again quickly. But still, Yasuko-san doesn't have what I'd call a happy relationship. I wonder how she came to marry that prize turd? They seem totally ill-matched. Even here, where all major marriages are arranged for political reasons, there has to be an overshadowing reason to outweigh an incompatibility as massive as that. I wonder if they allow divorce. . . .

A sudden roar split the air as a flight of machines wheeled round overhead and headed off. It was Sadamasa's squadron, flying off towards Kanoya City. Some hours later they watched them return.

According to Yasuko, the report was made to Hideki Ryuji in the Prefect's enclosure.

"Sadamasa reported that his men have seized the artesian water wells on the edges of the Lagoon of the Dragonflies," she said. "They now control a pumping station and an overland pipeline that supplies the city."

"That's good. Maybe the Kan will see that and realise they can't last out. Maybe there'll be a peaceful settlement after all."

But two pieces of news from the scouting parties and spies who covered the countryside to the south had come to enrage them as night fell. First, the Kan had sent a force from the city and impudently recaptured the shores of the lagoon and restored their water supplies long enough to fill the city's cellars as emergency reservoir tanks. Second, and more important, the monitoring station at Naha had detected a message drone transiting Teth-Two-Eight, and had picked up a tight-beam broadcast from Yu Hsien. He had dispatched reinforcements from Satsuma. Thirty thousand Kan drop-troops and seventy thousand on freezee—veteran Kan infantry all hard-uniformed and equipped with 30-kV arms.

The news made Hayden Straker's mouth go dry.

At the Council of War in Hideki Ryuji's magnificently appointed temporary Residency, Sadamasa assembled his generals and they in turn brought in every officer until the inflatable hall was packed with three or four hundred men.

"The Prefect is outraged," Sadamasa told them all, speaking for his father, who watched grave-faced. "No one has ever dared question his authority before. He is the rightful overlord of Kyushu, granted his position by the Shogun himself. These *yabanjin* leaseholders are filthy traders, inside Sacred Yamato by his permission alone, guests of Kyushu. Yet they do not behave as guests should.

The Kan delight to ignore lawful commands, they have made war on our Quadrant's capital world despite Hideki Ryuji's explicit prohibition, and now they intend to face us with even more troops!"

There was total silence. Then the generals pored over the visualisers, denouncing the gall and stupidity of the Kan commander, as Sadamasa, heedless of spies, put his plan before them all.

"As my father wishes, our main headquarters position will be here, at the burial ground of the Hideki ancestors eighty *ri* south of the city. Ground forces will scatter in the form of a new moon, her cusps touching the Western Ocean. Our *ashigaru* regiments will dispose themselves so as to contain any Kan units seeking to escape across country."

He paused instinctively, looking for small signs from the older heads that would tell him what they really thought of his strategy.

"The important idea is this: at present the Kan have very little that is airborne. Apart from a few shuttles and orbit landers that we can force down, they possess only surface skimmers. It is possible they still believe our vehicles have only skimmer capability, since we have not yet revealed their full potential. Therefore, if we use our *sora-sensha* in a lightning attack to destroy all the landers on the apron and all the skimmers we see, they will be immediately confined to the ground within the area of the Lease."

One of the white-haired *fundai* frowned, and Sadamasa caught it.

"You have an opinion, Toraiwa-san?"

"A question, Lord. While it is true that the Kan do not have atmospheric craft, they still have a fleet of powerfully armed ships in orbit. May I ask how you have overcome this problem?"

"It is certain their beam weapons will not be able to target our sky tanks from orbit with any accuracy when we are performing random avoidance maneuvers, and even if they could, there is an optimum time when most of their ships will have set, like any celestial object, over the horizon. The presence of the Amerikan facility called Fort Baker, parked at the Kanoya City zenith, has driven the smaller Kan vessels down from the prime standing orbit. All their warships overfly Kanoya City regularly, but only the biggest ship, the White Tiger Class vessel, can afford to come within a few thousand *ri* of the fortress. It has adopted an inclined Osumi-synchronous orbit centered twelve hundred *ri* over the Western Ocean. From here—"

Sadamasa reached overhead and described a generous figure-eight with his finger "—the ship appears to move like this.

"The commander will have two options, either to bring his ships down from orbit to engage us—and if the Kan attempt to use the apron, here, we shall have enough meson equipment in place to disable them—or he can do nothing and rely on his ground forces' falling back on the city until a settlement can be negotiated." He looked around their faces proudly. "Since we do not seek any compromise, and since the Kanoya dome has been rendered useless by the Kan themselves, should that happen, we will sweep down and destroy them."

"No quarter!" someone shouted.

"No quarter!!"

The cry had been taken up by several voices.

"No mercy for the interlopers."

Hideki Ryuji nodded once, his foremost son's handling of what was a difficult moment pleasing him. But Hayden Straker was shocked pale by the decision as the celebration of warlike intent erupted around him. There was a cruel

justice that haunted him, and he almost laughed. Now,
irrevocably, there would be a battle, and that meant he
would have to stand alongside Shingo in his sky tank,
and Yasuko would be there also, and Shingo would take
deliberate delight in plunging the ship into the thickest part
of the battle, and down below there would be a terrible
carnage as the sky tanks carved up the Kan ground forces.
He would have to witness the deaths of a thousand men,
deaths he had summoned like an evil *kami* from the false
amygdala. It was as Yasuko had said: there was a special
psi magic on Osumi. A dark, powerful magic that controlled the affairs of men.

As the cries died down around him, he had begun to
understand their intention. It was to be a mantrap, set
and sprung, into which Yu Hsien's ground forces would
blunder. If the Kan were to attempt a withdrawal, Sadamasa's sky tanks would fall on them and massacre them,
and if they were to attack they would be caught in the open
and cut to pieces. It was surely an impossible option,
he thought. What infantry commander could conceive of
fighting across endless tracts of knee-deep paddy water
and then facing an airborne army that at present outgunned
his own firepower by a factor of more than ten to one?

At the climax of the council, Hideki Ryuji called for
his Shinto divines to pronounce on the auspiciousness of
coming events. They came forward out of the south-facing
crowd before him, black-robed and crimson-hatted, one
simpering, one arrogant, and one wise. This last was an
old man, hairless, the skin tight on his face and leathery
as an ancient Chinese; high cheekbones guarded empty
orbits, but also shadowed a benign gape. This man had
lived hard and lost his eyes with the armies in Hainan
many, many years ago.

The procession entered with *gohei* and yarrow stalk bundle and book carried high. Three young acolytes—just into their teens—followed. The last dabbed on a drum whose notes bent and soared. The middle one blew windy notes from a *shakuhachi*. The first and tallest twanged on a wire-stringed instrument.

The robes of the three older men glittered as they approached the dais. They all bore the *mon* of their exalted Shugendo Order, the triple-curving teardrop of the Ying-Yang-Null surrounded by an aurium thread–embroidered border of electric blue in which the eight trigrams glittered. It was the Sequence of Earlier Heaven, known in Amerikan comparative psi texts as the Primal Arrangement of Tao.

They made obeisance to the Prefect, then unwrapped the ancient "Book of Dark Learning" from its silk covering, bowed repeatedly to it, lit an incense burner, and asked the Prefect to pass their fifty sticks three times through the smoke. This he did.

The eyeless one asked, "What is your question, Lord?"

Hayden Straker knew that the consultation was intended to illuminate the psi parameters that would govern events in the next few hours. It was not prediction so much as a pointer towards the critical moments of the Prefect's conduct, and the desired flavor of his inner composure during that time. How he should be if events were to be influenced towards the desired outcome.

"What should be my spirit's Way if I am to achieve my military goals within the next seven days?" the Prefect asked.

"That question is worthy, Lord," all the divines said in unison.

After that the Principal took one of the sticks and laid it aside. It was included only to ensure that the magically significant number fifty was arrived at; once it was gone there were seven times seven remaining. With his right hand he divided these active sticks into two unequal piles. It was a nonchalant motion, but Hayden Straker knew that this was the so-called deterministic moment of chaos and that to divide the sticks without forebrain interference, with the true "innocence" of a young child or a consummate artist, required years of training. It was more difficult to accomplish than responding honestly and obediently to the seventh-rank Zen shout, "Don't think of an elephant!"

The divine took one stick from the right pile and placed it between ring finger and little finger of his left hand. Then he took away sticks from the left pile four at a time until only four remained. He put those between the middle and ring fingers of his left hand. He repeated this with the right pile until only one remained, and placed these between the index and middle fingers of the right hand.

Hayden Straker watched as this accomplished chief psi divine laid some sticks aside and repeated the whole process twice more until he had gathered three piles. Then a quickly chanted calculation fixed the bottom line of the hexagram they were searching for. Meanwhile, the First Assistant divine had pegged out a blank paper scroll with silver weights and the Second Assistant divine had mixed up bright red ink from an ink block, recording the Yang line with a bold slash.

The ritual was repeated six times, and each time a new line was added to the hexagram, either Yin or Yang, Old or Young, Uncalm or Tranquil. Each of the eight combinations of line types had a distinct ritual.

"That which is past becomes lesser. That which is yet to come becomes greater. By this process we move away from what was and towards what shall be. Where they meet is."

A murmur passed round the gathering as they saw the especially significant combination of Old-Yang-Uncalm had appeared in Hideki Ryuji's scroll. The interpretation would be complex.

Hayden Straker saw that all six lines in the hexagram were broken Yin, with the exception of the line second from bottom, which was Yang.

Shih . . . a troop of soldiers!

The foremost savant told the daimyo in flowery phrases that his psi was presently ruled by a most fortunate combination of trigrams, that "earth" was lying upon "deep water"—K'un upon K'an in the original Chinese reading. Most favorable and poetic in form—and best of all, was the astonishing Judgement.

"Thus is the unborn spring where soldiers lie concealed until they are needed."

The First Assistant spoke the Commentary. "Lord, inner danger and outer devotion are symbolic of military organization. Righteous action. Yours is the initiative. Given a wise leader of great moral strength, there will result a fortune outcome that no one may reproach."

The Image was translated by the Second Assistant. "Water seeping deep beneath the earth is the hidden army that shall spring forth. The important man shall win over his followers in the market, the city, and the university by his great heart."

The First Assistant explained the lines. "In the bottom line the sixth ritual signifies: The soldiers must set out in good order; if there is disorder there will be misfortune."

Hideki Ryuji seemed well pleased by this. The Principal told him, "Your army functions on discipline. This is the essence of victory."

"In the second line the ninth ritual signifies: He stands surrounded by his forces. There is good fortune and no reproach. Three times the lord awards battle honors."

The Prefect of Kyushu seemed troubled. "Do you advise

I abandon my plan to designate the hill of my ancestors as headquarters and rallying point?''

"So sorry, Lord. I cannot advise. I only say that this line shows a leader in the midst of his forces, neither prominent in the attack nor hidden.''

''In the third line the sixth ritual signifies: The army that carries corpses in its wagons is assured of failure.''

This time Hideki Ryuji's eyes flashed to his second son.

The Principal turned his blind eyes heavenward. ''As it is the Kan custom to carry a young boy in place of the body at their funerals, so it must be with an army. Tradition must be honored. Also, let it be remembered that in an army where all are generals, there will be no one left to do the fighting.''

''In the fourth line the sixth ritual signifies: The army withdraws without disgrace.''

"There is no shame in withdrawing before a stronger force. Even if defeat is certain, it is better to preserve the strength one still possesses. This does not conflict with the Way of the Warrior, only with the Way of Fools.''

A hundred sword hands clenched at that remark, but the Prefect's calm stayed them and not a hand touched a hilt. While his respect for the *shugendo* priests remained, many interpretations supplanted that which insulted *bushido*.

''In the fifth line the sixth ritual signifies: When wild beasts roam the field there is no disgrace in capturing them. The eldest son is in command. The youngest carries away the dead: Persistence brings misfortune.''

Hayden Straker realised that this was as difficult a line as the fourth. At some point the Prefect would have to make his decision to trust Sadamasa-san utterly. The youngest and the eldest sons were mentioned, but what of the middle son?

''The enemy occupation is bestial. The moment is ripe to

attack and destroy them. But there must not be unnecessary killing.''

"In the top line the ninth ritual signifies: The lord issues his commands, grants estates and titles of nobility; but power should not be given to the inferior.''

The Prefect listened as an accused man listens when a correct verdict is read out by the *heishi* and he is shown to be innocent.

"Victory, then,'' he said at last.